Praise for Rosanna Ley

'A gorgeous, mouth-watering dream of a holiday read!' *Red*

'Sun-soaked escapism' *Best*

'Unabashedly romantic . . . slips down like easy-drinking vino infused with Mediterranean sunshine' *Saga*

'A beautifully crafted slice of escapist fiction' *Heat*

'A perfect summer read' Rachel Hore

'Impeccably researched and deftly written' Kathryn Hughes

'Holiday romance at its most evocative and escapist' *The Lady*

'A wonderfully relaxing sun lounger read' *Sunday Express*

'I loved the sultry sensuous feeling . . . a fascinating story with engaging themes' Dinah Jefferies

'The ultimate feel-good read, perfect for fans of Santa Montefiore, Victoria Hislop and Leah Fleming' *Candis*

'Completely beguiling and beautifully told' Kate Furnivall

'A great page-turner' Lucinda Riley

'Romantic, escapist and mouth-watering' Veronica Henry

'A glorious read that feels like a summer holiday in a book' *People's Friend*

Rosanna Ley works as a creative writing tutor and has written many articles and stories for national magazines. Her writing holidays and retreats take place in stunning locations in Spain and Italy. When she is not travelling, Rosanna lives in West Dorset by the sea.

Also by Rosanna Ley

The Villa
Bay of Secrets
Return to Mandalay
The Saffron Trail
Last Dance in Havana
The Little Theatre by the Sea
Her Mother's Secret
The Lemon Tree Hotel
From Venice with Love

Quercus

First published in Great Britain in 2021 by

Quercus Editions Ltd
Carmelite House
50 Victoria Embankment
London EC4Y 0DZ

An Hachette UK company

A CIP catalogue record for this book is available
from the British Library

HB ISBN 978 1 78747 632 5
TPB ISBN 978 1 78747 633 2

10 9 8 7 6 5 4 3 2 1

Typeset by CC Book Production
Printed and bound in Great Britain by Clays Ltd, Elcograf S.p.A.

Papers used by Quercus are from well-managed forests and other responsible sources.

To Ana and James with love

CHAPTER I

Holly

West Dorset, February 2018

Holly flipped through the crumpled and stained pages of her mother's old recipe book and there it was, peeking from inside a yellowing envelope. As if somebody (her mother?) had half wanted the recipe to be a secret one, half wanted it to be seen.

Carefully, she extracted the fragile sheet of paper from the envelope and smoothed out the folds with her fingertips. The original recipe was written in Spanish; she recognised a few of the words. Under this, the ingredients and instructions had been written much more clearly and in English, all of it in handwriting she did not recognise.

Seville orange and almond cake, she read. *For an occasion.*

Well, she thought, if this wasn't an occasion – the day she made her big announcement, the day she told her parents what she'd been planning, what she'd been working towards this past eighteen months without them having the slightest idea what was going on – then she didn't know what was.

Holly consulted the English version of the recipe. *First, scrub and roughly chop the Seville oranges.* She glanced over at them. They were sitting in a bowl on the kitchen counter, glowing like orange lanterns in the dim February afternoon light. The oranges weren't the prettiest; they were misshapen, rough and knobbly. But the colour . . . It was so vibrant, so bright. The first time she'd seen a box of Seville bitter oranges in the farm shop just outside Bridport, she'd been smitten.

Holly selected one now and sniffed the thick skin. *Ah.* The Seville orange was too bitter to be eaten fresh – it was as sharp and sour as a lemon. But the scent of this orange . . . It transported her to the possibility of an intoxicating summertime. *Here's hoping* . . . Holly began to scrub.

She had first discovered her mother's old Spanish recipe as a teenager. Other girls spent Saturday afternoons in town having coffee with their friends, buying make-up, chatting about which boy they fancied or what film was showing at the local cinema . . . Holly baked – fruit cakes, crumbles, batches of brownies. There was nothing quite as satisfying, she'd always thought, as a tray of pastries fresh from the oven.

OK, so she had been an unusual teenager. She smiled to herself. Sifting through her mother's recipe books had been her idea of a wild time.

Almost reluctantly, Holly placed the scrubbed oranges down on the chopping board. She sliced firmly into the first one. The bitter juice squirted, releasing more of its citrussy-fresh scent.

Holly had found the recipe, studied it, been fascinated by it, but she had never baked the cake – never dared, after the way her mother had reacted to the suggestion.

She gathered the aromatic and thick-skinned orange pieces together and pushed them to one side of the board with the back of her hand. The juice felt like an astringent on her skin. She could understand why Seville oranges had numerous uses, many of them medicinal – their scent, their flavour when cooked was both complex and intense.

And then there was marmalade. Holly had been using them to make marmalade for years. Seville oranges were considered the best in the world for it, because the high natural pectin content helped the marmalade to set correctly. And Holly had certainly never had any complaints. Making and baking were activities she turned to when she was tired or anxious. Far from sapping her energy still further, marmalade-making invigorated her, it always had.

She vividly remembered her fourteen-year-old self, waving the Seville orange and almond cake recipe in front of her mother, already excited about the prospect. 'Can I make this, Mum?' she'd begged.

'What?' Her mother stared at the piece of paper, almost snatched it from Holly's grasp. 'No,' she said.

She'd never said 'no' to a cake before. Holly had frowned. 'Why not?'

Her mother hesitated. 'Your father doesn't like it. It's not a great recipe.'

'But—'

'And we don't have any Seville oranges.'

'I could—'

'No, Holly.'

Even at fourteen, Holly had known her mother was protesting too much. What was it then about this old recipe? What was the big deal? Her mother's refusal only increased its allure. Where had it come from exactly? Why had her mother kept it? And why was it out of bounds? As far as she was aware, her mother had no Spanish friends. So, who had written it out for her, first in Spanish and then English? Holly was determined to find out more.

She wasn't stupid, though – she waited a few days before asking her mother about Spain.

'Of course I've been to Spain,' her mother said breezily. Too breezily? Holly wondered. 'I went with your father.'

Was that when someone had given her the recipe for the Spanish orange and almond cake? Holly decided that it was wiser not to ask.

'When did you go?' she asked her mother instead.

Her mother's expression changed. 'Oh, I don't know exactly, Holly. Does it matter? Back in the 1980s, I can't remember the exact year.'

Was that suspicious? Holly supposed not. No one ever remembered the exact year they went away anywhere. 'Whereabouts in Spain did you go?'

There was a pause. 'Seville.'

Was it Holly's imagination, or did her mother glance over towards the kitchen shelf, to where her old recipe book sat in the corner? 'So . . . ?'

But her mother didn't give her a chance to ask any more. 'Come on now, Holly,' she said. 'Enough. Dinner's almost ready and the table won't lay itself, you know.' She'd swept into full chivvying mode. Not only was she frowning, but Holly thought she could detect a tear in her mother's eye. That was it then. Her mother had never been a strict parent exactly, but she was a teacher and she'd always maintained boundaries. Enough said. The subject was very definitely closed.

That was fifteen years ago. At the moment, Holly lived in Brighton, but she was back here in Dorset on one of her regular weekend visits, because apart from wanting to see her family, she missed the landscape of her childhood too. Fortunately, she still had baking rights in this kitchen.

Holly put the vibrant orange pieces in a small pan, picking out the pips with a wooden spoon. She added water, covered the pan and switched on the gas. The recipe promised that after thirty minutes the oranges would be soft and the liquid would have evaporated. Holly felt the small hum of excitement that she always felt when baking. It was the process of creation, she guessed. Alchemy. It was something she never felt in the office in Brighton.

She glanced at the recipe. Maybe this old, crumpled piece of paper had been the start of her dream all those years ago. So, she'd decided to make the Seville orange and almond cake this afternoon while her parents were out. It seemed appropriate somehow.

She still felt bad about not telling them what she'd been planning, what she'd been doing. But her grandmother had advised against it, and with her parents living here where Holly had grown up, and Holly in Brighton, it hadn't been too hard to keep things quiet. But now, everything was about to change.

Holly cracked the eggs, carefully separating them into white and yolk. She put the whites into a bowl and whisked them into stiff peaks. Gradually, she added the castor sugar, beat the remaining sugar with the egg yolks until the mixture thickened and then added her fragrant chopped orange mixture and the ground almonds. Already it smelt heavenly.

She folded the egg whites into the mix, carefully transferred it to the greased and lined baking tin and sprinkled the top with flaked almonds. She checked her watch. It would be ready by the time her parents came back with her grandmother for tea.

And instead of tea . . . Holly took the bottle of champagne she'd brought with her from Brighton from her tote bag and put it in the fridge. She was sure that her grandmother would approve.

Seville orange and almond cake – for an occasion. She fancied she could already smell the almonds toasting, already sense the sugar combining with the oranges to make the cake perfectly bitter-sweet.

And when they came back? When they came back, she would try to explain to them why she was so dramatically turning her life around. She would tell them – finally – what had happened to her in Brighton and what she had decided to do.

CHAPTER 2

Holly

Brighton, one year earlier

It began one evening after work. Holly was late leaving the office – as she so often was – and hadn't had time to think about food. On the way home, she stopped off at the supermarket, her mind still full of work, recalling an email that she hadn't had time to answer, replaying in her head a phone conversation she'd had earlier with a client who was proving tricky.

She pulled a trolley from the line and made her way inside. The supermarket was bright, busy and disorientating. She steered the trolley past the newspapers and two quarrelling children and picked up a green salad from the fresh veg section. Tomorrow's lunch, she thought. She never had time to leave the office, always ate salad at her desk or heated up soup in the microwave.

She wasn't quite sure how her job as an accounts manager in Brighton had come to dominate her life, to consume every waking hour – there didn't seem much left after it had taken its fill.

And no matter how drained Holly felt, Russell, her boss, never seemed totally satisfied.

She headed for the deli counter. She had left West Dorset in her early twenties, drawn to the edgier, more bohemian buzz of Brighton, home of her boyfriend, Jack, who had become an ex-boyfriend after a year or so – fortunately with no one's heart being broken – by which time Holly had made friends, found a job and was earning good money. She was content to stay in her newly adopted city; she'd just never been sure that it would be forever.

She selected a few bits and pieces, checked the sell-by dates, paused in front of the chilled soup counter. Holly liked Brighton – she relished wandering down North Laine at weekends, meeting friends, dipping into the little bars and independent boutiques, exploring the vintage centre. She liked the music scene here, the arty crowd, the open houses and festivals, and she enjoyed living by the sea, which reminded her of her childhood. There was no one special for Holly right now. But nevertheless, she'd made a good life in Brighton.

Only . . .

She continued to hover in front of the chilled soup counter. Which one should she buy? How could it be so difficult to decide? Her mouth was dry and she swallowed and licked her lips. If only she hadn't left her bottle of water in the car. *Tomato and red pepper, Stilton and broccoli* . . . There was so much choice – too much choice – and oddly, she couldn't remember which one she preferred.

She felt dazed, not present almost, as if a part of her was floating above the shopping trolley watching her other self down below. And the lights – they were so bright, surely brighter than usual? Holly took a deep breath. She was working too hard, that was all; she needed to take a break, relax, she needed to . . . Escape, she thought.

Because something was going wrong. She was working long hours (but she was hardly alone in that), she wasn't sleeping well and she was stressed. Somewhere along the line in her twenties, this had become the norm – for her and more than a couple of her friends. She went to the gym, she'd taken up yoga, but rather than being relaxing, it felt as if she was always just desperately trying to fit more in. And then . . .

Holly began to feel dizzy; the chilled soups were swimming in and out of focus. She blinked hard. But now, without warning, she couldn't think, she couldn't breathe and there was a rapid inner pounding somewhere that could be in her heart or could be in her head – she didn't know. All she knew was that she couldn't stay in the supermarket, no way; she had to leave right there and then, shopping or no shopping. And she also knew that she felt scared.

'I think you had a panic attack,' her GP told her when she went along to the medical centre the following day.

Panic attack . . . Fight or flight. Holly closed her eyes. Remembered that moment, that strong urge she'd had to escape.

She listened to what her GP had to say about self-help, management and therapy. 'Try to ride it out,' he advised. 'Breathe. Confront your fears. Remind yourself it's only anxiety.'

Only anxiety, she thought. She admitted that she was stressed, overworked, exhausted. He gave her a look. *Aren't we all?* it seemed to say. Helpful . . .

Later, she looked up 'panic attack' online, recognised the feelings described by so many: the inability to decide, to think, the sudden overwhelming fear. Her GP had suggested that hopefully it would be a one-off incident, especially if she could cut down on stress at work, but Holly couldn't help thinking, was this what she wanted her life to be?

That Friday evening she went back to Dorset for the weekend. It was late summer and, unusually, the green hills were pale and parched from lack of rain. As she drove over the ridge between Dorchester and Bridport she looked out across the familiar landscape – sheep grazing in the fields, stone cottages and wooden barns, the limpid, blue-grey sea glimmering like moonstone in the distance. And for the first time in ages, she felt a sense of peace unexpectedly steal over her.

During the weekend, she visited a few of her old friends – Will and Susie still lived in a village just outside the town and were making a living from Will's art and sculpture and Susie's vintage furniture business, while Jess still lived with her parents and worked in the beach café at Burton. Holly also spent time with her family. It was so reassuringly normal, she could almost forget what had happened a few days before.

Her father, Felix, was still managing the garden centre; he'd been there most of his working life. He loved growing seeds and tending plants and Holly suspected he'd probably have been even happier if he'd never been promoted. Her mother, Ella, was as busy as ever. She was a primary teacher in the local school and if she wasn't teaching or marking books, she was going to staff meetings or lesson planning – nothing new there.

And Holly's grandmother, Ingrid . . . Holly's father's mother had always been an indomitable presence in Holly's life, but she seemed a bit softer these days, more mellow. And maybe more observant too.

'You look tired, my dear,' she said as Holly sat down in her grandmother's old-fashioned sitting room decorated with china dogs, shepherdesses and ornamental Toby jugs.

Like Holly's grandmother herself, the room smelt faintly of musty lavender. The covers her grandmother kept on her best chairs had preserved the fabric, stopping it from becoming faded in the sun, and the antimacassars protected the chair wings from wear and tear. The walls were painted ice blue and the carpet was what Holly's father would call 'scrambled egg and fireworks'. Still, that too was reassuring somehow. The entire house was a time capsule from the 1950s. Holly found herself breathing more easily.

It was pointless pretending – her grandmother's eyes were much too sharp. And it was a relief to let her bright 'I'm fine' smile slip a little. 'Yes, Gran,' she said, 'you're right, I am tired.'

In contrast, her grandmother's face was glowing. Eighty-five years young and despite her losses along the way, Gran's blue eyes were still as strong and determined as ever.

'Have you been burning the candle at both ends, my dear?' Her grandmother bent her head slightly to one side. Her hair was soft and white these days but she kept it cut short and neatly styled; she'd never been one to let herself go.

Holly knew her mother had had her moments with Gran over the years, but although her grandmother was still a force to be reckoned with, Holly had always felt safe, one generation removed and knowing she was unconditionally adored. 'It's mainly work,' she admitted. 'It's so stressful.'

'That's not good.'

'I know, Gran.'

It came out easily after that – the never-ending stream of emails to be answered, the constant client queries and demands, the thorny work relationship with a colleague, the unrelenting pressure, the long hours . . . She didn't mention the panic attack – she didn't want to worry her grandmother unduly. But perhaps, Holly thought, that was why she'd decided to come home this weekend.

'If it's so bad, why on earth are you doing it, child?' Her grandmother clicked her tongue. 'Why not do something else instead?'

'I don't know.' Gran made it sound so simple. But Holly needed to earn that salary so that she could continue to live in her Brighton flat and have the lifestyle that she currently enjoyed. And did she still enjoy it? The truth was, she was on a treadmill. 'What else could I do?' She spoke half to herself.

'The question is,' her grandmother said, 'what is it that you want to do, my dear?'

Holly thought about this conversation a lot after she got back to Brighton. *What is it that you want to do . . . ?* What she'd always loved doing was baking. She missed it so much. She still baked occasionally on Sunday afternoons after the gym and before she had to start preparing for work the next day. But it was snatched time and that spoilt the good feeling. And how could anyone make a living from baking cakes and making marmalade? How could that ever be more than a hobby?

So, what else could she do? She couldn't give up work, at least not yet. But she could make some changes. Slowly, gradually, she began to develop strategies for coping, some of them gleaned from online threads she was following. She tried to be nice to the colleague giving her a hard time – however much the woman glared at her. She walked away from her computer every thirty minutes – even if only to go to the loo – and she tried to focus on one task at a time instead of checking her emails constantly. She pushed herself into being firmer with Russell about just how much she was capable of doing and, to her surprise, he responded more positively when she was confident and assertive than he had ever done before.

She started to meditate once a day. She cut down on social media time. And when she started feeling a bit stronger, Holly bit the bullet and enrolled in an online course to develop her business studies. That had been Gran's idea. 'You could always think about getting some different qualifications, Holly,' she had said. 'Something to enable you to take control?'

Control . . . None of it was easy. But Holly knew that she was beginning to make a difference.

Quite a few phone calls passed between Holly and her grandmother in the months following that first chat in Gran's sitting room at the end of the summer. Holly had made the decision to change her life, but it was taking much longer to decide exactly what to do instead.

Holly visited her grandmother too, every time she was in Dorset, and they discussed strategies. Holly sensed that she was relishing the excitement of being Holly's confidante. Gran had always been so sure of what she thought, so strong-minded. Gradually, with her help, Holly began to make a plan. At last, she'd decided on the way forward.

'We won't tell your parents though,' her grandmother had said. 'Not yet. We don't want them to interfere and spoil things, do we?' And she shot Holly a conspiratorial smile.

'No, Gran. I suppose not.'

But now, they had agreed it was time to come clean and tell her parents everything. What would they say? Holly was about to find out.

CHAPTER 3

Ella

West Dorset, February 2018

Ella opened her back door and stepped into the kitchen. In seconds, the familiar scent of cake-baking filled her nostrils with sweetness.

She breathed in deeply. 'Oh, Holly, that smells heavenly! What—?' She stopped abruptly. The fragrance was indeed heavenly – and it didn't just remind her of the marmalade Holly used to make in this kitchen. It reminded her of so much more besides. It was intense, heady. *Orange blossom*. Ella steadied herself with a hand on the kitchen counter. It had been such a long time ago. And yet . . .

'I thought you wouldn't mind if I made it just this once.' Holly's voice wavered.

And Ella's heartbeat quickened. 'Made what, Holly?' Oh, she had seen the pitted, twisty oranges in the fruit bowl this morning, but thought very little of it. Holly was planning to make some marmalade. Nothing new there. But this . . . this was something else.

'In you come then, Mum.' All of a sudden, Felix was behind Ella, ushering his mother into the room.

Ella moved out of the way. These days, Ingrid needed a stick and couldn't spend so long on her feet.

'Hello, my dear,' Ingrid said to her granddaughter. And there was something in her tone . . .

'Hi, Gran.' Holly came over to give her a hug.

'What are you baking, Holly?' Ella asked again. She kept her voice casual. But the scent of almonds was threaded through that of the oranges: sweet, rich and nutty. Surely she wouldn't have?

Her daughter's expression said it all. 'Sorry, Mum, I know you were never keen on me making it.'

So why do it then? 'It doesn't matter.' It had been so long ago. Shouldn't Ella have got over it by now? Though the scent of the cake drifting in the air was already having an effect on her. She shrugged off her jacket, hung it on the hook by the door.

'Tea, everyone?' she asked brightly. She mustn't show she cared. And over the years, hadn't she become so very good at pretending?

Ella looked around. Felix's mother was smiling, eyes gleaming as if . . . as if she knew something Ella didn't. Ella caught the conspiratorial glance that passed between her mother-in-law and her daughter. They'd been as thick as thieves lately, these two. What were they up to?

'Good idea. I'll do it.' Felix beamed. 'Mmm. What've you made for us then, love?' As usual, he had missed the subtext, had no clue what was going on. Not that Ella was much wiser. She waited.

'Mum's Spanish Seville orange and almond cake,' Holly said. She shot a worried glance towards Ella. 'I wanted to make something special. For an occasion.'

'Quite right.' Ingrid nodded her approval.

'Something special?' Felix raised an eyebrow at Ella. 'What occasion might that be then, love?'

So, she'd been right. Ella shrugged at Felix. She'd never made the cake herself, of course – didn't want to lower the drawbridge and risk all those memories flooding back in.

She shouldn't have kept the recipe at all, she supposed. Only, she had so little and it had meant so much. It had seemed such a small thing. And whenever she'd seen the little envelope as she flicked through her recipe book, whenever she'd gently pulled the old Spanish recipe from its hiding place and read through the list of ingredients, it had made her smile, sometimes even made a tear come to her eye. Ella's emotions were never far from the surface where this cake and the city of Seville were concerned. But sometimes, it was good to remember.

Felix rubbed his hands together in that characteristic and hearty way he had. 'Is it somebody's birthday?' He chuckled. 'Let me take your coat, Mum.' He helped his mother off with her coat and settled her in what they called the comfy chair, putting her walking cane to one side. 'Are you going to let us in on the secret then, love?' He turned to Holly and laughed – but not unkindly. Felix wasn't the sort of man to be unkind.

The secret. Ella realised she was holding her breath. What was this all about? And why did she feel a sense of foreboding? Something was definitely up. She busied herself with cups and saucers; over the years, distraction techniques had been more useful than she cared to admit.

'Yes.' Holly straightened her shoulders. She glanced at Ella and then back to Felix again. 'Mum, Dad, I've got something to tell you,' she said.

'Go on then, love.' Again, Felix looked at Ella. Again, she shrugged.

But Felix smiled. Some young man, he was thinking, Ella could tell from the expression in his grey eyes. Was his daughter about to announce her engagement to someone they hadn't even met? Ella knew the way his mind worked. It worried her sometimes how well she could follow its patterns. They'd been together thirty-six years, but had he ever considered that her brain even had a pattern? She wasn't so sure.

'Well . . .' Holly began.

Ella shot her a look. There wouldn't be any young man. Holly had told her only yesterday that there was no one special. Her last date had been with someone called Liam she'd met at the gym. Holly had apparently run out of things to say to him after two drinks, made an excuse and left the bar. Ella knew some things.

Holly cleared her throat. She looked anxious. Ella wanted to reassure her but she also needed to know what this was all about.

Felix was frowning. Now was about the time he might suspect that their daughter was pregnant, Ella thought. It wouldn't be that, though. Holly had been unusually quiet this weekend, and Ella had certainly detected an undercurrent of excitement, which had made her ask in the first place if there was someone new. What else could it be? A new job perhaps? Promotion? She shook her head at Felix, but was a microsecond too late.

'You're not . . . ?' Felix's frown deepened.

'Dad!' Holly looked indignant.

Ingrid clicked her tongue. 'There are other kinds of announcements, Felix,' she said reprovingly.

For once, Ella was in full agreement with her mother-in-law.

She tried to say, *A work thing, is it, darling?* But strangely, her throat closed under the assault of the fragrance of the Seville orange and almond cake and no sound emerged at all.

'The thing is, I've come to a decision. I want to do something different with my life.' Holly turned to open the flowery cake tin that was on the kitchen counter. She lifted out the cake; Ella noticed it was already standing on one of her more decorative plates. Holly held it out in front of her like an offering.

Ella couldn't help smiling. It looked just like the other Seville orange and almond cake that had been made all those years ago, the only difference being that the icing sugar on the top of the other one had been dusted more finely.

She brought herself back to the present. 'What is it that you want to do, darling?' Ella tried to sound encouraging. She knew Holly had been finding things hard lately, though she hadn't opened up to her mother as much as Ella would have liked. 'Have things been tough at work?'

'I've given in my notice,' Holly said. 'And yes, they have.'

'Blimey.' Felix went to put the kettle on. 'Have you got something else lined up then, love?'

'Well . . .'

Ella noted another glance passing between her daughter and her mother-in-law. She tried not to feel resentful. But how come Ingrid knew something that Ella did not? Ella had always been a busy mother – her career was important to her; she loved her teaching work even though it could be very full-on – but she'd never been a bad mother. Had she? Had she been too busy to listen? Too busy for Holly to come to her with her problems, her fears? She tucked her hair behind one ear and away from her face. It was warm in here – from the baking, she supposed. She was certainly feeling a little dizzy.

'I'm starting my own business.' Holly looked from one to the other of them, clearly unsure of their reaction.

'Your own business?' Felix echoed.

Ella blinked at her. 'Just like that?' Where had all this come from so suddenly?

Holly seemed to stand a little straighter. 'I know it's risky. But I've given it a lot of thought. And actually, I decided some time ago.'

'You didn't say a word,' Ella murmured. But her mother-in-law had known, she was sure.

'I didn't tell you before, because I didn't want either of you to try to make me change my mind.' Holly spoke in a rush. 'But the thing is, I've done a business course—'

'A business course?' How come Ella didn't know anything about this? Neither did Felix, she presumed; he seemed as bemused as she.

Holly looked down. 'Like I said, I didn't want to say too much too soon. And I didn't know if anything would come of it. So . . .'

The kettle was boiling. 'What kind of business, love?' Felix threw in four bags – he always used too many – and poured the boiling water into the teapot.

'I'd like to open a shop.' At last, Holly put the Seville orange and almond cake down on the kitchen counter.

Ella tried not to look at it. 'What kind of shop?' she asked.

'An orange shop.'

Ella gazed at her daughter, trying to understand. 'An orange shop?' What was she thinking? It sounded more like a phone company.

'All things orange, that is.' Holly took a breath. 'I want to call it Bitter Orange. I'll be making marmalade, sourcing toiletries and beauty products – all made from oranges. I'll import orange wine and liqueur, candles. You wouldn't believe how many products there are.'

Ella would actually. 'Where?' she asked. 'Where would you open this shop?'

'Bridport.'

'I see.' So, she'd be close by. A smile crept onto Ella's face. That felt good. Ella and Felix had brought their only child up to be independent, to be brave enough to fly from the nest, but that didn't mean Ella didn't miss her, didn't often brood about how different her life would be if Holly lived just around the corner.

'Sounds like you've got it all worked out, love.' Felix looked pleased too, though the crease of worry hadn't quite gone from his brow. Understandably. Their daughter was giving up a good career and a more than decent salary in a city buzzing with opportunities. And for what? It was true that there were opportunities here too, especially for something a bit more unusual, more artisan, more . . .

Orange, she thought. She shook her head.

'I've done loads of research,' Holly said. 'I really think I can make it work. And it's something I'd enjoy. Being creative, being my own boss, being back here in Dorset close to you guys.'

'Attagirl!' said Ingrid, nodding enthusiastically.

'Great!' Felix rearranged the cups on the tray. He was no doubt relieved that at least their daughter was neither pregnant nor engaged to be married to someone they'd never met.

Ella, though, seemed incapable of moving. She was still taking it in. An orange shop. Holly back here in Bridport. And the scent of a Seville orange and almond cake that was bringing back so many mixed memories she didn't quite know what to do with.

'But, er . . . how would you finance it, love?' Felix glanced across at Ella. 'Me and your mum, we don't have much spare.'

'Oh, I know that, Dad.'

'And you've given in your notice already?' He gave a little sigh. 'I don't want to put a dampener on it, and obviously we'd love for you to move back here. But have you really thought this through?'

Ingrid cleared her throat noisily. They all looked at her sitting, back erect, in her chair. 'That's where I come in,' she said.

Ella stared at her mother-in-law. Ingrid would have encouraged this idea of Holly's, of course she would, especially if she thought for a second that Ella might raise any concerns. Maybe that was unfair. But . . . Ella thought of all the times Ingrid had interfered in their life, in their marriage. Sometimes on behalf of Felix – well, he was her son after all – but sometimes selfishly too. And now Holly . . . She was still young. She had so much of her life in front of her. Ella had been hoping their daughter would be able to save some money for a deposit on a flat or house, that with their help Holly would have some security, that she might get a promotion, that she . . .

Felix was looking from his mother to his daughter. 'In what way, Mum?' he asked mildly.

'I'm financing the project,' Ingrid said proudly. 'I'm a sleeping partner.'

'What?' Ella did a double-take. 'Without consulting us?'

'I'm sorry, Mum. I know I should have told you before.'

Holly hadn't wanted to confide in her. That stung. 'Darling, I know things haven't been easy at work—' she began.

'Worse than you know,' Holly blurted.

'But . . .' Ella would love for her daughter to be back here in Dorset. She just didn't want her to throw any opportunities away, that was all. She was her mother. She couldn't help but worry.

'I've thought it through. I told you. I've done the course on starting your own business. I've done masses of research, like I said.' Her daughter looked defiant now and Ella couldn't help feeling proud. She hoped that was something she might have given Holly – because there were times when she'd had to be defiant too.

'OK,' she said. 'I'm sure that you have. I'm sorry. It's just . . .' – she hesitated – 'a shock, that's all.' Ella looked to Felix for confirmation.

'A shock,' he confirmed. 'We only want the best for you, love.'

'I know you do.' Holly took a deep breath. 'I've already located some sources for products I want to stock.' She looked around the kitchen from face to face. 'And now, some business premises have come up.'

Ingrid clapped her wrinkled hands. 'Excellent news,' she said.

'Blimey,' Felix said again.

'I didn't want to bother you, Mum.' All of a sudden, Holly was talking to Ella alone. 'You were busy. I know you worry about me. I wanted to sort things out first and then tell you.' Unexpectedly, Holly's eyes filled.

Ella took a step towards her. Perhaps this was her daughter's big opportunity after all. And as she knew only too well, chances for happiness should never be passed by. 'So, where are you planning to live?' But she smiled as she said this, hoping she already knew the answer.

'Here?' Holly's voice was small. 'Just for a while – until I get on my feet.'

Ella nodded. She took Holly in her arms and felt the softness of her daughter's hair against her face. 'That's wonderful,' she whispered. Because it really was.

Felix too was grinning as he poured the tea. 'Well,' he said. 'This really is a turn-up for the books.'

'Forget the tea, though, Dad.' Holly slipped out of Ella's arms and opened the fridge. She waggled a bottle of champagne in the air. 'We should celebrate with something a bit more exciting than tea.'

They all laughed.

'But first, Mum' – and now Holly sounded serious – 'you have to answer me a question.'

Ella felt a twinge of alarm. She was busy, but of course, she would help all she could in her daughter's venture. What mother wouldn't? She was proud. She was excited. She'd even managed to push the scent of the Seville orange and almond cake to one side. So, so long ago, she reminded herself again. And it had nothing whatever to do with what was happening now.

'Yes, darling?' She reached up to the glass-fronted cupboard for the best champagne flutes – they'd been a wedding present and were reserved for special occasions.

'I have to go on a trip to meet some producers,' Holly said. 'I've made a list. In fact, I've contacted some of them already.'

'That sounds exciting. And?' Ella stood there, champagne glasses in hand.

'And I wondered if you'd come with me?'

'Oh.' Ella beamed. 'Really?'

'Really.' Holly grinned back at her.

'I don't know how much help I'd be,' she demurred. 'I don't know anything about starting up a new business, darling.' She put the flutes on a tray and took it over to where Holly was standing.

'I wouldn't want you for that, Mum.' Holly twisted the wire on the bottle of champagne. It was so chilled Ella could see the condensation rising from the wet glass. 'More for company and moral support.'

'Hmm, well, in that case . . .' Ella was beginning to feel really good about this.

'I thought maybe during the Easter holidays?' More twisting of the wire.

'Just for a few days, do you mean?' Ella couldn't help thinking of the lesson-planning that wouldn't do itself – there was just so much of it these days. And what about Felix? 'I don't want to leave your father on his own for too long.' Though Felix was perfectly capable of managing without her.

'Don't be daft.' Felix passed around plates. 'You go. Take as much time as you need.'

'Can we fit in two weeks before you go back to work? After Easter? They say it's lovely there in the springtime.' Holly's face took on a dreamy expression. She began to ease the cork out of the bottle.

Ella did a quick calculation; she knew the term dates off by heart. 'Just about,' she said. 'Where are we going then?' She felt a warm dart of excitement. A holiday with her daughter. What could be nicer? Well, not a holiday exactly, but . . . She reached over to put the tray of glasses on the counter.

'Seville.'

There was a crash as the tray and four champagne flutes fell to the floor. Ella stared at the hundreds of tiny shards of glass. No one spoke.

'Ella?' Felix said at last.

Ella heard Ingrid's unmistakeable click of disapproval from behind her. 'I'm sorry,' she said. For goodness' sake, how could she be so clumsy? Only, she knew it wasn't just clumsiness that had made her drop the tray of glasses. 'Seville?'

'That's where most of the products come from.' Holly looked down in faint alarm at the broken glass covering the kitchen floor. 'There are over thirty thousand orange trees in the city alone,' she said. 'That's why I made the cake. I need to go to Seville. And I want you to come with me.'

CHAPTER 4

Ella

West Dorset, February 2018

'Well!' Ingrid clicked her tongue again and sighed in that way she had. Ella felt she had been listening to that sound her entire married life.

She looked down at the broken flutes; shards of glass were shining like silver all over the kitchen floor and the scent of the Seville orange and almond cake still hung in the air. 'Sorry,' she said again. 'That was so clumsy of me.' She looked at Felix.

He was regarding her steadily. 'Are you all right, Ella?' His voice was gentle.

'*She's* all right,' Ingrid said pointedly. 'But we can't say the same about the champagne glasses, more's the pity.' She laughed.

'Sorry,' Ella said for the third time. Because there was rather a lot to apologise for. 'Yes,' she said to Felix. 'I'm fine. The tray just sort of slipped out of my hands.'

Holly was staring at her, a little frown on her face as if her mother was one of those difficult fractions that she had always found so bewildering in maths lessons. Ella had helped her with maths, though, managed to stop her being number-blind, taught her that it was just another form of language like all the rest and that there were tricks. She did the same with the children she taught; it had often helped them too.

Holly bit her lip. 'Mum,' she said in a small voice. It was as if she knew – or guessed – what had made her mother drop the tray.

Ella supposed it had been rather dramatic. She wasn't usually so careless, and these glasses had survived thirty-five years without even a chip. She felt awful. She looked again at Felix. The fact that the glasses had been a wedding present made the breakage seem a much worse crime. Thirty-five years was a long time.

Felix gave a little shake of his head and she hoped this meant it didn't matter. *They're only glasses*, he might say to her later. *No one's died.*

'Stay where you are, everyone.' Felix held up a hand and took charge. 'Henry to the rescue.' He opened the utility cupboard door and pulled out the cheery-faced vacuum cleaner, plugging it in and pulling off the brush in favour of a more appropriate nozzle.

'Sweep as much as you can into a dustpan first,' Ingrid advised. She looked expectantly at Ella.

But Ella was still rooted to the spot, broken glass around her feet.

'Right you are.' Felix fetched the dustpan and got to work.

Holly took a cautious step towards her mother, managing to avoid the worst of the glass. 'Are you upset, Mum?' she asked her. 'Do you think I'm doing the wrong thing? Is that it? Tell me.'

'You're doing nothing wrong, Holly, my girl,' Ingrid said.

Felix glanced up from where he was sweeping. His expression was mild but slightly concerned.

'No, of course I'm not upset.' Ella wished they could have this conversation on their own rather than with her mother-in-law listening in. 'It was an accident.' She caught Ingrid's eye; her mother-in-law was giving her a very strange look indeed.

'So, you don't think it's a totally crazy idea – to give up my job and start my own business?' Holly was looking anxious.

'Absolutely not,' Ingrid chipped in.

As he had done before, Felix looked up from his sweeping, but said nothing.

'No. You should do what you like, darling.' Her daughter was still young. Ella was married and a mother when she was her age. 'I only want you to be happy.'

'We both do,' echoed Felix from his position on the floor.

'I know.' Holly smiled back at her father and gave Ella's arm a squeeze.

Again, Ella caught her mother-in-law's eye. And again, she felt uncomfortable under her scrutiny. 'I just wish you'd felt able to confide in me and your dad, that's all.'

'Sometimes it's easier to confide in a grandparent,' Ingrid put in helpfully. 'Sometimes your parents are too busy to listen.' She smiled fondly at Felix, as if to exonerate him – he was a man after all and it was his job to bring in the money, not listen to family problems.

'I've never been too busy to listen.' Had she? Well, perhaps, sometimes. Lessons wouldn't plan themselves and then there was the marking. Paperwork seemed to be the larger part of teaching these days.

'It's not that,' Holly reassured her. 'I told you before, I just didn't want to worry you.'

Had Ingrid asked Holly to keep quiet? Was that it?

'But what made you drop the glasses like that, Ella?' Ingrid's voice cut across Ella's thoughts. She sounded suspicious, though of course, she couldn't possibly know.

Ella glanced across at the cake. 'Um . . . slippery fingers, I suppose.' Seville, she thought. That was quite a prospect.

Holly treated her mother to one more probing look and then opened the drawer and took out a knife. She was going to cut the cake. Ella braced herself – on cutting, even more of the rich scent of orange and almond would be released.

Sure enough . . .

'Mmm.' Felix and his mother spoke in unison.

The fragrance was as intense as she remembered. Ella distracted herself by getting more glasses out of the kitchen cupboard – the everyday wine glasses this time. Felix had finished sweeping up the bigger pieces of glass and now he had switched on the vacuum, so thankfully, further conversation was paused.

Funny, thought Ella. She had put Seville – not entirely successfully – to the back of her mind for so long. The sunshine, the music, the scent of orange blossom. She glanced across at the cake once more. Really, it looked just like that other one. She remembered exactly how it would taste too.

Felix switched off the vacuum. Holly poured out the champagne and passed around the glasses.

'To Holly and her new venture,' Felix said.

'To Holly,' they echoed, taking a sip of the wine.

Holly began to pass around the plates, a piece of the cake on each one. The ceremony was so like the previous ceremony that Holly might almost have been there to witness it. Ella couldn't wait to taste the cake; at the same time she had the almost irresistible urge to run from the room.

'So, will you come with me?' Holly asked Ella.

Ella took the plate that her daughter was handing her. She breathed in the scent of orange and almond. She'd been waiting for the question, aware that she hadn't yet replied. 'I'm not sure, Holly,' she said. She didn't want to disappoint her daughter and of course she would love to have the time with her. But it wouldn't be easy to go back there.

'Oh, Mum.' Holly looked crestfallen. 'Why not?'

'Your mother's busy,' Ingrid said. *Isn't she always?* her expression seemed to add. 'Isn't there someone else you could take, my dear? An old schoolfriend perhaps? I'd have thought most people would have jumped at the chance.' She shook her head in despair.

'Ella?' Felix raised his glass to her. 'You were always so keen on the place. Don't you want to go back to Seville? You loved it, didn't you?' His grey eyes were kind and understanding.

But of course, he didn't understand at all. How could he?

'Did you, Mum?' Holly was on it immediately. Her dark eyes brightened. 'What was it you loved so much about the city?'

'Yes, I loved it,' Ella said. 'Even more than I thought I would. It was . . .' – she shrugged – 'alive.'

There was a pause, as if everyone was reflecting on her choice of words.

'I don't want to interfere . . .' Ingrid began.

'But you are,' Felix said.

They all stared at him. Ella had never heard Felix say anything like this to his mother before.

'Felix?' Ingrid looked extremely taken aback. 'Whatever do you mean?'

He straightened his shoulders and looked directly at his mother, who was still sitting in her chair, though the rest of them had remained standing. 'I mean that you should let Ella and Holly decide what they're doing,' he said firmly. 'You should keep out of it.'

Ingrid let out a little gasp. 'Keep out of it?'

Ella and Holly exchanged a glance – part complicit, part horrified.

'Yes,' said Felix. His eyes were steely. There was clearly no way he was backing down.

'That's some way to speak to your mother, my lad,' Ingrid spluttered. She made as if to get up from her chair but then seemed to remember the champagne and cake and sat down again. 'Especially when *I* have been the one to help Holly.'

'I know you have.' Felix went over to her and put a gentle hand on her shoulder. 'And believe me, we're all very grateful to you – me, Ella and Holly. Very grateful for your kindness and your generosity.'

Ingrid stared at him, bemused.

'Yes, Gran,' Holly echoed. 'Very grateful.'

'But whether or not Ella goes with Holly to Seville,' Felix went on, 'that's up to the two of them. Ella works really hard, you know that; the school, the children – they all depend on her.'

Ella blinked at him in astonishment.

'So, it's nothing to do with you or me. OK?'

Ingrid nodded. She pursed her lips but said nothing further. She was clearly so shocked that if she'd been holding four champagne flutes, she probably would have dropped them too.

Well done, Felix . . . It might seem a small thing, but to Ella it was a mountain. Their whole life together she had been waiting for Felix to stand up to his mother, to challenge her, to defend Ella. He had tried to mollify, to be a diplomat, to please everyone. At times – and here, Ella couldn't help but think of Seville back in 1988 – he had even risked his marriage in order to keep his mother happy.

'So, will you come with me, Mum?' Holly asked. 'I could go on my own, but . . .'

'Sometimes every girl needs her mother,' said Felix.

Her mother . . . Ella saw a pointed shard of glass on the floor by her foot; it looked like a tiny dagger. She bent to pick it up and put it in the kitchen bin, but once again she was careless and the pointed end caught at the flesh on her fingertip. A bubble of blood appeared.

'Ella.' Felix sprang forwards with the kitchen roll. He tore off a piece and held it to her finger, which was bleeding freely now. 'You should be more careful,' he said.

He was right. But perhaps she'd forgotten that sometimes you also had to take a chance. 'I'd love to come with you, darling,' she told Holly. She couldn't let this effort of Felix's be wasted.

'That's brilliant, Mum!' Holly flung her arms around her.

Ella held her close for as long as she could. She was terrified and she was excited. Seville always seemed to have that effect on her. But . . .

No. She wouldn't think about the 'buts'. She'd face them when she got there. Neither would she take any notice of Ingrid, who gave another little despairing shake of the head but thankfully remained silent.

Instead, Ella smiled at Felix. 'Thank you,' she whispered. She had the feeling he would know what she was thanking him for.

And finally, she took a bite of the Seville orange and almond cake. The taste of the almond oil was sweet on her tongue, the orange as bitter-sweet as ever. It took her back there immediately – just as Ella had known it would.

CHAPTER 5

Holly

Seville, 2018

Holly and Ella took a taxi from the airport to their hotel in Santa Cruz. Holly wanted to be in the old town, in the centre of things; she already had a couple of meetings lined up, but there would be plenty of time left over, she hoped, for seeing some of the city. Their trip had slotted into the gap between Seville's famous *Semana Santa* festival, culminating with the processions on Good Friday, and the *Feria de Abril* a few weeks later which sounded like an incredible spectacle but might not, Holly suspected, be the best time to be having business meetings in the city.

'Where did you stay when you came here before?' she asked her mother as the taxi bumped over the narrow cobblestones of the old town, nearly taking out several tourists on the way. 'Can you remember?' Or are you willing to tell? she silently added.

Although she had agreed to come to Seville with Holly – after some persuasion it had to be said – her mother had remained cagey on what exactly had happened here the first time around. Perhaps it was nothing remarkable after all. But going by her mother's reaction when Holly had baked the Seville orange and almond cake, not to mention the dropping of the champagne flutes, Holly suspected the opposite.

Her mother turned to face her. Like Holly, she'd been staring out of the car window at the cafés and bars lining the narrow street, at whitewashed houses and shops where crimson shawls and multicoloured fans seemed to dominate what was on offer. Plants trailed from terracotta pots on little tiled patios and climbed along wrought-iron balconies to cascade over the skinny pavements. There was a strange look in her mother's hazel eyes, almost of longing.

'I remember,' she said. 'It was a hotel in the Alameda de Hércules.' She pointed. 'Over in that direction. About fifteen minutes' walk from the centre. The tapas bars there were always crammed full of locals.'

Hmm. This was the most her mother had ever said about their trip to Seville. Perhaps she was opening up at last?

Holly was looking forward to sampling the tapas. They were bound to be more authentic than anything to be found in the UK. 'What did Dad make of the tapas back then?' she asked her mother. Holly's father was very traditional in his tastes; it was her mother who had always been the adventurous one.

'Oh.' Her mother looked as if she wasn't quite sure how to reply. 'He was a bit cautious at first, but . . .' Her voice trailed. She glanced at Holly as if about to say more, then clammed up again.

Which seemed to sum up her parents' visit to Seville, thought Holly. They had certainly made it into a mystery.

They were driving now through a warren of white alleys and patios. Every so often she caught sight of a seductively tiled porch, a wide wooden doorway allowing a peek beyond of stone walls and fountains.

Holly had known that making the Seville orange and almond cake – which had tasted delicious as it turned out – was a risk, because clearly it meant more to her mother than she was saying. Which suggested perhaps that Seville meant more to her too . . . Holly smiled at a guitarist playing to a small audience outside what seemed to be a flamenco museum. Flamenco – that was another thing she would definitely be making time for, she decided. Their driver had his window open and a few chords crept into the car as they drove past. Her mother heard them too and Holly saw her expression change once more – into nostalgia this time.

Perhaps Holly had made the cake in order to try to force something out into the open? Her mother had always been so odd about that recipe, keeping it half hidden in her recipe book as if half-hoping it would be found. No wonder Holly had been tempted.

She craned her neck to get a better look at the whitewashed buildings with window grilles and colourful flowers blossoming in window boxes. A strong scent wafted in the air. Holly let out a small gasp as it stole into the car. She turned to her mother.

'Orange blossom,' her mother said. And she closed her eyes.

Of course, thought Holly. What else?

Holly may not have learnt much about her parents' trip to Seville in the 1980s, but her mother was here with her now and that was the important thing. Holly had almost two weeks in which to find out more.

'And look!' Her mother was pointing to the top of a tall spire back in the direction they'd come from.

Holly craned her neck to see. 'What is it?'

'The spinner on La Giralda.' Her mother was smiling now. 'It's actually a weathervane, you know. They say you can see it from almost everywhere in the city.'

On impulse, Holly leant over and hugged her. Perhaps her mother was happy to be here in Seville after all.

After that weekend visit to Dorset when she'd made her announcement and baked the cake, Holly had given notice on her Brighton flat and moved back home. Leaving Brighton had been easier than she'd expected – perhaps the city had only ever been a temporary stopping place for her, a chance to test out her independence. Moving back home, though, that had been a strange turnaround.

Her old childhood bedroom looked much the same, though her father had painted the walls a natural pinkish shade called 'setting plaster' and her mother had placed a purple hand-woven Indian cover on the bed. Holly's bookshelves still contained some of her old books – and she soon filled them up with the rest. Her old wardrobe was almost empty, since her mother had nagged her to take clothes she no longer wanted to the charity shop on previous visits home; but this too soon filled up again. The same little stained-glass tortoise bedside lamp sat on top of the same bedside table and the dressing-table drawers were soon filled once more with her underwear, sweaters and tights.

By the time Holly had put her prints up on the walls, her old bedroom had become an updated version of its former self and she almost felt she had never left home at all. Just, perhaps, grown up a little.

How would she fit in with her parents now that she'd come back? she wondered. So far, so good. She took her turn with the cooking and clearing up. She felt more secure somehow, coming back to the town in which she'd been born; wrapped in her roots once again. She spent hours walking the cliffs between West Bay and Hive Beach, climbing the hill at Seatown to Golden Cap, revelling in the landscape of her girlhood. It was spring but still cold and the sea was as wild as it had been in wintertime. Sections of the crumbly ginger cliff at the bay had eroded and fallen a few weeks ago; someone who had underestimated the power of the sea had got stranded, sucked into the ocean by a freak wave and drowned. The landscape was not always a peaceful one.

Holly spent time sorting out the premises that would become her shop, Bitter Orange, for she was hoping to open in May, ready for the summer season of visitors. She continued to plan her business, she made the appointments for the sources she had found and which she would be exploring further on this trip to Seville, and she continued with all the other countless administrative tasks that running your own business entailed. She made batches of Seville orange marmalade too, filling her mother's kitchen with the sweet scent of boiling sugar and fruit. It was a time of new beginnings. Holly was nervous but also couldn't wait for Bitter Orange to be properly up and running.

In the cab, Holly glanced across at her mother and reached for her hand to give it a squeeze. She still felt guilty that she hadn't confided in her parents earlier. It was a big thing to have kept quiet about; no wonder her mother had been hurt and upset at first. Perhaps Holly shouldn't have let Gran persuade her to keep it a secret? She'd always known there was some bad feeling between her mother and grandmother and the last thing Holly wanted was to be in the middle of it. She loved them both; she didn't want home to be a battleground.

Her mother turned to her. The expression in her eyes was impossible to read. 'You haven't really told me, darling,' she said. 'What made you choose . . .' – she hesitated – '"all things orange"? For your shop, I mean.'

That was easy. 'Marmalade,' Holly said.

They both laughed.

Holly decided not to mention her mother's old recipe, which had played a part in it, for sure. 'The first time I saw a heap of bitter oranges in the farm shop,' she continued. 'They were so bright. So full of promise.'

Her mother nodded as if she knew exactly what she meant.

'And then there was the marmalade, and I realised how many other things were made from oranges.' She shrugged. 'The idea just came to me.' She only hoped it would prove to be a good idea.

They arrived at the hotel in Santa Cruz a few minutes later. The taxi driver parked right outside in the middle of the road, careless that he was holding up traffic. He pulled their bags out of the boot and Holly fished in her purse for some euros with which to pay him.

They made their way towards the hotel. There wasn't much traffic actually, because the hotel was at the bottom of the street, in a plaza, so it was kind of a dead-end road. The hotel itself looked charming. Its old door of burnished wood was half open, revealing a porchway lined with tiles.

'Oh, Mum, come and look at these.' Holly was immediately enchanted. They were blue and yellow, wound with images of flowers and snakes.

Her mother, though, was staring towards the plaza, towards

the cobbles, the faded grandeur of a fine building that stood opposite the hotel and looked towards an orange grove. The sun was lighting up strands of her dark hair into shades of mahogany. And there was that expression of wistfulness, of longing, in her eyes again.

'Mum?'

'Sorry, darling.' She seemed to come to, followed Holly, reached out to touch the tiles in the porchway. 'Yes,' she said, 'you're right, they are lovely. Well, let's go inside, shall we?'

The foyer of the hotel was light and airy, painted white with creamy pillars and arches, a big and dramatic picture of a flamenco dancer in a red and black dress positioned on one wall. A candelabra sat atop a baby grand piano and in the centre of the foyer was an ornate marble fountain with water trickling through, cane chairs scattered around the cool space. At the back in the centre was another decorative tiled facade, while terracotta pots of vibrant orange amaryllis and early-flowering lilies softened every corner. It reminded Holly of Marrakesh where she had gone with Jack, her Brighton ex, some years ago to stay in a riad; here, there was the same sense of light, space and tranquillity as in the central core of a Moorish stone building.

They checked in and soon settled into their two adjacent single rooms ('We'll probably both need a bit of space,' her mother had said when they'd made the booking) which were on the first floor with a good view of the cluttered white street, the maze of the old town beyond and, of course, the plaza and the orange grove. And it was still only early afternoon.

'Where to first?' Her mother looked slightly anxious again now. 'The cathedral? The palace? A bit of sightseeing before you get down to business?'

Holly consulted her phone. 'I thought we might take a look around Triana,' she said. 'Did you go there when you came to Seville, Mum? It's the best place for ceramics apparently.' It wasn't exactly on the tourist trail, but to Holly, the area sounded creative and exciting.

'Ceramics?' her mother said. She sounded out of breath, though they hadn't gone anywhere yet. 'Triana?' She paused. 'Yes, I did go there.'

'One of my contacts lives in Triana,' Holly said. 'Tomás. I'm not due to meet him till tomorrow morning, but I could text him and see if he's free.' She glanced at her mother. She looked terrified. 'Or are you too tired, Mum? We could just wander around the old town, if you like?'

'Yes.' Her mother was like a drowning woman grasping a lifeline. 'Yes, please, Holly. I'm feeling a bit wiped out from that early morning flight. Can we leave . . .' – she hesitated again before saying the word – 'Triana until tomorrow?'

'Yes, of course. But let's go and explore for a bit in the old town, shall we? And maybe get a late lunch at one of the delicious-looking tapas bars we saw on the way here?'

'Perfect.' Now her mother looked relieved.

And so they returned to reception, left the cool of the white foyer of the hotel and stepped out into the warm and honey-scented sunshine of Seville.

CHAPTER 6

Ella

Seville, 1988

'Look, Felix!' Ella clutched his sleeve. 'Flamenco!'

'Oh, yes.' Felix seemed lost for words. Perhaps he was feeling as overwhelmed by their surroundings as she. The Plaza Nueva was a peaceful cobbled square lined by tall, decorative buildings including the imposing Seville City Hall, gilded in the sunshine. The square was planted with elegant plane trees and fragrant orange trees and in the centre of the plaza stood a bronze statue of a man on horseback. Ella consulted her guidebook. Ferdinand III of Castile.

But on the far edge of the marble and granite mosaicked cobbles, under the glossy leaves of a white blossoming orange tree, a young black-haired woman in a scarlet dress, her dark hair threaded with flowers, had set up a tape recorder and was already adopting the haughty flamenco stance, waiting for the crowd to gather.

Ella and Felix drew closer. It was irresistible. The scent of the orange blossom filled Ella's nostrils, heady and sweet. 'Oh, darling. Isn't it marvellous?'

And Felix squeezed her hand with such affection that Ella glanced at him in surprise. It was getting to him then. The magic of Seville was working. So perhaps things could be all right between them after all. Maybe their marriage could be saved, and they could find a way through.

The taped music began with a drumbeat, little more than a pulse. The dancer clicked her fingers – once, twice, as if summoning the people to her show. Maintaining her dramatic posture, she waited.

Ella shivered with anticipation – for the dance; for this time in Seville with Felix which still lay ahead of them, glorious and unknown, because they had only arrived this morning and now they were here, in Spain, just as she'd longed for, having their first holiday together abroad. It was just the two of them, Felix was being as attentive as he'd been when they first met six years ago and now there was a flamenco dancer in the square. It was almost impossibly romantic . . .

The soft drumbeat was joined by the rhythmic strum of a guitar and Ella watched as the dancer shifted her erect pose, moving from side to side, swirling the flounces of her gauzy red dress in time with the beat, slowly at first then gradually building to a rapid tempo. She tossed her head back defiantly, lifted her chin and began to move to the music, her poses stylised, her arms writhing slowly like serpents, her heels tapping on the pink, grey and white cobblestones.

Ella fancied she could read the expression in those dark, arrogant eyes. *I will perform this dance for you, but do not doubt it, you tourists will pay.*

And quite right too. The dancer's shoulders tipped and

rocked, her head jerked, she twisted and kicked, she spun. She threw her black shawl out from side to side; she drew it in front of her and behind. She leant and she circled in a fluidity of movement that was both sensuous and mesmerising. And all the time, the drumbeat and the delicate plucking of the guitar went on, accompanied by a voice that was, Ella thought, more wailing than singing.

Ella couldn't take her eyes off the dancer. What would her mother have said if she could see her now, here in Spain, watching flamenco? As the restless beat got faster, as the red shoes tapped and clicked more loudly on the cobbles, the dancer's movements, her countenance, became more emotional, more urgent, more frenzied. The rhythm of the music was complex and unpredictable; Ella found it impossible to follow. And still, the dancer danced on, her body as fluid as water, her expression at first proud, then passionate, then full of suffering and pain.

Ella found herself holding her breath. She felt that she was living the dance somehow, experiencing for herself the suffering of the lone dancer. It was incredible. How on earth had Ella managed to persuade Felix to come here?

They had been sitting, one evening last winter, in the lounge of his mother's house – the lounge which the three of them shared, since Felix and Ella were living there too, saving up to buy their own home. Felix was in the big maroon velveteen armchair with the white antimacassars, Ella was at the dining table marking a set of her class's exercise books. *A Place I'd Like to Visit*. That was the title of the composition the children had written for their homework. Ah, thought Ella, she'd quite like to tackle that subject herself.

Felix's mother Ingrid rose from the sofa to prepare the hot chocolate she always made at ten p.m. – her signal that it was time for everyone to go to bed. She always made it clear that she disapproved of late nights in front of the TV, or anywhere else for that matter, Ella thought uncharitably.

Ella waited until her mother-in-law had disappeared through to the kitchen. 'Where would you go?' she asked her husband of five years. Though actually, shouldn't she know?

'Hmm?' Felix had one eye on the news. He didn't have the strong political opinions of his mother, but he liked to know what was going on in the world.

Ella repeated the question and told him about the homework she was marking.

'Ilfracombe?' he said. 'St Ives?'

'Oh, Felix.'

'Devon and Cornwall are both lovely.' He looked affronted. 'All right, North Wales then.'

Ella sighed. When they went away during the school holidays – only a week; it was hard for Felix to get time off from the garden centre and he didn't like leaving his mother alone for too long – they always went to Devon, Cornwall or North Wales. Felix was entirely missing the point of the exercise. Ella was talking dreams.

'Well, where would you like to go?' Felix asked her.

That was easy. 'Spain,' she said.

Felix pulled a face. 'Stuck in some characterless costa del something with a load of lager louts? Really?'

Ella couldn't help appreciating the alliteration. But sometimes, Felix sounded like his mother. Sometimes he sounded fifty-five, not twenty-five.

'Not on the coast,' she said crisply. 'I'd go to Seville. It's a beautiful city. It's warm, sunny and has a wonderful sense of history.'

It wasn't just that. Ella had recently read a novel that was set in Seville and it had contained a passage about flamenco that had given her goosebumps. She had a musical jewellery box her mother had given her as a child and it had a flamenco dancer on the top who danced to the tune of 'Spanish Eyes'. Ella loved that box; it had always seemed so exotic to her. And the day her mum had given it to her was a rare perfect memory among many others that were far from perfect and probably best forgotten.

'I've never been to Spain,' her mother had said wistfully. 'But you will, Ella, one day, you will.'

Even then, Ella had longed for it. And now, she longed even more for the colours of Seville that had been described in the pages of the story she'd read – the shiny yellows, oranges and greens of the fruit trees, the dramatic black, red and gold of the flamenco. Perhaps she longed for the passion too.

Felix grunted and Ella sensed the chink of an opening. 'Couldn't we?' she tried.

'What?'

'Go to Seville? Next spring? For a real holiday? Abroad?' She launched herself from her chair and went to perch on the arm of his.

Felix blinked and drew back slightly as if to absorb the attack. 'We're saving up, Ella,' he reminded her, 'for—'

'I know.' As if she could forget. Anytime she wanted anything, he reminded her. She felt as if she were living half a life, a life of waiting. So, it was up to her to change things. She leant closer, whispered in his ear. 'We could go in the Easter holidays.' He smelt faintly of earth and foliage.

'But—'

'I don't want to grow old before my time, Felix.' Where had

that come from? But Ella knew. It had come from five years of living with Felix in his mother's house.

She shouldn't be ungrateful. Her mother-in-law wasn't a bad person. Ingrid had strong opinions, yes. She lived her life according to a strict set of rules and expected others living under her roof to do the same. Fair enough. And she was also kind. Hadn't she allowed Felix to rescue Ella? Hadn't she taken Ella in, thereby giving her security and choices that Ella was in danger of losing? Ella had much to thank her mother-in-law for. But even so . . .

Ella suspected that living with Ingrid was slowly but surely driving her insane. And as for Felix . . . He didn't stand up to his mother. She knew that he couldn't bring himself to. Ingrid was still grieving for the death of Felix's father, or so Felix had told her, and Ella privately suspected that her mother-in-law had made Felix the replacement before Felix and Ella had even met. But why hadn't Felix prevented this from happening? Ella was in danger of fast losing all respect for her husband. She didn't want to, but it was happening anyway.

Felix seemed taken aback. 'What on earth do you mean, darling?' He took her hand, checked the doorway to see if his mother was on her way back in – Ingrid didn't approve of easy affection either. Hardly surprisingly, over the years this had made Ella and Felix less and less affectionate with one another. And . . . But Ella wouldn't think about the 'and'. Not now.

'I want . . .'

'What do you want, Ella?'

'I want . . .' She regarded him helplessly. 'I don't know exactly. But not this.' She looked around the dingy, claustrophobic living room. 'I want to live, Felix. I want to have fun. I need to get away – just for a week, that's all.'

Ingrid returned to the room then and the subject was dropped. But some of Ella's desperation must have got through to Felix, because before the week was out, they'd visited the travel agent, withdrawn the money from their precious savings and booked this holiday to Seville. And off they flew, leaving a tight-lipped Ingrid behind them.

Ella's triumph couldn't be sweeter. They were here for a week – and what a week they would have. Nothing could spoil it now.

'Isn't it wonderful?' Ella said, as the music rose in its final crescendo before dropping to a murmur of wistfulness. 'Aren't you so glad we came?' Ella edged closer to Felix. He didn't smell of earth and foliage now that they were in Seville. He smelt of something fruity, sweet and almost seductive. Or perhaps that wasn't Felix at all – it might be the orange trees in the square. But what did it matter? She was breathing it in and it felt as if she were breathing in life itself. 'I'm so happy to be here. Alone with you.'

As the music finally faded, Felix glanced at her with a look of what seemed to be affectionate tolerance. 'Me too,' he said. 'It's really nice.'

'Mmm.' She took his arm and snuggled closer. Though he could sound a bit more enthusiastic.

'Still, I didn't like leaving her,' Felix said. 'She's been so good.'

Oh, why did he have to spoil things? 'Yes.' Ella was tired of being grateful. She was young – she wanted to rant a little. Yes, and enjoy this time alone for once without thinking of everything – and everyone – they'd left behind.

He frowned and drew her away from the horseshoe of tourists. Ella sighed.

'It is nice,' he said again. 'But . . .'

'Yes, I know.' It had cost them more than they could afford. Already, the intensity of the music and dancing had dissolved. Already, the tranquil atmosphere of the Plaza Nueva seemed spoilt.

She saw the frustration in his grey eyes. 'Don't you want us to get our own place, Ella?' He was hurt. He really didn't understand. And that was partly Ella's fault, because it was so hard to explain. 'After all, when we have children—'

'Yes, of course I do.' But that was another issue that had come between them. Felix wanted them to start a family as soon as possible, while Ella wanted to wait – not only because they hadn't got their own home yet, but also because of her career. She wanted to establish herself first. They'd married so young. She wanted to gain some sense of independence, make a place for herself at the school. What was wrong with that? And besides, what was the hurry? She was only twenty-three years old. She didn't want to get pregnant and leave when she'd been there less than a year. But that was another thing. How would she get pregnant if they hardly ever made love?

'I want us to have our own home,' she reiterated. *But not if it destroys us in the process*, she silently added. She looked up at Felix. The sun was filtering through the leaves of the plane trees, highlighting the fair hair that kept flopping into his eyes, no matter how often he brushed it back.

Ella had read in her guidebook that this square was the site of an old convent. No wonder it was so peaceful. She didn't want to argue here. She didn't want to say anything that would spoil things, that would acknowledge how much had already gone wrong between them. If she didn't say it, the feeling wouldn't be real.

She nodded towards the dancer, to the basket she'd placed in front of her makeshift stage, and they moved forwards together. Felix threw in some pesetas and the dancer favoured them with a small nod of acceptance.

Ella squeezed his arm. The important thing was that she still loved Felix, didn't she, with his tall gangly frame, already slightly stooped with bending to pot plants and tending to seedlings? She'd liked him from the moment she'd first seen him in the cinema queue, since he offered for her and Mandy to go ahead of him because the seats were mostly taken, since he overcame his own awkwardness with a gentle smile.

The film was *The Elephant Man*, the sad and moving story of a man living with deformity in late nineteenth-century London. John Hurt's performance had brought Ella to tears. Bumping into Felix again outside the cinema, seeing the warmth in his grey eyes and accepting his offer of a drink in a nearby pub (he'd invited Mandy too, of course), had been the catalyst for them to start seeing one another.

When Ella trusted him enough to open up a bit more about her life, her unhappiness living at home with her mother and stepfather, her desire to go to teacher training college, her desperation to get away . . . Felix couldn't have been kinder. And then more than kind. They got on well, they began spending more and more time together.

Within weeks he had told her that he loved her; within months he had proposed. He'd insisted that she still go to college as planned, but perhaps as a day student rather than a boarder? Within a year of their first meeting, they were married and Ella had moved in with Felix and his mother, Ingrid. And weeks later, Ella's mother and stepfather had moved to

Scarborough, his old family home. Her stepfather at least was relieved to be rid of her, no doubt.

Ella never saw her mother again. A year later, Kenny, her stepfather got in touch to tell her that her mother had died from a stroke. Once, they had been so close. And there had been good times – before Kenny. Ella was heartbroken. Felix took her to Scarborough for the funeral and Ella suffered Kenny and his family, who were as loud and disrespectful as Kenny had always been. Ella could barely remember her real father. And in truth, she had lost her mother a long time ago.

Now, Ella and Felix sat down on a wrought-iron bench under a palm tree and Felix held her hand. In front of them, two pigeons strutted, looking for food, moving their heads in that funny jerky way that pigeons do. They were slimmer and whiter than pigeons at home. More like doves, she thought, an appropriate symbol of love and peace here in the tranquil Plaza Nueva.

Ella felt a sense of serenity wash over her. She'd been so right to persuade Felix to come here. In Seville they could sort out whatever had gone wrong between them. They could spend quality time together; reconnect in all the ways they needed to. In Seville, there was no Ingrid to dictate their every move, no looks of faint disapproval, no eggshells to negotiate.

They would eat tapas and drink rich, fruity Spanish wine and absorb the colours and flavours of Seville; the sensuality. They would be restored. Ella would find whatever was missing between them and she would slot it back where it belonged. That lost piece of jigsaw that was threatening to ruin the picture. She was sure of it.

They headed back to the hotel to change for dinner, wandering through the winding street of Calle Sierpes where an old woman was playing the accordion, staring sightlessly in front of her but smiling all the while. The extravagantly gilded and marbled Sierpes shopfronts fascinated Ella and she made Felix loiter as she took photos of the cakes, pastries and sweets in the elaborate Confitería La Campana, as she examined the old timepieces displayed in the clockmaker's El Cronómetro, and explored the beautiful art and jewellery shops, before entering the shop selling thousands of traditional Spanish fans.

'Let's find a souvenir,' Felix suggested and they studied the huge variety on offer before plumping for a red, black and gold fan made of a light varnished wood featuring the image of a flamenco dancer, the obvious choice for Ella.

They dipped into the Sombrerería Maquedano, a hat shop with no counter, just two seats, a large mirror and lots of hat boxes. Ella giggled while Felix browsed the catalogue from caps to sombreros, though of course he wouldn't be buying anything, it was all far too expensive. Then she pulled him into Papelería Ferrer, which was, according to her guidebook, the oldest stationer's in Spain, founded in 1856 by a Catalan family.

Finally, they wandered back to their hotel in the Alameda de Hércules. It had been such a lovely afternoon and Ella was content. She felt as if she were floating. For a whole week nothing would bother her. She wouldn't let it.

'*Señor, señor.*' The hotel manager was flapping about in reception when they got back. He wiped his sweating brow.

'*Si?*' Felix had grown an inch or two this afternoon, she thought. Back at home he seemed to be infinitesimally shrinking. Back at home, through no fault of his own, he seemed somehow less of a man.

'There has been a telephone call,' the manager said.

'Yes?' Ella felt Felix's body stiffen beside her.

'It is your mother, *señor*.'

'What is it? Is she ill? Has she had an accident?' Felix's face drained of colour.

But Ella knew already. She felt her sense of contentment beginning to drain from her. Ingrid was not going to allow them to enjoy this holiday together. She had found a way of preventing it.

'A fall, I think.'

'Is she badly hurt?'

'I am afraid I do not know.' The manager coughed politely. 'But it was your mother who telephoned, so . . .'

So, not badly hurt then. But already, everything was spoilt. Ella went into the bar and ordered two brandies. She had the feeling that they would both be needing a drink.

CHAPTER 7

Holly

Seville, 2018

Holly and her mother strolled over the Puente de Isabel II, known as the Triana bridge because it led to the district of the same name. It was a warm and sunny day; canoeists were striking out through the placid River Guadalquivir and people sat on the riverbanks and ambled along the sandy pathways below. The sun glinted gold on the green water and the intricate wrought iron of the bridge cast delicate shadow-patterns on the ground at their feet. A saxophonist was playing a mournful tune that Holly half recognised; waves of music carried on the gentle breeze.

Her mother lingered, dark hair loose around her shoulders, her arms resting on the balustrade, gazing nostalgically out into a distance that might or might not contain whatever it was that had happened to her here, whatever it was that had made her scared of coming back. Because she had been scared, Holly was certain of it. But why? And if her mother was scared, or even anxious, then was this a reason for concern? Holly hoped not.

She thought of the recipe for the Seville orange and almond cake. Had it originated here? Presumably so. But so far, her mother had said so little about that previous trip to Seville. Which was strange, to say the least. It suggested – didn't it? – that all had not gone well when her mother was here before.

Holly walked on into Triana. The tall buildings immediately made the street more shadowy than the open riverfront. Was this *barrio* a darker place than the rest of the city? She suspected so. In the distance, she caught sight of a statue and as she got closer, she saw that it was a sad-eyed bullfighter; some local hero, no doubt, a gaping hole in his belly testament to how he had gained his fame and lost his life. Holly checked the map she was following on her phone. And this must be the Plaza del Altozano, its glass-fronted balconies providing a perfect venue for people-watching.

She took a photo and waited for her mother to catch up. There was a vibrancy about this area – Holly felt it immediately. The *barrio* had a strong sense of history and of real life too. These were working people thronging the streets and going about their business this morning. Triana might cater for tourists, but it had retained a firm sense of identity. It wasn't just the bustling main road ahead of them, or the street performers and musicians she'd already spotted in the plaza; not even the plethora of colourful and decorative *azulejo* tiles on the facades of the buildings everywhere she looked. Holly took another picture. It was something in the air, she thought. Something about the spirit of the *barrio*. If every place had a soul, Holly was drawn instinctively to Triana's.

She turned to her mother. Was it her imagination or was there a new gleam of excitement in her mother's eyes? She hoped so. 'What do you think, Mum?' she asked.

'It's hardly changed,' her mother said. 'But what do *you* think, Holly?' She had her head to one side and she was smiling.

'I like it,' Holly said decisively. She smiled back. There seemed to be something special that the two of them were sharing in this moment, in this place.

The street was lined with orange trees, many in fruit, and there was still enough blossom to send an intoxicating scent their way. Holly breathed in deeply. If she had all these bitter oranges, just think how many jars of marmalade she could make . . .

'Isn't it heavenly?' Holly realised that her mother too was breathing in the aromatic fragrance.

'It really is.' They linked arms and walked on.

'Why do you think they planted only bitter oranges in Seville?' Holly asked her. 'Was it just a tease – seeing as no one could eat them, I mean?'

'I think they were grown originally because the trees are so decorative.' Her mother looked up into the branches as they passed by. 'As well as for the fragrance, of course.'

'They are pretty.' Holly had always been attracted to the bumpy-skinned, almost startlingly vibrant variety of the Seville orange – not just for marmalade but for the look and scent of them too – but she could see now how colourful these trees made every street in Seville. At the moment, some of the fruit was a paler orange, some as green as a lime, but they were a long way away from harvesting time, she knew. 'Plus, they'd provide some welcome shade in summer when the temperatures soar,' she added.

'Hmm.' Holly's mother had that dreamy wistful expression on her face again. 'In China they believe that orange trees bring their owners happiness and good fortune,' she said.

'That's nice.' She seemed to know a lot about it, Holly thought. 'Do you think it's true?' She hoped so, for her own sake.

'Who knows?' Her mother came to with a start. 'So, who did you say you're meeting, darling?' She took a firmer hold of Holly's arm as they continued to stroll down the Calle San Jacinto.

'Tomás,' Holly reminded her. 'He's one of my main contacts here.' She'd exchanged several emails with him over the past weeks and he had sounded friendly and knowledgeable about many of the local products that Holly was interested in. What she was most interested in, though, were those organic and natural soaps, cleansers and body oils made with neroli orange blossom and Andalusian herbs that Tomás's mother Sofía made – and in her own kitchen apparently.

'Tomás?' Her mother frowned. 'Does he have a surname?'

'Of course.' Holly glanced at her mother curiously. 'Why do you want to know his surname, Mum?' Another part of the mystery? she wondered.

'Oh, no reason. Look, Holly.' Her mother drew her attention to a pretty wrought-iron balcony riotous with vivid red flowers hanging down almost to the ground.

'What are they?' Holly supposed that with a father who'd worked in a garden centre all his life, she should know, but she had no idea.

'Trumpet vine,' her mother supplied. 'Your father would know the Latin name but I can't help you there.'

'They're stunning.' Holly manoeuvred a pathway around a long-haired musician playing classical guitar, his instrument propped on his shoulder. 'And it's Pérez,' she said. 'Tomás Pérez.'

'Pérez. Ah, yes.' Her mother nodded vaguely. 'And where does he live?'

Holly had no idea, though she guessed it was in Triana. 'We're not meeting him at his home.' Tomás hadn't suggested it. Perhaps he was protective of his mother. At any rate, he managed the business, ran the website Holly had found some months ago and dealt with all enquiries; so far Holly hadn't had any contact with Sofía at all.

'Where are you meeting him then, darling?' Her mother was looking around as they walked; she seemed to be scrutinising every face.

'In a bar just round the corner, I think.' Holly consulted her phone. 'Yes. And *we're* meeting him. You're coming with me, aren't you?'

'Well . . .' Her mother looked uncomfortable now.

'Mum!' Holly was beginning to get annoyed. What was she so anxious about? Was it something that Holly should be anxious about too? And really, what was the point of her coming to Seville if she wasn't even going to offer Holly any support?

'Do you honestly want me hanging around? I thought I might just go somewhere, get a coffee, and—'

'Yes, I do want you around.' She turned to face her. 'What are you so afraid of, Mum?'

'Nothing. No one.' But her mother looked so chastened that Holly softened and pulled her into a hug.

'I'm sorry,' Holly whispered. 'But I'm new to this, remember? You might think of something I've forgotten to ask him.'

'Yes, I know you are and you're right. I'm sorry too, darling.'

Holly drew back. Was that a tear in her mother's eye? She shouldn't have been so short with her, she realised.

'And of course I'll come.' Her mother gave a little smile and squeezed her arm. 'If you want me to.'

'I do. You could make notes or something.' She knew her

mother always carried a notebook and pen around with her in case she thought of an idea for a lesson plan.

This would be her first proper business meeting and Holly didn't want to admit it, but despite what she'd learnt on her business course, despite the thoroughness of her research, despite her assumed confidence . . . she was nervous.

She looked up. Ahead of them a magnolia tree – of the large and glossy-leaved Mediterranean variety – stood in front of a terracotta church, which according to the map on her phone must be the Iglesia de San Jacinto. She steered them left down the Calle Pagés del Corro, where the bar was situated a little way up on the right.

'And, Holly?'

'Yes, Mum?'

'You'll do just fine, darling,' her mother said. 'I know it.'

As business meetings went, Holly supposed it was unusual. The bar was busy; from the outside it looked simple and old-fashioned, painted navy blue with old lace curtains at the windows; inside, strikingly patterned *azulejo* tiles of blue and ochre lined the walls from floor to ceiling.

Tomás was already there. He came over to greet them immediately – they must, Holly supposed, be instantly recognisable as the only non-Spanish people in the place.

'Holly, yes?'

'Yes. And this is my mother, Ella.'

'So happy to meet you. I am Tomás.'

They all shook hands. Tomás was dressed casually in a black T-shirt and blue jeans. His thick dark hair was brushed back from his face and he had brown eyes and a pleasant welcoming smile.

'You would like something to eat and drink?'

She'd known from his emails that he spoke perfect English, which was a relief to Holly. 'Coffee would be lovely,' she said.

At which Tomás yelled out an order to the barman for café cortado and tostada con tomate. 'A small snack,' he said. 'Business, it is never good on an empty stomach.'

He led the way over to a battered wooden table in the corner. They exchanged pleasantries and Tomás welcomed them to Triana – 'the best part of the city,' he said. The food and drinks were brought over and Tomás rubbed his hands together in anticipation. 'To business then,' he said, taking a large bite of tomato toast.

'To business.' Holly wasn't quite sure how she could make herself heard in this noisy bar, but she smiled and her mother pulled her notebook and pen from her bag.

In the end, it wasn't difficult at all. The buzz going on around them stopped Holly from feeling nervous; it felt more like a friendly conversation between two acquaintances. The coffee was intense and bitter and the *tostado* delicious – improved by the addition of sherry vinegar, according to Tomás. They discussed the products and the quantity Sofía and her small team could feasibly produce for export. Holly wanted to think of the environmental cost too; was it possible that other products from other makers could be exported at the same time? This might be something they could explore.

Tomás had a bag of samples with him. Holly had seen everything online, but that was no substitute for seeing, touching and smelling the real thing. She and her mother spent some time examining the soaps and bath and sleep oils, feeling the textures, sniffing the fragrances and assessing the quality.

'This essential oil smells amazing.' Holly dabbed some onto the pulse at her wrist and breathed in deeply.

'Lavender and neroli orange blossom,' Tomás told them. 'The velvety white petals of the bitter orange tree breathe out one of the most important and ancient scents in perfumery.'

Holly raised an eyebrow. He was a bit over the top, but the oil did smell wonderful, it was true. 'Sleep oil is certainly on trend.' She passed it to her mother. Holly knew plenty of people who claimed to have trouble sleeping. It must be the stressful world they all lived in, she supposed.

Her mother followed Holly's lead. 'Divine,' she echoed, a dreamy look in her eyes. 'Who wouldn't want to breathe in this scent every night?' She smiled at her daughter.

'Orange blossom is iconic for our city,' added Tomás. 'The flowers of the bitter orange – both spicy and sweet-smelling – are known to help insomnia, anxiety and depression. It is the same lift that we get from the springtime, *non*? The lift of hope and new beginnings.'

Hope and new beginnings. Considering most of his business dealings, by his own admission, were with local shops, Tomás had a good line in sales patter. Not that he needed it; the quality of the products spoke for itself.

Holly picked up the light orange blossom water which Tomás told them was intended to be a daytime *azahar* perfume spray.

'Wholly natural,' he said, 'made during the process of extracting the essential oil from oranges and blossom. We will try it, *sí*? The scent of neroli is powerful and floral, yet also light and refreshing.'

Holly misted some in front of her and immediately the air filled with the very fragrance he had just described. '*Azahar*?' she asked Tomás.

'When the trees blossom in early spring,' he said, 'you know they produce the delicate white flowers, some we can still see outside?'

'Yes.' She certainly did.

'That is the *azahar*, from the Arabic for "white flower".'

'Ah, yes, I see.' It was that distinctive scent, definitely part of the Seville spring experience, she thought. That was what she was looking for. *Hope and new beginnings* . . .

There was also a facial wash guaranteed to relax and revitalise skin, according to Tomás, a toner, a facial oil – 'to help dry skin stay soft and supple' – neroli bath salts and a neroli and geranium soap made from goat's milk, which was soft and kind to problem skin. Altogether, an enticing mixture.

'And it's oranges I'm interested in,' Holly reminded them all. 'But the packaging . . .' The branding could be more professional, she felt. She peered at the label. 'There needs to be more emphasis on the organic aspect. And it might be better if it was more . . .' She hesitated.

'Orange?' suggested her mother.

Holly smiled. 'Definitely more orange.' She had a vision for the shop and ideally, she wanted everything she sourced to reflect that. Even more crucial, though, was the naturalness of the ingredients and a quality that would shine through. People wanted to be sure that there were no unpleasant chemicals in their beauty products these days. They cared about their bodies and they cared for the environment too.

Tomás shrugged. 'Any change, it is possible,' he said. 'But first, we should talk figures.'

'Yes, of course.' Holly took a final sip of her coffee and braced herself. This was the part she wasn't so confident about. She needed to make money – obviously, she must maintain a decent profit margin – but these were not rich people and she wanted, above all, to be fair. Holly met her mother's gaze. Her mother knew what Holly was thinking, she could tell.

She gave Holly a little nod of encouragement.

Holly straightened her shoulders. 'How much are you looking for?' she began. 'As I explained before, my business is only just starting up, so I'll have to see how everything goes, and I don't want to overcommit too early. But if I were to order . . .' She looked down at the notes she'd made on her phone about quantities and margins.

He named a figure, she considered, he named another figure, she juggled the quantities, and so the discussion went on. She need not have worried, Holly realised. Tomás was clearly capable of driving a hard bargain on his mother's behalf. He was a good businessman.

An hour later, they seemed to have come to an agreement and Tomás stuck out his hand. 'It is a pleasure doing business with you,' he said. 'We appreciate that you have made a special trip to come and sample the products.'

'No problem at all. It was good to meet you.' Holly took his hand and they shook on it. She'd completed her first business transaction. At least, the initial stages and verbal agreement of it. She beamed first at Tomás and then at her mother.

'I am, of course, my mother's business manager,' Tomás said as they all got to their feet. 'But she also would like to meet you.'

Holly didn't hesitate. 'I'd love to meet her too,' she said. In fact, she had been hoping to.

'Excellent.' Tomás grinned. 'In that case, I will invite you both to our house. Now, if that is convenient?'

'Perfect.' Holly had another meeting this afternoon but the rest of the morning was free. 'OK with you, Mum?'

'Of course. I'd like to meet her too. Thank you, Tomás.'

'Then *por favor*, please excuse me for one moment while I make a call.' Tomás took out his phone and went over to the door.

Holly and her mother exchanged a grin.

'Well done, darling,' her mother said.

'Thanks.'

'I knew you could do it.' She drew Holly into a hug. 'I'm really proud of you. Your father will be too.'

Holly could still smell the fragrance of Sofía Pérez's products in her mother's hair. 'It really helped, having you here,' she confessed.

'You don't need me.' But her mother was still smiling.

Holly looked at her mother carefully. She was wrong, Holly did need her. She needed all of her family, and if something had happened between her parents when they came to Seville the first time, she'd really like to know what it was – especially if it had affected her mother so deeply. She realised how rarely she thought about her parents having a relationship of their own. They were her parents; they might not be overly affectionate towards one another, but they had always seemed to get on well enough. And they were still together after all these years, which meant a lot.

'Did something happen in Seville, Mum?' she found herself asking. Because she couldn't just let it lie. 'Between you and Dad?'

'What do you mean, darling?' Her mother took a step back. They both glanced towards Tomás, who was still standing by the door talking into his phone. It was a moment of truth between them – at least, potentially.

'I don't know exactly . . . That's why I'm asking. You seem

so . . .' Holly gathered up her things. She couldn't explain it. But she knew there was something.

'No,' her mother said firmly. 'It was just . . .'

'Yes?'

'A different time,' she said.

A different time? Holly glanced again back to where Tomás was now making his way towards them, all smiles once again. When was her mother going to stop being so mysterious? That told her nothing at all. A different time indeed . . .

CHAPTER 8

Ella

Seville, 1988

'Did you speak to her?' Ella asked Felix when he finally came into the bar. He looked tired. He looked very different to the way he'd looked half an hour ago.

He brushed back his hair with one hand and sat down on the high bar stool next to her. 'Yes, I did.' He turned round to eye her warily – a bad sign.

'And? How is she? What happened?' Ella sipped her brandy. It was too sweet and strong and made her feel slightly nauseous after their afternoon in the sun. She felt guilty too. She shouldn't have assumed that her mother-in-law had done this on purpose. Surely she wouldn't have?

'She fell down the stairs.' He shook his head. 'Not from the top, just the last few. She tripped on that damn stair carpet.'

Ella knew the bit he meant. It wasn't far to fall, but it would have shaken her up. She glanced across at Felix. She knew what he was thinking. The carpet was worn and frayed, Felix was the man of the house, he should have dealt with it – his father would have.

'It's not your fault,' she said automatically.

'If we hadn't come here—'

'It could still have happened.'

'Yeah, I know.' He picked up the other glass and drank his brandy down in one gulp. 'But then we would have been there.'

Ella let out the breath she'd been holding. 'But she's not seriously hurt?' she asked. Her next thought was a selfish one. *Let it not be bad.* Ella didn't want to go home.

'I don't think so, no. She went in a taxi to A & E.' He sighed. 'I just wish I'd been there to take her.'

'I know.' Ella gave up on the brandy and put a hand on his arm. 'Has she twisted or sprained something then? What did the doctor say?'

'I'm not sure. I think it's her ankle. She didn't really tell me much.' Felix gave a little shrug which didn't convince Ella in the least.

'But she's back at home now? She's all right?'

'Yes.' He got up from the bar stool. 'I suppose so. Yes.'

Ella followed him up to their room overlooking the buzzy and tree-lined Alameda de Hércules. It all seemed very vague. Already in the bar below the *Sevillanos* – for most of them seemed to be locals – were gathering for Saturday night drinks and tapas, chatting and laughing uproariously. Ella didn't mind, though; she liked the fact that the city was so alive.

And as for her mother-in-law's accident – what else could she say? Felix should be relieved that it wasn't any worse, but he didn't seem relieved at all. His mood had altered; he'd become morose and quiet. But from what he'd told her, Ingrid was more or less OK; she'd had a bit of a shock, obviously, maybe even a small sprain. But if that was all it was, then why was Felix punishing himself?

Dinner was subdued that evening, despite their surroundings. They went to a noisy bar around the corner which had huge hams hanging from hooks on the ceiling and old photos pinned on the walls, where the bar staff yelled out orders to the kitchen, somehow making themselves heard above the hubbub of the bar, and chalked up the tapas tabs on the counter itself just as they'd probably done for decades. The raucousness made it easier for Felix and Ella to be quiet, because how could they compete?

Ella christened the place 'Shouty Bar' and tried to be bright and cheerful as they chose their tapas from the spoken menu of what was on offer. Who knew what each dish contained? *Pescaíto frito* was clearly 'fried fish,' but this didn't do the tapas justice; dusted in flour and fried in olive oil, Ella guessed they'd tried cuttlefish, sardines and anchovies, along with a variety of hams and croquettes. But Felix didn't get into the swing of it; he continued to brood.

After breakfast the following morning, he phoned his mother again. 'Just to check everything's OK,' he told Ella. 'She's on her own, don't forget.'

As if she could forget . . . Ella could only hear one half of the conversation, but she could imagine the rest.

'But you are all right, Mum? You are resting? Brenda has come in to make you some breakfast?' Felix asked a string of questions and listened intently to his mother's replies.

Thank goodness for Ingrid's next-door neighbour, thought Ella.

'How is she?' she asked Felix as soon as he got off the phone.

'She says the swelling's gone down.' He frowned. 'But she

decided to spend the night in the living room to be on the safe side.'

Ingrid had a downstairs toilet in her house, so that was probably a good idea, Ella thought. 'But she hasn't broken anything?'

'Oh, no, it's just a bit of a twisted ankle, I think.' But Ella couldn't tell if Felix was reassured by the phone call or even more worried than before.

This morning, they'd planned on visiting the Alcázar – the oldest royal palace still in use in Europe and the jewel of Seville, according to Ella's guidebook, with its Mudéjar patios and halls, richly decorated apartments and glorious gardens. It was the natural place to begin sightseeing: the hub of Seville, the heart.

When they arrived there after another stroll through the characterful Calle Sierpes, the street of the snakes, Ella was immediately charmed by the gorgeous plasterwork tracery in the patios, the delicate fountains, the decadent gold and red ceilings displaying coats of arms above richly tiled floors. It was, she thought, the most incredible building she had ever seen.

'Isn't it stunning?' she asked Felix as they wandered into the gardens, laid out with terraces, fountains and pavilions. 'Don't you just love it?'

'Yeah. It's great,' Felix said.

Ella understood that he was still worried about his mother. But her husband's lack of enthusiasm was beginning to irritate her. 'Felix? Aren't you glad we came?'

Ella needed the reassurance. This morning, it had felt as if he weren't with her. He'd walked through the magnificent vaulted rooms of the palace beside her, he'd nodded as she admired the golden domes and the gilded, interlaced wood, he'd agreed that yes, the diamonds of blue and white with orange stars created a striking pattern on the *azulejo* tiles. But she knew that he was with her in body alone. The rest of him had already returned to Dorset.

'Glad?' He shot her a glance that said it all.

'Felix . . .'

'Look.' He paused beside a lemon tree with ripening yellow fruit and glossy green leaves. 'It's obviously easy for you, Ella.'

'What do you mean?' Ella felt a twinge of disquiet in her belly. She could smell the sharp citrus of the lemons mingling with the scent of old plaster and the all-pervading fragrance of the orange blossom. The sweet smell of orange trees was everywhere in this city, musky and intense, increasing the sensation that she had escaped, that here, they were in another world.

Felix kicked at the ground in front of him. 'It's easy for you to enjoy yourself,' he said. 'To forget about Mum and what's happened to her.'

Ella was stung. She felt tears come to her eyes. That wasn't fair. 'I haven't forgotten,' she said. 'I'm just trying to . . .' She walked on along the narrow, gravelled pathway. What was she trying to do? Distract him? Make him want to stay? She certainly hadn't forgotten. Apart from anything else, Felix's hangdog expression had been reminding her all morning. But she mustn't be unkind, she told herself. She turned back to him. Felix was standing with his hands in his pockets looking more than a bit fed up.

Ella sighed. 'You said she was all right. If it's only a slight sprain, I can't really see why . . .' Her voice trailed. *Why we can't enjoy ourselves now that we're here*, she was going to say. Was that so selfish? She supposed that it was.

They continued down the formal path past the sculpted

cypresses laid out in geometric patterns, towards the magnolia trees in the next garden. It was wilder here. The tall palms waved gently in the breeze and she could hear a blackbird singing his heart out.

'But *I* can't.' Felix continued as if she hadn't spoken. 'I keep thinking of her lying there at the bottom of the stairs, all alone.' His voice broke.

'Hang on, Felix, isn't that a bit . . .' *Melodramatic?* But that wouldn't go down well either. Once again, she held back. They passed a little pond surrounded by old stone walls, the orange flash of a fish darting to the surface.

'Lying there, unable to get up, with no one to help her. While we're here . . .' He flung out his arm in a gesture that encompassed the lavish gardens, the palace, the entire city of Seville. 'While we're here having a good time.'

They had entered another garden now and the pathway had turned to sand. The bird of paradise plants were tall and stately, and normally she knew Felix would have been excited at the sight of them, but now, he barely gave them a second glance. The sound of water trickling from a fountain should have been soothing and would have been at any other time. But not now.

Ella did get it, of course she did. She wasn't heartless. She didn't want her mother-in-law to be hurt or upset. Ingrid and Felix were her family now. Ella had grown up with only part of a family and now even that had gone. There had been a few short years when she and her mother had lived on their own and taken on the world together – at least that was how it had felt. Her mother had struggled to make ends meet in those days; it must have been hard being a single parent on a low income and, in hindsight, Ella couldn't blame her for taking the opportunity of a better life when one came along.

Although since Ella had been fast approaching her teenage years, she certainly had blamed her at the time.

At the bottom of the garden was another orange grove with cheese plants – Ella would have asked Felix the Latin name if he'd been in a better frame of mind – a turreted wall, and eucalyptus trees interspersed with salmon and white oleander. They were away from the crowds here, which was perhaps a good thing, she thought.

Kenny . . . He was her mother's 'opportunity' and that was when everything had changed. Ella was only twelve years old when they'd met and she'd disliked him on sight. He was short, dark and bullish in appearance and he always tried to make everything into jokes that weren't funny. At first, it wasn't too bad, but within months Kenny had moved in and Ella's brave, cheerful mother had become nervous and desperate to please.

How had it happened? Kenny had never been physically violent – at least as far as she knew. But he had a way of spoiling everything. It was his snideness, the small cruelties, the exclusion. He resented Ella. He wanted a woman without the baggage of a child, she supposed now, and eventually, he had got one. As for her mother . . .

Ella would never understand how she could have altered so much. Perhaps it was the hardship, perhaps it was losing her first husband after only five years of marriage. Perhaps she thought she was doing the right thing – finding a replacement husband and father. Was that how she saw it? Ella didn't know, because her mother never told her. The mother and daughter who had taken on the world together had lost their unity the first time Ella's mother didn't stand up to Kenny, didn't take Ella's side or protect her. That's when Ella knew she was on her own.

They were walking now towards a small pavilion. Ella took

Felix's arm, trying to make amends. She understood that Ingrid depended on her son, she appreciated their closeness and she wasn't trying to take Felix away as Ingrid seemed to suspect she was. But Felix was married now. Ingrid needed to let go a little.

'But she coped without you,' she told Felix as they surveyed the elegant dome of the pavilion, the tiled walkway, the exuberant planting. 'And isn't that a good thing? You wouldn't want your mother to be helpless and wholly dependent on you, would you?'

'No, of course not.'

'She got herself to A & E, she's been checked over by a doctor, and now Brenda's keeping an eye on her.'

'I know all that.' He sighed. 'I just feel bad, Ella,' he said. And he looked it.

'Are you going to feel bad for our entire holiday?' She was hoping to laugh him out of it.

But he shot her a look of reproach and something snapped inside her. It was such a waste, she thought. To be here, in this beautiful place, and not even properly see it.

'Are you going to continue being miserable, just because you didn't fix the stair carpet and because you weren't at home to help her?'

At that, his face closed up even more and Ella knew she'd gone too far. It was the story of her life. She kept quiet, bottled up her emotions and then when it all came out there was way too much of a kick in it.

'I can't change the way I am.' Felix began to walk back towards the more formal gardens of the palace and Ella walked quicker to catch up with him.

She knew that too. And more than once, she'd had reason to consider: had she been right to marry this man? She had to be honest with herself. What if she hadn't been desperate to leave home? Would she have fallen for him so readily? Would she have accepted his proposal with such little hesitation? Might she have reminded herself that she was only eighteen, that she had hardly lived? Might she have warned herself not to tie herself down too young? Might she have been looking for fun and adventure rather than a kind man she knew she could rely on?

'I don't want you to change,' she whispered when she was beside him once again.

He took her hand at last as they walked on. Ella tried to take in the pretty cobbled pathways and decorative tiled grottos, the blossom, the little galleries, but . . . She and Felix seemed to have lost so much of what had once bound them together. In her mother-in-law's house, Ella felt like a lodger rather than Felix's wife. And in the bedroom . . . She pushed this treacherous thought aside. Who could blame him, with such a thin wall separating their bedroom from his mother's? No wonder Felix was inhibited, no wonder he hardly touched her these days.

Even last night here in Seville . . . It might have been different if he hadn't received that phone call. And of course, he'd been worried. Ella could think up any number of excuses. But it had been five years since they'd spent a night away from his mother's house and she'd had high expectations for the sort of night it might turn out to be. They had made love (though Ella couldn't help wondering if Felix would have instigated it; in the event, she'd been the one who had made it happen) but it had lacked the passion she'd been dreaming of. It was good to be held by him – it was always good to be held by him – but Felix was on edge, almost as if his mother was still sleeping in the room next door.

'And I don't think I can stay here.' Felix's mouth was set. 'Not while Mum can't look after herself properly.'

'What do you mean?' Though Ella knew.

'I mean we'll have to change our flights. Get home just as soon as we can.'

'Felix!' Ella felt a surge of anger. She pulled her hand from his. Their first holiday abroad. The splurging of their precious savings. Their escape route. Was it all to be for nothing?

'It's only fair,' Felix was saying. 'It's so hard for her to manage. She's putting a brave face on, but after everything she's done for us, we can't just leave her on her own.'

Everything she's done for us. He was right, of course. But . . . 'Has she asked you to go home?' Ella whispered. In the background she could hear the screech of parrots in the palm trees. Were they mocking her or simply joining in with the debate?

'Not in so many words,' he said.

'But?'

'She did say it couldn't have come at a worse time.' Felix lowered his voice as a party of visitors tripped blithely past them. 'She said she doesn't like to keep asking Brenda because she's so busy with the kids. She said . . .'

'Yes?'

'She said, don't bother about me. You two just stay there and enjoy yourselves.'

Emotional blackmail, thought Ella. She sat down on a bench in front of a fountain. The clear water sparkled in the sun, hitting the surface of the pond with a soft fizz. 'Do you think she did it on purpose?' she heard herself asking.

'Ella!'

'Well, it's a bit of a coincidence.'

'Don't be ridiculous. No one falls down the stairs on purpose.' Felix was looking at her as if he didn't know her at all. 'For heaven's sake, Ella. How can you be so selfish? If I'd known you were—'

'If you'd known I was what?' She braced herself. She closed her eyes until the sunshine and the water fountain were just bright lights inside her eyelids.

'Nothing. Forget it.'

'Felix?' She opened her eyes again.

'Just stop.' He shook his head. 'I've had enough of this. I can't stay here. She needs me. We're going back home and that's the end of it.'

Ella couldn't believe they were in this glorious setting of the palace gardens arguing in a way they'd rarely argued before. Perhaps, though, that was because they were always in Ingrid's house and there was never any space to argue, never any room to let your thoughts be known, for your voice to be heard. Barely room sometimes to breathe. Ella realised that she was shaking. She thought of all the things they'd been planning for this time away. She thought of the spring sunshine and the scent of the orange blossom. She couldn't bear it. She really couldn't.

'Only it's not,' she said.

'Not what?'

'Not the end of it.' Ella got to her feet. If she had learnt anything from being stepdaughter to Kenny, she had learnt that no man was going to tell her what to do anymore – at least not as far as her private life was concerned.

'What are you talking about?' Felix got up too and checked his watch. 'We'd better get back to the hotel and see about changing those flights. I'm sorry, Ella. I know how much you wanted this holiday. But she needs me and that's more important. You do see that, don't you?'

‘I do see that, yes.’ She walked away from the bench under the crumbling archway towards the palace and the way out. A magnificent peacock with blue and green jewelled feathers was strutting across the lawn but she barely noticed him through the tears in her eyes.

‘Ella?’ He frowned, picked up his pace as he followed her.

‘You can change your flight,’ Ella said, and to her surprise there was no tremor in her voice, though she could feel it like an earthquake inside. She turned back towards him. ‘You can go back home if you need to. But I’m staying here.’

‘What? Don’t be silly.’

‘I’m not being silly.’ Ella walked on along the pathway inset with tiny tiles and lined with hedges and flowering gerberas. *On the contrary* . . . And she wouldn’t cry. She took a deep breath. She’d never been surer in her life that this was the right thing to do. ‘This is my holiday,’ she said. ‘And I’m staying till the end of it.’

‘But what about Mum?’ He seemed bewildered.

‘Your mother will manage – she already is managing. There’s nothing wrong with her that a bit of a rest won’t sort out.’ Ella looked over towards the pink and ochre walls of the palace. ‘I’d go back if it was anything serious, you know I would. She doesn’t need you, Felix, she’s just exercising control.’

It was the first time she had said anything like this – and perhaps she should have said it before. Hadn’t she seen first-hand the damage a controlling person could do? Sometimes it wasn’t obvious. But when someone always responded in a certain way . . . well, you were being emotionally manipulated, weren’t you? It was like training a dog, with the treats being smiles of approval instead of dog biscuits.

He scowled at her. 'You can't stay here on your own,' he said. 'I won't let you.'

Ella met his gaze head on. 'I'm sorry, Felix,' she said, 'but that's exactly what I'm going to do. I'd rather be here with you. I thought that this would be our chance to . . .'

'To what?' Felix looked more baffled than ever.

But somewhere inside him, she thought, somewhere, he must understand. 'To get close to each other again,' she said softly. The scent of the orange blossom seemed even stronger now. And wasn't spring a time of new beginnings? 'To reconnect. To save our marriage.'

'Ella?' He was staring at her now, disbelieving.

'But if you won't stay here with me,' she said, 'I'm going to stay here on my own.'

CHAPTER 9

Holly

Seville, 2018

Tomás led them out of the bar and down the busy street. 'We live very close,' he explained. 'And my mother, she is preparing to show you how she makes her products.'

'How exciting!' Holly forgot to sound like a business-woman. She felt like skipping along the cobblestones. She couldn't believe how well her first meeting was going. She'd made a deal. And who would have thought that she would be discussing contracts in a buzzy little bar in Seville, eating *tostada de tomate*, or that she'd be invited to the home factory itself to witness the goods being made. She thought of her old office back in Brighton, the constant emails she could never keep up with, the churning in her stomach before a client meeting. This informality under the sunny blue skies of Seville was very different and Holly was loving it.

'I hope you will think so,' Tomás replied dryly.

Holly turned to her mother. She was smiling too, but Holly

sensed she wasn't entirely comfortable now that she no longer knew exactly where they were heading.

'Here we are,' said Tomás.

They had arrived at a three-storey building painted dark pink with green shutters at the windows. Above the wrought-iron balcony on the first floor was a row of decorative tiles and on the very top of the house was a rooftop garden. Ceramic urns were positioned on the pink sculpted stonework of the roof and there were flowers everywhere: in terracotta pots at the front, creeping through the ironwork, peeping over the edges of the rooftop garden. It was a little shabby but utterly charming.

Tomás pointed to the pots. 'Mama's herbs,' he said. 'They are everywhere. On the roof and in the back courtyard too.'

'Your mother puts all these plants into her products?' Holly bent to sniff. She didn't know all the names, but she recognised fennel and mint among the more unfamiliar varieties.

'Yes, and she travels outside the city to gather even more,' Tomás said glumly. 'It is I who must take her.'

'How lovely,' Holly's mother said.

'Oh, yes. Gathering herbs from a natural habitat, that's amazing.' Holly had been so lucky to find this family whose production process seemed to have gone back in time, or never moved on from the old-fashioned way of doing it, she supposed.

'Perhaps you could send us a few photographs, Tomás?' her mother suggested. She gave Holly an enquiring look.

For publicity purposes, Holly realised. Of course. Lucky that her mother was on the ball. She grinned. 'Could you, Tomás?' she asked. 'That would be brilliant.' She could envisage a small notice placed above the beauty products in Bitter Orange, explaining – with pictures – how the ingredients were sourced. That would make them even more appealing to her customers.

'No problem,' said Tomás. 'We will be out one day this week. I can take some pictures for you. Mama will love it.'

He opened the front door and they followed him up the narrow and rather rickety staircase. The light was dim and the walls painted a grungy beige. But as they got to the upstairs apartment, a middle-aged woman with a thick mass of dark hair tied back with a red scarf opened the door with a welcoming flourish. She beamed at them.

'Mama, this is Holly Hammond. And her mother Ella.' Tomás made the introductions.

'Welcome, welcome.' Sofía clasped their hands and kissed them on both cheeks. She beckoned them inside. 'Would you like some fruit juice?' she asked. 'Coffee? A beer?'

'Fruit juice would be lovely,' said Holly's mother and Holly decided to follow her lead. She needed to keep a clear head for this afternoon and her meeting with Axel the wine merchant. There would, she was sure, be some tastings there to look forward to.

'*Gracias* . . . Thank you for coming.' Sofía led them into a spacious but cluttered living room furnished with two worn armchairs and a big but tired-looking sofa, a dining table covered in paperwork, at least eight dining chairs, a wooden cabinet, a bookcase, a coffee table and an extremely large TV. On the wooden floor was a frayed multicoloured rug. 'Sit down, *por favor*,' Sofía said.

'Thank you.'

Her mother sat down on one of the armchairs but Holly continued to look around the room, fascinated by all the framed photographs of what looked like family gatherings adorning the dark red walls. She could see that several had been taken at flamenco shows.

Holly went up to take a closer look. In one photo, a young woman, a flamenco dancer, posed in a flouncy dress, one leg bent to reveal her shapely calf and ankle and black dancing shoe, her dark hair wound in a tight bun around her head. The group of onlookers were clapping and tapping their feet. The dancer wasn't smiling and her expression was haughty. She had been caught, Holly supposed, in the moment of the dance.

'My mother,' Sofía said quietly, from behind her.

Holly swung around. 'She was a dancer?'

Sofía laughed. 'Most of the women in my family were dancers,' she said.

Holly turned back, captivated by the image. She was just about to ask Sofía more when her mother spoke.

'But not you, Sofía?' she asked.

'Not me, no.'

'So, what led you into making your wonderful soaps and your sweet-smelling oils?' her mother continued.

Reluctantly, Holly turned away from the photo. She had only seen the flamenco danced a couple of times and that was on film, but she'd been drawn by the spirited dance, the strength and the ardour that these women seemed to hold deep in their beings. But of course, her mother was right. They were here to discuss Sofía's work, not the history of the family flamenco.

'*Mi madre*, she teach me natural products are best.' Sofía seemed pleased to talk about this subject and she nodded and beamed at Holly's mother as she spoke. 'My brother, he has problems with his skin, you know' – she pulled a face – 'and so it was necessary for us to find a cure from the garden outside the city.'

Holly's mother nodded. 'The old traditional ways are often the most effective,' she said.

'We're all turning away from chemicals,' Holly added. 'And about time too.'

'*Si, si.*' Sofía nodded even more energetically at this. 'And so, for me, the gathering of the herbs, the flowers, it became my interest,' she said, 'from when I was a girl.'

At this point, Tomás came back into the room with the drinks and a plate of biscuits on a wooden tray. 'My mother, she likes to experiment,' he added. 'She is, in fact, a scientist.' He put the tray down on the coffee table and passed the drinks around.

'Oh, Tomás.' Sofía laughed. 'I only learn as I go along.'

'Perhaps that's the best kind of learning,' Holly's mother murmured.

Holly shot her a curious glance.

'You are right,' said Tomás. 'And my mother here, she has perfected the technique.'

Holly sipped her juice. 'But how many hours a day do you work, Sofía?' she asked. She was wondering how easy it would be for Sofía to keep up with demand – that's if there was demand.

'My mother, she has a good team,' Tomás said smoothly. He always seemed to have a ready answer. He brought the biscuits over and offered them to Holly and her mother. 'Ginger and turmeric,' he said. 'There are plenty of girls around here who are keen to earn a bit of extra money.'

Holly could imagine. It didn't appear to be a wealthy neighbourhood. She took a biscuit from the plate and smiled her thanks.

Sofía looked doubtful. She shook a warning finger. 'Not all to be trusted,' she added.

Tomás frowned. 'That is no problem,' he said. 'With the right management. With you and I to watch over them . . .'

'Ah, yes.' Sofía seemed to get his drift. The last thing they wanted was for their new client to think they couldn't get the goods to her on time or in large enough quantities.

Holly smiled to herself. It hardly mattered. Holly was even more inexperienced than they were. And she wasn't worried. With Sofía's passion and knowledge and Tomás's business acumen and management skills, she had no doubt that they would be able to supply what she needed.

'Delicious biscuits.' She swallowed the last bite. 'Did you make them, Sofía?'

'Of course.' Once again, Tomás answered for her. 'It is another of her most famous specialities.'

'But now,' Sofía said, changing the subject, 'you must come to my working kitchen. You must see where the magic takes place.'

Willingly, they complied.

In the kitchen, Sofía showed them her ingredients: the herbs and the oils, the heaps of neroli blossom, the large cooking pots and mixing bowls she used for her recipes, and finally the airing cupboard on the landing in which she dried out bunches of herbs by hanging them from the shelves. 'They must be warm and away from the sun,' she said. 'And if you grow your own, you know they are pure.'

'How do you produce the essential oil?' Holly asked. 'From steaming, or . . . ?'

'Pressing.' Sofía showed them the machine. Of course, it wasn't up to any kind of industrial scale and it looked as though it had been cobbled together from all sorts of bits and pieces, but clearly it did the job. 'Oil is squeezed, mainly from the peel,' Sofía said, 'There are other ways, but . . .' She shrugged. '*Si*. This is the best, I think.'

'And the bath salts?' asked Holly's mother. 'How do you make them, Sofía?'

'Ah, this is a secret recipe.' Sofía looked guarded and the other two women smiled.

Holly found herself thinking about her mother's secret recipe – one so secret that she hadn't wanted that cake ever to be made. And when Holly had made it . . .

'I start with a basic bath salt recipe,' Sofía relented. 'I use the Epsom salt, the sea salt and the baking soda. After that' – she smiled mysteriously – 'you can add what you will.'

Sofía picked up an orange from the counter. It had several leaves attached. 'Look,' she said. She pointed, and spoke to Tomás in Spanish. Holly guessed that what she had to say might be beyond her English.

Tomás was nodding. 'On the leaf you can see the pale ovals here. These are the oil glands,' he told Holly. 'The peel of the fruit, it too is most aromatic.' He held it up for Holly to sniff.

She did so, remembering all the times she had sniffed bright and misshapen Seville oranges before making her marmalade.

Sofía was nodding enthusiastically. 'The scent of the neroli, it is restorative,' she said. She gave Holly's mother a long look.

'The essential oil could be used in the bath too,' Holly's mother said. 'Or in a room diffuser, do you think?'

'*Si, si*. For a new lease of life,' said Sofía.

'Oh, yes,' agreed Holly's mother. 'A new lease of life indeed.' They gave each other a warm smile of shared camaraderie.

'For the emotions,' Sofía began, 'it will give the energy.' She put a hand on Holly's mother's arm. 'But the mind, it will calm.'

Holly raised an eyebrow. Sofía seemed to know something about her mother that she did not.

'And that is not all. For the Seville orange is both sour like a lemon and yet warm like an orange.' Sofía was getting even more into her subject. She spoke once again in Spanish to Tomás.

He listened, nodding and smiling before turning to the other two women. 'It is a long list my mother gives me,' he said. 'The therapeutic properties of bitter orange include treatment of poor digestion, constipation, acne, colds and coughs, heartburn. It is even an antiseptic.'

'A wonder cure contained in a little orange globe.' Holly turned the orange around admiringly.

Her mother was watching her, but this time, saying nothing.

'And where do you get your oranges, Sofía?' Holly asked. 'I know they're everywhere in the city, but . . .' The oranges from the streets must surely be polluted, she thought.

'Some from the local market,' Sofía told her. 'But they must be pure.'

Holly nodded.

'I have a supplier.' She touched her nose. 'If you go on the back road . . .'

'The back road?'

'Homemade produce stands,' Tomás said. 'Single sellers waiting by the road with sacks of fresh oranges.' He held up his hand. 'But do not worry. My mother, she is vigilant. Even if they have not passed official controls and certification processes, she knows what is good.'

Holly didn't have any doubt about that.

'Your products are so vibrantly coloured, Sofía.' Holly's mother was holding a small bar of orange soap. 'How do you achieve that?'

They certainly were. The orange was marbled around the soap with a deeper red that was warm and satisfying.

'With that one I add paprika and a thread of saffron.' Sofía smiled. 'The true orange, it is more delicate.' She held one up for them to see. 'For yellow, there are calendula petals and maybe a hint of turmeric or yellow clay. For green, powdered parsley, rosemary or sage. And so . . .' She gave a little shrug.

'Perfect,' said Holly.

They were just about to leave the flat when the door opened and a beautiful young Spanish girl, probably in her early twenties, walked in. She was unsmiling, though, and when she saw them, she scowled. Family, guessed Holly, though this girl clearly had neither the people skills of Tomás nor the friendliness of Sofía.

The girl narrowed her eyes and shot a torrent of fast Spanish in Tomás's direction. He replied in the same vein. There was much shrugging and gesticulating; the girl seemed very aggrieved about something. Holly hoped it wasn't anything to do with their visit. She and her mother looked from one to the other of them and then at each other. Who was this firebrand?

'My sister, Valentina,' Tomás said at last, in English.

'Pleased to meet you,' Holly's mother said.

The girl gave a small nod of acknowledgement. As if the pleasure should indeed be theirs, thought Holly.

'Hi,' she said, trying out a friendly smile.

Valentina looked back at her; her raking gaze seemed to take in every detail of Holly's appearance, from her flowery top to her denim skirt and low-heeled chunky leather sandals. The girl was several years younger than Holly but she was making Holly feel decidedly uncomfortable.

Sofía seemed unaware of the tension in the room. 'Valentina, she is a dancer,' she said, flinging out her arms in an expansive gesture. 'An excellent dancer, if I may say.'

Valentina graced her mother with a half-smile from pouting lips.

'Oh? Flamenco?' Holly tried to be polite for Sofía and Tomás's sake.

Instead of replying – though Holly was sure that the girl must speak English – Valentina turned to her mother and spoke in Spanish.

Sofía nodded. '*Si*,' she said. 'Valentina is mistress of many forms of dance.' She smiled proudly. 'She continues the family tradition we spoke of.'

'Well, it's been very nice to meet you all.' Holly's mother spoke with a note of finality in her voice and Holly could see her edging towards the door. Her mother had always been good at bringing conversations to a natural close when she'd had enough, and on this occasion, Holly had no objection. She didn't want to stay here any longer, and besides, she had appointments to keep this afternoon.

'Oh, but what am I thinking?' Sofía hit her head with her hand. Holly saw her mother wince. 'What kind of a welcome to Seville is this? What must you think of me?'

They both looked at her blankly.

'Naturally, you must come tonight,' Sofía said.

'Tonight?'

Valentina glared at her mother and let out another stream of Spanish. Tomás joined in, then Sofía, and suddenly they were all three talking at once and very loudly. Holly gave a little shrug to her mother, who was still inching closer towards the door.

'*Si, si*,' said Sofía in a voice that must have held some authority because both her offspring stopped talking at once. She patted her daughter's arm in a placatory manner, bent close and spoke to her, soft and reassuring.

What a prima donna. Holly shot another glance her mother's way. *What now?*

'My mother wishes to invite you to the flamenco tonight,' said Tomás.

'Oh, no!' exclaimed Ella.

Tomás and Holly looked at her enquiringly. Even Valentina stopped her protestations for a moment or two.

'I mean, we wouldn't dream of intruding on a family occasion,' she corrected herself.

Holly smiled inwardly. She could understand her mother's reluctance – Valentina was a drama queen and rude with it – but even so, they were talking flamenco here. She felt a leap of excitement. Who could resist a real and authentic flamenco experience?

'It is not only family,' Tomás assured them. 'It is a gathering for friends too.'

This didn't appear to reassure her mother at all. 'But, we're not—' she began.

'And business associates,' Tomás said firmly, cutting her off. 'In fact, we would be honoured if you could join us.'

'Well then . . .' Holly was keen to accept without further ado, but her mother looked terrified at the prospect. Whatever could she be scared about now?

'And perhaps even offended if you do not.' And although Tomás said this with a chuckle, Holly had the feeling that he meant it.

She decided to make an executive decision. 'In that case,' she said, 'we'd be delighted to come along. Wouldn't we, Mum?'

Her mother's expression was unreadable now.

'Mum?'

'Yes, of course.' Though this didn't emerge quite as enthusiastically as Holly would have liked.

'Excellent.' Tomás rubbed his hands together. 'I will give you the address and we will see you there at nine. You will watch Valentina dance and hear some wonderful music. You will see flamenco at its best.'

Valentina gave a little flounce of her head and walked away.

Tomás shrugged. 'The creative temperament,' he said. He pulled his phone from his pocket, tapped in an address and bent closer towards Holly so that she could see.

Holly typed it into her own phone. 'OK, great,' she said.

Tomás grinned. 'See you later then.'

Speaking for herself, the haughty Valentina notwithstanding, Holly couldn't wait.

CHAPTER 10

Ella

Seville, 1988

What had she done?

It was the following day and Felix had already left for the airport.

After their visit to the Alcázar palace, after his announcement that he would go, and hers that she would stay – which felt like a live enactment of exactly where they were in their marriage at this moment – Felix had at first maintained a stubborn silence.

They'd walked together – but oh, so far apart – back to their hotel, without loitering in Calle Sierpes this time, without enjoying the warmth of the spring sunshine on their heads and their skin, without admiring the architecture and street life of Seville.

As they got to the wide tree-lined Alameda de Hércules, Felix turned to her. 'Ella,' he said. 'I know you're upset. I didn't want this to happen either. It's the last thing I wanted.'

Ella nodded warily. She knew that. All the same, she thought, he had made a choice and she had emerged second best.

'But how can I leave you here on your own?' He spread his hands; his grey eyes were pleading.

How easy it would be, she thought, to walk into his arms, to say, *Of course I'll come home with you, Felix.*

And then maybe regret it for the rest of her life . . .

She'd wanted this for too long. It wasn't just about coming here to Seville, it was the getting away, the escape. She needed it. Perhaps she needed to assert herself too. And so, she wasn't going to change her mind. Around them, the *Sevillanos* and tourists were going about their business: drinking coffee or beer in the cafés that lined the long rectangular plaza, standing around chatting and smoking or strolling under the plane trees. On the surface it was a tranquil enough scene. Smart, colourful villas jostled with less elegant apartment buildings on the wide street and some young boys were playing football in the cobbled plaza.

'I'll be fine,' Ella said. She kept her tone breezy so that he wouldn't make a fuss, but inside, she wasn't so confident. This was supposed to be a holiday for the two of them, a chance to reconnect, not a story of abandonment or a one-woman adventure.

'Ella—'

'I know you have to go home to her.' It struck her how much she'd made her mother-in-law sound like the 'other woman'. But who exactly was the other woman in this relationship triangle? 'I know if you stay here, you'll feel miserable and guilty. So . . .'

'So?'

So, what was the point of trying to make him change his mind? 'But you see, Felix' – she took his hands in hers – 'if I go home with you now, then I'll be miserable too.'

'Yeah, I know.' And his mouth turned up, just slightly.

'And this gives us a solution.' At least, she thought wryly, it could be viewed that way.

'But . . .' Felix continued to hesitate. She could see how torn he was. His mother and his wife were pulling him in opposite directions. What was he supposed to do? Ella almost felt sorry for him. She lifted her face up to the spring sunshine. It felt so warm, so different from the chilly spring weather they'd left behind.

'I'm not a child,' she said. 'I've got a map and a guidebook. I'll be all right on my own.'

Still, he looked doubtful.

'At any rate,' she said, 'it's better than going home. That would be such a waste.'

'Hmm.' They walked on, taking the side street that led to their hotel, and this time, he held her hand. It was a peace pact of sorts.

'But you and me?' He bent his fair head towards her as they negotiated the narrow and potholed pavement. 'What you said about our marriage . . . ?'

'It doesn't matter. I was upset.' Ella didn't want to dwell on that now. It wasn't the right time – or place. She needed to think, but she'd be able to do that much more easily when Felix was gone.

'You didn't mean it, though, did you?' he pressed.

They stopped outside the hotel foyer and she reached up to kiss him briefly on the lips. She couldn't lie to him. 'It's not easy sometimes, that's all,' she said.

He nodded, smoothed her hair gently from her face. 'When you come home,' he said, 'we'll talk about it then. I promise.'

*

After Felix left for the airport, Ella had coffee at a café on the Alameda and studied her guidebook. She was excited, but she also felt very alone. *Come on, Ella*, she told herself. *What are you waiting for?*

Triana, she decided. She would walk down to the bridge and do some exploring on the other side of the River Guadalquivir, an area famous for its ceramics and Sunday market. She paid her bill and set off.

As soon as she crossed the Triana bridge, over the wide river so thick, dense and green, Ella could tell that Triana had a very different character from the rest of Seville. It wasn't just the narrow, cobbled streets or the bustling market on the riverside, it was the independent and authentic feel of the place, as if working-class people still lived and worked here, as if it was still their own.

She turned right down the street of San Jorge and took her time exploring the ceramic shops in this little area. At the end of the road was the charming Nuestra Señora de la O church, which she dipped into to admire the sculptures and the belfry decorated with locally made *azulejos*. The tiles were so beautiful, each one a separate work of art. She inhaled deeply; breathed in the scent of soft musk from the incense burning.

From her guidebook Ella knew already that Triana was the *barrio* that had once housed Seville's gypsy quarter and produced many great and famous bullfighters, sailors, musicians and flamenco dancers. It was quite a legacy. And she imagined that she could feel that legacy living on in the vibrant mood of the place, the colourful flower-filled streets, the decorative tiles and ceramic lettering on walls and shopfronts, the undeniable air of creativity and romance.

At the next ceramic shop, she was drawn in by some old and

unusual tiles on the wall; she stepped inside to examine them more closely. The colours might have faded a little, but the delicate hand-painted artistry remained glorious. The shelves of the shop were crammed with more contemporary ceramics – vases, dishes, jugs and plates in bright glazes of red, yellow and green; flower motifs, geometric patterns, bird and animal images – Ella had never seen anything like it.

In the corner of the shop, a young man was working on a potter's wheel, his dark head bent in concentration. He threw a lump of pink clay onto the wheel, dipped his hands in a bowl of water and cradled the clay on the rotating circle – almost tenderly – between his palms.

Ella watched him, fascinated, as he worked the clay through his fingertips, stretching it, wetting his hands again, leaning on the side of the wheel and pressing on the centre of the form he had created with his thumbs and palms. All the time, he was smoothing, moulding; increasing and lessening the friction and pressure on the clay, gradually easing it into the shape he wanted. He seemed totally absorbed in his task, all his attention focused on the clay, the slip, the rotating wheel.

Ella was mesmerised. His brown hands were coated in the slippery pink clay; each part of them seemed to have a special role to play in this balancing act, this evolution, this creation. Working on the centre of the form now, the rest of his body still and stable, the potter moved his long fingers up and out, sweeping his fingertips across the outside of the pot with gentle strokes now, deft and true. He slowed down the wheel and Ella held her breath as magically the shape appeared – it was a bowl of some kind, she saw. She almost wanted to applaud – it was such a transformation, such a delight.

He slowed the wheel still further, drew a wire under the

pot, lifted it between his wet palms, placed it carefully on the side, looked up and met her gaze.

Crikey. Ella was immediately flooded with embarrassment. What was the matter with her? Clearly, she'd been staring – which was rude and could also be badly misinterpreted. Perhaps Felix was right, she thought. Perhaps she wasn't safe to be here on her own.

The young potter's dark eyes gleamed with humour. Could he read her mind? '*Señora*,' he said.

She smiled back at him, gave a little nod. 'Sorry,' she said. 'I was fascinated, watching you.' But of course, he wouldn't speak English, she realised. She flushed again. *For heaven's sake*. She didn't want to be thought of as one of those unbearable English tourists who didn't even bother to make an effort, who expected to speak English and be understood in a foreign culture as if they had superior rights or something.

'*Lo siento*.' She apologised again, in Spanish this time. Thanks to her guidebook, she had at least learnt a few words and phrases.

He laughed and held up a clay-stained hand. 'Please, no,' he said. 'I understand English. And I am very happy that you have interest in the ceramics.'

'Oh, I do.' She came closer, forgetting her embarrassment. 'Will this bowl be glazed like these others?' She gestured towards the jam-packed shelves.

'Yes. Glazed and fired and made beautiful.'

And yet it was beautiful already, she thought, in its own simple way – the shape was classic and elegant and this man had created it from the raw material in minutes.

'Let me show you some more things we make.' He spoke softly, as if she were the only person in the shop, when in fact there were a few others browsing the shelves, looking towards the potter and his wheel with some curiosity. Ella guessed he had learnt English in order to answer all the questions he must get asked as he sat here in the direct line, as it were.

'OK,' she agreed.

He moved from behind the wheel. 'One moment, please.' He turned, washed his hands at a small white basin behind him and took off his clay-smeared apron, hanging it on a hook on the wall. Suddenly, he was just an ordinary man. But rather an attractive one, Ella thought. What was she doing?

'But really, there's no need . . .' She let her voice trail off as she decided against British politeness. This was what she was here for, she reminded herself. To find out things, to experience the culture, to see the real Seville – and this was surely part of it? Perhaps in some ways it was almost a good thing that Felix wasn't here. He wouldn't have wanted to speak to this pleasant young man for a start.

'My name is Caleb.' He stood in front of her now, a head taller than Ella, eyes almost as black as his curly hair which grazed the collar of his blue shirt. He was wearing jeans and black trainers. He extended his hand for her to shake.

'Ella,' she said, taking it. His hand felt cool to the touch from having just been washed, his skin slightly grainy as if some of the clay remained. She could see the pink of it in his nails too, and she could feel the dryness of his palms.

'I am pleased to meet you,' he said gravely.

Did he expect her to make some serious purchases from his shop? Ella knew there was a lot of poverty in Spain. No doubt they saw the tourists as rich and easy pickings and who could blame them? But she didn't want to give the wrong impression.

'And you, Caleb,' she said. 'But I should warn you, I don't

have much money. I may not buy anything. I'm not even a proper customer, not really, I was just interested in watching you make the pot. Sorry.'

Had he understood her? Now was the time for him to leave and talk to someone more useful, but instead the black eyes gleamed once more. 'Do not worry,' he said. 'It is for the information only. I like telling people how we work and why we work. If you buy or not . . .' – he shrugged – 'it is not important.'

'OK then.' Ella was absurdly pleased.

'These then are the *azulejos*. The root of all our work in ceramics.' He showed her the decorative old tiles on the walls and in the shopfront window. 'We use them on our interior and exterior walls for many years.'

'Yes, I've seen them. There are some amazing facades here in Triana,' said Ella. Over and under arched windows, around door frames, proclaiming the name or occupation of the resident or shop worker.

'Facades, *si*.' He spoke as though trying the word on for size. 'The techniques, they were introduced by the Moors. *Azulejo* from the Arabic *az-zulayi*.' His voice was soft and seemed to caress the strange Arabic syllables. 'Little stone,' he said.

'Little stone?' Ella looked more closely at one of the tiles. 'As in mosaic, do you mean?'

'But, yes.' He nodded with enthusiasm. 'Traditionally, Moorish *azulejos*, were made with tiny stones in a pattern of one colour alone.'

'So, when did all the other colours come into it?' Ella laughed. Because these tiles in Seville were the most multicoloured she'd ever seen.

He smiled an enigmatic smile. 'The tiles evolved,' he said.

'Processes, they became different. Tiles were painted, colour was added. Seville made them her own.'

'She certainly did,' Ella agreed.

'You have visited the Real Alcázar?'

'Oh, yes.' The tiles in the patios had been stunning.

'And you must also visit Casa de Pilatos,' he informed her, 'for some good examples of Mudéjar tiles.'

'I definitely will.' She made a mental note.

He reached out his hand and gently touched the tile they were both looking at. It was a gesture of affection, almost a gesture of love. The tile was blue, green and white and its geometric design looked a bit like a symmetrical jigsaw puzzle, she thought.

'And perhaps the tobacco factory.' His eyes clouded over with an emotion that took her by surprise.

'The tobacco factory?' she repeated. Hadn't she read about that in her guidebook? Wasn't it something to do with Carmen?

'My great-grandmother, she worked there,' he said. 'And there is a perfect example of a decorative sign made from tiles right outside the entrance.'

'I'll go there too,' she promised.

'Even billboards were made from tiles.' He grinned. 'There is an excellent one of a Studebaker motor car in Calle Tetuán.' He sighed, as if regretful that Ella had so many tiles still to see, while he was stuck inside the *ceramica* making his pots and bowls.

Ella loved his enthusiasm – though at this rate, she'd be spending the entire week tile-hunting. She decided to veer off the subject slightly. 'But rather than tiles, you make bowls?' she asked. 'Like this?' She pointed to the one he'd just made, still standing beside the wheel.

'*Si*. Among other things.'

'And you make your living from it?' She hoped she didn't sound rude.

'I make enough, yes.' She saw the pride flash briefly in his dark eyes. 'But this is not all I do.'

'Really?' Ella was intrigued. He seemed to know a lot about the history of the city too. Clearly, he was a man of many talents.

'Perhaps . . .' He gave her a look that was very direct, almost an examination.

Ella stood up straighter. 'Yes?'

'How long do you stay in our city?' he asked.

'I'm here for just under a week now,' she said. And it was beginning to feel like such a short time. She thought of Felix, already winging home to his mother. What a waste. What a damned waste.

'It is long enough,' he pronounced.

Long enough for what? she thought. Not long enough to see everything, surely?

'To have the taste. To find the flavour of Seville.'

'I hope so.' Ella looked away from him, from those dark eyes that seemed too knowing. She should leave the shop now; after all, he'd given her a demonstration and provided plenty of information too. But something kept her there. It seemed to Ella that the more she spoke to Caleb, this talented potter who felt so passionate about this place, the more she would find out about what made Seville tick, the more she would discover the heart of the city.

'And you are alone?' His voice was lower now, more confiding.

'My husband had to go back to England,' she said quickly. She didn't want him to think she was looking for a Spanish boyfriend while she was over here. She'd heard from Viv, a colleague at work who had been to Spain on holiday a few times and who had become a good friend to Ella over the past year or so, that Mediterranean men often thought they had a good chance of a fling with British girls. They often weren't Catholic, they had lived through the swinging sixties – or at least part of them – they didn't always get treated so well by their English boyfriends so sometimes they might easily be swept off their feet; flattered and seduced into a holiday romance.

'Ah, yes, *señora*. I saw the ring,' he said.

She guessed he was the kind of man who didn't miss much. He had called her *señora* rather than *señorita* when he'd first spoken to her this afternoon, she recalled.

'It was such a shame,' she added for good measure. 'We wanted to see Seville together, of course.'

'Of course,' he echoed. 'This is natural, *no*?'

'Yes.' Or at least it should be.

'But you must be careful, Ella.'

'That's what my husband said.'

'He is right.' Caleb frowned. 'I tell you this. Me' – he thumped his chest dramatically – 'I would not leave you alone in a strange city.'

Ella smiled. It was silly, but she liked that flare of protection, that sense of drama. Sometimes British men were just so . . . well, British.

Caleb was still looking rather emotional. 'If you like,' he said, 'I will take you to a special flamenco performance. The best in the city.'

Ella's immediate response was to back off. She knew it. She'd given him the wrong idea. And it must have shown on her face, because he literally took a step backwards as if releasing her from any commitment. 'No rules,' he added.

Rules? Ella frowned. 'Strings?'

He frowned too. 'No strings?' he tried again.

Maybe she was being naive, but Ella instinctively trusted him. She had listened to him explain about the *azulejo* tiles and she had watched him make something beautiful. She felt as if she knew him already – just a little. 'An authentic flamenco show?' she asked.

'Not a show exactly. It is more personal to our community. More intimate.' He stepped closer to her again. 'It is the most real flamenco you can ever see in Seville,' he said.

'When?' she asked. She was tempted. Of course, she was tempted.

'Tonight. Late. At ten maybe.'

Ella shivered. But she knew that the Spanish ate dinner late and partied late too. It was normal. It was how things were. 'Where?' she asked.

'Here in Triana. Just around the corner from this shop,' he said.

'But I'm staying over the river, up at Alameda de Hércules,' she said. It was too far to come alone and a taxi would be far too expensive on her budget.

'I will send a car to your hotel,' he said. 'My cousin, he will drive it, for I must be at the club for the music.'

'Really?' Still, she hesitated. What would Felix say? But then again, Felix had chosen to leave.

Caleb nodded. 'He will take you back too. You will be quite safe. I promise you, Ella.'

She'd already made one rash decision today, so why not another? A real flamenco club in the *barrio* where the pulse of the flamenco still played, alive and well. Who could resist an offer like that? Not Ella.

'OK,' she said. 'You're on.'

CHAPTER II

Felix

Dorset, 2018

Felix wasn't going to work today. His mother was occupied with an old friend from London and his wife and daughter were in Seville, so he decided to go for a walk.

Although it was still chilly outside, there was a sense of springtime in the air that drew Felix to the clifftop at Burton Bradstock. Springtime had always felt hopeful and obviously signified new beginnings; everyone knew it. Felix could do with some of that. He drove past the village and the pink farmhouse and parked the car at the top of the dead-end road. He got out and looked down to where the waves crashed onto the sandstone rocks below.

Time was when it was possible to walk down from the grassy clifftop via a narrow, rocky path that led directly to Hive Beach. Felix had always loved that path, loved standing there on a narrow ledge, looking out past Chesil Beach to the great shimmering ocean beyond. In those days of his early adulthood that view had seemed to represent so many possibilities; a future lying open and ready in front of him, blank pages of an open book that he, Felix, would make his mark on. Now, though, that future was more than half lived and the cliff had eroded – so much so that the path was closed and the beach could only be reached across the fields by a much more circuitous route.

Not that Felix felt that he had failed exactly. What constituted a successful life anyway? Money? A sense of achievement in any given field? Happiness in your personal life? There had been happy times, and many of them, though no vast sums of money and no achievement that anyone might find memorable. But . . . It was all about grasping opportunities when they presented themselves to you – or at least recognising them as they threatened to flit past. Perhaps that was where success really lay.

Because the path no longer existed, Felix trudged instead across the field behind the upmarket restaurant that had replaced the run-down hotel where he and Ella had held their wedding reception. It was cheap and it had the best view of the sea – with Ella by his side, what more could Felix have possibly asked for?

He went on towards the National Trust car park and Hive Beach. The thing was, though, he thought, if you missed the moment – made a bad decision or simply didn't notice the opportunity that was presenting itself to you – then it was gone. It wouldn't come back. He supposed that in a way you always had to be ready. Open to life, Ella might say.

The grass was damp underfoot and Felix could feel the early morning wetness seeping through the small tear in his walking boots. No matter. At the car park, he strolled down the hill to the golden shingle beach. It was quiet; although it was still the Easter holidays, it was too early for any families to have ventured onto the beach. A good time for hiking. Felix looked out over the ginger stones. He was – as far as he could tell – alone.

Seville, for example, thought Felix. Should he have done things differently in Seville, back in 1988 when he and Ella had gone there on what had seemed to be a whim (Ella's)? Felix had somehow known that he must take her – he'd looked into her hazel eyes and recognised something in her expression that he simply couldn't ignore. He couldn't explain the expression or its significance. He just knew he had to act on it.

He'd never fully understood Ella, he realised now; she was like an elegant but mysterious black calla lily or Queen of the Night tulip. It was as if some deep, dark part of her had always remained on the other side of a door and Felix could never quite locate the key. Sometimes, such as on the day that he discovered she was pregnant and certainly on the day that Holly was born, he thought he'd found it, but the key had never quite fit. In reality, of course, there were no truly black flowers – most were shades of very dark purple or red – but this fact only added to the mystery and the magic as far as Felix was concerned.

What Felix had questioned after the Seville visit was not whether he should have taken Ella there, but whether or not he should have come back to Dorset after his mother's fall.

Ah. Felix took a deep breath and headed up the hill. He relished the effort, the reward of getting to the top of the cliff. He blew out his cheeks, was conscious of the slight straining of his leg muscles, the tingle of the breeze on his face as he lifted his head, looking towards the summit. *Mother*, he thought.

His family had come here for picnics when Felix was a boy and his father was still alive. Felix, Colin, Mum and Dad:

a family that had always felt complete. His father had cooked sausages on a primus stove up here in the grassy valleys of the cliff, Mum had buttered slices of fluffy white bread and they'd eaten the sausages hot from the pan, smothered in ketchup. Happy days, he thought. Life was simple then: nothing to worry about, nothing to fear.

Felix looked back to the west from where he had come, at the high ginger cliff at Freshwater, Golden Cap beyond, great drifts of purple thrift cloaking the hills. He loved that thrift; it could withstand all the rain and salt winds and it came back again and again, whatever was thrown at it.

Their father had died when Felix was still at school. Then Colin – three years older than his brother – had gone off travelling only six months later. Felix remembered their mother crying and begging Colin not to leave, but Felix's brother put a hard look on his face and left anyway. Why? Felix wondered now. Why had Colin left so soon? Why had he left at all?

Felix turned back and continued along the path towards Cogden. There were cows in the fields to his left. Once, the family had been walking up there and run a mile when a bull came charging towards them. They'd all laughed – but only when they reached the other side of the fence.

By the time Felix had met Ella, Colin had been gone almost two years. He'd gone to Australia – backpacking at first, in the early days – and he'd never come back. Felix had never understood why Colin had more or less cut all ties with his family, but he had. Colin had always been reserved, always difficult to read. He was his father's son and when Dad died . . . something seemed to break loose in Colin too. Perhaps that was why.

Colin was married now – he had two kids, but Felix had never met them and neither had his mother. Felix reckoned she'd never forgiven Colin for leaving. Anytime Felix wrote and made noises about the families getting together, his brother just left a long silence before he got in touch again. He didn't have to say more.

Felix kept to the top path with the best views. The sun was warming up now and he unzipped his jacket. The water below gleamed blue-grey and the silvery early morning sky was deepening into a pale, pastel springtime blue. *Mother*, he thought again. His father's death, Colin's departure . . . Obviously, it had been left to Felix to do what he could to save his fractured family.

When Felix met Ella – oh, God, how he had fallen for her; it was corny but it was a thunderbolt all right – everything started to make sense again. There were Felix and his mother – just part of a family, really. And there was Ella – needing a family, needing a home.

Felix had never looked back. But should he have left Ella in Seville and run to be by his mother's side? It had seemed the obvious response at the time, but now, well, Felix wasn't so sure. Whichever way he looked at it, whichever way he'd jumped, it seemed that it would be a betrayal of either his mother or his wife. And Felix was so accustomed to doing whatever his mother asked of him. He sighed. It was true, he had to admit it. Did that make him less of a man? Probably. And what about Ella? Had he been fair to her? Probably not.

Felix trudged on with a little shake of his head. Because these two women . . . They'd never got on as well as he'd hoped they would. Even after they had Holly. Two broken families did not make a whole, it seemed.

Felix passed the caravan park on his left. A bit of a blot on the landscape, he supposed, but there again, everyone should have the chance to live by the sea, even if it was only for a week or two once a year. And now . . . It was natural that Seville had come into his mind. But it was a long time ago. As for Ella . . . when she got back from that trip, she had been different. Softer somehow. So perhaps the turning point – if that was what it was – had been for the best after all.

The gigs were out. Felix could see them in the ocean below, sweeping forward in a smooth rhythm, oars slicing through the water. Beyond, he looked over towards Portland. The sun always seemed to shine in Portland; even now the island appeared almost luminescent in the morning light.

Felix paused to take a swig from his water bottle. He was approaching Cogden Beach and the land was changing. He loved that, the way the cliff dipped down into flat shoreline, the beach becoming more desolate here: a long lonely stretch of sandy grass and pebbles, with clumps of frothy-flowered sea kale dotted over the ground like giant cauliflowers, more purple thrift and the jagged silvery-green leaves of poppies soon to flower. Most of the beach plants at Cogden grew on the sheltered landward side of the shoreline. This was a protected area and plants with long roots that loved the shingle and could stretch deep in their search for fresh water thrived. There was sea campion too, its white trumpet-shaped flowers just coming into bloom, and clumps of sea sandwort, which was one of Felix's favourites with its starry white blooms.

Felix wasn't going in to work today because he'd given up work. Or to be more accurate, work had given up him. The garden centre – owned for generations by a local family – had been bought by some large, national company. So many businesses were going that way; it was a depressing fact that many smaller companies were unable to compete with the big boys.

He thought of Holly. Hopefully that wouldn't apply to her – the business she'd planned was very niche.

Could Felix have taken any action to save the garden centre? It was hard to see what he could have done. For a while, they had all thought it would still be a garden centre, still requiring experienced staff to run it. But then word had crept out that it wasn't to be a garden centre at all. It was to be a furniture warehouse.

Felix shuddered. As if there weren't enough of those already.

He gazed over the broad shingle beach and out to sea once more. It looked so peaceful out there. The sea, the rowers, a few people on the beach now, the occasional seagull crying overhead, soaring with the thermals. The salt freshness was in Felix's nostrils, in his throat as he breathed the blustery air in deep, the sun warmer now on his face.

He hadn't told his family. He wasn't sure why. There had been chances to do so . . . But he'd been looking for something else. So that he could say, *I've been made redundant* (a demeaning word, it had to be said, and not easy to bounce back from). *But it's OK, because look what's come up, look what I can do instead . . .*

Only he hadn't found anything he could do instead. Felix paused in his thinking as he caught the steady, pulsating song of the chiffchaff coming from the hawthorn and bramble undergrowth to his left. The chiffchaff's song was a sure sign that spring was here. He looked and looked but he couldn't see the little olive-brown warbler. Felix walked on.

There were jobs around, all of them much less well paid than his long-standing position as manager of the garden centre. And none of them had anything to do with horticulture. Felix wasn't an ambitious man, but he'd always loved plants and he'd never wanted to do anything else; it satisfied him. But now . . .

Had he failed? Had that promising future come to nothing after all?

His notice had flown by and now here he was, unemployed and walking. What next? Felix was at a loss. He knew Ella would worry. They were comfortably off these days but there wasn't much spare. Holly was with them now and they didn't want to take anything from her while she was setting up a new business. But without Felix's salary it would be more difficult. He had a lump sum payment, but for how long would that last?

When Holly's Seville plan had come up, he was even more determined to keep quiet because if Ella knew about the redundancy, she'd never go. And Felix had wanted Ella to go to Seville. Those two needed some time to themselves.

Felix made his way down the steep shelf of stones to the shoreline. There was a strong swell. The waves were swooping onto the pebbles in deep arcs, foaming, hissing, creeping back. A woman was throwing a ball for her dog and the golden retriever was launching himself into the water with so much energy and enthusiasm that Felix had to smile. The dog swam out, shaking his coat when he came back and re-emerged, wild droplets of water leaping into the air around.

Mother, Felix thought again. He loved her, but she'd driven a wedge between Felix and Ella on more than one occasion – or tried to – and she was doing the same to Ella and Holly now. That was what had compelled him to speak out. Felix realised he was gripping his fist tight. He relaxed it, picked up a smooth pebble and skimmed it across the waves. It bounced: once, twice, three times. So, some skills he hadn't lost then. And the new feeling of this springtime day was giving him some hope. Felix was enjoying being out in the open air; it was invigorating and reminded him of his early days at the garden centre when he'd spent most of his time tending to the plants outdoors.

He wouldn't let it happen this time. He understood why his mother had issues, he knew she always needed her special someone and that she worried about losing them after what had happened with his father and Colin. But she wouldn't drive a wedge between Ella and Holly because he wouldn't let her. Felix could do that at least.

CHAPTER 12

Holly

Seville, 2018

After their meeting with Tomás and Sofía this morning, Holly and her mother had a late lunch in a small bar near the metal-arched Triana Bridge and congratulated themselves on how well it had gone. Holly was thrilled. It was only her first source, but because of the variety of products Sofía produced, as a whole it would be an important element of her stock for Bitter Orange.

After lunch, Holly's mother yawned. 'Do you need me at this wine tasting, darling?' she asked. 'If not, I think I'll give it a miss, if you don't mind.'

Holly shot her a suspicious glance. But then she softened. Her mother did look tired. 'Don't you fancy it, Mum?'

'I fancy a siesta back at the hotel more,' she admitted.

'That's fine. All the more wine tasting for me,' Holly teased. She didn't really mind. Despite what had happened this morning, she didn't expect her mother to trail around the city with her every day. And anyway, this was an initial meeting – no promises had been made. In fact, when she'd contacted him online, Axel Gonzáles had seemed rather wary. Didn't he want another outlet for his orange wine?

Axel's bar and little shop selling wine and liqueurs was back in Santa Cruz quite near the hotel and Holly found it easily enough amongst the maze of narrow streets of the colourful Jewish quarter. It was, she thought, the most seductive part of the city in many ways, with its old Moorish buildings, its little plant-filled courtyards and picturesque alleyways, the cave-like tapas bars and sunny street cafés. She was already, she realised, getting rather attached to Seville.

The front of Axel's bodega was painted white and ochre, and flowers spilled down from the wrought-iron balcony above. There were grilles at the windows and red geraniums on the sills and the name of the bodega was made up of tiny blue ancient mosaic tiles. Outside, people were eating and drinking beer at rustic wooden tables. The tapas were listed on two blackboards in the window. It was a long list and Holly scanned it quickly. Amongst the usual suspects of *gambas* and *calamares*, there were plenty of more unusual offerings to tempt her here for lunch another day.

She ventured through the battered old doors into a dark cavernous interior with gnarled beams. There was only one man standing on the other side of a wooden-topped counter fronted with cracked glazed tiles, while a couple of waiters were whizzing in and out of the bodega, slipping past each other – somehow avoiding a collision – and going to and fro through another doorway which led to a busy and steamy kitchen.

'Good afternoon. I'm looking for Axel Gonzáles,' Holly said

to the man. Another blackboard proclaimed *hay vino de naranja*. She was certainly in the right place for orange wine.

'And here you find him.' The man stuck out his hand. Holly shook it. His skin was rough and dry, his grip firm.

Thank goodness, she thought, another person with a good grasp of the English language. But Holly felt slightly ashamed. Perhaps she should have taken Spanish lessons before coming out here?

Axel was tiny, around fifty years old with sharp eyes and a mass of black hair threaded with white and silver. He was wearing a huge white wine-stained apron that almost enveloped him entirely. 'You want to taste?' he asked. 'You want to buy?'

'Well, yes, sort of.' She looked around. The shop was as tiny as its owner. Behind Axel, narrow shelves were lined with numerous bottles and glasses and in the corner stood an ancient fridge-freezer and a scruffy old wooden cabinet. The counter also looked as if it had stood there forever; on it sat some small pots of herbs and a bowl of oranges glowing under the lamp above them. 'I'm Holly Hammond. From the UK. I emailed you to let you know I was coming?'

'Hammond? *Que . . . ?* Ah.' Axel Gonzáles's expression altered immediately. He looked swiftly from right to left and then his gaze scanned the tables outside. Finally, he brought his attention back to Holly. His behaviour was reminding her a bit of her mother's, come to think about it. And Holly was determined to get to the bottom of whatever was going on with her mother and the mystery of Seville, even if she had to cross-question her throughout this entire trip.

'Hammond,' she confirmed.

'I did not know you come today.' He frowned.

'Isn't it a good time? I could come back another day?' Holly was confused. Perhaps he had misunderstood her email?

'*Si,*' he said. 'No. I am sorry. I am pleased to meet you. Come in. Come in.'

'Thank you.' Though she was in fact already in.

She took in the many photographs on the walls – evidence of the bodega's long and illustrious history, she supposed – so many that Holly could hardly tell what colour the paintwork was underneath. The bottom half of the walls were tiled too and the panelling of the street door had been scribbled on with white paint: *hay carne con tomate, higaditos con salsa, hay migas con chorizo . . .* Holly wasn't sure what it all meant, but presumably this panelled wooden door had served as the tapas blackboard many years ago. Once again, time here seemed to have stood still.

'This,' declared Axel, 'is my orange wine.' He put a bottle on the counter in front of her. His obvious pride in his product had apparently overcome his previous misgivings.

The bottle was black, the foil and lettering orange. It was simple but effective; the branding and the packaging was good. But the question was, what did it taste like? At this point, Holly rather wished she had her mother here for a second opinion. Had her mother really gone back to the hotel for a siesta? Or had she sneaked off to do something that she wanted to keep quiet from her daughter? Holly worried that she was getting paranoid.

'Some people, they say orange wine is an after-wine, a dessert,' said Axel. He rolled his eyes to indicate how stupid those people must be. 'But in fact, it is an *aperitivo*.'

'Really?'

'Yes, it is so.' He nodded energetically and Holly thought of Sofía, who'd shown similar enthusiasm for her products. Holly had really liked her and Sofía had appeared to take to them too. Especially to Holly's mother . . . She had seemed to sense that something was going on there. Holly pushed the thought away – she mustn't brood. Tomás was nice enough too. Very capable, very charming. Holly wondered if he had a girlfriend. Perhaps she would find out tonight.

'We have it with the ice,' Axel pronounced. 'The taste and the aroma of the orange – it awakens the senses so you are ready for the food,' he explained. He turned to the ancient fridge-freezer behind him and removed a scoopful of ice from a bucket inside the door. 'Here.' He took a small tumbler from the shelf and poured the ice carefully in. He then uncorked the bottle.

His hands, Holly noted, were brown and swarthy, but at the same time rather delicate. She wondered if he had been a bar tender and a winemaker all his life. She would ask him later, if she got the chance. At the moment, she didn't want to distract him from the task in hand.

'We have the wine,' Axel said. 'We have a slice of orange, yes?' He looked at Holly enquiringly.

'Yes, why not?' she said.

He took an orange from the bowl on the counter and sliced it in half on a wooden chopping board. He sliced again and dropped a single segment into the tumbler. 'And we have the mint?' One eyebrow was raised enquiringly.

'Lovely,' said Holly.

Axel snipped a two-leafed sprig from one of the plants on the bar next to the oranges and dropped that into the mix. 'And now . . .' he said.

He certainly knew how to build up the anticipation, Holly thought.

She watched as he poured the dark orange wine over the ice,

mint and orange. ‘It looks amazing,’ she said. The colour was rich amber; in fact, it looked rather like a very strong Aperol Spritz without the bubbles, and she could imagine it looking even better in an elegant wine glass. Perhaps it might even catch on in Bridport?

‘And now you taste.’ Axel pushed the tumbler towards her.

Holly took it and sniffed it first. As though she knew what she was doing, she thought. It smelt wonderful. Rich, aromatic, a slight vanilla tang and heavy on the oranges. She took a sip.

Axel was waiting.

‘Delicious,’ she said. And she meant it. It coated her tongue with the taste of orange and honey.

He beamed back at her, his nonchalant shrug belying his obvious pleasure at the compliment. ‘It is good,’ he agreed.

It certainly was. The wine could be drunk as a dessert wine, she thought, but it was bitter-sweet with just the slightest hint of vanilla. And as an *aperitivo* with ice it was perfect.

‘I’m definitely interested,’ said Holly, cutting to the chase.

‘Oh.’ He muttered something in Spanish. Was he changing his mind again? ‘You mean, you want to buy . . . ?’ He trailed off, once again did his quick scan of the immediate vicinity, inside and out.

‘How many bottles do you produce each year?’ Holly asked him.

He stared back at her.

She leant in closer. ‘Are you interested in discussing a deal, Axel?’ Because if not, she was wasting her time.

‘England . . .’ His voice was low, Holly had to strain to hear it. ‘I have always wanted it,’ he said. ‘But . . .’ He bowed his head.

‘Then what’s the problem?’ Holly asked brightly.

Axel looked up. He regarded her steadily. 'We can talk again,' he pronounced at last. '*Si?*'

She nodded. 'Yes.' Because this product was worth pursuing.

'You come to see me again perhaps? I must talk with some people, there are other . . .' – he seemed lost for words – 'concerns to think of.'

'OK,' said Holly. 'That's fine.'

He seemed to cheer up at that. 'And the liqueur?' he asked. 'Will you try?'

Holly was glad she'd had lunch; she needed something to have lined her stomach. 'I'd love to,' she told him.

Axel produced a much smaller bottle from behind the counter this time, also black with an orange label. He poured the thick liquid into a shot glass.

Holly raised it to her lips. She sipped. Wow, this was strong stuff. Incredibly rich and velvet-smooth on the tongue, it was somehow powerful and delicate, fruity and fresh – all at the same time. She didn't know an awful lot about wine or liqueurs but this was a pure citrus burst on the palate with hints of marmalade and a zesty lingering finish. And orange, very orange.

'It's excellent,' she said. 'I really like it.' It could probably be used in desserts too – it might even give her mother's orange and almond cake an extra zing, if she was ever allowed to make it again. It could be an ice cream or pancake topping and it could certainly be a component of a classy cocktail.

Axel seemed satisfied. 'And now.' He shrugged towards the doorway where some people were loitering, obviously also keen for a taste of his orange wine.

'I won't hold you up any longer,' Holly said. 'But when shall I come back to see you?' She got out her phone and consulted her calendar. 'I understand that you need to think about it, but

I'm only here for a short time.'

Axel looked nervous at this.

Holly persevered. 'Tuesday? Wednesday? Or is the weekend better for you?'

'Ah, always I work.' Axel spoke with mock-sadness. He frowned. 'But perhaps early in the morning before we open? Ten? On Wednesday?'

'Agreed.' Holly shook hands on it.

'*Muchas gracias*.' Axel bent his head once more. 'Thank you very much.'

'*Muchas gracias*,' Holly repeated. 'And is it OK if I just' – she indicated her phone and the two bottles on the counter – 'take a picture?'

'But of course.' He opened his arms expansively. 'These things, they can always be changed, but—'

'No,' said Holly, looking at the bottles. 'No, I don't think I would change a thing.'

CHAPTER 13

Ella

Seville, 2018

Back at the hotel, Ella was getting ready for the evening ahead. What did you wear to the flamenco in 2018? She surveyed the choice in her wardrobe – a knee-length little black dress that was flattering and which she could still get away with, thank goodness; a floaty white linen that hung in the way that only Italian dresses seemed to hang; or a close-fitting cotton dress in leaf-green and yellow that she'd shoved into her case at the last minute. She sighed. She'd had this particular problem once before. And she had never expected the exact same thing to be happening again.

She selected the black dress and added dangling silver earrings. This was Seville – it was definitely permissible to dress up for the flamenco . . .

Flamenco. For a moment, she closed her eyes and allowed the memories to flood in. The music, the dancing, the strumming of the guitar. She could feel the heat suffusing her body and quickly she opened her eyes again, dragged herself away from Seville in the past and back to this hotel room, to now.

It had, she conceded, been an interesting day. She had been shocked to discover that not only was Holly focusing all her attention on Seville, but she'd even narrowed it down to the *barrio* of Triana. Ella shook her head. *Of all the places.*

In the bathroom, Ella smoothed some moisturiser into her skin. But why wouldn't her daughter have been drawn to Triana, just as Ella had been? It was the natural hub of creativity in Seville. It was alive with energy.

As they'd approached the district, Ella lingering on the bridge, unwilling to take that step towards the past, she'd felt the same mix of excitement and terror that she'd felt ever since she'd promised to come here with Holly. It was known and yet unknown. It might remind her of what she'd lost, but also of what she'd found. It was dangerous in all sorts of ways. But . . . how she wanted it.

Ella added her usual light foundation and finished it with a dusting of loose powder. What was Felix doing now? she wondered. She thought again of how he'd stood up to his mother and she smiled. Felix was a good man. He had always been a good man and she knew she was lucky to have him.

To Ella's relief, the day had gone smoothly, with nothing, surprisingly, to be terrified about. She had appreciated being part of her daughter's business meeting, even though she'd tried to slink off to drink a solitary *café cortado* in the back of a bar somewhere she'd never be spotted. It had appealed to her – to be in Triana and to be anonymous. But she'd enjoyed talking to Sofía and learning more about soaps, salts and oils. Ella applied just a hint of blusher. It had been an impressive package – all the more so, since Sofía had no idea how good it really was.

Ella paused. And if the scent of the neroli blossom in Sofía's kitchen had brought back emotions and memories long buried . . . that was inevitable. Besides, the orange trees all around this city were already doing exactly that for themselves.

And she was surviving it.

She used a light neutral shade on her eyelids with a dash of purple at the corners and a quick stroke of mascara. Not only surviving it; she was reliving that past, which was bringing pleasure as well as pain. It seemed that where Seville was concerned, there would always be ambivalence.

A knock on the door cut into her thoughts. 'Hi, Mum. Room service.'

Ella smiled. 'Come in, darling.'

She peered around the bathroom door. Holly was holding two glasses of white wine. She looked stunning in a blue dress the colour of lapis lazuli. The fabric clung to her figure, emphasising her height and her slim curves. Her dark hair was loose and her lipstick a fiery red.

'You look fabulous,' Ella told her. Tonight, Holly would get noticed, for sure.

'You too, Mum.' Holly came to the bathroom door. She eyed her mother speculatively.

Ella applied her own lipstick in a more discreet shade of caramel and smoothed her hair into place with her fingertips. At the roots of the dark brown were definite smudges of grey. In the mirror's reflection, she could see Holly looking at her. Her daughter was wearing her thinking face.

Ella returned her attention to herself. She looked a bit afraid – like a deer caught in the headlights. How much was she kidding herself? How much had she always been kidding herself?

'So, when are you going to tell me, Mum?' Holly sipped her wine and put the other glass on the side for Ella.

'Tell you what, darling?'

'What happened in Seville. The first time you came here, I mean.'

She'd been expecting this. Ella picked up her wine glass and took a sip. She needed the pause. The wine was very cold and dry, just as she liked it. 'As in?' she said lightly.

'As in why you were so reluctant to come back here. As in what happened last time. As in why you're scared.'

Once again, Ella glanced at her daughter in the mirror. It was only slightly safer. But Holly looked troubled now.

'Why you didn't want to come to Triana this morning. Why you didn't even want to come to the flamenco.'

The flamenco. This time, Ella thought of her mother's jewellery box. The little dancer on the top. The music: 'Spanish Eyes' . . . She still missed her mother, even after all these years. Not the mother who had married Kenny, but the other mother she'd been before. And Ella often wondered, what would have happened if her mother had lived longer? Would she have recognised what living with a man like Kenny was doing to her? Would she have left him? Would she and Ella have been reunited – properly reunited? And would Ella ever have understood the reasons why . . . ?

She hoped so. Because everyone made mistakes, Ella knew that as well as anyone. And there were always reasons why.

Her lipstick had left an imprint on the cold glass. Ella took a tissue and blotted the colour on her lips. Holly shouldn't be troubled on this business trip. She should have a clear head and be feeling confident and unstressed. After all, her daughter's anxiety and stress were what had started this chain of events off in the first place. She certainly shouldn't have to deal with any of Ella's problems. Holly didn't need to know any of it. What good would it do?

So, Ella put on a careless smile. 'It was just the thought of not having enough time to do all my lesson-planning, that's all,' she said breezily. 'You know how I worry.' She eyed her own reflection once more. She looked pretty convincing, she decided. That was half the trouble – she always had.

'So, it was nothing to do with the past?'

Ella couldn't quite meet her daughter's eye. 'How could it be?' she said.

'Then . . . ?'

'I wasn't sure at first that Triana was the right place to find what you wanted, darling, but . . .'

Ella saw her daughter narrow her eyes. 'But?'

She turned to face her. 'But Sofía certainly proved me wrong.'

Holly nodded warily. She didn't look entirely convinced. 'And the flamenco?' she asked. 'Surely that's a chance not to be missed?'

Ella smiled brightly. 'You're right,' she said. 'But that Valentina . . .' She pulled a face. 'What a little madam. I wasn't sure I wanted to give her the satisfaction of being admired.'

'Good point.' Holly seemed to relax. 'But now that we've said we'll be there . . . It'll be quite an experience, don't you think?'

'I'm sure it will be,' Ella agreed. There was no way of avoiding it now. And there was no reason to suppose that Tomás's family had any connection to that other family from the past. Though how many family and friendship groups were there in Triana? They were a close-knit group of people, in her experience. Did everyone know everyone else? She shivered. But then again, everyone would look very different now.

What were the chances? Once again, Ella picked up her glass and took another sip of the delicious wine. At any rate, she was about to find out.

CHAPTER 14

Ella

Seville, 1988

To Ella's surprise – because she had half expected it wouldn't happen – the car, a beaten-up Seat, arrived exactly when Caleb had said it would.

Ella scrutinised the driver carefully before getting in. In the past few hours, she had doubted her own decision and changed her mind several times before finally deciding to go. She was in a foreign city alone and this was her first ever trip abroad, but it was an opportunity she couldn't miss.

'Hello? You are Ella?'

'Yes, I am.' He looked safe enough. He had kind eyes and an endearing gappy grin.

'I come to take you to Triana,' he said. 'Yes? Welcome. Please.' And he gestured to the passenger seat beside him.

'Thank you.' Ella climbed in. Although it was ten o'clock and dark, the air was still warm, and she'd opted to wear her blue puff-sleeved dress with wide black belt, and matching sandals with a narrow ankle strap. She had her black cardigan with her in case it got chilly later. It was the most up-to-date outfit she'd brought here. Since they'd been saving to get their own place, fashion hadn't been high on Ella's agenda. Though come to think of it, it never had.

Her driver expertly negotiated the narrow streets surrounding her hotel, where cars were parked in every tiny space, often on pavements, squeezed in so tightly together that she couldn't imagine how they'd ever get out again. They passed the old Convento de Santa Clara that she and Felix had discovered on their first afternoon – how long ago that seemed already! – and were soon on the main Avenida Torneo which ran along by the river and led right into the heart of the old city. In the distance she could see what she guessed were the lights of the bullring and the bridge that led to the district of Triana.

'What's your name?' Ella asked her driver, aware that Caleb had neglected to mention it.

'Sergio García at your service.' He tipped an imaginary hat. 'As the English say.' He laughed.

Ella laughed with him. 'You speak good English too,' she said.

'It is important for me.' He glanced across at her. 'I am taxi driver here in Seville.' As if to demonstrate his skills, he jammed the palm of his hand onto the horn and manoeuvred neatly from one lane to the other.

'Oh, I see.' She should pay him, she realised. It wasn't fair to expect the man to take her and bring her back for nothing. This was his livelihood.

Sergio indicated right and soon they were sweeping over the bridge with the rest of the traffic.

'You like our city, *señora*?' he asked her.

'Ella, please,' she said. 'And I love it.' She hadn't seen much of it yet, but already she was hooked. Seville was such a fascinating mix of the old and the new. She adored the tapas bars and the cafés and she'd been blown away by the Real Alcázar. She'd enjoyed exploring Triana so much that she had decided to return to spend the whole day there before she left. There was such a buzz to this city; it was noisy and exciting and yet on every street there was greenery – flowers or orange trees – and often some ancient and beautiful building that made you stop, take a breath and simply stare.

'Then you will love the flamenco,' he told her. He pulled up outside a small bar. 'This is the place.'

Ella peered out of the window into the dark night. The bar was lit up, though, and it was heaving, inside and out. It was clearly the place to be in Triana tonight.

Sergio reversed the car, parking predictably half on, half off the narrow, cobbled paving. As Caleb had told her, the bar was situated near to his ceramic shop, but goodness, Triana appeared very different at night. Ella gazed up the street. It was dark, moody and a bit mysterious. The bar itself was painted black on the outside and in the window, a blackboard was scrawled with the menu of tapas and drinks. Above, a balcony woven with vines was illuminated by an old lantern. The door to the bar had been flung open to reveal the bright and crowded interior and people had spilt outside to sit on wooden chairs and tables as they chatted, smoked and drank beer.

Sergio seemed to be waiting for her to move, so Ella got out of the car with some trepidation. It seemed to her that everyone outside the bar was staring at them. She glanced into the open doorway. It was noisy with the babble of conversation and raucous laughter, but there was no music, at least not yet.

She leant back into the car. 'Thank you so much, Sergio,' she said.

'And when it is over,' he said. 'I take you back.'

'OK, thanks.' She hesitated.

He gestured towards the bar. 'It is no problem,' he said. 'Go in. Get a drink. Enjoy.'

'And you? Aren't you coming in?' She wasn't sure she wanted to run the gauntlet of all these people alone.

His eyes twinkled. 'I have work to do. But I will return. Go.'

Ella turned, took a deep breath and edged her way through the crowd towards the bar. She stepped inside, jostled by two older Spanish men and their female companions. Some beer got spilt on the floor. '*Lo siento*,' she said. 'Sorry.' No one took any notice and so she inched further in.

There were so many people inside that the room seemed airless. Clearly this was a Spanish-only bar; there were no tourists here as far as she could see – apart from Ella herself, that was. Everyone seemed to be talking at once and the volume was getting louder and louder as they all tried to make themselves heard. On the far side of the bar she noted the makeshift stage, with three chairs placed on it and a guitar, half in shadow.

She shuffled through the crowd towards the bar where terracotta sangria jugs and gleaming rows of glasses stood ready on high shelves above the blue-tiled counter. *Azulejo* tiles decorated the white walls and there were pictures too – of dancing and of bullfighting. Ella craned to see, but it was nearly impossible. And where was Caleb? He must be here somewhere. She looked around the ocean of faces. Caleb was nowhere to be seen.

As she stood there at the bar, there was a hush as the lights dimmed.

Ella glanced towards the makeshift stage. Too late. It looked as though the show was starting. Two men walked onto the platform to the enthusiastic applause of the audience. The first, dressed in a red satin shirt with black trousers and shiny patent shoes, sat down and placed the drum he was carrying between his knees. The second man, dressed all in black, picked up the guitar. Caleb. He looked over. For a moment, his gaze seemed to lock onto hers. But the lights were so low and a lone spotlight was shining onto the stage, so surely it was impossible? She must be imagining it.

Caleb sat down on one chair and hooked his right foot onto the rung of another, placing his guitar on his thigh. He flexed his long fingers as if to get the blood circulating more freely and then began to play, rhythmically and slowly, the fingers of his right hand plucking notes that rang stridently across the floor. The drummer picked up the beat with a slow slap; Caleb too was tapping his other foot in time. The pulse was building. It was a sound unlike any Ella had ever heard, a sound of anticipation; almost of waiting.

The two men glanced across at one another and the drummer closed his eyes, then began to sing in a low, raspy voice. It was an anguished sound, almost a soft wail, and Ella winced at first, but as the sound continued to resonate around the room, she started feeling the emotion. It was impossible not to. The singer seemed to be reaching inside himself to a place deep in his soul. And the emotions were of nostalgia, of sadness and of pain.

The two men were in harmony; the music matched the singer's voice, the rhythm from Caleb's guitar both underlining it and structuring it. Ella wished she was closer to the stage. Caleb's facial expression had altered too; it had grown more intense and more focused, as his fingers moved deftly over the strings, as the beat switched once more and the tempo of the complex harmonies got faster. Ella couldn't believe that so much sound, so much tone and feeling could come from one instrument. Her heart seemed to be beating faster too.

As the music paused and the singer slowed, just clapping out the beat now with his feet and hands, the dancer entered from a back door on the other side of the stage. She wore a polka-dot red and black dress with red shoes, her raven hair flowed over her shoulders and, to Ella's surprise, she was at least middle-aged, but still a fine figure of a woman, tall and handsome with generous curves. Still and defiant, she took up a commanding stance at the front of the stage.

An air of expectancy filled the room as the music slackened once more. Quick, slow; quick, slow . . . The dancer's gaze was fixed trance-like above the heads of the audience, and her first movement was a gentle sway and rustle of her dress as she raised her arms above her head, moving into her starting pose. She thrust out her jaw, head held high. There was a long pause, a silence.

Caleb played a musical chord, almost as if in speculation. The dancer clicked her heels on the floor in reply and she began to move, slowly at first, twisting like a flame, then staccato, her feet pounding as the tempo grew and the music built in complex layers around her. She snapped her fingers to the beat, she tossed her head, she wove and stamped and took charge of the stage. She was strong and powerful; she was responding to the throbbing and strumming of the guitar music just as Caleb seemed to be responding to her. Almost as if this dance was improvised, Ella found herself thinking. But how could it be improvised when it was so professional, so good?

The dancer's expression became more tormented, her

movements smouldering, then frenzied, as she spun and clicked, faster and faster, reaching the climax of the dance in a burst of explosive heat. Finally, she came to rest, standing on the edge of the stage as before. Ella let out a breath of pure release. Such precision and control. Such passion. It was a powerful combination.

And now the singer moved into the spotlight and closed his eyes, preparing to begin again. Around the stage, the audience remained silent, waiting. The deep guttural wail was low in the back of his throat. Slowly, slowly. Then he took a gasp, threw back his head and let out a primitive moan. And began to sing. This time, he seemed almost to be telling a story. He was looking at his audience, engaging with them, while the other two stood apart. There was a lonely melancholy, almost an agony in his voice that moved Ella although she couldn't understand a thing. On and on he sang, while the plaintive notes of the guitar rang out and the dancer stood frozen as a statue.

At last, the singer let out another cry that snatched Ella's breath away. The dancer followed his lead and once again she began to move to the beat, her body unfurling, her arms lifting above her head, her movements growing more rapid, more feverish. While Caleb played on, sweat beading his brow as the music became freer, as the rhythm accelerated into a frenetic and blistering pace. Ella was close to tears. It was such a charged and theatrical experience; so raw, so poignant. All three of them played their parts like actors, all three were thoroughly immersed in the piece. And Ella too felt part of it. She couldn't repress a shudder. So, this was flamenco.

In the break, Ella managed to get herself a beer and perched on a stool by the bar where she wouldn't feel too conspicuous.

Caleb appeared as if by magic at her side. 'Ella.' He kissed her on both cheeks. 'You are here.' He had wiped the sweat from his brow but his lips felt hot on her skin.

'Of course.' She laughed, although the intensity of his performance had made her feel shy with him. 'But you didn't tell me you were the musician.'

He smiled modestly. 'I spoke to you of my other interest,' he reminded her. 'I make the pots and I make the music.'

'And you make it very well,' she told him. Which seemed rather an understatement. She was still reeling from the performance she'd witnessed from all three of them.

'Ah, you enjoyed it then?'

Enjoyed didn't seem the right word somehow. 'I loved it,' she assured him. 'The atmosphere in this place . . .' She looked around the bar. It was buzzing. 'The emotion of the singing, the playing, the dancing . . . it was incredible.'

'Good.' He seemed satisfied. 'But there is more to come. There are many different *palos* – styles of the flamenco. And much more emotion too.'

'Bring it on.' Though Ella wasn't sure she could stand too much more emotion. She had almost cried at the end of the last section. Cried for herself, for Felix, for all the pain in the world. How had the flamenco inspired all that?

'We will.' Caleb gestured to the barman for a drink. 'Can I get you something, Ella?'

'I'm fine,' she assured him.

'And you will stay to the end?' He took the beer the barman passed to him and drank thirstily.

'I certainly will,' she said. Now that she was here, there was no way she was missing a minute – whatever the emotional consequences.

'Excellent.' He touched her arm and she felt the warmth of him again. 'I will take you back in the car with Sergio.'

'Oh, there's no need to do that.' Ella felt safe with Sergio. In fact, it occurred to her that it was Caleb she didn't feel quite so safe with, especially after his mesmerising performance tonight. Not because she didn't trust him. But because she was drawn to him. Right at this moment, Felix and her marital problems seemed an awfully long way away, but the last thing she intended to do was put them into even more jeopardy than they were in already.

'Please,' he said. 'I only want to talk with you. Do not worry. It is all arranged.'

What was arranged? But Ella couldn't help smiling as Caleb clicked his heels together briefly and disappeared again to prepare for the second set.

Ella put her glass down on the bar and waited.

The second half went much the same way as the first, with alternating rhythms, singing, dancing and a surfeit of emotion. The dancer had changed into a dress of forest green and the singer, rather than telling a story to the audience, seemed to be setting the tone for the dancing. Once again, there was sadness and there was pain in the rough and wailing voice, but this time there was passion too. The dance was slower and more sensual at first; the dancer's eyes glazed over as if she had indeed been transported into another world and was determined to take her audience with her.

Ella glanced around her. The audience were with her, she could tell. Right now, the audience would let her take them anywhere. The pace quickened, Caleb's fingers flew over the strings, the singer let out a gravelly moan and the excitement rose. It rose to a crescendo, a climax. The dancer's skin glistened with sweat, her hair was damp and unruly. Absorbed in the music, living the beat, she danced on.

Ella closed her eyes for a moment and let it wash over her. There was such a charge in the air, such raw emotion – it felt almost sexual. The dancer spun, the tension grew. And then abruptly, the wild dance came to a juddering close. Caleb played the final haunting, shivering chord and the singer let out his final groan. The show was over and Ella felt as exhausted as if she'd been dancing herself.

She waited for Caleb and Sergio by the bar and after several minutes or so they arrived together. Although she was feeling wiped out, Ella knew she was wearing the biggest of grins. This was an experience she would never forget.

'You liked it then, Ella?' asked Sergio.

'It was amazing.'

'And Caleb here?' He clapped his cousin on the shoulder. 'He is a brilliant flamenco guitarist, *non*?'

'He is.' Ella watched Caleb. His black eyes were still glittering with adrenalin and energy. And something else. There was a sensuality about this man that Ella found very disturbing.

'Did you feel it?' Caleb asked her.

'Feel it?' Though some part of Ella knew instinctively what he was referring to.

'The *duende*,' he said. 'The height of the emotion.'

'Yes,' she said quietly. 'I think I did.'

'Good.' His smile seemed to hold a note of triumph. But he deserved it, she thought. He had been magnificent.

Caleb turned to his cousin and spoke to him in Spanish. He turned back to Ella. 'I will drive you back to your hotel,' he said.

What could she say? She was hardly in a position to refuse a lift. 'Thank you,' she said.

Sergio tossed him the keys. 'OK. See you soon, Ella.'

Would she? These two seemed to take an awful lot of things for granted. 'I hope so,' she called.

And now, here she was, alone with Caleb, flamenco guitarist and potter, a man to whom the heightening of emotions obviously meant a great deal. Help, she thought.

Caleb drove as quickly and confidently as all the Spanish seemed to do, back towards the Alameda and Ella's hotel. She thought about making conversation, but there was a tension in the atmosphere between them that she wasn't sure how to break. She supposed that he was still living the intensity of the flamenco performance and she could understand that, because she was still affected too. The pulse of the dance seemed to lie there still between them.

As they arrived outside the hotel, he cut the engine. 'Thank you for coming tonight, Ella,' he said.

'Thank you,' she said. 'It was a wonderful experience. I'm very grateful.' Which sounded lame. It seemed that words were inadequate to describe what had just taken place in that bar in Triana. She just hoped he understood.

Caleb shrugged. 'It is important for me to give people who visit our city a taste of the real Seville,' he said. 'We have a history, a culture to protect. We must not undervalue it or sell it cheap.'

Ella nodded. 'I see that.' She thought of how some Spanish resorts had already lost their character in the name of tourism. Yes, the Spanish were poor and no one could blame them for picking up on the tourist business as a way out of poverty. But wasn't the very charm that had attracted the tourists in the first place in danger of being lost in the process?

She wondered, though, did Caleb show everyone he met the authentic side of Seville?

Once again, he seemed to know what she was thinking. 'I am trying for another job,' he said. 'I know the history of our city. I could do the real tour for visitors. Why not?' He frowned. 'Do you think people will like that, Ella? Not just you, but other people too?'

So that was what he had wanted to talk to her about. He wanted to get the tourist's point of view. Ella was partly relieved that this was the case and partly put out by his words. She had assumed he'd singled her out because he was attracted to her – and what English girl wouldn't be flattered by the attentions of such a good-looking and talented Spaniard? – but clearly that wasn't it at all. So, was he concerned about the authenticity of the tourist experience per se or was he thinking of his own future?

'It's a great idea, Caleb,' she assured him. 'You would be really good at it.'

'You think so?' He raised one eyebrow.

'Oh, yes, I do.'

'But how do you know?'

'Sorry?' Ella was confused.

'You have watched the flamenco, yes. You have listened to the music. You have felt it, *sí*?'

'Yes.'

'But you have not yet heard me talk about my city.'

'Well, yes, that's true, I suppose.' What now? Ella fidgeted on her seat. She should go inside. What was she doing even having this conversation in the early hours of the morning with a man she hardly knew in a city she knew even less? She was married, for heaven's sake.

'So, Ella, may I take you tomorrow for a short tour?' he asked.

'Oh, I'm sorry, Caleb.' Now she got it. He was after business. 'I really don't have enough money for a tour guide.'

Which reminded her – she'd entirely forgotten to give anything to Sergio for taking her to Triana tonight. She groped for her purse.

'Ella!' Caleb sounded so hurt that she stopped what she was doing and looked at him. In the dim light from the lamp post by the hotel foyer, his eyes still shone. 'What are you doing? I do not want money.' He spoke in a hushed voice. And she could tell that he was offended.

'No, I—'

But before she could explain, he had got out of the car. He came round to her side and opened the door.

Ella took hold of her bag and climbed out. 'I'm sorry, Caleb,' she said. 'But—'

'Not everything is about money,' he said. His frown deepened. 'Some of us may be poor, but we all still have our dignity.'

Ella faced him. 'I know,' she said. 'But I don't want to take advantage of anyone. And I just wanted to give your cousin something for coming to collect me tonight. He is a taxi driver after all.'

'He does not want it,' Caleb said.

'Really?' Though shouldn't Sergio be the judge of that?

'He and I, we are family.'

'I know that. Even so . . .' Really, he was very difficult to deal with, thought Ella.

'If I take you,' he continued, 'it is because I want you to see our city and because I want you to learn the truth about Seville.'

'OK . . .' Somehow, he had managed to put her on the back foot, she realised. Clever.

'So, you will come?'

Ella couldn't make out his expression now. He'd made it almost impossible to refuse – she'd be bound to offend him again. She was tempted to go, of course. It would be wonderful to be shown around Seville by a knowledgeable guide. But on the other hand, what about Felix? How would he react? Caleb was young and he was attractive. And he seemed to practically make a business from sensuality and emotion. Then she thought of how quickly Felix had given up on her and Seville and rushed home to his mother. Felix's first loyalty would always be to Ingrid. Ella would always take second place. It was the way things were. So . . .

'I'd love to,' she said. It was only one tour. What harm could it do?

'Good.' He kissed her on both cheeks as he had done before. She breathed in the warmth of him just for a second before he drew away. 'You are alone in the city and this is not good,' he said. 'So, I will take you on a tour tomorrow.' He eyed her appraisingly. 'And maybe the next day too.'

'That's not necessary,' she said firmly. 'I'm more than capable of managing on my own.'

'Capable, yes,' he said. 'But how will you know where to go and what to see?'

'I have a guidebook,' she retorted. 'And anyway, what about your work? Your ceramic shop?'

'We have enough pots for now.' And suddenly, to her surprise, he smiled and the smile transformed his face.

Ella couldn't help but smile back. She thought of all those pots, bowls and dishes stacked on the shelves. 'Actually, yes, you have,' she agreed.

'Until tomorrow then,' he said. 'Sleep well, Ella. Shall I pick you up at ten?'

'Perfect.' Ella stood for a few moments watching the car speed off down the narrow street.

Oh, my goodness, she thought. What had she done? She stepped into the foyer of the hotel. She had just experienced what was perhaps the most exciting evening of her life. She had felt herself transported into a world of heightened sensuality and desire. And Felix, her husband, was so very far away.

CHAPTER 15

Holly

Seville, 2018

In the taxi, heading once more to Triana, Holly settled back to watch the sights of the city pass by. It was almost nine p.m. and people were mostly just starting their evening meal in the restaurants and bars; others, maybe just out for drinks, were chatting and laughing together. It was another warm, cheery and tapas-fuelled night in Seville.

Holly thought of her mother's reaction when she'd questioned her earlier. So cool, so calm . . . But Holly wasn't convinced. After what had happened when she'd made the Seville orange and almond cake, not to mention the fact that her mother had kept the recipe half hidden for so long, there had to be something more to it than worrying about lesson-planning. And as for the way she'd been acting since they'd arrived in Seville . . . Holly just knew she wasn't imagining it.

She sneaked a glance at her mother. She seemed composed enough now.

The taxi drew up at the address Tomás had given them – a club, just around the corner from the Pérez family's apartment. Holly felt a shiver of excitement as she looked out of the window. The door to the club was wide open and she couldn't wait to get in there.

They got out, paid the man and made their way over. Holly glanced at her mother – there was a discernible tension in her body as if she was waiting for something. Once again, she looked excited – and scared.

'All right, Mum?' Holly asked.

Her mother composed her face. 'Absolutely.' She squeezed Holly's hand. 'Shall we go in?'

The club was dimly lit, with a tiled floor and dark ginger-painted walls. Wooden chairs and tables had been placed in a rough horseshoe shape around a stage. People were sitting chatting; others were ordering drinks at the bar. There was a general atmosphere of bonhomie. Holly peered through the crowd. On the stage were two chairs. A guitar was propped against one of them, a shawl thrown on the back of the other. There was no music playing yet, but the buzz of conversation filled the air. Everyone seemed in very good spirits.

'Good evening.' Tomás was standing in front of them. He must have been looking out. 'Welcome.'

'Hello, Tomás,' said Holly. 'Thank you.' They did the usual kissing greeting. Holly caught a whiff of his pine aftershave and found herself wondering if his mother had made it.

Tomás looked rather debonair tonight, she thought, watching him greet her mother. No longer in jeans and T-shirt, but now dressed in smart grey trousers, a black shirt and jacket.

'Let me get you a drink,' he said. He seemed very solicitous. 'Come through. I have saved two places at a good table for you.'

'*Gracias*. Thank you,' they both said.

Holly and her mother shared a conspiratorial look as they followed Tomás to their table. Her mother, Holly noticed now as they made their way through the room, was once again glancing from left to right, a fixed smile on her face. She looked ready for anything.

Tomás introduced them to the other people at the table, neighbours of the Pérez family, who spoke as little English as Ella and Holly spoke Spanish, but who were welcoming and nodded and smiled a great deal. Once again, Holly was struck by the friendliness of the Spaniards. Everyone they'd met so far had been so hospitable, so warm.

Tomás disappeared to get their drinks and Holly looked around the room. It was no surprise to see lots of pictures on the walls – mostly featuring the flamenco, some in black and white, some in colour: a dancer receiving a huge bouquet of flowers, a dancer adopting a haughty stance at the beginning of the show, a dancer posing with her fan half covering her face. But Holly also spotted a few images of bullfighting; there was a young matador swinging a red and gold cape as a bull charged. There were ceramics too: brightly coloured plates and urns on high shelves, a display of antique fans, a beautiful gilt mirror worn with age, and old lanterns hanging from the ceiling. As always, there were decorative tiles – in this case, surrounding the shuttered windows of the club and below the dado rail on the walls.

Tomás returned with glasses and a carafe of white wine. He poured them both a glass. 'I must leave you now,' he said, looking disappointed. 'But I will see you later. Enjoy the show!'

As if on cue, the lights dimmed and a hush spread quickly around the room. Those who had been standing at the bar joined the horseshoe of tables or just came and stood behind. All was quiet; everyone was waiting.

A man walked onto the stage. People began to clap and he gave a little bow and a half-smile. He was young and attractive and his black hair curled around the collar of his white shirt. He was wearing close-fitting black trousers and shiny black shoes, but no jacket, no tie; his shirt was open at the neck . . . He was hot.

Holly thought she heard her mother let out a little gasp, but it was drowned by the applause and when Holly turned to her, she was smiling and clapping like all the rest. Holly turned back. Her gaze was drawn again to him, irresistibly.

With a loving touch, the young Spaniard on stage picked up the guitar and passed the straps over his shoulder. He placed one foot on the lower rung of the chair and played a chord.

As if summoned by the music, an older man appeared beside him. Again, there was clapping and he smiled and gave a small bow. This man, dressed similarly to the first but with none of the younger man's easy charisma, Holly found herself thinking, sat on the vacant chair and stared into space. He was the singer, she supposed. He seemed to be putting himself into some kind of meditative state.

The guitarist played another chord. Then another. For a second only, he looked up and she could have sworn he was gazing straight at her. Holly swallowed. She felt something. She wasn't sure what it was. Some sort of intangible connection. Was that crazy? Was that even possible?

Then he looked down and began to pluck the strings of his instrument, slowly at first, then building, building . . . The pace quickened. The guitarist's hand lashed out on the body of his instrument, across the taut strings. The second man tapped his feet and slapped his palms on his thighs.

After a few minutes, the older man, eyes closed, began to sing – soulfully, mournfully. Holly blinked. It wasn't in any way the kind of singing she was used to hearing, and it seemed to belong to some bygone age, some long-ago time and civilisation. And yet there was something about it . . . It seemed to touch her somehow. Once more, she felt that sense of connection. But perhaps, she thought, that was all part of the powerful experience that was the flamenco.

The song moved along faster and finally came to a climax. The audience applauded and the two men smiled and bowed their heads in acknowledgment. As he looked up again, for the second time, Holly had the distinct impression that the Spanish guitarist was staring straight at her, searching somehow. But it made no sense. And what would he be searching for?

There was another hush, a pause that hung in the air. And then a young woman strode onto the stage. It was Valentina – but not the same Valentina that they'd met earlier. She no longer looked surly and resentful, just beautiful and proud. She was wearing a red and white satin polka-dot dress with tiered flounces and black and red dancing shoes. The dress clung to her slim body and trailed on the ground behind her as she moved. Her eyes were smoky and her dark curls hung down her back, shiny and free. She swished her way to the very front of the stage and stared down at her audience imperiously. She owned it.

The guitarist played a chord, the singer nodded his head, Valentina seemed to go into a trance just as the singer had done before. And for the third time, the young Spaniard playing flamenco guitar, lifted his head, looked straight at Holly. Slowly, very slowly, he smiled.

CHAPTER 16

Ella

Seville, 2018

Ella watched Valentina strutting across the stage. She was confident. And she was good – very good. She knew all the steps and all the moves. She used the fan, the shawl like weapons; changing direction, changing pace, one moment rapid and aggressive, the next slow and sensual. Her heels clicked, her body spun. Her gaze flicked from side to side, her wrists twisted, her hands unfurled. She had some sense of power, some elegance and grace. But for Ella, there was something missing. Perhaps it was the pain; perhaps it was the passion. Valentina was young. Ella wondered if she had not yet learnt to dance from within. The performance, this music . . . It took Ella back, though.

In the dim light, she let her gaze wander around the faces of the audience, though most of them were in deep shadow. Just to check – once again. She exhaled in relief. There were no familiar faces belonging to that family from long ago. Although – and she felt the accompanying stab of disappointment, that ambivalence once again – would she even recognise them now?

As for the Spaniard playing flamenco guitar . . . Ella watched him, observed the intensity in his expression as he plucked the strings, saw him frown, felt him feeding off the emotion of the flamenco even as he delivered it – in spades. Oh yes, he had it, this one; she could tell.

Her breath had caught in her throat when he'd made his entrance. Because he reminded her so much of that other flamenco guitarist, that other night. The same dark hair, the same intensity, the same way of crouching over his instrument as if it were some live creature he must tame.

But of course, that other flamenco guitarist would no longer be young, like this one. Ella closed her eyes for a moment to let the music wash over her and felt the soar, the quickening pulse that she remembered so well. Pretty soon, her feet were tapping and the years were fading away. It had been a long time but there were some things that you never forgot. The music ended with its usual point of high emotion. Ella heard the audience let out a small sigh in unison, before the applause commenced.

'*Olé!*' someone shouted. '*Olé!*'

Duende, she thought. She remembered all right. She remembered everything.

She glanced across at Holly, who was clapping with enthusiasm. Ella had seen the excitement in her daughter's face as they'd entered the club, felt her thrill as the music began. She was, it seemed, her mother's daughter.

Ella leant closer. 'What did you think?'

'It was amazing!' Holly replied. Her dark eyes were shining. Holly loved the flamenco, just as Ella had known she would.

It was the interval, the lights went up and, smooth as a

well-oiled machine, Tomás was once more standing beside their table, checking they were OK for drinks, asking if they were enjoying the show.

'It's wonderful,' Holly breathed.

Ella had rarely seen her daughter sparkle as much as she was sparkling tonight. Was it anything to do with Tomás? Ella wasn't sure.

'Can I get you more wine?' Tomás was asking. And he was smiling as if he too had noticed the change in Holly.

Holly got to her feet. 'No. You must let me buy you a drink, Tomás,' she said.

'No, no.' He seemed shocked at this idea. 'Please, no.'

Ella couldn't help smiling; Holly was at serious risk of offending him now. The Spanish were a chivalrous race; they did not relish that opportunity for gallantry being taken away from them, as she remembered only too well.

'But—'

'No.' He held up a hand. 'Please. You are my guest.' And now, he was no longer smiling.

'OK.' Holly sat down again. 'Thank you.'

Tomás appeared to have won. 'And Valentina?' he asked them both.

'She was sublime,' said Ella.

He nodded, as if the compliment was for him alone. '*Muchas gracias*,' he said.

'And the musician . . . ?' Holly's voice trailed.

Ella glanced sharply across at her. She knew her daughter rather well.

'Ah, Rafael,' said Tomás.

'Rafael.' Holly murmured the name as if committing it to memory.

Ella frowned. 'Rafael?' What was his surname? There was such a similar look to him. But it couldn't be. Surely, it couldn't be?

Tomás didn't seem to find her question strange, though Holly shot her one of those quick and curious glances that she'd been sending her way ever since they'd arrived in this city.

'Rafael Delgado,' Tomás supplied.

Ella fanned herself with the same black and red Spanish fan that Felix had bought her in Seville all those years ago. Thank goodness. He wasn't a direct relative at least.

'Shall I introduce you?' Tomás asked.

'Oh.' Holly blushed. 'Oh, yes, that would be nice.'

'Stay there,' said Tomás, and off he scurried.

'Holly?' There might not be any connection. Nevertheless, Ella felt a sense of foreboding. Rafael Delgado had reminded her so much of that face from the past.

Holly shook her head and then her expression changed. The spark came back to her eyes; Ella could feel the fizz of her excitement almost as if it were her own.

Ella looked up. And there he was, the young Spaniard: dark, brooding and intense, a glow of heat suffusing his attractive young face. Ella shivered. She looked back at Holly. Of course, she thought. Of course . . .

Tomás made the introductions.

Rafael took Holly's hand and brought it to his lips. 'Enchanted,' he said softly. 'For a moment, I thought we had met before. But, no. I would remember you. Without doubt, I would remember you.'

Ella could almost feel Holly's world rock on its axis. *Enchanted . . . I would remember you.*

Oh, my goodness, she thought. This was all they needed.

'You play very well,' Holly told him.

'Thank you.' He inclined his head. 'The music – it takes you over. That is how it is with flamenco.' He raised his head and held Holly's gaze. The atmosphere was electric.

Heavens. Ella raised an eyebrow and sat back in her seat, still a bit concerned but content to let them talk. From the look on both their faces, they wouldn't hear her anyway. Once again, here she was in Seville at the flamenco . . . Her thoughts drifted to that music box her mother had given her.

Home and Felix seemed so very far away. And not only Felix, but the school: Viv and her other colleagues, the banter in the staffroom, the meetings, the marking and the children themselves – the freshness and innocence that she loved, alongside the naughty, the cheeky and sadly sometimes the lonely too. At any rate, Ella did her best to make their primary school experience a positive one, and one that hopefully provided a good base for all the learning and growing that was to come.

Ella's thoughts came back to the present moment as Tomás, who seemed unaware of whatever was happening between Holly and Rafael, disappeared to get more wine. Ella hoped his nose wouldn't be put out of joint at this latest development.

She watched her daughter and the young Spaniard. She had probably been worrying unnecessarily, she decided. Triana was a big district. Although the flamenco community . . . That was a lot smaller, she guessed.

She tuned in again to the young people's conversation. Heard the word 'ceramics'. Ella listened more closely.

'I work with ceramics by day,' he was saying.

Oh, my. Ella put a hand to her head. Another link? Another parallel? She could feel her hard-won composure slipping away. Another coincidence . . . ?

Surely then he must know Caleb? How many ceramicists were there in Triana? It must be an even smaller community than that of flamenco.

Ella leant forwards. 'Where do you work?' she asked Rafael. 'Which shop?'

Rafael looked at her in surprise as if he'd been so wrapped up in her daughter that he'd almost forgotten she was there.

'Not a shop,' he said. 'A small factory on Calle Alfareria.'

'Ah.' Ella sat back. A different place. *Alfareria* . . . A potter was an *alfarero*; his workshop an *alfareria*. A different place. But even so . . .

'My father, he wanted me to take over the family bar,' Rafael was saying.

'Your father?' Ella's voice was weak. It was ridiculous, but she couldn't get the notion out of her head. Because, really, he was so like him.

'He passed away many years ago now,' Rafael said.

Ella felt a jolt. There was, as she kept reminding herself, no connection. And Rafael's father had owned a bar, which the other family had not. But supposing . . .

'Oh, I'm so sorry.' Ella saw Holly instinctively put a hand on his arm.

Rafael gave a sad smile. 'I still miss him,' he said.

No. His father wasn't Caleb, of course he couldn't be. Ella was letting her imagination run away with her. And Caleb was still alive – she felt quite sure that he was. She thought of Holly's continual questions. For how long could Ella hold out against her daughter's interrogation? As for Caleb – wouldn't she love to see him again, love to find out how his life had taken shape, whether he was happy? Yes, she would. But there were obvious reasons why this would not be a good idea.

Ella blinked as Tomás returned with their drinks and at the same time, Valentina, still wearing her flamenco dress, arm in arm with another girl, approached their table.

One moment, Valentina was standing next to the other girl, perfectly balanced; the next she seemed to topple over, shoving right into the girl, pushing her arm out as she did so. The other girl had been holding a large glass of red wine and this flew into the air.

'Valentina!' The girl reached out to help her friend just as the glass landed on their table, the red wine sloshing over the wood and splashing onto Holly's dress.

Valentina immediately regained her balance and assumed a look of innocence. Her friend, realising what had happened to her wine, put a hand over her mouth and began apologising profusely in Spanish.

Holly had got to her feet and was dabbing ineffectually at her dress.

Rafael righted the glass, which fortunately hadn't broken, and spoke to Valentina and the girl, rapidly in Spanish. He looked angry.

'It's fine,' said Holly. 'I'll just go to the bathroom and—'

But Ella could see the dull red wine stain spreading and sinking into the fabric. 'Hang on.' She grabbed hold of the carafe of white that Tomás had just brought over and chucked the contents over the stain.

Everyone gasped.

'It's the only thing,' Ella told them. Red wine was so difficult to get out once it had sunk right in. And she was right: the white wine had immediately taken out most of the red stain even though now poor Holly was soaked.

'Mum . . .'

'Come on, I'll give you a hand.' Ella took her daughter's arm.

Rafael and Tomás seemed equally distraught. 'Holly, can I—?' Rafael began.

But they were already heading towards the bathroom and hopefully a hand-drier. 'Please don't worry,' Holly called back to them. 'It was an accident. No harm done.'

Was it an accident? It hadn't exactly looked that way; Ella was sure she'd done it deliberately, the little madam. She turned to glance at Valentina. Sure enough, the young Spanish girl was looking at Holly with pure venom. As Ella watched, she turned, took Rafael's arm – a gesture of possession, Ella noted – and spoke to him, pointing at the stage. She must be telling him they should go back to prepare for the second half of the show. And she was telling him something else as well. Telling Ella too.

Rafael cast a final glance towards Holly and Ella as they crossed the floor. He seemed reluctant to go, but Valentina pulled him away.

So that was how it was, thought Ella. Perhaps she had been right to feel concerned. She had better warn Holly to tread carefully.

CHAPTER 17

Holly

Seville, 2018

Over breakfast the next morning, Holly was jumpy, checking her phone every few minutes, a kind of nervous energy still fizzing through her veins from the night before. What an experience it had been; every bit as exhilarating as she'd hoped. The flamenco, she felt, had crept just a little bit into her soul.

'He had quite an effect on you, didn't he?' her mother observed dryly as she poured more coffee. They were sitting at a table on the little terrace at the back of their hotel, surrounded by pots of flowers. Vines and bougainvillea clambered up the trellised walls; in the corner, water trickled from a small stone fountain beside a lemon tree and the scent of citrus was in the air. More hotel guests occupied a few of the other tables, but Holly and her mother were in the far corner, tucked away.

'Hmm?' Holly helped herself to another pastry. She allowed herself the brief snatch of a memory. Rafael coming up to her when the show had ended, just as she'd hoped he would, his skin warm and his hair damp with perspiration from the energy, the passion he'd put into his playing.

'Holly.' He was still buzzing with adrenalin, she could tell.

'A brilliant performance.' Holly had beamed at him and given a little clap of the hands. Fortunately, she and her mother had managed to dry out her dress quite quickly without having to miss any of the second half of the show. And her mother's dramatic intervention with the white wine – though rather a waste, it had to be said – had saved the dress and the day.

'I told you.' He grinned. 'It is the flamenco, not me.'

'But you are part of it.' Watching him, hearing the waves of sound coming from his guitar as his fingers strummed, plucked and rippled over the strings, feeling the quickening rhythm of the music, the building of emotion . . . Holly had been mesmerised.

The dancing was wonderful – she had to admit that Tomás's sister Valentina was an excellent dancer. The singing was incredible too; it had seemed strange at first but the raw and emotive purity in the sound had soon captivated her. But for Holly, Rafael was the star of the show. He had something special. Allure. With his playing, he had captured the heart of the flamenco. Yes, he was a good-looking man. But more than that, there was something about him that caught at her, that made her want to know more.

'Holly.' He reached out and held her wrist, his thumb light on her pulse. It was an intimate gesture and it almost shocked her. 'Are you free tomorrow?'

She felt a rush of exhilaration. 'Yes,' she said instinctively. Then she remembered. 'Or at least, I'm planning to go and visit an orange farm.'

'An orange farm?' He seemed surprised.

'I'm over here on business,' she explained. 'I want to visit the Ave María farm.' She consulted her phone. 'In Mairena del Alcor.' The Ave María farm specialised in growing the best, most organic fruit in the region and they already supplied a certain upmarket UK store that was close to Holly's heart. She'd been buying Seville oranges there for years – for her marmalade – and it was a complete thrill for her to be able to visit the farm at last.

'You have a car?' he asked.

She shook her head. She'd thought about hiring a car on this trip, but driving and parking in Seville was a nightmare, so she'd decided to rely on public transport instead.

'I can take you,' he said.

'Oh.' Holly hadn't been expecting that.

'Will you give me your number?' He pulled a mobile from his back pocket. 'I will text you tomorrow morning. Yes? OK?'

'But . . .' Suddenly Holly couldn't think of any reason why not. She hadn't been sure how she was going to get to the farm; a taxi would be expensive, though when she'd emailed José Manuel at the Ave María farm, he had told her that if she got a bus to Mairena del Alcor then he could easily pick her up from there. But she wasn't going to refuse Rafael's offer. She wanted to see more of him, she realised. 'OK then,' she said. '*Gracias*.'

'I must go.' And he'd given her another burning glance that seemed to penetrate a lot further than a glance could normally go – at least in Holly's experience. 'Tomorrow then?'

'Tomorrow.'

And only after he was out of sight, lost among the rest of the people still milling about in the club, had Holly remembered to breathe.

Her mother laughed. 'I rest my case. Look at you. You're lost in a dream.'

Holly took a bite of the pastry and dabbed her lips with a napkin. 'Well, he was quite something,' she said.

'Does that mean you're expecting to see him again?' Her mother leant back in her chair. She was watching Holly appraisingly.

'Would you mind?' Holly countered. She was, after all, meant to be on a business trip with her mother, not dating hot flamenco-playing Spanish men.

'Of course I wouldn't mind.' Though, despite her words, her mother was looking slightly concerned. 'But take care, Holly. Remember you hardly know him. And there's someone else who most certainly would mind.'

'Who's that?' Holly sipped her coffee and resisted the urge to check her phone – again. He hadn't said what time he'd message her. And she had to get on. She'd give him till twelve, she decided, then she'd make her own way to the farm.

'Valentina.' Her mother pulled a face. 'I was watching her last night. She wasn't at all happy that you and Rafael were getting on so well.'

'I can't imagine her being happy about anything.' Valentina might be a great dancer, but she could do with some improvement in the personality department. Perhaps her beauty and her dancing skills had made her spoilt, arrogant even.

'A good point,' her mother conceded. She picked up her coffee cup and took a sip. 'But if looks could kill, you wouldn't just have had wine thrown over you, my lovely, you'd have dropped down dead on the spot as well.'

'Really? Do you think she did it on purpose then?' Holly hadn't noticed. But then she wouldn't have. For most of the evening she hadn't really been watching Valentina.

'Yes, really. And yes, I do think she did it on purpose.

At least it looked that way to me.' Her mother put a hand on Holly's arm. 'I know she's just a silly young girl who's had her nose put out of joint. I'm sure Rafael doesn't feel the same way . . .'

She sounded serious. Holly frowned as she pushed her plate away – that was more than enough pastries for now. 'What do you mean, Mum?'

'She thinks she's in love with him,' her mother said. She sat back in her chair. 'Trust me. It was written all over her face.'

'Was it?' Holly thought about this. 'We were only talking. But . . .' She didn't owe any loyalty to Valentina. Rafael was a grown man – couldn't he do what he liked?

'It's the *way* you were talking.' Once again, her mother picked up her coffee cup and took another sip.

Hmm. Fair point. Holly frowned. She didn't want to jeopardise her relationship with Sofía and Tomás. All the same . . .

Her phone pinged in a text.

She picked it up. *I can collect you at eleven. Where are you staying? Rx*

Holly grinned – she couldn't help it. 'I'll be gone in less than two weeks,' she reminded her mother. 'Valentina has nothing to worry about. I'm no threat.'

'If you say so.' Her mother gestured towards Holly's phone. 'Rafael?' she asked.

'How did you guess?'

'Are you serious?' Her mother shook her head in mock despair. 'I can see him in your eyes.'

Holly laughed. 'He's offered to take us to the orange farm.'

'Take you to the orange farm, you mean,' her mother corrected.

'Mum . . .' Holly wasn't going to let her start that again.

Her mother put up a hand to stop her. 'Don't pretend you want company. I plan to go back to the Alcázar Palace and sit under the orange trees in peace. You go to the farm with Rafael.' She frowned. 'That's presuming he can be trusted.'

'Oh, Mum.' Holly didn't know him but she did trust him. And the thought of seeing him again this morning was making her feel very warm inside.

'So, I'll see you back here later this afternoon. OK?' Her mother pushed her coffee cup to one side and got to her feet, unhooking her bag from the back of the chair.

'OK.' Holly sent a quick text in reply.

'And take care,' her mother reminded her. 'Remember, we're the outsiders, Holly. Whatever you think and however friendly everyone may seem, the fact is, we don't belong.'

CHAPTER 18

Felix

Dorset, 2018

'Thanks. We'll let you know.'

That's what the young woman who was manageress of the café had told Felix after his interview. Only, she hadn't let him know, so he'd gone back there. He used to be a manager too, he wanted to tell her. But he didn't. He just explained that he'd heard nothing since.

She peered at her computer screen. 'You must have slipped through the system.' Her gaze moved from the screen and slid past him. That showed, thought Felix, how insubstantial he was becoming, more so each day. At what point might he fade away completely?

'Sorry,' she added as an afterthought.

'And?' Felix sat up straighter, damned if he was going to accept this explanation and become yet another statistic that had failed to make its mark.

'And?' She flicked her pen between her fingers, a sign perhaps that it was time for the discussion to end.

'And what's the situation now?' Felix wouldn't grovel. God knows, he didn't even want to work in a café. But he had to do something. Would Ella believe that this job was in any way a true choice? He could see her now, fixing him with her hazel-eyed gaze, saying, *Really, Felix? Is this what you want?* As if wanting had anything to do with it. What he actually wanted . . . But he looked steadily at this young woman, as if to impress on her his reliability, his honesty, his transparency. At least, let her give him something.

'We don't have any positions to offer,' she said. 'I'm really sorry. But I can keep your name and details on file in case anything comes up.'

That was his cue to thank her and leave. That's what anyone would do.

She was already looking beyond him again, thinking of her next email or morning coffee, he supposed. That's what happened when you had slipped through the system. You were no longer important enough. That's what happened when you'd spent the best years of your life in one place with one company and expected it to go on forever. That's what happened when you were past your sell-by, Felix supposed.

'Fine.' He got to his feet. 'Thanks for your time.'

She nodded. 'Not a problem.'

She was wrong, he thought – it was a problem.

At the door, he turned; he couldn't help it, fool that he seemed to have become. 'I do have a lot of experience with sales,' he said. 'People skills, you know. If you read my CV . . .' *Shut up, Felix. Take no for an answer, why don't you?*

'I'm sure,' she said. 'And if anything comes up . . .' She let her voice trail. Really, she was being very patient. Felix could be patient too. Patience was always required when working with people. People could drive you crazy after all. But not plants, he thought. Never plants.

Felix walked out of her office. It was only a beach café but it was always busy. It wasn't even seasonal; it stayed open in winter too. He sighed, marched out of the main entrance and straight onto the pebbles of Chesil Beach. Perhaps a café wasn't the right place after all. Though to be fair, he'd already got to the stage where he'd consider anything. What would he do? What *could* he do?

His feet crunched over the stones. The sea was as grey and calm as a sheet of pale corrugated iron today, barely rippling – there was no wind. The sky above was grey too. Spring grey, he thought. Seagulls were hovering around the harbour where a fishing boat was coming in; their strident cries pierced the stillness of the air. Ahead, the block of grass-topped ginger cliffs stood serrated and golden against the skyline. Unchanging, bar erosion.

Felix was tempted to continue walking, to trudge on through the pebbles, on to the caravans at Freshwater, over the stream, up the cliffs and across to Hive. But his car was here, so he'd have to walk back again. And he had to stop all this aimless walking that was filling his days and stopping him from doing what should be the real stuff – getting sorted, finding a job.

He was head of their household, wasn't he? It might be an old-fashioned notion, but it still meant something. If he couldn't earn a wage, what did that say about him? Felix didn't want to think. He just knew he couldn't be that man, that man who told Ella when she returned from Seville, *I've been made redundant. I can't find another job. No one wants me.* Why not? Why couldn't he? Because then, she might not want him too?

Instead of a walk along the beach, Felix cut back through to the harbour and bought a local paper from the newsagent's – he knew that jobs were more likely to be found online these days, but old habits were hard to break and looking in a newspaper seemed more of a substantial effort somehow.

He drove home, made himself a cup of tea and drank it while going through *Situations Vacant*. There was even less on offer this week. But he made a couple of phone calls, tried to sound positive. Maybe he wouldn't say that to Ella. Maybe he wouldn't say anything. Maybe he'd become one of those men who pretended to go out to work each day and then stayed out nine to five, walking and wandering, and kept that up until the money ran out and the questions couldn't be avoided any longer. And what then?

The rest of the day stretched out in front of him still, full, not of possibilities but of emptiness. He couldn't even go and see his mother since he hadn't told her about his redundancy either. It was tempting and he might have told her before . . . But since Ella and Holly had gone to Seville, since that bombshell of Holly's – the news that not only was she starting up a new business but that her grandmother was providing the funds to enable her to do it . . . Well, he knew he should tell Ella anything important first. His first responsibility should be to her. His first responsibility should always have been to her. He hadn't done right. He had got things in the wrong order somehow.

Felix decided to do something useful – he'd mend the drawer in Ella's chest of drawers in the bedroom upstairs; she was always complaining that the drawer no longer fitted properly and was almost impossible to shut. Brownie points for him when she returned? Felix smiled. It couldn't hurt.

He took the drawer right out and spent some time diagnosing the problem. The runner wasn't working properly, a bit of wood had broken and he would have to replace it. Felix wasn't a carpenter. He wasn't, in fact, a practical man at all, but over the years he'd practised DIY out of necessity and he could now put his hand to most jobs around his house and his mother's house too – as long as they didn't include plumbing or electrics.

In fact, he had some wood in the garage that might do the job.

Felix worked slowly and methodically, focusing on the task in hand. By the time he'd finished, the drawer was running smoothly in and out and, what's more, it hadn't cost them a penny. *Not entirely useless then . . .*

He was whistling as he replaced Ella's woollens in the big lower drawer. This red sweater he hadn't seen for a while – Ella didn't wear red as much as she used to. Funny, that. Felix folded it carefully. This blue one was her favourite, though. He brought it close to his face and sniffed; he could smell the faint but familiar scent of Ella's rose perfume. Already, he missed her.

When the drawer was full, Felix tested the other drawers. Job half done and all that. The top left one was a bit sticky, so, flushed with his earlier success, he tipped socks and tights onto the bed and took a closer look. It wasn't broken, not like the other one; a bit of filing and it was as good as new.

He was just about to replace the contents of the drawer when he noticed a raising of the drawer lining, just old wallpaper that Ella had used to line the drawers with – his mother had always done the same. He ran his fingertips over the wallpaper to smooth it down; it was a flocked affair, one they'd had in their dining room when they first moved in and he'd had at least half a roll left over.

There was something underneath, he realised. He hesitated for a moment. Felix had never been one to rock the boat. He was the man who would always try to keep it steady. *Nevertheless* . . . He had to see what it was, he realised. Why did anyone ever put anything at the bottom of a drawer under the lining? This wasn't a hard question to answer. Because it was something they needed to hide.

He pulled up one corner of the wallpaper lining and took it out. Under the lining was a photograph. He took this out too, stared at it.

It was a picture of Ella – a young Ella, in her twenties, with a man of about the same age. Felix stared at him. He didn't recognise the man. The two of them were standing under an orange tree. Something slipped into place in Felix's mind. It had been taken, he realised, in Seville.

He got to his feet and went over to the window to examine the photograph more closely. Both Ella and her companion looked uneasy. They were standing close together and he had slung an arm around her shoulders like you do when someone's about to take a photo. Ella – and he knew Ella, Felix reminded himself, at least he knew her as well as anyone could – appeared slightly uncomfortable about this. Nevertheless, the two of them looked . . . Felix stared out of the window into the small back garden where daffodils and tulips were determinedly reminding him that it was spring. They looked together.

Felix didn't like the new thorniness that was running through his body, his mind. He was angry, but he didn't know what he was supposed to be angry about. Or at least he did, but . . . Who was this? What had happened between them? And why had she kept this photograph? To remind her? To remind her of him – this Spanish guy?

Felix brought his attention back to the photograph. She had hidden it at the bottom of a drawer. Hidden out of sight like a wild violet. And when you saw it . . . He felt some part of him sliding out of kilter. First the loss of his job. And now Ella? Did it take just one thing or a succession of things? How many things in total?

He had always been half afraid that she'd leave him, he realised. He'd never been sure of her. Why was that? Had he been a disappointment to her? How come he didn't know? It was, he supposed, an insecurity that was rooted deep within their relationship; it was part of what they had, who they were.

But she hadn't left him. He must hang on to that.

Felix replaced the photograph in the drawer. He put the wallpaper lining back exactly as it had been before and levelled the surface with his fingertips. He put all the socks and tights back in the drawer and he closed it. It closed smoothly now. There was no need, he realised, for her ever to know.

CHAPTER 19

Ella

Seville, 1988

Ella needn't have worried. The next day as Caleb walked her to the cathedral, he was the perfect gentleman and there was no hint of the intensity in his black eyes that she'd glimpsed the night before.

'If only you had come to Seville for the *Semana Santa*,' he told her. 'Every year there are such processions with the floats and the images of the Virgin and of Christ.' He shook his head sadly.

'I've heard of it,' Ella admitted. And she'd wanted to, but Felix hadn't liked to leave his mother alone at Easter and since she'd got her way over Seville, Ella had willingly complied.

'Or the *Feria de Abril*!' Caleb threw his hands up in despair. 'The dancing and the *casetas*, the *Sevillanas*, the flamenco.' He sighed dramatically.

'Yes, I know about that too,' she assured him. 'But I have to get back before the start of term, you know.' And besides, her first trip abroad would be exciting enough already without the chaotic frenzy of Seville's crazy Spring Fair.

They approached the cathedral via the wide, grand and tree-lined Avenida de la Constitución where two uniformed men on horseback were parading up and down the street in front of the vast and ornate buildings. Ella let out a small gasp when they came to the entrance. The tracery around the enormous arched doorway was quite magnificent.

Caleb nodded as if her reaction was only to be expected. 'The work on the new Christian cathedral, it took over a century to complete,' he said.

'A century?' Some project then, thought Ella.

'Yes.' He led the way into the equally immense entrance hall with its sculpted pillars and paintings decorating the walls. It had vibrant stained-glass windows and a black and white marble floor that made Ella feel a little dizzy.

'The new Christian cathedral?' She picked up on what he'd said. 'Do you mean there was something else here before?'

'Certainly. This' – his gesture encompassed the entire building – 'was the site of a great mosque created by a Moroccan tribe, the Almohads. They made Seville their capital,' he added proudly.

'And contributed hugely to the Moorish flavour of the area,' Ella guessed.

Caleb gave her a sharp glance as if he thought she was trying to take over his job and she smiled inwardly. He was surprisingly sensitive.

'You are right, Ella,' he conceded. 'La Giralda – the bell tower – and the Patio de los Naranjos are indeed legacies of this period of power. The Moors from Northern Africa built their beautiful palaces on top of the Roman remains after they conquered the city in 712. The Moorish-style buildings, the decorative ceramic tiles, the fountains in the courtyards, these are all part of that legacy.'

Further into the cathedral, Ella was especially struck by the golden *Capilla Mayor*, the Great Chapel. It was dominated by a vast Gothic altarpiece, made up of forty-five carved scenes from the life of Christ, according to Caleb, who seemed to have all the facts at his fingertips. And it was protected by a monumental iron grille.

'Who made it?' she asked him. A whole army of craftsmen, she suspected.

But, 'It was the lifetime's work of a single craftsman, Pierre Dancart,' Caleb told her. 'It is a Gothic masterpiece. And the amount of gold that was used in this chapel . . .' He shook his head. Clearly, he was as overwhelmed as Ella. 'It is staggering,' he said.

It certainly was.

They moved on to Columbus's tomb, the coffin carried in triumph by four allegorical figures representing the four kingdoms of Spain during Columbus's life. This was also impressive. Nevertheless, Ella felt a distinct sense of relief when Caleb led the way outside to the patio of the orange trees. There was only so much magnificence she could absorb in one go. The now familiar scent of orange blossom swept into her senses and she paused to breathe it in.

'This is an interesting fountain.' Caleb pointed to the circular stone structure in the centre of the patio. 'We spoke of Moorish fountains, Ella. In those days, you see, worshippers at the mosque, they must wash their hands and feet under the orange trees before praying.'

Ella moved closer. Water was so peaceful, the sound of it

and also the clarity. 'But that's not required today, I hope?' she teased him, for sometimes he was so solemn.

He smiled. 'Not required today, no.'

'That's good.' Despite this, his words had given Ella a mental picture of the scene and, once again, she felt transported back in time. That was the power of an old building or artefact, she reflected. It was as if everyone who had touched it somehow lived on in the ancient stone. Thoughtfully, she ran her fingertip around the grey rim of the fountain, found herself wondering how she could convey this concept to her class in a history lesson.

'We must take a picture,' Caleb announced. He pulled a camera out of his bag and spoke to a man who was standing nearby. 'A memento,' he said.

He came to stand beside her by the fountain amongst the grove of orange trees. He put an arm around her shoulder and although she felt a little awkward at the sudden physical proximity, Ella smiled obediently into the camera being held by the stranger, trying to ignore the strange effect Caleb's touch was having on her. It must be the scent of the orange blossom, she decided, that was making her feel so giddy.

Caleb thanked the man and took back his camera. 'And now,' he said, 'we will climb the Giralda tower.'

Ella looked up. It was awfully high.

'It is not as difficult as you think,' Caleb assured her. 'And if you look at the tower, you can see it is a history book. You simply need to know how to read it.'

'Show me.'

'It is written in the stones,' he explained. 'You start at the bottom and work your way up.' He pointed. 'The large sandy-coloured blocks of the foundations were originally from Roman temples in the area.'

She nodded. 'And the narrow bricks that come next?'

'That is the Moorish time I told you of.'

'And the decorative stuff above that?'

He smiled at her description. 'The Christians,' he said. 'And it was they who added the spinner.'

'The spinner? The statue at the very top you mean?' Ella peered up to the pinnacle of the bell tower. 'She's looking out over the entire city, isn't she?' It was a powerful emblem.

'Yes, she is.' Caleb put his head to one side as he too stared upwards. 'You can see glimpses of her from almost anywhere in Seville. But she is not a statue. She is a weathervane. She spins.'

'The spinner,' Ella repeated.

'She represents faith,' Caleb said softly.

There was no answer to that.

To Ella's relief, it wasn't too claustrophobic climbing the thirty-five floors and Caleb was right: it wasn't difficult either, because there were no stairs inside until they were almost at the top. They walked around the outside perimeter and Caleb pointed out all the landmarks – the river, the bullring, the Real Alcázar. The frosted spires of the cathedral encircled them, and as Ella looked down, she saw that in the orange-tree patio below, a man had put up a ladder and was collecting the oranges that fell from the tree in a huge net laid out on the ground. Ella could see even better from this vantage point how many of the trees were already laden with fruit.

They were standing close beside one another peering over the edge when a sudden and very loud clang made her jump a foot in the air and clutch at his sleeve.

Caleb laughed. 'It is the bell.'

He wasn't joking. The sonorous sound continued reverberating around the tower. Ella let go of him and, with a smile, she stepped away.

Later, after an afternoon exploring the labyrinth of streets in Santa Cruz, Caleb took Ella back to the hotel. She could hardly believe it was past six o'clock already – the day had flown by.

'So, what do you think?' he asked her.

'Of Seville?'

He smiled. 'I hope I know what you think of Seville. Who would not be impressed by this city?'

True enough, thought Ella.

'No,' he said. 'I mean, how did I do? What do you think of your tour guide, of me?'

Of me. That was a question she didn't want to dwell on. But the tour guide bit was easy enough and Ella realised that despite his apparent confidence, even his slight swagger, as he showed her around and displayed his considerable knowledge, at heart, Caleb was vulnerable and unsure.

'You're very knowledgeable, thoughtful and polite,' she told him. It was important for a guide to notice when someone was tired or needed a pick-me-up coffee or a sit-down. 'And you have a lot to say about the history of the city.'

'Too much to say, you think?' He looked worried now.

'No, not too much. Not for me anyway.' Ella wanted to know everything.

'So, you were not bored?'

'No, I definitely wasn't bored.' Caleb had the gift of making every little detail sound interesting. Whether he could maintain this with a new group of tourists every day was another matter, but it was a good start.

'Excellent,' he said. 'Then you will come on another tour with me tomorrow?'

'Well . . .' Ella had decided not to. She was independent enough to want to do some exploring on her own and no matter how well behaved Caleb had turned out to be, wouldn't it be safer to put any temptation aside? But today had gone so well and she'd really enjoyed his company. So . . .

'Please,' he said. 'I want to show you the *azulejo* tiles at Casa de Pilatos – remember I told you about them?'

She remembered. 'If you're sure?'

'*Si*,' he said. 'I am very sure.'

'All right then, I'd love to.' Perhaps it was wrong of her. But she'd had such a lovely day. And already, she was looking forward to tomorrow.

CHAPTER 20

Holly

Seville, 2018

It felt strangely intimate, sitting in the passenger seat next to Rafael as he drove to the Ave María orange farm in Mairena del Alcor, only twenty kilometres outside the city. Holly glanced across at him. He looked very casual, very confident and very different today, dressed in jeans, a faded red T-shirt and trainers. He seemed like a stranger – which of course he was – and yet on another level, Holly felt almost as if she knew him. For a first date, though – if that's what it was – it felt more than a little unusual.

'It's kind of you,' she said, 'to take me to the farm.'

He smiled, gestured to the blue sky outside. 'It is a lovely day,' he said. 'Too nice to sit inside, making pots, do you not think?' His dark eyes twinkled.

'Perhaps.' Holly smiled back at him.

'And besides . . .' – he gave a little shrug of the shoulders – 'it was a chance to see you again.'

On hearing these words, Holly felt a glow of pleasure.

She certainly hadn't expected this when she'd made her plans to visit Seville.

As they left the outskirts of the city, and the landscape became one of rolling hills, valleys, orchards and vineyards, Rafael asked her about her business venture and Holly told him about her plans for Bitter Orange.

He banged his palm on the steering wheel. Holly jumped.

'What a brilliant idea,' he said. 'Soaps, oils, potions, wine . . . And everything, it is orange.' He laughed.

'That's the plan.' Holly appreciated his enthusiasm. She just hoped that the people of Bridport and all the tourists who came to the town to visit the lively market, the popular vintage area, the literary festival, the film week and all the other events happening there, felt the same way.

'So, you will sell the oranges?' he asked.

'And make marmalade.'

'Marmalade?'

Holly explained that this was what had first sparked her interest. She decided not to mention her mother's Seville orange and almond cake – that would make things far too complicated. 'It's a great British tradition,' she said. 'After the war, Winston Churchill apparently recommended it be eaten every morning for breakfast – sunshine in a jar, guaranteed to lift the spirits.'

Rafael laughed. 'You British,' he said. 'You are hilarious. And the marmalade, it has led you into a business, yes?'

'Exactly.' Holly sat back in her seat and watched the countryside as they passed through. Already, the landscape was more rural and very unlike the city they had left behind.

'And what about candles?' Rafael asked.

She glanced across at him. She liked the way he drove: fast but not too fast; calm and not fazed by some of the crazy

Spanish drivers on the road. 'Funny you should say that, because I have been looking for a supplier for neroli candles,' she said. She and Rafael must be on the same wavelength.

She'd found a couple of candlemakers online. And a perfumier too, as well as a fabulous producer of sweet orange neroli body scrub and bath bombs that she had yet to investigate. But the candlemaker hadn't seemed quite right and she hadn't yet fixed up a meeting.

'I know someone.' He glanced across at her, a glance that lingered and made her feel very warm inside. 'I could introduce you. If you want.'

'OK.' She shrugged. 'Thanks.' Did he have an ulterior motive? She sneaked another look at him, noted the way the sun slanted onto his face, highlighting the sharp cheekbones and sensual mouth. *Oh, God.* Yes, he probably did. And did she mind? Not one bit.

Holly thought of her mother's warning. Perhaps she was right to be wary. And she was certainly right in saying that Holly and her mother were both outsiders here in Seville. But this trip was also about making contacts. Seville seemed to be the heart of all things orange – Holly thought of all those orange trees lining the streets of the city – so this was most definitely the right place to be. And anything else . . . She smiled to herself. Was a bonus.

They arrived at the Ave María orange farm, drove through the rather grand stone and iron gateway, and parked outside the main factory building where they met José Manuel, who was welcoming, friendly and spoke excellent English.

'First, would you like a tour?' He gestured to the surrounding orchards.

'Yes, please.' Now that she was actually here, Holly wanted

to find out as much as possible. She breathed in deeply. The fresh country air was heavy with the aroma of oranges.

And José Manuel proved to be the man for the job. He told them first about the geography of the area and why this landscape with its gentle hills was such a perfect location for orchards. 'Mairena del Alcor, it is from the old Arab word *mairena* for *maharana*,' he began. 'That is, the water of the fountain, the source; this generous flow of natural source water which circulates underground.' He looked round admiringly at the landscape. '*Alcor* means rolling hills. We call this area *Los Alcores*, meaning rounded hills. You see?'

Holly saw. The abundant water helped make the landscape perfect for this sort of planting and it seemed it had always been used so, since Roman times at least.

'The water, it brings the nourishment – the fluid, the minerals,' José Manuel explained as he led the way into the orchard. 'Oranges are not only rich in vitamin C, they are even richer in potassium, and they provide calcium too. This all comes from the natural sources.'

It was all about the land, thought Holly. She loved the way he spoke about their trees; he seemed to have a real nurturing spirit. She had, she felt, come to the right place.

'Our oranges mature and ripen naturally according to the seasons of the year,' José Manuel went on. 'Trees need cold as well as warmth.' Tenderly, he stroked the bark of one of his orange trees.

Holly smiled at Rafael. You couldn't mistake the love.

'And when are they harvested?' Holly asked. She too reached out to touch the trunk of a nearby tree.

'December and January is the main crop,' he said. 'After this, the trees, they will have the sweet-scented white blossom.'

'Neroli,' murmured Holly.

'Exactly.' José Manuel put his fingers to his lips and blew a kiss. 'The scent, it is perfection. The blossom, it is harvested by hand in late March and early April for the essence, the perfume.'

'It is wonderful,' Holly agreed.

The farm comprised ten hectares, José Manuel told them, and surrounded the family home. He pointed to where the house stood, in a prominent position looking down over the glorious hills and valleys. 'It was built where a Roman villa once stood two thousand years ago,' he said.

'Wow.' And standing here, looking out at the magnificent view over the hills and orchards, Holly could feel that sense of history.

'In the beginning for the family,' said José Manuel, 'it was a hobby. And it grew.'

It certainly had.

Rafael was watching her. 'A bit like your marmalade,' he said.

Holly smiled. 'Exactly like my marmalade.'

The Ave María farm, though, was a huge success story. José Manuel's family was the fourth generation to farm the oranges commercially and José Manuel certainly knew his stuff. He explained the history of citrus and hybridisation from the original four citrus plants and as he spoke, the three of them continued to wander around the orchard, José Manuel pointing out the different varieties, such as the Buddha's hand being cultivated in what he called the 'experimental area'.

Everything must always move forward, Holly found herself thinking. She bent to sniff – the fruit was yellow and smelt as sweet and heady as a ripe peach.

At the Ave María farm they grew other oranges too but *los naranjos*, the bitters, were clearly their speciality. 'They are long-lived,' José Manuel told them, 'and can grow up to ten metres in height, the highest of all citrus fruits.' He indicated one particularly tall tree as they passed by.

Holly could see for herself that the flowers were abundant, large and aromatic. And she also knew from her own experience that the colour of the fruit was intense. The oranges seemed to have an almost magical quality, especially when they lit up her fruit bowl in the gloom of wintertime.

What impressed Holly the most about this family-run farm was the emphasis on the organic, their respect for and reliance on nature and especially the bees, and their determination not to use pollutants or chemicals.

This meant, José Manuel told them, that they must lose some trees to disease. 'This is life,' he said. 'And death. But it is the natural way. And it is our way.' Furthermore, they were inspected every month, he told them, to ensure that standards were being maintained.

As they walked around the orchard, José Manuel occasionally pulled out a weed here and there. 'Some weeds, they are OK for the air and the oxygen,' he informed them. 'Too many and they take water from the tree.'

Holly could see that looking after the farm was an ongoing and everyday activity for all concerned.

'These trees are living things,' José Manuel reminded them, as he patted another tree trunk affectionately. 'They communicate with one another through their roots. They are not alone. They have each other.'

And although it seemed a bit mad, there was undeniably a calm and tranquil atmosphere in the orchard, a sense of everything being in harmony and at peace.

'Sometimes,' José Manuel confided. 'I walk around here with my transistor radio. The trees, they like the music, you see.'

Somehow, Holly wasn't even surprised.

'Any particular kind of music?' asked Rafael.

Holly shot him a sharp look but he seemed completely serious.

'Classical,' said José Manuel. 'Always classical.'

Inside the factory, José Manuel showed Holly and Rafael how the oranges were weighed and cleaned (though not with water as this would destroy their organic status, he said) and how they were then sorted into different calibres or categories, depending on the buyers and the price.

He introduced them to Mari, a sixty-something selector who had worked at the farm since she was sixteen and who was so quick and dexterous that Holly's eyes could hardly keep up. Finally, the oranges were packed, ready for shipping.

Traditional orchards were, however, disappearing each year. One reason, José Manuel told them, was the unregulated picking and selling of the street oranges, clearly inferior and frequently polluted by traffic.

Holly recalled what Sofía had told her about the need to check the source and quality of the oranges she used for her natural products.

These inferior oranges, as José Manuel referred to them, were often sold to factories in the north of Spain for pulping, for extremely low prices, before the pulp was exported to marmalade manufacturers, and mostly to the UK. Holly shivered. Not only did this practice undermine the business of Ave María and affect the price they could charge for their oranges, but the end consumers would have no real idea of where their marmalade had come from.

When the tour was finally over, they sat down at a table outside the factory to drink fresh orange juice and talk business and, at this point, Rafael tactfully drifted away to chat to one of the workers who was taking a break nearby.

Holly appreciated the gesture. Not that she minded him being by her side – in fact, she was enjoying it – but this was her business and she wanted José Manuel to know that she was independent, that this was strictly between the two of them.

Four hundred and fifty kilos comprised half a pallet and this represented a part-load, José Manuel told her. She would have to order this amount, Holly realised. Anything less would be too expensive. So . . . she would be making an awful lot of marmalade. But she could sell the Seville oranges on to other makers – and there were plenty of those in the surrounding areas of Dorset, Devon and Somerset – and according to José Manuel, the Sevilles could be kept in a fridge for three months without losing any flavour and could also be frozen.

Four hundred and fifty kilos sounded a lot, but Holly knew she had to think big.

José Manuel had spoken about the soil here at Ave María, which was red, sandy, grainy and apparently contained plenty of iron and phosphorous – vital, because under that fifty centimetres of topsoil, he told her, there was solid rock, the *albero*, formed in the Guadalquivir River basin five million years ago, and used to make country roads.

The phosphorous apparently gave a special sweetness to the oranges. 'It is what makes Ave María Sevilles so special,' José Manuel said. 'It makes them stand apart from all other oranges. In finesse, flavour and aroma.'

It wasn't just sales patter; Holly believed him. Seeing the orange trees, walking among the glossy green-leafed orchards, breathing in the natural citrus scent of the fruit, had entirely convinced her.

José Manuel had also talked a lot about the water and the organic nature of the growing. But now, sitting at the table in the warm Spanish sunshine, he spoke freely about the passion – about his family, their principles and their truth. 'We have respect for our trees and our fruit,' he said. 'We do it this way because this is the right way – this is what we believe.'

And that, Holly thought, was the reason why the farm was a success.

When they finally left, José Manuel presented them both with a bag of beautiful radiant oranges – not the bitter Seville variety, but sweet oranges they could eat.

They stopped for lunch at a small bar in the village and this time, Holly took the opportunity of asking Rafael more about his life, his work, his family. She didn't want to talk any more about her business – at least not today. What she most needed now was a period of reflection; to sit down and work out some figures, to consider how far she'd got and what exactly she should do next.

As for Rafael . . . He told her how he had got into making ceramics and playing flamenco, he spoke of his mother and his sadness at losing his father, and he talked about Triana and his life there.

'And is there . . .' – she wasn't sure how to say this – 'someone special? Do you have a girlfriend, I mean?'

He gave her a long look. 'There is no one,' he said at last.

By the time they got back to her hotel, Holly felt she knew him rather better. He was no longer a stranger. But what was he? She was undeniably attracted to him, and from the way he kept looking at her, he seemed to feel the same. But he lived in Seville and she lived in the UK. And it was probably a mistake to mix business with pleasure. Was there really any point in taking things further? It would be so easy. But couldn't she just enjoy his company, flirt a little and keep her heart intact? Because she sensed that a relationship with someone like Rafael could never be a light-hearted romance or a one-night stand, and besides, Holly didn't do one-night stands.

'Thanks so much for taking me to the farm, Rafael,' she told him. 'I'm very grateful.' She got out of the car; he got out too and came round to her side. They kissed, cheek to cheek.

Just for a moment, Holly closed her eyes. He smelt of oranges – maybe she did too? – and the sense of a promise.

'Holly . . .' He put his hands lightly on her shoulders. She still felt the pressure though.

She looked up at him. 'Yes?'

'I like you,' he said.

'I like you too.' She smiled.

'Yes.' He tilted her chin and maintained eye contact. 'But I really like you.'

'Uh-huh.' Holly had a feeling this was going to get more complicated whether she wanted it to or not.

'I like you, as in I want to see you again. I want to get to know you better. I want . . .' He let this hang.

Did he even know how seductive he was being? Holly remained silent. It seemed the safest option.

'But what do *you* want?' he asked her. 'This, I do not know.' He let go of her and took a step away.

It was a big question. The ball was in her court. 'I don't want anything to get in the way of what I need to do here,' she replied honestly. That was what she didn't want. What she wanted . . . she wasn't quite ready to admit to that yet.

'And you think I would be a distraction?' His voice was soft but intent.

'Wouldn't you be?' She searched his expression. This was

definitely not how she'd been planning on spending her time in Seville.

'Maybe.' He gave a little shrug. 'But I can help you too.'

'Oh, yes?'

'Yes.' He spread his hands and stepped closer once again. 'I can teach you about the city of oranges.' He bent so that he was whispering into her hair. 'I can introduce you to the candlemaker. You know you will have to see me again if you want that introduction.'

'Isn't that blackmail?' she teased. His face was so very close to hers. If she wanted to, she could trace the outline of his full lips with her fingertip; if she wanted to, she could close her eyes, lean forwards just a little and . . .

'No, just gentle persuasion,' he murmured.

Holly took a step back. If she went any further forwards, she would, she felt, have little choice about what happened next.

'And you're very good at gentle persuasion,' she said.

He shot her a reproachful look. 'I am only trying to help.'

Hmm. 'Well, thank you.' Holly felt on slightly safer ground now that there was a pace between them. 'And in that case, I would like to meet your candlemaker. Tomorrow maybe?' Why not? she thought. And if anything were to happen between them . . . She was free and single. He too was apparently free and single. So . . .

'Of course.' He tucked a stray strand of hair away from her face, kissed two fingers and put them to her lips.

His touch was warm and she couldn't help wanting more. She waited. If he were to move any closer now . . .

But he held her gaze and took that step away. 'I will text you,' he said.

'I'll be waiting,' she replied. And whatever she told herself to the contrary, she knew very well that this would be true.

CHAPTER 21

Ella

Seville, 1988

There was something rather different about Caleb the following day as they wandered around the charming patios and gardens of Casa de Pilatos, which was, in Caleb's opinion, he told her, the finest palace in Seville with its gothic balustrades, delicate plasterwork and, of course, the fine *azulejo* tiles. It was as if yesterday, he had been on his best behaviour and today, he could relax. Ella wasn't complaining. She liked the tour guide but she preferred this more chilled-out version of the intriguing man from Triana.

After the sightseeing, when they were once again almost back at Ella's hotel, Caleb suggested a drink in a local bar.

'Why not?' It seemed natural enough to Ella. After several more hours in his company, she still wasn't in the least bored. In fact, she continued to be curious about him. He was a bit of a mixture – confident and yet unsure; quiet and yet flamboyant; charming and also serious at times.

'Tell me about yourself,' she said as they sat down opposite one another at an outside table, two glasses of pale-gold *fino* in front of them because, 'you must try it,' he had insisted. 'Who is the real Caleb? Tour guide or flamenco guitarist? Ceramicist or historian?'

He was silent for a few moments. It must have been a difficult question, she thought.

'I have not spoken to you yet of Triana,' he said at last. 'It is more than just the other side of the river. It is my background and it is a place with a special complexity, a unique spirit. The old gypsy *barrio*, the home of bullfighters, flamenco dancers and explorers. If you have the time, I would like to show you round it one day.'

Ella had to admit that she would like that too. 'Have your family always lived there?' she asked.

'Yes, as far back as I know.' His eyes grew dreamy.

She wondered what childhood adventures he was thinking of, which night he had discovered how deeply the flamenco was embedded in his soul.

'I spoke to you of the Royal Tobacco Factory,' he said.

'Yes?' Ella remembered very well. She sipped her *fino*. It was rich and sweet. She could easily develop a taste for it, she decided.

'My great-grandmother worked there,' he said. 'She was a *cigarrera*, one of the women who rolled the cigarettes back in the day.'

'Like Carmen,' breathed Ella.

He laughed. 'In some ways, yes,' he said. 'My great-grandmother also lived in Triana – although she did not fall in love with a bullfighter and no one killed her out of jealousy.'

'I'm relieved to hear it.' Ella laughed with him. 'I'd like to go there too,' she said. Though she had read that the building now housed a university, she'd still like to see it. There were so many places to visit – and such little time.

He inclined his head. 'And you,' he said. 'I also wonder, who is the real Ella?'

Ella didn't want to speak about her mother or her upbringing – it was still too painful. She thought of Felix and the life they led at his mother's house. 'I wish I knew,' she said. 'I'm a teacher.' That part was easy. 'And I love my job.' She thought of the children at the school and what would be waiting for her when she returned to Dorset after this holiday; this strange, almost surreal time away that was so different from the holiday with Felix she had envisaged and planned.

'I can see that in your eyes, Ella,' Caleb said. 'I recognise the passion. And it is always good to have that – the passion.'

She couldn't quite meet his gaze this time. This man was having a powerful effect on her. Maybe it was the *fino*, but she was sharply aware of his hands resting on the table between them, the shape of his mouth, the way he smiled.

When they arrived back at her hotel, Caleb seemed to hesitate. Without any warning, he drew her into the shadows of the orange trees that lined the street. 'You can smell the scent, Ella, *sí*?' he asked her.

'Yes, of course.' It was everywhere in this city. The fragrance of orange blossom hung in the air, seductive and intoxicating, an integral part of the charm of Seville.

Caleb reached out a hand to the trunk of the nearest orange tree. 'They came originally from China and India,' he said dreamily. 'The Indian name for orange is *narayam*.' He seemed to roll the word around on his tongue. 'It means perfume within.'

'That's lovely.' *Perfume within . . .*

'It is said in Roman mythology that Juno received orange blossoms when she married Jupiter,' he continued.

Ella could understand why. Not only was the orange blossom pretty, but the scent was literally divine.

'The pure white of the blossoms signifies pure love,' Caleb continued. 'While the evergreen nature of the tree stands for the everlasting nature of that love.'

Oh. Too late, Ella realised where this was going. Though perhaps she had known and let it happen anyway.

'Ella . . .'

'What is it?' But she didn't even have to look at him to know.

'Sometimes, Ella,' he said, 'you have to follow your heart.'

There was a moment as they stood there, close together, but not touching, not quite, when Ella could have pulled away. There was a moment when she could have laughed it off, when she could have turned and headed instead for the safety of the hotel foyer. But she hesitated. And in another moment, all she was conscious of was the warmth of his skin, the touch of his hand and the scent of orange blossom, overpoweringly sweet above them.

Then his hands were on her shoulders, his lips were on hers, still sweet from the *fino* they had just drunk together. She closed her eyes and he pulled her closer. She felt that she was falling, drowning in a thick mist of desire, and nothing else seemed possible, apart from the fact that she wanted to kiss this man.

His mouth on hers grew more urgent and Ella let out a small moan. But a shout from somewhere on the other side of the street made her instantly come to her senses. She pushed him away. 'No, Caleb.'

His eyes glinted. 'Ella.'

Just the way he said her name . . . 'No.' She kept her voice steady. 'Sorry, but, no.'

'No?' His voice betrayed his doubt.

'I'm sorry if I gave you the wrong impression.' She sounded so stilted and polite. She hated that.

He waited.

'But that's not what I want.' Though this emerged weaker than she would have wished and she wasn't sure that either of them believed her words.

'It did not feel that way, Ella, to me,' he murmured.

'But it's true.'

'Sometimes,' he said, 'we do not know what we want. Until it is there. It is here. In front of us. Between us.' He seemed to be willing her to understand.

He needn't worry. She did understand. That was the problem.

'I'm married.' Ella stood up straighter. She forced herself to remember her marriage vows. *Till death us do part*. 'I don't want to betray my husband. I love my husband.' She stared at him, daring him to question it.

But he only nodded. 'I see,' he said. 'Then I am sorry too. I thought that you and I . . .'

She turned away. She couldn't think about the 'you and I'. 'No,' she said again.

He grimaced and she wanted to take back her words, wanted to hold him, comfort him, tell him that yes, she understood, that yes, she felt it too, this magnetic attraction, this bond.

'Do not worry, Ella,' he said. 'I will not be a nuisance for you. You have made it perfectly clear.'

Inside, she felt a wave of desolation. It wasn't perfectly clear at all. It was a mess – a blurred, confusing mess.

'I'd better go inside.' She began to move away.

'And tomorrow?'

She turned back to him. He stood under the orange tree just watching her and waiting. How easy it would be . . . 'I'll explore on my own tomorrow,' she said firmly. 'I've taken up enough of your time. It's for the best.'

'It was bad then,' he said glumly. 'I will never be a good tour guide.'

She grasped his hands, although she knew he was only half joking. 'You will be a wonderful tour guide,' she said. 'But you can't make a pass at the tourists.'

He smiled. 'Only you, Ella.'

'Goodbye, Caleb.' She knew she wouldn't see him again. Caleb had far too much pride to run after anyone, he wouldn't take rejection lightly.

'Goodbye, Ella,' he said. He turned and with a final and brief wave of his hand, he was gone, leaving only the bitter-sweet fragrance of the orange blossom behind.

CHAPTER 22

Ella

Seville, 2018

Ella had returned to the hotel, having spent her day reacquainting herself with Seville. She had revisited a few old haunts, including the Alcázar Palace and the Parque de María Luisa. After all the recent emotional upheaval, this was exactly what she needed, she felt – to simply relax and enjoy. Of course, it was conceivable that she might run into Caleb in one of the tourist hotspots (he had said he'd intended to become a tour guide after all) but this was a big city and even if she did, what did it matter now? Even if they were to recognise one another after so many years . . .

And somehow, she felt that she would recognise him. The image of him had never quite left her. Even now, he occasionally surprised her by haunting one of her dreams; dreams whose vague wistfulness tended to make her cross and out of sorts all day long.

But there had been no sign of anyone who looked remotely

like Caleb – even the older version that he would be now. Apart from those rare night-time visits, Ella reminded herself, Caleb belonged to the past. What had happened between them also belonged to the past. Perhaps, she thought, it was just the memories she was scared of after all.

In the palace, she'd enjoyed seeing again the incredible array of traditional *azulejo* tiles. She paused as she reached the famous Peacock Arch in the Hall of Ambassadors – the tiles on the arch as flamboyant as the bird itself – and remembered how she had felt on her previous visit here with Felix. Frustrated mainly, that he wasn't seeing it as she was seeing it. Sad about the growing distance between them. Disappointed that their precious holiday together was already slipping away from them.

Thinking of Felix had made her want to speak to him, so she'd phoned him from one of the quiet little patios but he hadn't sounded quite himself. Perhaps he was missing them. Ella smiled. That was no bad thing. She thought of the way he'd urged her to come here – almost as if he knew she had to relive the memories before she could totally banish them. Perhaps he was wondering if he should have come too and this time stayed in Seville a while longer.

In her hotel room, Ella stared out of her bedroom window which looked out onto the front street. Since she'd been here, she'd begun to tentatively let those memories back in . . . And they hadn't hurt quite as much as she'd expected, so perhaps Felix was right. She felt a little sad, a little reflective. But she'd made her choice, and there was no room for regrets.

She was just gazing out at the French consulate building opposite, which had old millstones built into the vintage-pink painted wall – perhaps a relic of a time when any old blocks or stones were used as building materials, she thought – when a rather beaten-up-looking car drove towards the front entrance of the hotel and parked by the plaza.

Holly and Rafael, she realised. Ella wondered how the day at the Ave María farm had gone, what had happened between them. She hoped she had no reason to worry.

She continued to watch as they spoke briefly and then both got out of the car. Rafael came round to Holly's side; they were standing very close to one another, and even from her vantage point, Ella could sense the tension between them. He put his hands on Holly's shoulders and they exchanged a light kiss which from this distance felt like much more. Ella just knew she was right about these two. She shivered. What a strange parallel it was. Another Spaniard making pots and playing flamenco. As if some deity on high was having a huge joke with them all. *If you don't succeed first time around, try, try again.*

She saw them move even closer. They were talking very intently, oblivious to what was going on around them. Holly's body language was a giveaway. She looked as though she couldn't decide whether to move closer or run away. Ella sighed. That brought back the memories again.

Suddenly, Ella felt like a voyeur, an intruder. She stepped away from the window and, as she did so, another movement from the street corner caught her eye. A young woman . . . And she seemed familiar. Ella stiffened. Surely that was Valentina walking away now in the opposite direction from the plaza? She recognised the long dark hair, the stiff back, the angry stomp of her footsteps on the cobbles.

But perhaps she was mistaken. Why would Valentina be there?

A few minutes later, there was a light tap on the door. Holly was smiling as she came in.

'Hello, darling. Good day?' Though she hardly need ask – it was written all over her daughter's face.

'Wonderful. And look.' Holly dangled a bag in front of her. 'I have oranges.'

'Great.' Ella laughed. 'How did it go at the farm?'

They went down to the bar for a drink and Holly told her about the visit. 'So, it's full steam ahead with the Ave María oranges,' she said. 'It's a fabulous place. And it's all coming together, Mum. It really is.'

'Well done, darling. I'm so pleased for you.' Ella beamed. 'And . . .' She hesitated. 'What about Rafael?'

Holly toyed with the stem of her wine glass. 'I'm seeing him again tomorrow. He's going to introduce me to a candlemaker who uses neroli.' She wouldn't meet Ella's eye.

'Ah.' Holly needn't say more. Ella wondered if she should disappear again tomorrow, or if that would count as aiding and abetting. She wasn't even sure whether she should be colluding in this blossoming romance or trying to prevent it from happening. It was inevitable, she supposed. But where could it possibly lead?

'And what about you, Mum?' Holly asked.

'Me?'

'Yes. What have you been doing this afternoon? Dreaming of the past?'

Ella blinked at her. That was far too accurate for her liking. 'The past?' she said lightly.

'Your mysterious trip to Seville all those years ago.' Holly leant forwards. She was teasing, but there was a serious question in her eyes.

Ella laughed. 'Hardly mysterious, darling.'

'You mean apart from the fact that you've hardly told me a word about it?'

Fair point, thought Ella.

Fortunately, at that moment, Holly's mobile rang. Holly plucked it from her bag, looked at the screen and raised an eyebrow as she read the name of the caller.

'It's Tomás.' She picked up. '*Hola*, Tomás. How are you?'

He said something and Holly frowned. 'What, now?' She listened to his reply, glanced at Ella and muted the sound. 'Tomás wants to come round. Now. He says it's important.'

Ella shrugged. 'Why not? He can join us for a drink.'

'OK,' Holly said into the phone. 'See you soon.'

'What do you think he wants?' Ella thought of the girl she'd seen in the street. Had it been Valentina? And if so, could she have been watching Holly and Rafael, even spying on them? Ella wondered whether to mention it to Holly. Probably best not to, she decided. After all, why on earth would Valentina be hanging round their hotel? It was unlikely, laughable even.

'I don't know. But I hope Sofía hasn't changed her mind about our deal.' Holly chewed her lip. 'I thought it was all going a bit too well.'

'Why should she change her mind?' Ella squeezed her daughter's shoulder. 'It's an excellent opportunity for her. No, it's probably something quite different. A chat about the packaging perhaps?' She hoped she was wrong. But Ella was beginning to get a bad feeling about this.

Ten minutes later, Tomás strode into the bar. He seemed uneasy, lacking his normal confidence.

'What's the matter, Tomás?' Holly asked him as he approached their table. 'Is there a problem? Is it your mother?'

'No, no.' He stood beside them, looking decidedly uncomfortable.

'Sit down then,' said Holly.

He gestured towards the bar. 'Can I get you a drink?'

'We're fine, thanks,' Holly told him.

'One moment then.' He ordered a beer and then joined them at their table.

Ella and Holly waited. 'So . . . ?'

'It is difficult,' he said. 'It is delicate.'

'Go on,' said Holly. 'What is?'

'Someone told me,' Tomás began, 'that you spent a long time with Rafael Delgado today.'

'Someone?' Holly frowned.

'Someone,' confirmed Tomás. Clearly, he wasn't going to elaborate.

Ella shifted uneasily in her chair. Valentina, she thought. So, she'd been right all along.

'And is that a problem?' Holly sounded calm, but Ella knew her daughter and she knew that behind that unruffled exterior, Holly was angry. She had never liked people interfering in her life or telling her what to do. And why should she?

'Well, yes, it is,' said Tomás. He paused as the waiter brought over his beer. '*Gracias*,' he said. He took a long draught.

'Why?' Holly's gaze was steely now.

'I hesitate to say.' Tomás looked down. Ella realised that his knuckles were white.

'But isn't that why you're here?' Holly challenged him. 'To say?'

'Yes, you are right.' He sighed, spread his hands as if protesting his innocence in all this.

'Out with it then,' Holly suggested.

'I do not want to upset you, Holly,' he said. 'You are my new business partner. My mother, she is so excited. But . . .'

'But?'

'Rafael Delgado. I have to tell you. He is not always what he seems.'

Holly's eyes glittered. Ella realised that she was keeping her composure with some difficulty.

'What on earth do you mean, Tomás?' said Holly.

He shrugged. Took another gulp of his beer. 'We like Rafael,' he said. 'He is part of our community. But he is . . . how can I put it? A bit of a Don Juan.'

'Don Juan?' Her voice was cold now.

Ella sipped her wine. She was beginning to feel slightly sorry for Tomás. Her daughter could be a formidable force.

'What can I say?' He made a gesture of defeat. 'He likes the ladies – a little too much, I fear.'

Holly remained silent. She picked up her glass and took a small sip of wine.

Her lack of response clearly made Tomás feel more uncomfortable than ever. He drank some more of his beer. He was nervous and drinking rather quickly, Ella noticed.

'I do not want him to take advantage of you, that is all.' He spoke in a rush.

Holly sat up straighter. 'Take advantage?'

Ella felt distinctly worried now. Surely all Holly's plans weren't going to fall apart so quickly? And over a man?

'Yes,' he said. 'You see—'

'I don't want to upset you either, Tomás,' Holly cut in. 'But I should tell you that I'm perfectly capable of looking after myself. And I'm not sure it's any of your business – who I choose to spend time with, I mean.'

'Naturally, you are right, but—'

'As a matter of fact, and not that it has anything to do with you or anyone else,' Holly continued as if he hadn't spoken,

'Rafael was giving me a lift to Mairena del Alcor to visit an orange farm there. It was business. It wasn't . . .' – her lip curled – 'some sort of romantic liaison.'

'No. Yes. Sorry.' He seemed confused. He drank more beer. 'Forgive me, please.'

'And even if it was . . .'

Even if it was, thought Ella. Nothing was uncomplicated, was it? Nothing was easy.

'Then that would be my affair,' said Holly.

Tomás finished the last dregs in the glass. He seemed to be considering what to say next. 'It is only that my sister Valentina, she is affianced to Rafael Delgado,' he said stiffly.

'Oh.' Ella and Holly stared at him.

Affianced. Well now, thought Ella. She leapt instinctively into protective mode. 'I'm surprised,' she said tartly, 'if he is such a *Don Juan* that you even want him in your family.'

'Once again, you are right.' Tomás bowed his head. 'For myself and my mother, I say, no, we do not. Although he is a friend,' he added swiftly. 'He is one of us.'

One of us. Ella remembered what she'd said to Holly about them being outsiders. Then she remembered the recipe for the Seville orange and almond cake that she'd been given. She hadn't realised back then the significance, nor quite what an honour it had been.

'But for Valentina . . .' Tomás rolled his eyes. 'My sister, she is madly in love.'

So madly in love that she was jealous enough to wait around for hours outside her rival's hotel, Ella found herself thinking. And she certainly seemed like the kind of girl who wouldn't react well to anyone taking what she considered to be her property.

'Rafael, though, is an adult,' Holly pointed out. 'He can decide for himself who to see, where and when, can't he? He's responsible for his own actions, don't you think?'

'But of course,' Tomás agreed. 'I wanted to warn you, that is all. He cannot be trusted, you see.' He shook his head sadly. 'I felt responsible since it was I who introduced you to him. Some men, they simply cannot resist a beautiful foreign girl.'

Foreign girl. Ella and Holly exchanged a glance.

Tomás looked from one to the other of them. 'I apologise,' he said. 'I have offended you.'

'No. I'm not offended.'

She was hurt, though, Ella could see that. She was hurt and she was struggling. Ella's heart went out to her daughter. She willed her to stay strong – at least until Tomás had walked out of the door.

'And as I said,' Holly continued, 'I don't want to upset you or any of your family, you can be sure of that.'

At last, he smiled. 'So, you will not see him again?'

Ella saw Holly hesitate. She had no idea which way her daughter would go.

'I have heard you, Tomás,' she said at last. 'Thank you for the warning.'

Gracefully done, thought Ella. And making no promises.

Tomás got to his feet. His smile had slipped a little, but some of the old confidence had returned. 'I will be in touch,' he said.

'Of course.'

Ella and Holly watched him go.

'Well?' said Ella.

'You heard him.'

'But, darling.' She reached for her daughter's hand. 'Do you like him? Rafael, I mean. Because . . .' Because if you do, you should follow your heart, she was going to say. She still felt ambivalent, she still felt protective. But she wasn't at all convinced that Rafael was involved with Valentina. It hadn't looked that way at the flamenco club. He'd only had eyes for Holly.

'It doesn't matter if I like him or not.' Though Holly's eyes were huge and sad. 'I can't risk offending Tomás and Sofía. I'm a businesswoman now, Mum. I can't risk losing that contract.'

'No, I suppose you can't.' Ella sighed. 'Though perhaps you should sleep on it, darling, and decide in the morning?' She couldn't help wondering what Sofía thought about it all. Don't give up, she wanted to say to her daughter. If you really care, then don't give up until you absolutely have to, until there's no other way. But she didn't say it. How could she? When she had done the complete opposite? When she hadn't been brave enough to follow her heart at all?

CHAPTER 23

Felix

Dorset, 2018

Felix was chopping onions. He had gone round to his mother's for supper and she had agreed to let him prepare the vegetables. He knew she loved him being in the kitchen, as much as she loved cooking for him. He supposed that she didn't get the opportunity as much as she would have liked. She had put on her best apron and she was humming as she floured the beef for the casserole.

Ella had phoned him from Seville this morning. 'Sorry to disturb you, darling,' she'd said. 'Are you busy? I thought I'd just give you a quick call.'

Felix had been out in the garden hoeing his small vegetable patch ready for planting some salad leaves. He had to remind himself quickly that he was supposed to be at work. 'No, it's fine,' he said. He nipped inside before she heard the birdsong. 'How's it going in Seville?' He tried to make his voice sound careless and breezy, but since he'd found that photograph, the word *Seville* had acquired new meaning.

He listened to her voice as she told him how Holly had been getting on so far and he thought, *What about you, Ella? What's it been like for you – to go back?*

'And where are you now?' he asked. 'Where's Holly?'

'I'm in the Alcázar gardens,' she said. 'Sitting under an orange tree.'

Felix's breath caught. *Under an orange tree . . .*

'And Holly's gone to the orange farm. With someone she met at a flamenco club.'

'A flamenco club . . .' Not only had his side of the conversation become an echo, but Felix himself felt like an echo, a mere shadow of some former self. Perhaps it was the former self who used to stand on the cliff at Burton and imagine all those future possibilities?

'But that's another story,' Ella said and laughed.

She sounded cheerful. Felix guessed that the two of them were getting on well and that was good. 'I miss you,' he said.

'Felix? Are you all right?' Her voice changed.

'Yes, yes, of course,' he said. He fought to find his usual cheery bluster. Where had it gone? It had always served him well. 'I'm fine. Just about managing without the two of you.' His laughter sounded so hollow that he wished he hadn't even made the attempt.

'And your mother?' Her voice changed again. 'How is she?'

'She didn't mean to upset you.' Felix found himself answering a different question. This was a feature of his communication with his wife about his mother and vice versa; there was just so much damned subtext between those two.

'It doesn't matter,' Ella said.

Though of course, it did.

'She'd never intend to come between the two of you,'

Felix said. Because he knew that this was what had happened – at least to a degree. 'She loves Holly, but—'

'I know.'

There didn't seem much else to say to this. And Felix didn't completely believe himself anyway – he never had. The truth was that he wasn't always sure of his mother's motives, especially where Ella was concerned. What he didn't really understand, though, was why.

'OK, well, give my love to Holly,' Felix said.

'Will do. And I'll call again soon. Bye, Felix.'

And she had gone before he could even tell her that he loved her.

Felix's mother's voice brought him sharply back to the present.

'Felix? How was work today, I said?' She turned to face him. Her hands were floury, almost as white as her hair. Her eyes were large behind her glasses. The meat was sizzling in the pan, already giving off a rich aroma.

'Work?' he said. He blinked away an onion tear. Even men were allowed onion tears, weren't they?

'Work,' his mother repeated. She gave a little despairing shake of her head, a mannerism he was used to. He knew she didn't mean anything by it.

'Oh, yes, fine, thanks.' He'd gone blank for a minute there. Felix hated lying to her. But how could he tell her about the redundancy when he hadn't even told Ella? He'd made up his mind to get his priorities – and the women in his life – in the right order. Only sometimes it got rather complicated and hard to manage.

His mother clicked her tongue. She bustled over to the sink to wash her hands. 'I don't know what's got into you,' she said.

'Ella and Holly being away, I suppose it is. Hard to be without them, is it?'

'Mum . . .' He hated the sarcasm in her voice. She was like an orchid, that diva of the plant world. Why did she always demand so much of him? Why did she always have to be first in everything? He gave the onions a final chop. But it wasn't her fault. It was losing Dad, losing Colin, losing those she loved. Why shouldn't she cling on to whatever was left?

'Oh, take no notice of me,' she said.

Felix took the onions over to the stove, giving her shoulder a squeeze as he passed by. 'I always take notice of you,' he said. 'But Ella's my wife. Of course I miss her.'

'Hmph.' She dried her hands on the tea towel. 'And don't I know it,' she said.

Felix turned his attention to the carrots. He began peeling first with long smooth strokes. 'Why do you mind so much, Mum?' He'd often wondered this. 'Why can't you two ever just be friends?'

His mother let out a deep sigh. Felix waited for her to bat his comment away, as she did so often, but this time her shoulders sagged and she remained silent.

Immediately, Felix felt guilty. 'Mum?'

'It isn't that I don't like her, son.'

Surprised, Felix turned around. His mother had her back to him. She was taking the browned beef out with a slotted spoon and putting it into the base of the casserole dish. 'What then?' he asked.

'When you first got together, I was worried,' she said.

'What about?' Felix genuinely had no idea. His mother had never allowed this conversation before – or maybe he'd never initiated it.

'Ella needed rescuing,' she said. 'She was grateful to you, to us.'

Felix let this sink in. He turned back to the carrots. 'Meaning?'

'Meaning I wasn't sure that she loved you in the way I wanted her to love you, son.' The onions hit the pan with a loud sizzle.

Felix didn't want to think too much about this. Because Ella had loved him, he knew that. 'You thought she might hurt me?' he asked. A dog-eared corner of the photograph he'd found in the drawer began to edge into his mind and, crossly, he pushed it away.

'Yes,' she said. 'Yes, I did.' She sounded very sure.

It was strange to be having this conversation with his mother when they were standing back to back in her kitchen, but perhaps they couldn't have it any other way.

Felix allowed the photograph in. Who was that man? Why had Ella hidden the photo of the two of them? What had happened in Seville? Was this how she had hurt him? Without him knowing a thing about it?

'But that was a long time ago,' he said to his mother. And to himself really.

'Yes.' She turned the onions in the pan. 'And you've made a go of it, I know.'

'Yes,' he said firmly. They had. What did some ancient photograph matter in the grand scheme of the life they'd built together?

'And if she makes you happy . . .' – his mother's voice trailed off – 'then that's the main thing, I suppose.' She sounded doubtful, though.

'Yes,' he said again. That was the main thing. It absolutely was.

'Only . . .'

'What?' Felix chopped the next carrot much more ferociously than necessary. His mother liked small cubes, and consistency was key.

'That work of hers,' she said swiftly, and Felix had the distinct impression she'd been going to say something else.

'She works hard, Mum,' he said. 'Teaching is a vocation. I'm proud of what she does.'

'Yes, well, I'm old-fashioned, as you know.'

He took the carrots over to the casserole preparation area by the stove. 'I know.' But without Ella's job, he thought, where would they be now?

'Thank you, dear.' His mother treated him to a smile.

Perhaps they should get off the subject of Ella, Felix thought. 'Grated parsnips?'

'Please.'

Had something happened between Ella and the man in the photograph? *Well, obviously, Felix*, he told himself. Why else would she have hidden the damn thing all these years? Felix thought of what his mother had said about Ella being grateful. Had Ella stayed with him out of a sense of duty? He couldn't bear it if that were true.

'But I always wondered . . .' his mother said.

'Hmm?'

'There was something . . .' Her voice wavered. 'Of course, it's not my place to say, but—'

'Then don't.' Felix didn't want to hear any more. What could his mother possibly know about anything anyway? But he knew his voice was louder than he'd intended. And this was the second time in only a few months that he'd told his mother not to speak. He turned around.

His mother turned around too. They faced each other.

She wiped her hands on the apron. 'Don't you want to know, Felix?' she asked.

'No,' he said, 'I don't.'

She gave him a long look. 'As you please.'

Felix turned back to the kitchen counter. He started grating the parsnips. If he wanted to know anything, he would ask Ella. Until then . . . He scooped the parsnips up in his cupped palms and took them over to the casserole.

His mother nodded. She added the stock and put the dish in the oven. 'At least an hour,' she told Felix. 'We could do the crossword?'

'All right,' he said. It was a truce. And in this case, ignorance was very definitely bliss.

CHAPTER 24

Holly

Seville, 2018

Holly had slept on it as her mother had suggested, but after a restless night, nothing had changed as far as she was concerned. It didn't matter that Rafael might not consider himself 'affianced' to Valentina, as Tomás had so quaintly put it (what century were they living in anyway? she thought). There must be some sort of understanding between them – at least on Valentina's part – so Rafael had no right to be taking Holly to orange farms, nor should he be telling tell her how much he liked her and that he wanted to see her again. He wasn't free.

Holly sighed. Besides, this was a business trip and from now on, she'd remember that. She simply couldn't afford to antagonise all the contacts she was trying to make – that wasn't how it worked at all.

Straight after breakfast, she went back up to her room to send Rafael a text: short and to the point, she decided. *No need now to introduce me to your candlemaker.* She felt a pang of regret in the split second before she sent it. And not just about Rafael, she tried to tell herself. Would she even be able to find another candlemaker? *Thanks, anyway*, she added, realising how abrupt it had sounded, damn it.

A text pinged back almost immediately. *Why not? Have you found someone else? Lunch instead then?*

Holly let out the breath she'd been holding. He really had no idea. But why would he? If he made a habit of chatting up foreign tourists, as Tomás had suggested, then he must be confident of not being found out. She would have to make it even clearer.

It was nice meeting you, Holly wrote, *but I'll be busy for the rest of the trip. Sorry.* And thanks for making my heart beat a little faster, she thought. She was disappointed, but she'd get over it. For a short while she'd indulged in a bit of a romantic dream as far as Rafael Delgado was concerned – it must be the Seville sunshine and the scent of the orange blossom. Not to mention the effect his dark-eyed gaze seemed to have had on her. But no more, she told herself firmly. She would not be a pushover.

'Are you ready, Holly?' Her mother was standing in the open doorway. She glanced at the mobile phone in Holly's hand. 'See you down in the foyer in a few minutes?'

'Perfect.' She couldn't have come here with anyone more understanding, thought Holly, and it had been unfair of her not to confide in her mother earlier about her business plans, about Bitter Orange. So far, her mother had been helpful when Holly had needed it and yet hadn't seemed to mind at all when she'd gone to the orange farm with Rafael yesterday. Holly sighed. Suddenly, yesterday seemed a very long time ago.

They were heading out to visit a few small-scale perfumiers this morning, in search of the finest neroli. Holly was looking forward to spending the day with her mother, and two noses were definitely better than one.

Another text came in. *Holly? What's happened?*

She decided to ignore it. She didn't have the time or energy for explanations. Let him work it out for himself – it couldn't be that hard.

The morning went well. The first perfumier was pleasant enough but the products weren't as good as Holly had hoped. The second maker, however, seemed more promising. She talked a lot about values and standards and the necessity of choosing the best raw materials in order to achieve aromas of the highest quality. The perfumes were all natural, the young woman told them, handmade slowly and gradually, thereby respecting the process. This was more what Holly was looking for.

She examined one of the bottles. The branding and colours of green and orange were good on the neroli fragrance, which was the one she was interested in, obviously. She studied the list of ingredients – fortunately given in both Spanish and English.

'No chemical additives,' the woman assured her. 'And always inspired by our landscape.' She selected tester cards and sprayed liberally. The pungent scent of orange blossom seemed to fill the shop.

Holly's mother gave a small gasp. 'Wonderful,' she said, and just for a moment she closed her eyes.

Holly had to agree. The fragrance was fresh and flowery with a green leafy note and crucially seemed to hold that bitter-sweet scent of the Seville orange deep within. The perfume had caught the essence of springtime in Seville.

They sat down to drink strong and bitter Spanish coffee and discuss terms. It was an initial meeting, but Holly doubted she'd find a better product that would fit in quite as well with her developing portfolio.

At lunchtime, Holly and her mother made their way through the narrow streets to El Rinconcillo, a tapas bar that claimed to be the oldest in the city, having served tapas since 1670. While waiting for a table, Holly and her mother peeked inside to admire the elaborately carved wooden ceiling, the old photos of the bar's history on the tiled walls and the hundreds of bottles lined up on the shelves. Huge and richly fragrant Iberian hams hung from the ceiling and the waiters and bar staff chalked up the bills on the counter. The whole place belonged to a bygone age.

After they'd claimed their table and sat down outside, Holly checked her phone which had been on silent. Four texts and two missed calls, all from Rafael. He was persistent, she'd give him that.

She read the texts:

Can you tell me what has changed since yesterday afternoon?

Has someone spoken to you about me? Is that it?

Is there someone in England for you? Is that why?

I deserve some explanation, Holly.

Holly swore softly under her breath.

'Trouble?' her mother asked, transferring her gaze from the chalked menu board to Holly.

'Sort of.' Holly read her the texts.

'It doesn't sound as if Rafael has any idea what's going on,' her mother commented.

Before Holly could reply, the waiter appeared and they ordered beers and a selection of tapas. Holly was already becoming more accustomed to the different types of Spanish tapas and their names, and if she got anything wrong, well, wasn't it part of the fun to try something different? This time she thought she'd ordered spinach with chickpeas, manchego cheese tortilla and some fried cuttlefish, but she couldn't be sure.

'But, Mum.' Holly sat back in her chair and let the sun warm her face. 'You don't think I should ignore what Tomás told us, do you?'

'Well, no, but . . .' Her mother was watching her thoughtfully. 'We don't know that it's true.'

'Even so . . .' And why would Tomás lie?

'Part of me wants you to be cautious,' her mother admitted. 'But I don't like people interfering in my daughter's happiness.' She squeezed Holly's hand.

Happiness . . . Holly considered.

The waiter brought their drinks and Holly thanked him and took a grateful sip of the cold beer.

'If you feel something for Rafael . . .' – her mother was still talking, as if finding her way – 'then perhaps we shouldn't jump to conclusions, that's all. Perhaps we should give him the benefit of the doubt. Or ask him his version of how things stand between him and Valentina.' She sipped her beer. 'As he says, he deserves some sort of explanation at least.'

'Yes, I suppose so.' Holly had been too cross with Rafael to acknowledge this at first. And hurt. She was cross with herself too for letting her guard down so easily and allowing herself to be charmed by the first handsome Spanish guy she'd met in Seville.

But now, well, she knew that her mother was right. 'I'll call him when we get back to the hotel,' she said. They had another perfumier to visit this afternoon and afterwards, her mother had suggested a visit to Casa de Pilatos to see the patios and the tiles there, which were apparently among the best in the city.

The waiter reappeared at their table and began unloading

little terracotta bowls full of delicious-looking tapas in front of them. The enticing scents of whisky, roasted tomato and caramelised garlic, crispy potato, cumin, olive oil and cheese drifted their way. And Holly had thought she wasn't hungry . . . She and her mother shared an appreciative glance.

Holly decided to start with the *solomillo al whisky*: lightly-grilled tender pork loin doused in a garlicky whisky sauce, served with fried potatoes to mop up with. Rafael would have to wait, she thought. Although she couldn't help feeling gratified that he'd tried so hard to get in touch. That had to count for something, didn't it?

When they finally got back to the hotel at six, the receptionist greeted them. '*Hola*. Good afternoon. You have a visitor.' She gestured to the far side of the lobby.

Holly glanced over and there was Rafael, sitting next to the little white marble fountain. She smiled, felt a dart of excitement that she tried to push back to wherever it had come from. She turned to her mother, who gave a start of surprise as if she were seeing a ghost.

'You have to talk to him, Holly,' she said. 'I'll catch up with you later.'

'Yes, of course. See you later.'

Rafael looked up and saw her coming over. He jumped to his feet. 'Holly.'

Holly felt her heart soften at the sight of him. He was wearing his usual jeans and faded T-shirt and his dark hair was a little unkempt. She didn't get too close. No kissing greetings this time, she vowed. 'I'm really sorry, Rafael,' she said, aware that she sounded ridiculously formal. 'I hope you haven't been waiting long?'

'Not long, no.' He stared at her. 'I'm sorry too – for turning up like this – but you know, you gave me little choice.'

Holly raised an eyebrow. Most men would have just shrugged and accepted that she wasn't interested. It wasn't as if anything had even happened between them. They had shared a day together, that was all. But even as she told herself this, she knew it wasn't quite true. And perhaps Rafael was more emotionally honest than she. 'Shall we get a drink?' she suggested. She felt as if she needed one.

They went out to the little terrace with their beers and sat at a table by the fountain.

'I do not want to be a nuisance,' Rafael said sadly. 'But I like you, Holly. And so, I wanted to know – why?'

Holly was finding it hard to meet his gaze. 'You're not a nuisance,' she said. Never that.

'And I thought you liked me,' he added. He touched her arm and a shiver ran over her skin. *Damn it.* She pulled away. Distance, that was the key.

'I did,' She sipped her beer. As always, it was just the right temperature. She knew that she must be honest too. 'I do. But . . .' She hesitated. How could she put this exactly? She didn't want Rafael to blame Tomás.

'But?'

'But this is a business trip.' That was true enough.

'And so, you do not have time for love?'

Love? She blinked at him. 'Look,' she said. She'd had enough of whatever game he was playing. 'Don't waste any more of your time. I know about you and Valentina.'

He stared at her. 'What about me and Valentina?'

'That you and she are . . .' – she hesitated – 'involved.'

'Pah!' He made a gesture of frustration. 'Valentina? She is

a friend, nothing more. I have known her all my life. She is a little sister to me. What are you thinking?'

'But she likes you.'

'What?'

'In fact, she loves you.'

'Who told you that?' He looked angry now. He gave up glaring at Holly and frowned into his beer.

'I don't want to—' She didn't want to say, didn't want to get anyone in trouble and especially didn't want to cause further problems with Tomás. That had to be her main motivation now. It felt as if their new business relationship was delicately balanced and could topple over any moment into nothing.

'Tomás Pérez?' he asked.

OK then, she supposed it was obvious. She nodded.

'And you believed him?'

Oh, honestly. 'Why would he lie about it?' Holly spread her hands.

Rafael grabbed them. 'I do not know. But I will find out.'

'No.'

Their gazes locked.

'He and his mother – they're my business partners now,' she said. 'He was upset. I don't want to upset him or his family any further.'

He let go of her hands. 'Because if he is upset, then he will no longer do business with you?' His expression was scathing.

'Exactly.' She tried to force her emotions to one side. 'You probably won't understand, Rafael, but this new business venture means everything to me.'

'Clearly,' he said. 'I am not stupid. I think I understand you very well.'

Holly felt like crying. She mustn't, though. That would be

even more pathetic and unprofessional. 'I'm sorry,' she said again.

'So am I.'

'And for the record . . .' She put a hand on his arm. His olive skin felt warm to the touch. 'I do like you – very much.'

This time it was Rafael who shrugged her off. And she could hardly blame him.

'But there are so many problems with it, I can see you thinking.' He made an angry gesture that seemed to encompass the entire hotel terrace, which fortunately was empty apart from them. 'If I see this man, I lose my new business contact. This man, he lives in Spain, I live in England, so how can this possibly work? What point is there? Why take a risk on a pathway to nothing? So many practical problems. So much to overcome.'

Holly laughed at this speech – she couldn't help it.

'And you are British,' he added.

'So?'

'So, you are not impulsive, you do not have the romantic, the spontaneous temperament.' He looked sad. 'This is what I have to deal with.'

'I can be spontaneous,' Holly objected.

'Prove it.' He grinned.

She sighed. She'd walked right into that one.

'And can you be romantic too?' He gave her a sidelong glance.

'Yes,' she said crossly. She knew what was coming, but what the hell . . .

He leant closer. 'Prove it,' he said again.

Holly half turned. Their faces were almost touching. 'Rafael . . .' This wasn't going at all the way she'd intended.

He nodded as if she'd proved his point. 'I have an idea,' he said.

'I thought you might.'

He touched his nose. 'We do not tell Tomás or any of his family that we see each other. Simple, huh?'

Hmm. She wasn't sure that would work. She didn't know how they'd found out in the first place, but she supposed that everyone knew everyone else in Triana. Word had clearly got around.

'I have a better idea,' she said.

He pulled a face. 'I do not like your ideas so much, Holly.'

She ignored this. 'You introduce me to your candlemaker,' she said.

'And that is all?' He looked so disappointed. 'Always the business with you, is it not?'

'That's why I'm in Seville,' she said primly.

But it was difficult. Something in her heart had lifted when Rafael told her that there was nothing between him and Valentina. She couldn't help that. And if there really was nothing between them, then why shouldn't she see him? She wasn't doing anyone any harm – apart from possibly herself, by the risk of getting romantically involved with someone who lived in a different country. And she was willing to take risks, wasn't she? Wasn't this whole business venture a risk? A way to change her life?

She couldn't allow Tomás and his family to dictate her movements, no matter how much value their products could add to Bitter Orange. If they pulled out of the deal – and she hated this thought – there were other makers, other sources. No one was indispensable and she couldn't allow anyone to imagine that they were.

'And after I introduce you to the candlemaker?' Rafael's eyes were gleaming.

Holly got to her feet. 'Then we'll see,' she said.

His face lit up. 'You mean . . . ?'

'Shall we say tomorrow afternoon?' she suggested.

'Tomorrow afternoon,' he agreed. He got up too and took a step closer.

This time Holly didn't move away.

He lifted her hand to his lips and he kissed it. 'Until then,' he said.

And Holly knew that this was a promise.

CHAPTER 25

Ella

Seville, 1988

The following day, Ella felt ridiculously bereft as she visited the Plaza de España and the Parque de Mariá Luisa alone. She knew she'd done the right thing. She was married after all. But she missed Caleb already. The plaza – which according to her guidebook was created as a centrepiece for the 1929 Ibero-American Exposition – was splendidly theatrical, but despite the warm spring sunshine it somehow left her feeling cold and unsatisfied. Compared to what she'd seen with Caleb – the nuggets of detail she'd learnt that revealed the true history of the *Sevillanos* people and their culture – the plaza seemed inauthentic with the tourists rowing down a man-made 'Venetian' waterway. Although that, she supposed, was what theatre was all about. No one imagined that it was real.

She tried to shake off the feeling. The colourful ceramic footbridges over the green canal were very cute and the little alcoves around the perimeter, each representing a province of Spain and its history and decorated with tiles, were fascinating. But . . .

Ella sighed as she bought some ham *montaditos* from a bar near the plaza to take away for lunch. She had first sampled these small and delicious toasted sandwiches when she and Caleb had been exploring Santa Cruz the day before. What on earth was wrong with her? Here she was in a city she'd longed to visit, a city with which she had already fallen in love, and yet she felt unable to properly appreciate it.

Ella ate her *montaditos* in the leafy Parque de Mariá Luisa. She was sitting on a tiled bench overlooking a ceramic pool lined with orange amaryllis. No doubt all of these ceramics had been made in Triana, she thought, admiring the playful frogs that decorated the edges of the pool. Should she go back there tomorrow as she had planned? One part of her said 'yes', another 'no'. It depended on which part she decided to listen to tomorrow morning, she supposed.

On the other side of the pool, a young, long-haired Spanish boy was playing a mournful guitar. Ella watched the ducks swimming in the water: cooling down, fluffing up their feathers. Just beyond the pool where she sat, a decorative pergola was wound around with white magnolia and a pale lilac wisteria. In the tree behind, two grey and white doves settled on a branch next to one another, content. The guitar reminded Ella of the flamenco. Like everything, she thought.

Last night, she'd phoned Felix from the hotel. It hadn't been an easy conversation – not least because she guessed his mother was listening in.

'How's everything going, darling?' he'd asked, and she heard the concern and maybe even a tinge of guilt in his voice.

Did he feel bad at rushing back to Dorset the way he had, at leaving her here alone? If so, he'd never admit it.

'All right, thanks.' She told him where she'd been that day. And now it was her turn to feel guilty. 'It's not the same without you, though.' No, it wasn't the same. It had been very different. Though not perhaps in the way Felix would imagine. No, she thought now, she definitely wouldn't go to Triana. She daren't risk it. It would be like walking into the lion's den.

Felix had picked up on her tone. 'I really don't know if it was wise for you to stay behind,' he said.

Maybe it was unfair, but Ella thought she could hear Ingrid's voice behind his words. 'Perhaps,' she said coolly, 'it wasn't wise for you to leave me here.'

'Ella . . .' She heard his sigh. He wouldn't want to argue – not now, not when they were so far apart, and especially not if his mother was listening.

'I know you felt you had to go home,' she said quickly, to soften the blow. 'I do understand. But can't you see what a waste it would have been for me to come too?'

'Hmm.' He wasn't conceding. 'I do feel bad about it. And I'll make it up to you, darling, you know I will.'

As if he could. She wondered if he'd been brooding about their other conversation – about the sorry state of their marriage at this moment in time. 'And how is your mother?' she asked.

'Oh, fine.' Ella detected a note of embarrassment now.

'Nothing broken then?'

'Nothing broken, no.'

'So . . . ?' *So, you went back for no reason.* Ella pictured her mother-in-law reclining on the sofa, rather pleased no doubt that she had her son all to herself again, running errands for her and making tea.

'Nothing wrong that some rest won't put right.' His voice dropped to a whisper. 'I couldn't leave her here on her own, Ella,' he said again. 'I already explained that to you.'

Not like he had left Ella, in Seville, she couldn't help thinking. *All on her own . . .* 'I know. It's fine,' she said breezily. Suddenly she just wanted this phone conversation to be over. She didn't want to think about any of it anymore. 'And I'll be home before you know it.' She thought of her class at school. She missed them. But when she got back, would she even be the same person?

'Good. I just want everything to be back to normal.' She heard the relief in his voice. *Back to normal.* Ella wasn't sure about that. Would they ever be? What had happened with Caleb . . . Nothing seemed normal anymore.

Ella left the cool lakes with their goldfish, swans, ducklings and little stone bridges and the shady walkways of the Parque de Mariá Luisa planted with carob trees, exotic flora and lush greenery, still listening to the sound of parrots screeching in the tall palm trees and water pouring into the ceramic pools from stone fountains. She trailed back to the hotel. It was just after six p.m. and she was tired. She'd stay in tonight, she decided; she couldn't face negotiating for food and drink in Shouty Bar again and it wasn't quite the same going out for dinner when you weren't part of a couple.

The manager waylaid her as she came in. *Felix*, she thought. Something else had happened at home.

'Someone is waiting to see you, *señora*,' the manager said.

Someone? Oh. Caleb was sitting on a leather chair in the foyer. He got to his feet and came over. His dark gaze locked onto hers.

'May I talk with you for a few minutes, Ella?' he asked.

Ella couldn't help smiling at the solemnity of his tone. She was so pleased to see him, it was crazy. *Oh, Ella*, she thought.

'Yes, of course.' She was aware of the manager, hovering and curious. 'Shall we step outside for a moment?'

A glimmer of amusement flickered in Caleb's eyes. Clearly, he understood her thinking. 'Yes, we should do that.'

They went out onto the pavement. 'Have you been waiting for me long?' she asked him.

'Only an hour.' He shrugged.

An hour . . . 'So . . . ?'

'I want to say sorry, Ella.' He turned to face her. 'I crossed a line. It was wrong.'

She shook her head. 'You don't have to apologise.' It was she who had crossed the line. Whatever was there between them – and she could feel it even now, making her want to step closer to him instead of back and away – was no one's fault.

'But I do,' he insisted. 'You were right. I was less than professional.'

'Though strictly speaking, you weren't acting as a tour guide,' she reminded him. After all, he hadn't taken any money.

He put his head to one side as he regarded her. 'Anyway, I was sad not to see you today,' he said.

'Me too.' She didn't tell him about the sense of loss she'd felt amongst all the theatrical splendour of Plaza de España.

'And I still want to show you my Triana.'

My Triana . . . 'I still want to see it,' she whispered. She couldn't help herself. Caleb made the city come alive and that was what she had enjoyed the most about their two days together. It was exactly the life and vibrancy she'd imagined she would find here that had made her want to visit Seville in the first place. That and her mother's jewellery box, she reminded herself. This holiday destination had been – and still was – an escape.

'If I promise not to . . .' – he hesitated – 'cross the line again . . .'

'Yes?'

'May I show you Triana tomorrow? That is, if you have not made other plans.'

'I haven't made any other plans.'

'Then . . . ?'

'I'd love to.'

He grinned. 'And the tobacco factory?'

'And the tobacco factory.' She couldn't wait to hear all about his great-grandmother, the *cigarrera*, who had rolled cigarettes back in the day like the legendary Carmen.

'I know you will be leaving Seville very soon, Ella,' Caleb said softly.

She nodded, though the thought of leaving made her feel sad. But, yes. Of course she would be going home – to her job, to Felix, to the life they shared.

'And so, I am selfish,' he said. 'I want to see you as much as possible before you go.'

Ella watched him. Didn't that remark sound a bit like crossing a line?

'As a friend,' he added, with a slow wink. 'Cross my heart.'

Ella laughed. 'As a friend,' she agreed. 'I think that would be wonderful.'

CHAPTER 26

Holly

Seville, 2018

After their last conversation, Holly had thought things might be awkward with Rafael, but she felt at ease from the moment she met him outside the hotel at three p.m. the following day.

She had spent an enjoyable morning with her mother exploring the Museo de Bellas Artes which was situated in the quarter of El Arenal, an area dominated by the dazzling white bullring. A former convent, the Bellas Artes, had been restored to its former Baroque splendour and was now, according to their guidebook, considered one of the finest art museums in Spain; Holly was perfectly content to while away a couple of hours in the company of the impressive paintings and sculptures of Murillo, de Zurbarán and the like.

After their visit, they wandered back to Santa Cruz to call in again on Holly's chosen perfumier in order to finalise their deal. She hadn't found another perfume that could match this one; she and her mother were both in love with its zesty orange fragrance and agreed that Bridport would love it too.

They had lunch in a tapas bar nearby, savouring the sunshine after their morning in the museum and chatting about the Sevillian products they'd already found for the shop. Holly consulted her phone. The list was growing.

After they'd paid the bill, Holly's mother got to her feet. 'Time to leave you to it,' she said.

'Come with us to the candlemaker, Mum,' said Holly. With her mother there, it would be so much easier to resist Rafael's indisputable charms. Even Rafael would behave, with her mother around to chaperone.

'You don't need me, darling.' Her mother was firm. 'And there's something I want to do this afternoon.'

Ah, so she was being mysterious again. Holly hadn't stopped wondering about that. 'Oh, yes? Are you going back to the hotel for a crafty *siesta*, is that it?'

But her mother only smiled that enigmatic smile. 'Not today,' she said. 'I thought I might search out a few ghosts.'

'Ghosts?' But something told Holly that she wouldn't get anything more out of her right now. And this afternoon she had more than enough of her own issues to contend with – she had to decide if she even wanted to resist Rafael's charms.

She met him in the plaza outside the hotel and they walked together to the candlemaker's workshop which was tucked away in a nearby alley, behind the woman's family home. The workshop was crammed with an array of candles and equipment, including small brown glass bottles of essential oils lined up on a shelf, various waxes, wicks, candle-holders and moulds.

Behind the wooden counter, the young woman, Luciana, was working. She stopped briefly to greet Holly and Rafael but since she clearly spoke no English, Holly was relieved to have Rafael around as interpreter.

Luciana seemed equally glad of this as she chatted happily away to him.

He was clearly exercising that charm of his. But he was also giving Holly plenty of information as they talked: 'Her wax blend – it has been certified as organic.' More nodding and conversing as Luciana indicated various pots and jars. 'It is made up of organic coconut oil and mainly beeswax. She uses only sources that are pure.' Followed by: 'no glue or resin to fix the wicks . . . Only this artisan technique known as dipping.'

Holly watched carefully, but already Luciana had moved on.

'The candles, they are poured by hand.' Rafael spoke as Luciana demonstrated the process. The smell of hot wax filled the air, thick and intense.

'And the fragrance?' Holly asked.

Rafael spoke to Luciana some more.

'She will demonstrate in a moment,' he told Holly. 'It is a fragrance which is clean and complex and which comes directly from the orange blossom flowers. These are steam-distilled to produce the neroli.'

It all sounded good so far and Holly liked Luciana's working methods which, like Sofía's, were natural and transparent. She was a true craftswoman.

Luciana continued to explain the method of production to Rafael as she worked, while he talked to both of them and Holly nodded and smiled encouragingly.

It was a while before they progressed to financial details. Holly sensed that, as with some of the other makers and producers she had met so far in Seville, Luciana needed Holly to understand a lot more than simply how much the candles would cost her. Increasingly, it was about their respect for the natural elements of their landscape, their values, their patience in teasing out the best, the heart of the ingredients, from what they had to work with. It was about passion too and once again, Holly recognised that love in Luciana's dark eyes. Holly had no problem with that ethos – she intended to celebrate it.

Luciana lit one of the neroli candles she had made earlier. The soft but insistent scent of orange blossom slowly filled the air. Not just orange blossom, though; Luciana was right – under the citrus there were green and earthier notes. It was like nectar, Holly thought. A veritable food of the gods.

Once again, Luciana spoke and Rafael translated.

'Neroli has many benefits,' he told Holly. 'Plus, it is calming to the mind and emotions.' He waggled his eyebrows as if to emphasise the point.

'So I've been told.' Holly smiled. Though it could also be good at churning up the emotions, she'd found. 'And would you be interested in supplying candles to my shop?' She looked to Rafael for a translation. She liked the product and the maker. Now, it was time to get down to business. 'What would your costs be? And for how many units?'

Holly left with a verbal agreement she was more than pleased with. Another box ticked. Another natural and organic source. And she could still smell the bitter-sweet scent of the orange blossom, though whether it came from the workshop, their clothes and skin or one of the many trees in the city of Seville, Holly couldn't say.

'Thanks, Rafael,' she said, turning to him as they stood in the narrow alleyway. 'I couldn't have done that without you.' Language and communication – she had given so little thought to this before she came here, which only showed her naivety.

And yet, it was something she should have been aware of, something that had certainly come up in the business course she'd studied.

He grinned. 'Ah, but I wonder. I think, Holly, you are a very capable person. A woman who could do anything she sets her mind to.'

'If only.' Holly laughed. Most of the time she felt an awfully long way away from that woman.

He eyed her appraisingly. 'And now, if you want to return the favour . . .'

'Ye-es?' She was immediately wary.

'Will you allow me to show you some of our legends of Seville?' He glanced at his watch. 'There is time, yes, before you must return to your hotel?'

'Around here?' She gestured. Legends of Seville certainly sounded interesting. And she was reluctant to leave him just yet.

'Around here,' he confirmed.

'OK then, you're on.'

They began in nearby Plaza de Refinadores where Rafael invited Holly to sit on one of the circular tiled benches. She complied. The plaza was made up of cobbled squares, and lined by tall palms and smart villas with large overhanging windows and wrought-iron balconies. A honey-white jasmine wound its way around the trees, filling the plaza with a sweet perfume.

'So, here he is.' Rafael pointed to the dark grey statue standing in the square.

Holly looked up. 'Here who is?'

He shot her a wicked grin. 'Don Juan, of course.'

'Ah.' Holly folded her arms and regarded the statue curiously. She should have known from the self-satisfied smile on his face and the arrogance of his bearing. There was a certain tilt to his head that gave it away. 'And the legend?' she asked Rafael.

He adopted a posture not unlike Don Juan's, now she came to think of it. 'As you know, he was devilishly handsome and charming,' he said.

'Hmm.' That was one way of putting it. 'But was he fictional? Or was he a real person?'

'The legend of Don Juan was first introduced by Tirso de Molina in the 1630s,' Rafael told her. 'A Spanish writer. I have not read the story, but his Don Juan was definitely a bit of a rogue.'

'A womaniser, no doubt?' Holly assumed.

'Oh, yes.' Rafael looked up into the blue Sevillian sky as if it could provide him with inspiration. 'He had countless affairs with young Spanish women.'

Holly noticed the way Rafael's dark hair curled into his neck, barely touching the collar of his casual white linen shirt. It was an effective contrast. 'And who,' she wondered aloud, 'was the inspiration for this character, do you think?'

'There was a man,' Rafael told her.

She didn't doubt it.

'His name was Don Miguel de Mañara – he was Sevillian. He inherited a great fortune at a young age, and went on to lead an extravagant, public and very indulgent lifestyle.'

'Lucky old Miguel.' Holly stretched her legs out in the sun. This was all very pleasant and a lot more fun than writing business contracts.

'At first, yes,' Rafael agreed. 'But eventually he married.'

'And then he wasn't so lucky?' Holly gave him a questioning look.

'No, no. Not that. He loved his wife so much and so exclusively that when she died . . . when she died . . .'

Holly was on the edge of her seat. Her certainly knew how to spin a story.

'Mañara was so filled with grief that he turned to God.'

'You're kidding me?' This was, she felt, an unlikely ending to the legend of Don Juan.

'No, it is true.' Rafael sat down on the bench next to her and she inched slightly away. He had a manner of encroaching on her personal space – which was nice, but potentially dangerous.

'He founded the Hospital of Charity, which still looks after the poor and disabled to this day,' he said.

Holly stared at him. 'So, it turns out that Don Juan was a good guy?' Was he trying to tell her something?

'Exactly.' He jumped to his feet, held out a hand and pulled her up. 'And now,' he said, 'to the Jardines de Murillo.'

The gardens, right next to the ancient thick walls of the Alcázar, were lovely and some of the trees very old. It was surprisingly quiet in this part of the city; Holly could even hear birdsong. 'So, what's the legend here?' she asked Rafael, reaching out to touch the bark of an ancient magnolia tree whose roots were like the ribs of a giant skeleton half embedded in the ground.

She realised too late that he had whipped out his mobile phone and was taking a picture of her.

'Do you mind?' he asked, after he'd taken it. 'There is no legend. It is only a scented walkway that we take to our next destination.'

Intriguing. They walked past the orange trees, the figs and the magnolias, Holly inhaling the heady mix of perfumes. 'Jardines de Murillo? Named after the painter?' she asked

Rafael, rather pleased with her knowledge, gleaned from her visit to the Museo de Bellas Artes earlier today.

'I'm impressed.'

Holly allowed herself a secret smile.

He nodded. 'And you are right. As you can see, we are next to the walls of the palace. The Alcázar owned these gardens originally. Later, they were donated to the city and named after Murillo, who is buried in a church nearby.'

They walked on past the charming pink and white houses on the little street of Pimienta and down narrow alleyways, past water fountains, through patios and under arches. It was a whole world away from the Seville that Holly had seen up till now and she loved the pure romance of it. As for Rafael, he seemed to know instinctively when to talk and when she wanted to have a few moments of quiet reflection. She even liked it when they were forced to walk in single file – it gave her a good opportunity to look at his body unobserved. He was only an inch or two taller than Holly. She liked the way he dressed, the way he walked, his air of confidence and the dark, wicked gleam in his eye.

They passed a rather strange sign which she had already noticed several times in and around the city. It combined the Spanish syllables 'NO' and 'DO' with a figure 8 in between. Holly paused to examine it again. 'What does it mean?' she asked Rafael.

'It is the official motto of the coat of arms of Seville,' he told her. 'And another legend.'

Another legend? Seville, it seemed, was quite the city for them. 'Explain?' she suggested.

'Hmm, well, the number eight represents the threads of a . . . how do you say, like a ball of wool?'

'Yarn?'

'Yes, which in Spanish is *madeja*.'

'*Madeja*,' she repeated.

'Exactly.' He smiled – probably in amusement at her poor accent, she guessed. 'So, when you say, *no madeja do*, it sounds like, *No me ha dejado*, which means it – the city of Seville – has not abandoned me.'

'Clear as mud,' she said.

He laughed. 'You need to understand the language to get it,' he said. 'It is believed to represent the fidelity of the people of Seville.'

Fidelity again, she noted. It seemed to be a theme. And given what Tomás had told her about Rafael and Valentina, just how important was fidelity to this man? She frowned at him but he was still chuckling to himself and oblivious of her scrutiny.

'Shall we go on?' He gestured ahead.

Holly followed him down another narrow street.

'And now, Susona,' he said.

They had arrived in a small square. He pointed to a blue and white swirly-leafed plaque containing some Spanish writing constructed out of tiles on the wall.

'Susona?'

'This,' he nodded towards the plaque, 'is the last wish – or should I say warning? – of Susona, a young girl who lived in this neighbourhood in the late fifteenth century.'

'So, what's the story?' Holly had never heard of her. The square was sweet, though, with a very tall and rather random palm tree towering above the buildings.

'Susona's family were Jewish but forced to convert to Christianity. The conversion, it was a pretence for them. And then . . .' – he paused for dramatic effect – 'Susona, she fell in love with a Christian boy.'

'*Romeo and Juliet*,' said Holly. A story as old as time.

'You might say, yes,' he agreed. He assumed what Holly was beginning to think of as his storytelling stance. 'One night, right here where we stand, she overheard her father and a group of other men plotting against the Christians of the neighbourhood, who, they claimed, had been oppressing them for too long.'

'Was that true?' Holly asked.

He nodded. 'Very probably.'

'So, she was worried for her lover's safety?' Holly asked.

'She was.' Rafael gestured to the plaque on the wall. 'And so, she reported her father and the other men to the Spanish Inquisition.'

'Really?' That was a bit much. Holly resisted the impulse to slip into a Monty Python impression of *Not the Spanish Inquisition*. 'What happened to them?' she asked instead.

Rafael drew an imaginary blade across his throat and made a sound like a death rattle.

Holly flinched. He was too good at this. 'They killed them?'

'They had to set an example,' he explained.

'And what happened to Susona?' She must have felt more than a little guilty? Holly hoped the Christian boy was worth it.

'Ah.' Rafael frowned and adopted a sorrowful expression. 'Sadly, her lover rejected her.'

'After she'd saved his life?' That was a bit ungrateful, to say the least.

'But, yes. On the basis that he could never trust anyone who could betray their family in the way she had.'

Fair point, Holly supposed. 'So, what did she do?'

'Heartbroken and filled with regret,' Rafael went on, really milking it now, 'Susona confined herself to her house. She asked that when she died, her head be removed from her body and hung on this very corner as a warning to others to never betray their families as she had.'

Holly shivered. Poor old Susona had paid a high price for putting the love of a man in front of her family.

'Legend has it that the skull hung here for two hundred years before being removed and replaced with this plaque,' he added.

Holly gazed at the ancient tiles. They were rather attractive. 'Much less macabre than a skull, I suppose,' she said.

From here, they dipped into the pretty cobbled square of Doña Elvira, where she admired the fountain, orange trees and tiled benches as they refuelled with a cold juice. After their pit stop, Rafael led the way through more narrow lanes emerging at Patio de Banderas, Courtyard of the Flags, which revealed what Rafael told her was the narrowest alley of all, the Calle Judería. Holly was fascinated. It took them past the old gatehouse under arches so low that no one would be able to enter the Jewish quarter on horseback, according to Rafael.

Holly couldn't vouch for the accuracy of his stories but she was enjoying them, and enjoying this time with him too. He was good company, had a great sense of humour and she knew she wasn't imagining the spark between them.

They entered Calle Agua (even Holly knew this was Water Street), which ran alongside the old city wall. 'The pipes for the Alcázar water supply go through the wall.' He showed her where they could be seen at the end of the street.

And on to Calle Reinoso. 'It is one of the narrowest streets in Seville,' said Rafael. He stopped abruptly. 'And so, it has another name too.'

'Another name?'

He took a step closer, put his hands on her shoulders and kissed her firmly on the mouth. Holly was so taken by surprise that she just stared at him. He gave a little shrug. 'Kissing Street,' he said.

'What?'

'It is known as Kissing Street, because you can stand on the balconies on either side of the road and . . .' He pointed.

She looked up. He was right. On the opposite balconies you would be close enough to kiss. And Rafael still was close enough to kiss. She looked at him, he looked at her. He held her face gently between his hands and he kissed her again – this time so slowly, so tenderly . . . Wow.

When the kiss ended, they continued to stare at one another. They had reached a tipping point, Holly realised, and before she'd been fully aware of it, they had tipped right over.

CHAPTER 27

Felix

Dorset, 2018

Once again, Felix found himself walking the cliff path at Burton, this time from Cogden Beach along the green valleys and sandy ridges to Hive. Had he become a man without purpose? No. But right now, the days were long. And without Ella, without his job, he woke early, aware of the number of hours looming ahead, needing to be filled before the day was done.

He paused and gazed out towards the hazy grey shimmer of the morning sea. There was just a light breeze and the ocean was calm, stretching out towards a white horizon. But Felix had come to a turning point in more ways than one. It wasn't only losing his job – a job that had been such a huge part of his life for so long that now he felt as if he was walking around minus a limb. Neither was it the photograph – because surely whatever had happened was dead and buried in the past? He and Ella had forged a whole life together since then.

They had history. They had Holly. What danger could possibly be presented by one old photograph?

No. It was more as if he'd reached a moment where he had to make an important decision. It had taken most of his life to reach this point. And now, Felix didn't want to get it wrong.

The sky was grey too. Not dull, though. There was a silvery brightness promising to break right through the thin cloud cover. Felix thought about that conversation with his mother. What had she been referring to? It could only be trouble.

He began walking down the hill towards Hive Beach. It had rained last night and the new growth of grass was wet and slippery underfoot, with patches of mud that made his boots slide. He adjusted his backpack. Perhaps Ella would call again today. He'd spoken to her briefly yesterday. She'd sounded worried and he'd felt a flicker of concern.

'Is everything all right, love?' he'd asked her.

'Oh, it's nothing, just a bit of a hiccup.'

He could tell she didn't want to say more.

'What kind of a hiccup?' What was it about him, Felix wondered, that stopped people – and not just any people, his own family – from telling him things? Did he seem too weak, too needy? Did they think he couldn't cope with the knowing? Did he seem, to them, the sort of man who wouldn't understand?

'It's a man . . .' Ella hesitated.

Felix felt a little flip of panic. His senses sharpened. 'What man?' His mind zipped back to the photograph. Ella and a Mediterranean-looking man standing under an orange tree.

'Holly quite liked him, that's all. It was someone called Rafael. I think I told you – she went with him to the orange farm.'

'Oh.' *That* man. And *Holly* quite liked him. Felix felt the sweet dip of relief. Honestly. What was he thinking? 'So, what happened?'

He heard Ella sigh. 'Someone warned her off.' She'd lowered her voice so that the whole thing sounded even more sinister. 'It's a bit odd. I can't explain now, though, Felix. She's about to – Oh, hello, darling.' Her voice changed. 'I'm just talking to Dad.'

'Are you all right, Ella?' Felix asked her. He should be looking after them. Perhaps he should have gone with them to Seville. That would have provided some purpose. But it would have defeated the object of giving them time together and besides, Felix had needed time too – in order to think, to consider his next step. 'Is Holly all right?'

'Yes, we're fine.' Ella's voice was bright and cheerful again now.

Felix found himself wondering if he'd always been convinced by that brightness and cheer too easily. 'If you're sure . . .'

'Yes, I'm sure. Bye, darling. Speak soon.' And she was gone.

Down in the bay below, Felix spotted a man with a Land Rover parked on the edge of the car park by the shingle. National Trust. He'd seen him here before. He came to collate information, to chat to people, to give out leaflets and sign up more members, Felix supposed. To provide a presence. Felix and Ella already belonged to the National Trust, even though they didn't visit many of the properties; they didn't really have the time. It was more a matter of supporting the Trust's values.

Felix went on down the hill. He knew that Ella and Holly were capable of looking after themselves. All the women in his family were strong. And if Ella needed him, she'd say, wouldn't she? She'd always been independent. She'd needed him back when they first met, of course. After that, well . . .

Felix thought of what his mother had said about Ella needing rescuing. Some of it, at least, was true. He walked across to take a look at the National Trust Land Rover. The man had chalked up sightings of seabirds and plants. Felix moved closer, got into conversation with him; he was a friendly, weathered-looking bloke of around his own age, maybe a few years older.

After several minutes of pleasant chat, mainly about the flora and fauna of the area, a subject close to Felix's heart, Felix noticed a sheet of paper pinned to the noticeboard behind the vehicle. *National Trust representative required*, he read, followed by the hours. A full-time job then.

The man saw him looking. 'Interested?' he asked.

Felix was. But could he do it? 'What does the job entail?' he asked.

They carried on talking. The man was leaving – going to live closer to his son and family in Bristol, he said. He seemed to like Felix; gave him the information he needed, a form to fill in and a few tips. 'Seems to me, with your knowledge of the area, and your expertise on plants and what have you, that you'd be ideal for the job,' he said.

Felix grinned. 'I hope so,' he said. 'It could be exactly what I'm looking for.'

Could it be that easy? he wondered as he walked back along the cliff to Cogden, where he'd parked the car. Well, maybe it could. Sometimes things did happen at precisely the right time. And perhaps his luck was due to change.

When he got back home, his mother was waiting for him in the kitchen. They'd always had keys to each other's houses. Nevertheless, Felix was surprised.

'Mum?' Was she ill? 'Are you OK? What are you doing here?' He forgot for a moment that he was supposed to be at the garden centre, that he hadn't told anyone about the redundancy.

'Not at work today, son?' She was staring at him, a look of sadness in her blue eyes. Felix had seen that look many times and he hated to be the reason for it, he always had.

'Fancy a cuppa?' he asked her. If she could ignore a question, then so could he.

She nodded. Her mouth was a grim line of disapproval. 'You'd better tell me what's going on,' she said.

Felix sighed. She was far too good at making him feel five years old again. He went to fill the kettle. So much for telling Ella first. He felt the burst of elation that had swept over him after talking to the National Trust man evaporate. It had given him hope.

He switched on the kettle. Hope reminded him of that young boy on the clifftop considering his future possibilities. What had happened to that boy? Why had he always chosen safety over knowledge?

'I've been made redundant,' he told his mother. 'I've been looking for something else.'

'Oh, Felix.' She got to her feet – somewhat unsteadily – and held out her arms. 'Why didn't you say?'

He accepted the comforting embrace, breathing it in, smelling his mother's scent of lavender and geranium. 'How did you know, Mum?' he asked her. All-seeing, that's what she was.

'I'm your mother.'

Felix couldn't hold back a smile at that. 'Sit down, Mum,' he said.

She did so. 'I suppose Ella doesn't know?' Was it his imagination or was there a faint note of triumph in his mother's voice?

'Not yet.' He turned to face her. 'I wanted to tell her first,' he admitted. 'But I just . . . haven't.' He didn't want to explain the reasons why, didn't want to talk about his feelings of failure, didn't want to hear her reassurances either – and no doubt his mother would be able to guess all of it accurately enough.

Her features clouded with disappointment. 'Of course you did,' she said. 'Well, you needn't worry about me. I shan't say a word.'

And for a moment, it hovered between them. That other knowledge. Whatever else his mother wasn't saying, for whatever reason. And her resentment of Ella, of course. But that was nothing new.

'Thank you.' Felix made the tea the way his mother liked it: loose tea well mashed in the pot. He covered the teapot with a cosy she'd hand-knitted for them years ago, and left it to brew. 'I've been waiting for something to come up,' he said.

'And has it?' she asked.

'Not yet.' He gave a little shrug that he hoped would convince her how little it all mattered. As if. 'It's not easy,' he admitted. 'I'm not young, not qualified.'

'You can be trusted,' she put in. 'You've always been good with people. You know a lot about some things.'

Plants, he thought. He knew a lot about plants. He decided not to tell her about the National Trust job. He might not get it. But he'd apply at least. What did he have to lose? He straightened his shoulders. 'We'll see,' he said.

'If you need anything . . .'

'Thanks, Mum.'

'But they'll have given you a package, I suppose? Isn't that what they call it?'

'A package, yes.' Which wouldn't last for long. It was about much more than money, though.

Felix poured the tea, milk last.

His mother shifted in her seat. 'So, I suppose this isn't a good time,' she said.

'Good time?' What was she on about now?

She looked around the kitchen as if someone might be eavesdropping. She'd never been slow in coming forward, but now his mother looked distinctly nervous. 'Well, son, after you left the other day, I got to thinking.'

'Yes?' Felix was wary now. *Don't do it, Mum*, he thought. *Don't say it.*

'And I realised that I have to tell you. I should have told you a long time ago. We agreed, your father and I.'

'Dad? What's Dad got to do with it?' Felix was confused.

'It's no good hiding your head in the sand, son,' his mother said. 'You have to face up to things, it's part of what life's all about. And if anything should happen to me . . . Or when it happens to me . . .'

'Mum—'

'Then you wouldn't know,' she said. 'And in my book, that's not right.'

She was waiting. The speech was over and she was waiting. Felix knew that she was expecting him to try and stop her like he'd done before. But he didn't. He looked out into the garden he loved and he imagined himself back on that cliff. Future possibilities . . . She was right. How could he become his own person if he didn't face up to things? How could he have a strong sense of self when he was hiding from the world, from knowledge? Knowledge was power.

Felix passed his mother her tea and sat down. He braced himself. This was the decision then. This was it. 'Go on then, Mum,' he said. 'Out with it. What exactly is it that you think I should know?'

CHAPTER 28

Holly

Seville, 2018

The legends of Seville walk over, Holly and Rafael were strolling back to her hotel when they bumped into Tomás, who happened to be coming out of a nearby bar.

Just her luck, thought Holly. Or was it not a coincidence at all? At that moment, she and Rafael had not been holding hands, but were walking so close together that their bodies were touching all the way. But Tomás hadn't been spying on them, had he?

'Holly. Rafael.' Tomás didn't look in the least surprised to see them. 'I was going to call you, Holly.'

'Oh?' Holly blinked at him in the late afternoon sunshine. She moved slightly away from Rafael. Nevertheless, she really didn't want this time with him to end.

'Yes. There are a few details in the contract I would like to discuss.'

'The contract?' More likely it was Rafael he wanted to talk about.

'And I have an idea of how to change the packaging of our products.' He waited.

'Oh, I see.' She was aware that this was something that should be addressed at some point. But . . .

'We could go for a drink now?' he suggested smoothly. 'It will not take long. If that is OK with you, Rafa?'

Rafael's expression was giving nothing away. 'It is up to Holly,' he said. 'She is her own person.'

'Of course, of course.' Tomás cocked his head to one side and eyed Holly expectantly.

Holly looked from one to the other of them. She certainly was her own person. But why did this feel like a competition? Or a trap? 'OK, fine.' She made a sudden decision. Better to get everything out into the open. And the packaging did have to be discussed. She turned to Rafael. 'I'll text you later, shall I?' She smiled. She could still feel the warmth of his lips on hers.

His eyes seemed to burn into her. How could Tomás not see the strength of his feelings that he didn't try to hide?

'A very capable person,' he repeated, as if he needed to remind her. 'Yes, of course, please do.' They kissed on both cheeks and said goodbye. Giving no clue to Tomás – Holly hoped – of the sweet shivers running through her at his touch, at the delicious sensation of his breath on her skin.

'In here?' Tomás gestured to the bar he'd just come from.

'Fine.' Holly wondered if she should be nervous.

She waited until he'd ordered the drinks and they'd sat down at a table. Then she leant forwards. 'You're probably wondering why I was with Rafael, after what you told me,' she began. They might as well get the subject done with straightaway.

'I did wonder, yes,' he admitted. 'I did not think you gullible, Holly.' He raised an enquiring eyebrow.

She didn't much like his tone. And Tomás had been drinking, she could tell. 'I asked Rafael about your sister, Valentina,' she went on. 'And he told me it wasn't true. They're not romantically involved, and I have no idea why you told me that they were.'

The other eyebrow shot up at this. 'Well, he would say that,' he said dryly. 'Wouldn't he?'

Holly sipped her beer. It was a fair point, she supposed. But she had believed him. 'Couldn't it all be in Valentina's imagination?' she suggested. Besides, after the kiss they'd shared, she was sure that Rafael couldn't be involved with anyone else. She thought of the way he'd looked at her, the way he'd kissed her. No one could be that good at pretending. 'You know how it is,' she continued. 'A younger girl having a crush on an older guy. He doesn't reciprocate. She creates a fantasy—'

'It is not a fantasy, Holly,' Tomás cut in. 'It is a family agreement. You do not live here in Seville. You do not understand our ways.'

'You're right, I don't.' How could she not agree with him? She'd turned up here only five days ago; she knew nothing about the small community she'd thrown herself into. She still didn't believe it, though. Not of Rafael. Tomás, she was sure, had some ulterior motive.

'Well, then.' He sat back and took a long draught of his beer.

'But he's an adult, I'm an adult, and to be honest, Tomás, I don't take kindly to other people interfering and telling me what to do.' There, she'd said it. Again.

He was watching her closely. 'As you have already told me.' But his features were closed and she couldn't read what he was thinking.

'Exactly,' she said.

'Then I must tell you, Holly, I do not know if my family will want to do business with the woman who seeks to destroy my sister's happiness.'

'I can assure you that's not my intention.' Holly tried to stay calm. 'But according to Rafael, there is no agreement between them.' If only he'd be reasonable. She still wanted Tomás and his mother on board if at all possible.

'I am telling you how it is.' Tomás spread his hands. 'It is not my decision what happens next.'

Holly wasn't having that. 'Tomás,' she began. 'I love your mother's products and I would very much like to stock them in my shop, you know I would. I want to work with you both.' Though she was having her doubts about Tomás, it had to be said. 'But I won't let your family dictate my movements or my decisions.' She took a deep breath. 'Think about it, please, and let me know what you decide.'

She got to her feet too quickly, half stumbling. It was such bad luck to have run into Tomás today. But she meant what she said. And there was no point in talking about packaging or contracts until this was sorted out.

'Holly . . .'

She ignored him, but Tomás followed her out of the bar and onto the street. 'Holly, I hoped—'

'What did you hope?' She turned.

He pulled her into a clumsy embrace. 'I hoped that you and I—'

'Tomás!' He must be drunk. 'For God's sake. What are you doing?'

He didn't let her go. 'Why Rafael?' he murmured into her hair. 'Why him?'

'Goodbye, Tomás.' Holly pulled away and this time he didn't

stop her. He looked so mournful standing there on the cobbles that she almost felt sorry for him. But not quite.

'Think about it, Tomás,' she repeated. 'Let me know by the morning.'

'So that you have time to find someone else,' he said sadly. 'My mother, she will be desolate . . .'

'She doesn't have to be, Tomás. She really doesn't have to be.' And Holly walked away, down the street, back to their hotel.

CHAPTER 29

Ella

Seville, 2018

Ella crossed the metal-arched Triana bridge. The sun was sharp and bright, creating lacy shadows on the pavement. As always, there was a beat of trepidation in her step, but after Tomás's visit to the hotel, after listening to her daughter's account of her conversation with Rafael last night . . . Ella had come to a conclusion. Some people had to be stood up to. Some things had to be faced. There might come a time when you had to stop running from the past. There might come a time when it was necessary to embrace it.

And perhaps for Ella that time had come. She paused halfway across the bridge, as she had done before, leant on the balustrade and looked out across the dense green River Guadalquivir. It was another fine afternoon in Seville and there were canoeists out on the river, people sunning themselves on the banks. Everything seemed peaceful – except for the faster beating of her heart.

Caleb had explained to her something of the nature and history of Triana back in 1988 and Ella hadn't forgotten his words about how they had lived, often in poverty, amongst the blood of the bullfighting and the passion of the flamenco. The music of their soul, he had called it. History shouldn't be forgotten. It was, by definition, someone's story.

Ella had been frightened of seeing Caleb. But why? Now, being here in his territory had altered her perspective. Now, she had become curious. She found herself wanting to know what had happened to him, what he had become. She had plenty of reasons to be curious after all.

He might not even remember her. Ella smiled to herself as she took a right past the bridge and headed for the first ceramic shop en route. Just because his memory had stayed with her, it didn't follow that it had been the same for him. It would be different for Caleb. It always had been different for him.

Perhaps it would be enough to find out how he was, whether he had children, grandchildren even. Or perhaps she would need to see him, just to be sure. If she saw him, what would she feel? Would he be merely an old, bitter-sweet memory? Or would she still be drawn to him just like before?

And then?

She stood outside the ceramic shop. This wasn't the place where Caleb had worked, but he had brought her here, and introduced her to the owners. It was indirect and a little safer; as good a way in as any.

There didn't have to be an 'and then', she told herself. There didn't have to be anything like that at all. She took a deep breath and stepped inside.

The shop hadn't changed a bit. Bold ceramics of red, blue, green and yellow filled the shelves. Patterns of dots and stripes, swirls and squares; motifs of stars, birds and flowers. Bowls, plates, jugs, vases. Old tiles, new tiles; big tiles, small tiles. Everything that could ever be made from ceramic was here.

'*Hola*,' said the young woman behind the counter. 'Can I help? English, yes?'

Amazing, Ella thought, how fluent everyone was these days. It put her to shame. She recalled her previous visit and her stuttering attempts at mastering the Spanish phrases in her guidebook. The Spaniards must have given up on British tourists by now and learnt the English language for themselves – far easier.

'*Hola*,' she said. 'I wonder . . .' She hesitated. Took a deep breath. 'Do you know Caleb García?' How long had it been since she had even spoken his name?

The woman considered, head on one side. 'No, I do not think so,' she said. 'Caleb García, you say? He lives here in Triana, yes?'

'Oh, yes – at least he did.' Ella hadn't been expecting that. As she remembered it, everyone had seemed to know each other in this community. Certainly, Caleb had been greeted with hugs and waves wherever he went. 'But the family name? García? Do you know it?' she persevered.

'Sorry.' The girl shook her head. 'It is not an unusual name. And I do not live here in Triana, you see, I only work in the shop. I live on the other side of the river.'

'Ah.' Once, everyone who worked here lived here, or so it had seemed. So, things had changed much more than had first appeared.

Ella's mobile rang. *Holly*, was her first thought. Ella's instinct was that Rafael was trustworthy and she was glad that her daughter had stood up to Tomás, but something was going on and she was still concerned. However, she saw immediately that it was Felix.

She thanked the woman and took the call as she left the shop. Felix. It was almost as if he had known where she was, what she would be doing.

'Felix. Are you OK?'

'Yes. Why wouldn't I be?' He sounded defensive, which wasn't like him at all.

Ella glanced at her watch. It was three o'clock in England. 'Well, it's the middle of the afternoon. Aren't you at work?'

She heard him sigh. 'I just wanted to check that you were both all right,' he said. 'After what you said yesterday. I just wanted to hear your voice, I suppose.'

'Oh, Felix.' Ella couldn't remember how long it had been since he'd said anything like that to her. She'd thought he'd take their trip to Seville in his stride, that he'd make the most of her absence to do things he might like to do: visit his mother more often, watch more sport on the telly, spend all his time in the garden, that sort of thing. But he seemed on edge, as if he was all too aware of the significance of this trip for Ella.

'We're fine,' she said. 'Holly's gone off to see a candlemaker and I'm having a wander around Triana.' She felt a bit bad about the 'having a wander' bit but she could hardly explain.

'OK,' he said. 'Good.' But he didn't sound OK at all.

'Felix?' she said. 'Is something wrong?' She watched a couple of young men walking down the street, both looking down at their mobile phones. And here she was, on her mobile too. Yes, she thought again. Things had changed.

'I've got some stuff to tell you, that's all,' he said.

Stuff? Ella thought about the old recipe for Seville orange and almond cake still taped into her recipe book. She thought about the photograph too. But it couldn't be that. And these were the only clues.

'But it's nothing serious. It can wait till you get back.'

Nothing serious? A health problem did he mean? If so, it must be a minor one if it wasn't serious. Even so . . . 'Felix, you're worrying me now.'

'Nothing to worry about, I promise.'

'Really?'

'Really.'

'You're not ill?'

'No.' He spoke quickly – to reassure her, she guessed. 'I'm not ill.'

'So . . . ?' She clutched her mobile more tightly.

'They're things that need to be said face to face, Ella,' he said. 'But you'll be home soon.'

'Yes.' She couldn't imagine what these things might be, but she knew Felix well enough to know that he'd made up his mind not to tell her on the phone.

'No more problems with that bloke you were telling me about then?' he asked.

'No,' she said, thinking, *not yet*.

'Good.' He let out another little sigh. 'Right then, I'll let you go.'

'I'll phone you tomorrow,' she said.

'All right. Take care, Ella.'

'I will. Bye bye.'

Ella was thoughtful as she made her way to the ceramic shop where Caleb used to work. Into the lion's den, she thought. It wasn't like Felix to be secretive. And what could he possibly have to tell her that she didn't already know? Didn't she know everything about her husband? Felix was an open book;

he always had been. That had been a big part of the security he'd offered her and she was grateful for it.

She hesitated on the threshold of the shop. Imagined a younger version of Caleb who would look, she guessed, a bit like Rafael – standing by the potter's wheel, moulding a pot, the same look of intensity in his dark eyes. For surely Caleb would have had a family and she couldn't help imagining a son.

Ella put her hand to the door and pushed. Or would it be Caleb himself standing there, much older now, but still working with the ceramics rather than the tourists?

She went in. Stylistically, the shop was very different. The ceramics were still bright and colourful, but the look was much more minimal. The shelves were more spaced out and there was no potter's wheel. This was the biggest shock. She stared at the empty space where it had once stood.

'*Señora?*' A woman of about her own age was standing behind the counter eying her curiously.

She could, thought Ella, be Caleb's wife. Because of course he would have married as well as had a family. A man like him would never have stayed alone.

'*Hola*,' she said. She took a deep breath. The woman was smiling and seemed friendly enough. 'I was looking for Caleb García. I knew him many years ago. I just wanted to say hello.' *Don't gabble, Ella*, she told herself. She didn't have to justify everything.

'Oh, Caleb, yes.' The woman nodded and smiled.

Good. Ella exhaled. So Caleb wasn't just a figment of her imagination. 'Does he still work here?' she enquired. She heard the tremble in her voice and fought to control it.

'Ah, no.' The woman shook her head. 'He moved away some years ago. To Huelva province, I believe. I do not know his address. So sorry.'

Not his wife then. And he had moved to Huelva . . . The place he always went when he needed somewhere to escape to. The memory of that day in Huelva swam back into Ella's head, threatening to overwhelm all the orderliness she usually tried to keep there. A hot sun, a high golden sand dune, the vast blue ocean . . .

'Right. *Gracias.*' She felt relieved – and disappointed. 'And his family?' she asked. She thought of his diminutive mother, his fierce grandmother, the wife and children he might now have.

'I am sorry.' The woman shrugged. 'I do not know.'

So that was that. Ella thanked the woman again and said goodbye. Caleb had moved away and perhaps his family too. So, she needn't have worried about bumping into him; it wasn't going to happen.

Nevertheless, she took a circuitous route around Triana, following her and Caleb's footsteps of all those years ago, looking through the open doorways of cafés and bars, just in case she should spot a familiar face from the past.

She lingered once again outside the church of Santa Ana where there was a wedding. The bride was young and radiant, the groom smart and shy; their guests – the men in dark suits and white shirts, the women in extravagant hats and bold shades of turquoise and fuschia – threw rose-petal confetti and rice and cheered as the couple emerged from the church, blinking in the sunlight.

At last, Ella came to the bar where she had met Caleb's family that last night. She went in and slipped through to the back room, the venue for the family party. It was so very familiar to her, even though it had been so long ago. The walls were still painted deep red and lined with pictures of old

Triana, and the wooden chairs and tables were still placed in a horseshoe shape around the perimeter of the room. For the flamenco, she thought. But Caleb was no longer playing the guitar – at least not here.

Ella looked around the room and felt the memories flood back – the music that'd had such an effect on her, the dancing, the life-defining moment when she had walked out of this door . . .

Back at the bar, she asked about the Garcías once again, but the club had new owners and although they had heard of the family, they didn't know where they had gone.

As Ella was leaving the bar, her mobile rang again and this time it was Holly.

'Hi, darling,' she said.

'Mum? I just wondered where you were? Will you be back soon?' Holly sounded flustered and upset.

Ella felt a rush of concern. 'What is it, Holly? Is everything OK?'

'Yes, everything's fine. But where are you?'

'In Triana.' *Laying that ghost to rest.* But already Ella was making her way towards the bridge. 'I'll be back in twenty minutes,' she promised.

In any case, she had seen enough. She felt deflated that her search had come to a dead end. But at least she had tried. And, who knew, perhaps it was better this way? Not to know, not to face him, to let the past remain buried under the years that had followed.

CHAPTER 30

Ella

Seville, 1988

Ella and Caleb began their tour of 'his Triana' the next day by crossing the Puente de Triana, the oldest bridge in Seville. The decorative metal arches spreading over the wide and densely green River Guadalquivir were already becoming a familiar landmark to Ella. She couldn't help feeling relieved that she no longer had to do her sightseeing alone. Perhaps then she wasn't as independent as she'd hoped. Or perhaps it was just the effect Caleb García was having on her. But she needn't feel disloyal to Felix, she told herself firmly. All she had to do was ensure that Caleb kept his distance and there would be no harm done.

First, Caleb pointed out the Capilla del Carmen, a small chapel with intricate stonework and a pretty ceramic dome situated at the west end of the bridge.

'Carmen?' Ella's ears pricked up.

'Carmen,' he said, 'she is important to us too.'

Ella made a mental note to revisit Carmen's story – it would be so much more interesting now that she knew the landscape behind it.

'There is a unique spirit here in Triana,' Caleb explained as they headed down to the waterfront of Calle Betis. 'This is what I want you to experience.' He paused, as if breathing it in. 'Can you feel it?'

'Yes.' She certainly could. Simply breathing the air made her feel more alive.

Ella looked around her at the bars and cafés lining the riverbank. It wasn't even eleven in the morning and yet already the place was buzzing. This side of the river was less showy and more down to earth, but also more daring in its spirit, whereas the other side of the river – the centre of Seville – was classic and elegant with its gracious buildings and shady parks and orange groves.

She sneaked a look at the man by her side. Caleb was wearing blue jeans and trainers with a yellow T-shirt. His dark hair was as untamed and unruly as ever, his black eyes giving nothing away. Yes, she thought, this side of the river definitely held a hint of danger.

'From here you have the finest views of many landmarks.' Caleb paused, in full tour guide mode now, she noted, and clearly on his best behaviour as promised. 'Such as the Torre del Oro, the bullring, the Giralda.'

It was, she agreed, a bewitching view. And this was a bewitching city. Felix and her life at home, the school, the children, had never seemed further away.

'Why is it called the Tower of Gold?' she asked him. It was an iconic shape; unmistakeable on the skyline.

'The lower part of stone was originally decorated with golden tiles,' he told her.

'Ah, yes, I see.' Even now, the tiles were flashing in the sunlight.

'And some say that once upon a time, the tower was used to store gold plundered from the Incas,' he added. 'Perhaps that is the reason why.'

She nodded. So many facts, so many stories . . . Caleb would make an excellent tour guide, she was sure.

They drank *cortados* in a tiny café nearby and then turned right and away from the more open waterfront into the maze of inner Triana. Caleb shot her one of his deep, probing looks that she was gradually becoming more accustomed to; almost, she thought, as if he were trying to see into her very soul.

'And now,' he said softly. 'We come into the heart.'

Ella blinked at him. *The heart?* Where had he come from, this man, and what exactly was he trying to do to her? She felt as though all her reason, all her good intentions had flown back to England with Felix. But Ella's soul . . . that had remained here.

They were approaching a church and a small square. 'Iglesia de Santa Ana,' Caleb told her. 'This is the oldest church in Seville and a popular place of worship for many who live here in Triana.'

Was this the heart? she wondered.

They went inside and Caleb pointed out various features of note. 'This is the *Pila de los Gitanos*,' he said, gesturing to the stone font.

'Font of the gypsies?' Ella had wondered about the gypsy culture. This *barrio* had been their homeland, their heritage, and yet since the 1970s, she had read, the community had been moved to another area further away from the city – a new housing estate of cheaply built tower blocks on the southern edges of town unoriginally named Las Tres Mil Viviendas,

The Three Thousand Homes. Apparently, it was already a rough area, already renowned for its drugs and its violence as well as its music and creativity. 'But the gypsies don't live in Triana anymore,' she murmured. How had they felt about that? Being shunted from their homes?

'You have heard about this?' Ella couldn't read Caleb's closed expression.

She nodded. 'It must be hard for them,' she ventured.

He nodded. 'Many *Sevillanos* have no time for the *gitanas*,' he said. 'The gypsy culture – it is both revered and shunned.'

'How so?' she asked.

He considered for a moment. 'They are a people who can be rough on the outside, it is true. There is crime, there is violence, for sure, as there is everywhere. But beneath the surface' – he shrugged – 'there is the raw passion, the creativity, the art.' He looked at her closely. 'There have been many hardships for the *gitanas*,' he said. 'Throughout their history, they have been accused of being unconventional and problematic. They have not conformed. They have been marginalised, stereotyped, persecuted and glorified.'

'But they are all individuals too,' Ella suggested.

'*Sí*.' He said this with some feeling. 'The usual *Sevillana* view – it is too generalised, too sweeping. Yes, some gypsies, they are fortune tellers, con artists and thieves. But there are many other hardworking traders at local outdoor markets and in the ceramic workshops. And perhaps in the end, we all share the same common human experience.'

'Perhaps we do,' she said. And what about Caleb? Did he have some gypsy blood running through his veins? She wouldn't be surprised. There was, at times, an intense spirituality about him that took her by surprise. It was there, in the way he played flamenco, the way it seemed to transport him right out of this world . . . He had learnt to let go. He was unlike any man she had ever met in her life. 'And the font?' She reached out to trail her fingers along the stone surface. It was cool and rough to the touch.

'The font is believed to pass on the gift of flamenco song to the children of the faithful,' he told her.

'Were you baptised here?' she teased.

'No.' He chuckled. 'But I only play. I never sing. Although for sure, I would be faithful.'

Interesting, thought Ella, filing this nugget of information away to reflect upon later.

'Why is Triana so different from the rest of Seville, Caleb?' she asked him as they left the church. Her guidebook had given a certain view, but she'd like to hear the perspective of someone who had grown up here. 'Is it just because of the legacy of the gypsy community?'

He gave a little shrug. 'We were for a long time under separate rule,' he said. 'We are the working class. *Gitano* or not, we have lived with the blood of the bullfighting and the intensity of the flamenco.' His dark eyes flared. 'We have been poor and we have been desperate. It is a dark place, yes, but with a strong spirit.'

It was another passionate speech and Ella watched his face while he made it. She felt as if he was describing not just Triana but also himself, his upbringing, his life. And there was a sadness there that intrigued her. Getting to know Triana, she realised, would mean getting to know this man beside her. There was no other way. And there was no holding back.

They continued along Calle Pelay Correa, a narrow and pretty street decorated with flowers and hung with washing drying in the warm sunlight and in the gentle breeze. Ella breathed in the scents of jasmine and fresh laundry, of meat cooking in people's houses ready for lunch, the main meal of the day. The street smells seemed to Ella to invoke the close-knit feel of old Triana. Where Seville was cool and elegant, Triana was the fire in the belly. And as they walked the streets that must be so familiar to him, Caleb continued to talk to her about his home *barrio*; according to him, Triana was not so much a place as a spirit – which included the ritual of bullfighting apparently.

'It is seen as barbaric by many visitors,' he said matter-of-factly, but in a way that suggested he'd be ready to defend the practice if called on to do so.

Ella couldn't help but agree with those visitors; the idea of bullfighting made her shudder. But according to Caleb, the profession had long dominated family life in Triana. Since most local matadors came from this side of the river, it was practically a family legacy.

'Would you like to visit the bullring, Ella?' he asked her.

'No, thank you.' She couldn't think of anything worse.

He seemed surprised. He stopped walking and looked across at her, apparently curious as to why this should be. 'It is very exciting,' he said.

'And very cruel.'

His eyes gleamed. 'For the bull?'

Was he teasing her? She wasn't sure. 'For the matadors and the bull,' she said firmly.

Caleb gave another of his little shrugs. 'It is our tradition,' he explained. 'It is a way for a local boy to make a name for himself. If he does well in the ring, he may be carried on men's shoulders along the river and back over the bridge to Triana. He will have the glory and fame.'

'Hmm.' And if he didn't do well? She supposed that then he'd simply be gored to death and forgotten. This was one practice that illustrated the huge divide between her and Caleb, for Ella would never be able to celebrate bullfighting, no matter what.

They were walking along the Calle Rodrigo, a street lined with buildings of ochre and white. 'And who was Rodrigo?' she asked him. 'One of your matadors?'

He sent her a sidelong glance. 'He was a sailor,' he said. 'An explorer. For in Triana we have many famous explorers too.'

'Of course you do.' Was there anything they didn't have? she wondered. They were certainly an adventurous lot. But she envied Caleb his rootedness. Ella loved West Dorset, but she reckoned she could see its flaws as well as its plus points. It didn't have famous matadors or flamenco dancers, but it had creativity and a love of the land.

'Rodrigo, he was the first to catch sight of the New World,' said Caleb.

'Really? I thought that was Columbus.' Ella remembered the tomb she'd seen in the cathedral. Christopher Columbus and his famous voyages of discovery were well celebrated in this city. And she recalled the rhyme: 'in fourteen hundred and ninety-two, Columbus sailed the ocean blue'.

'*Si*. Exactly. But Rodrigo de Triana, he too was on the epic voyage of 1492,' Caleb told her. 'And he was the first one to see the land – or so they say.'

Hmm. Ella was fascinated by this stream of information, but she also longed for something a bit more personal. How could she get him to open up about himself? she wondered. How could she learn more about the real Caleb and what made him tick?

'And then there is the flamenco,' Ella said, half to herself.

Because that was what seemed to matter to this man more than anything.

'And then there is the flamenco.' Caleb's voice took on a dreamy note.

'So, tell me.' Ella grasped the opportunity. 'Tell me about flamenco.'

This time, Caleb didn't stop walking. If anything, he picked up pace and Ella had to half run to keep up with him. 'It is the music of our soul,' he said simply. 'It is the world of extreme passions – of love, of life, of death. And if you are feeling the pain of loss . . .' He paused to glance at her.

Why did he always seem to see so far inside her? Ella found herself wondering.

'Then it will heal you.'

Had the music of the flamenco healed Caleb? Were the shadows that she could sense in him due to some hurt or loss that he hadn't yet confided to her?

'The tourists, they may see the shows over the river, but here in Triana, our music plays every night. Sometimes a performance such as the one you saw, but more often it is spontaneous.'

'Spontaneous how?'

'How is anything spontaneous, Ella?' A half-smile appeared on his face and she knew he was thinking of the other evening, when they had kissed under the orange trees. 'Some people are eating and drinking perhaps, in a bar or a *freidura* . . .'

'A *freidura*?' She stumbled over the word.

'A *freidura*, *si*, a little one-room restaurant where they serve wonderful seafood fried in oil and washed down with thick red wine from La Mancha.' He smacked his lips together and she laughed.

'And what happens?' She wanted to hug this moment, his words, close to her.

'Someone begins a rhythm, someone begins to sing and someone will dance.' He turned to her. 'Always, someone will dance. Impromptu flamenco is the sound of that spirit of Triana.'

'The flamenco that night was wonderful. I felt . . .' She could hardly describe how she felt. She only knew that she would never forget that performance, that emotional hit, which was so unlike anything she had experienced before. It had gone deeper inside her somehow.

'You are right, Ella.' He caught hold of her hand, just for a moment, before once again he let it go. 'I am happy that you felt it too,' he whispered.

Oh, she felt it too. Just as she felt the warmth from his touch, the frisson that was like a spark of energy, a jolt. But she was married, she reminded herself. And she mustn't think like that.

Before they left Triana, they revisited the ceramic and pottery workshops and talked with some of the workers there. Caleb seemed to know everyone. Everywhere they went, he was greeted with a hearty slap on the back, a hug, a kiss or a cheery wave across the street and a shouted greeting. It was, Ella thought, quite a community. Caleb was right – Triana had a creative vitality about it that was special. And he was very much a part of it.

They ate a delicious lunch of *puntas de solomillo*, Iberian pork sirloin steak, beaten thin, lightly grilled in olive oil and served with coarse grains of sea salt on top of a piece of bread alongside a plate of the usual Spanish croquettes, which Ella had quite fallen in love with. They were simple spheres of béchamel sauce stuffed with anything the chef might fancy, from ham to spinach to squid, and were the tastiest snack ever, in Ella's opinion.

She'd pretty much fallen for the concept of tapas per se – she loved the story behind it, that tapas originated from the 'lids' of bread, cheese or ham served on top of glasses of wine back in the day, though whether this was to keep flies away or, as Caleb suggested, to stop the King getting too drunk at lunchtime, she really couldn't say. It summed up the Spanish for Ella, though – they ate tapas because it meant sharing plates of food while socialising with friends and family – clearly the highlight of any sociable Spaniard's day . . .

'Around the corner,' Caleb said casually, when they'd finished their meal, 'on the Calle Pagés del Corro, I could show you some *corrales de vecinos*, if you are interested?'

'*Corrales de* . . . ?'

'Traditional communal gypsy houses.'

'Oh, yes, I'd love to see those.' They left the bar and made their way to the street he'd mentioned.

Caleb pointed to a rickety and sprawling building with wrought-iron balconies and flowers growing everywhere. 'A large family would live here,' he said. 'On top of one another. All the living spaces and bedrooms lead off from a central courtyard – the home's social hub.' He chuckled. 'It would be used for washing and cooking – and often singing and dancing too.'

Ella tried to imagine. Triana was still a vibrant and special place, but what had it been like only ten years ago, in the late seventies, when the *barrio*'s scruffy but charming yellow, white and blue houses had been full of a thriving gypsy population of potters, sailors, flamenco artists and bullfighters?

They headed back over the river to the Royal Tobacco Factory, pausing to admire the decorative tiles on the high iron railings outside that Caleb had spoken of before. Although the factory was now part of Seville University, it was still possible to wander around the interior and admire the great stone staircases, vaulted ceilings and spacious patios.

'It's like a castle,' Ella said. 'And huge. I can't believe it actually has a moat.'

Caleb laughed. 'And watchtowers.' He pointed them out. 'It was all very serious. The King, he must protect his lucrative tobacco monopoly, do not forget.'

'But of course he must.' As Ella knew, at that time, Seville was Europe's gateway to the New World.

'Three quarters of Europe's cigars were once manufactured here,' Caleb went on. 'Rolled on the thighs of over three thousand *cigarreras*.' He raised his eyebrows and Ella distinctly saw him glance at her thighs – highly visible today in her blue shorts.

She felt the heat rise. 'Only women's thighs?' she asked. And dared a glance at his. He had a good body, there was no denying that. He was lean but not skinny, well muscled but in a way that suggested normal day-to-day exercise rather than hours spent in a gym.

His gaze was challenging. 'Women have daintier fingers.'

Ella couldn't deny that. And she decided not to look at his fingers at this point. It was his hands as he cradled the clay on the potter's wheel that had got her into this in the first place. Whatever 'this' was. 'What was your great-grandmother's name?' she asked instead.

'Rosalía,' he told her.

'That's lovely. And do you think she liked working here?'

He considered. 'Times, they were hard, and it was a job at least, although the production was more mechanised already.'

'And the girls?' she asked.

'The girls were all from a similar class, many of them Roma. Most of them lived in. If they had children, they often took them into work with them.' His expression softened. 'My great-grandmother, she remembers.'

'But it wouldn't have been well paid?'

His laugh was short and lacked humour. 'No, for sure not. The girls even used the silk material that the tobacco was packed in to make clothes, or so the story goes.'

Which would have been colourful at least, Ella supposed. Roma, he had said. So most of the girls were of the gypsy culture then. And Rosalía? What of her? She wondered how they had been treated, this great legion of girls who rolled the cigars at the Royal Tobacco Factory. Like lower class citizens, she suspected, perhaps not even considered respectable, just like Bizet's Carmen. Caleb had already pointed out to her the prison where the workers would spend time if they tried to smuggle out any of the goods. The factory had royal status, Caleb had reminded her, so they could dish out whatever punishments they liked.

Caleb also told her how the tobacco leaves would be dried on the roof then shredded by mills powered by donkeys. Ella only half listened to his words, though she was lulled by the sound of his voice, which was rich and yet gentle. She was thinking of a gypsy girl called Carmen in a red dress who fell madly in love with first a soldier and then a bullfighter – wasn't that how the story went? – before being murdered by her spurned lover. Carmen, the wild and sensual gypsy girl who had lived in Triana, seemed to Ella to epitomise the Spanish spirit of romance.

When they returned to the hotel at the end of the afternoon,

Ella braced herself for what might happen. It seemed to her that they had grown closer today, that learning about Triana and visiting the Royal Tobacco Factory had given her glimpses into Caleb's personal life and past.

But when they arrived, he made no attempt to draw her into the secrecy of the shadowy orange trees with their intoxicating perfume; he clearly had no intention of coming into the hotel or even of continuing their conversation in the more intimate setting of a nearby bar.

'Tomorrow night,' he said, 'my family is having a party. It is an anniversary of my aunt and uncle's wedding. They are the parents of one of my cousins, Sergio, you met him before.'

'Oh, that's nice.' Tomorrow would be Ella's last night. She didn't want to think about that.

'Will you be our guest for the evening?' he asked.

'Really?' Ella didn't know what to say. She had never expected to be invited into the inner sanctum as it were. Perhaps now she might get to meet some more of Caleb's friends and family; perhaps there might even be one of those impromptu flamenco performances he had told her about. She felt almost giddy with excitement.

'Unless,' he added, 'you have made other plans?'

'No, and yes.' She beamed. 'I'd love to. It would be such an honour.' Though this meant, didn't it, that he must have feelings towards her? This meant that, although nothing untoward had happened during the day, Caleb had felt their connection too. Here, though, her imagination ran out of steam. What was she thinking? Because it was all pointless. Nothing could happen between them because she was married. She didn't belong here in any way whatsoever. It was nothing but a fantasy, a dream.

He smiled. 'And in the daytime?'

Ella took a deep breath. 'What would you recommend?'

'That is easy.' He raised an eyebrow in that way he had. 'I will borrow Sergio's car and we can drive to the Huelva district where I spent time as a boy. We can go to the Asperillo Cliffs in the Doñana National Park. They are twelve hectares of high fossil dunes.' He made a gesture with his hand. 'More than a hundred metres high,' he confirmed. 'Formed by wind, rain, sand and other organic materials gradually deposited over the ages, and lifted by the forces of the earth.'

'Crikey.' He made everything sound so exciting, she thought.

'It is very beautiful,' he assured her. 'And it has always been our escape.'

Our escape . . . Ella wasn't sure what he meant by that. Perhaps it was a place that he and his family ran to when the bustle of the city became too much? A bolt-hole? Or could it be some sort of an escape for Ella and Caleb? She pushed the disloyal thought away. 'That sounds lovely,' she said. It would be a relief to get away from the city after so many days spent walking around it. Much as she loved Seville, sightseeing was a tiring business.

'Excellent. At ten then.' He leant closer to give her the lightest of kisses on both cheeks, just an echo of what had gone before.

Ella bit her lip. She hadn't expected more. She didn't want more – it would make things far too confusing. But somewhere deep inside her she couldn't help but feel bitterly disappointed that this time Caleb had not crossed the line.

CHAPTER 31

Holly

Seville, 2018

The last three days had passed in a whirlwind for Holly. There had been more business meetings – with Luciana the candle-maker and with Axel the vintner, as well as a baker of *tortas de aceite*, an olive oil biscuit containing orange, sesame seed, aniseed and wheat flour, with sugar sprinkled on the top so that as the *tortas* are baked the sugar melts and goes crispy. These were a delight, and since each *torta* was handmade, they all looked different, which was perfect for Holly's purpose. The more Holly explored this city, the more orange delights she was finding – olive and orange oil for cooking, orange vinegar, even orange-flavoured icing sugar – perfect for birthday cakes, Holly reckoned.

Terms had mostly been settled on. Even Tomás had come back to her and grudgingly conceded that his family wanted to go ahead with their original agreement. They'd had that chat about changing the packaging of the products and no mention was made of Rafael, Valentina or what had occurred between Holly and Tomás three days before.

Holly had expected him to apologise for making that clumsy pass at her, but he didn't. He was arrogant, she realised. She had given him no reason to think she was interested in him, and after all, he knew about Rafael. So, what was he playing at? But although his decidedly unprofessional behaviour had made her hesitate, Holly had decided to go ahead regardless. She didn't have to have a friendship with Tomás in order to do business with his family, she only needed to have a contract in place, and in any case, Tomás's mother Sofía was the real partner, the person who made the products. Tomás, and Valentina too, would no doubt get over it.

Her second meeting with Axel Gonzáles had been a little strange. Having been keen to do business with her when she'd first contacted him online, he now seemed to be having doubts over whether he could manage to produce enough wine – and he had put the price up too. They talked it over. Holly knew that there were other winemakers producing orange wine but Axel's was a cut above the rest and his was the wine she wanted. Finally, Holly convinced him to go ahead and now the matter seemed settled. But Axel was clearly ill at ease and Holly couldn't help worrying a little. She had thought, during her first few days in Seville, that everything was straightforward – but why should it be? Starting up a business was never easy; she'd learnt that much at least.

In the past few days, Holly had also explored more of the city with her mother. They'd visited the vibrant and colourful Calle Feria traditional indoor food market where the rich, ripe scents of fresh fish, meat, vegetables and flowers followed them down every aisle. And they'd continued out into a flea market running all the way to Plaza de la Encarnación, where they rummaged for antiques and other treasures. They dipped into random churches and chapels that they came upon while wandering the romantic streets of old Seville and they went to see the famous eighteenth-century bullring with its white and ochre Baroque facade. Finally, Holly persuaded her mother to walk with her to Alameda de Hércules where her parents had stayed first time around in Seville.

'Your father wasn't here for the whole holiday,' her mother confided. She'd brought them to the place where they'd stayed and Holly noted the wistfulness in her mother's hazel eyes as she looked at the building, a little run-down but still a functioning hotel.

'Oh?' This was news to Holly. 'Why not?'

Her mother hesitated. 'Your grandmother had a bit of a fall and your dad decided to take the next flight home.' She laughed as she said it, but Holly could tell that this was a hurt that had cut deep.

'I see.' Holly squeezed her mother's hand. She looked out over the ochre concrete benches, past the orange trees and plane trees lining the cobbled Alameda, towards the tall columns at the end of the plaza. As her mother had suggested when they first arrived, this area seemed to be mainly inhabited by locals, congregating in the lively cafés and bars.

She didn't see, of course, not everything. But she could make a guess at how it had been. Holly loved her grandmother, who had been incredibly good to her, but . . . As she'd grown older, Holly had also recognised that the relationship between her mother and her father's mother wasn't the easiest. Both of them seemed to have a grudge to bear.

As for Rafael . . . Holly thought back to last night with him. The playback made her go weak at the knees.

Over the past few days, since that kiss, Holly had seen much more of him. And she now knew for certain that Tomás had been mistaken. Sometimes, when he didn't have to work, Rafael had accompanied them on a sightseeing trip to 'fill in the gaps' as he put it; sometimes he'd joined them for lunch or a drink in a café or bar. But it was the evenings that meant the most to Holly. After dinner with her mother these last two nights, she'd slipped out from the hotel to meet him and they'd driven out of the city to a quiet bar where they'd sat drinking wine and talking into the early hours, sharing their life stories, their ambitions and dreams. He was so different from the men Holly had been out with before. He was funny, but also serious. He seemed keen to open up about his life, to let her in. Every time she saw him, he seemed to draw her closer.

That first evening, Rafael talked a lot about his upbringing, about the death of his father and about the family friend who had become his mentor when he was a young boy; who'd helped him on his pathway through life, become something of a father figure, she supposed. Like Holly's father, Rafael had been compelled to become the man of the house when he was probably too young to take on the role, and Holly felt the growing bond between them strengthen when she heard this. They were from diverse backgrounds, but there were many parallels between them. And an attraction that grew with every day that passed by.

That night, he took her back to the hotel and they kissed under the orange trees – long, sweet kisses punctuated by the heady bitter-sweet scent that filled the orange grove. Holly wanted more, but she also wanted to wait.

The second evening he took her to the same quiet bar, and again they talked and talked, drinking red wine, eating tapas and exchanging kisses.

Rafael was very clear that although he loved the city of his birth and certainly had no immediate plans to leave his friends and family in Seville, he was also hoping to do some travelling at some point in the future.

'Why would you ever want to leave such a beautiful city?' she asked him dreamily.

'Seville is beautiful, yes.' Rafael picked up Holly's hand and stroked the base of her thumb in a way that made it hard for her to concentrate on what he was saying. 'But I also want to travel one day. I want to see more of the world. It is possible for our generation, *si*? We are not trapped by geography.'

Very true. 'And where would you go?' Holly leant back in her chair and regarded him objectively. And would it just be travelling? She couldn't imagine him living anywhere else. Rafael had obvious skills – but where could he make such good use of his ceramic making and flamenco guitar-playing as in Seville? He seemed to belong here; he was very much part of the landscape.

'South America,' he said. 'Scandinavia. The UK.' He shrugged. 'I will have to save up. But I think you can do anything if you are determined to.' He eyed her speculatively, that humorous, half-serious glint in his dark eyes. 'Do you agree?'

It felt as if he was asking her something different, something even more important. 'Yes, I do,' she said. And she felt compelled to lighten the tone. 'But you'd hate the weather in the UK, Rafael.'

'It would depend,' he told her sternly, 'on what else was there.' He clasped her hand more tightly. 'Or who.'

Or who . . . It was the first indication he'd made that he'd like their relationship to continue beyond this short time in Seville. Holly waited. She knew they'd come to another point of significance. This wasn't just a friendship and a few shared kisses; they both knew that.

'Will you come back to my place tonight, Holly?' he asked. 'I want us to be private. I want us to be alone.'

Alone . . . There was a beat as she considered this. She wanted to – oh, how she wanted to. But once she took that step, she knew that she wouldn't be able to hold her emotions in check. She liked Rafael. She liked him an awful lot. And if they were to make love . . . She'd have to go into it knowing that this week together might be all they had. She couldn't possibly expect more. It wasn't realistic. It wasn't practical. But . . .

'Yes,' she said. Because she didn't want this opportunity to pass her by. She wanted to be held by him. She wanted to touch him properly, skin on skin. She wanted to feel whatever it was that was drawing her to him. She wanted to be loved by him, damn it, and she wanted to love him in return. Whatever the consequences might be.

CHAPTER 32

Ella

Seville, 2018

The next day, Holly had no appointments, but Ella was surprised all the same when her daughter suggested that she and Ella go to Córdoba.

'What about Rafael?' she asked her. Ella had been pleading the occasional headache to give them a chance to spend more time together guilt-free; she could see how much Holly liked him, guessed he was never far from her daughter's mind. She still had the occasional pang of concern – what mother wouldn't? – but how could she deny her daughter the right to experience love in Seville?

'He offered to drive us,' Holly admitted. 'But he also let slip that he should be working, so I thought you and I should take the train.'

Secretly, Ella was pleased. And perhaps it would be good for her daughter to spend some time away from Rafael today; it might give her the space to be more objective – to work out if he was what she really wanted. The relationship was hurtling along very fast, Ella felt; understandably, since they knew that very soon they'd be apart. And, more selfishly, Ella was looking forward to having her daughter to herself for a while.

They spent the morning exploring the charming patios and courtyard gardens dotted around La Judería, the old and cobbled part of the city. The streets were too narrow for cars and Ella had the sensation that nothing had changed here for hundreds of years. They admired the little niches and alleys, the intricate wrought-iron gates and balconies, the quaint silversmith workshops, the delicate stone fountains and the lemon and lime trees clambering up trellises in patio gardens, their citrussy scent filling the tiny tiled spaces.

They wandered down to the riverfront and found a restaurant for lunch where they sampled *salmorejo*, a thick, cold, tomato and garlicky soup closely related to gazpacho. For Ella, this dish summed up the wonderful simplicity of Spanish cuisine. They ate it with crusty white bread and fried aubergines with honey, washed down with glasses of cold beer.

'You and Rafael,' Ella said at last, 'you seem to have got very close?' She didn't want to intrude, but she was dying to know how Holly felt about him.

'Oh, Mum.' Holly put down her fork and gazed at her mother.

Stars in her eyes, thought Ella.

'I like him a lot. In fact, I think I'm falling in love with him.'

That was even more than she'd expected. Ella smiled. 'I'm not surprised.' It was strange, she thought, this way history had of repeating itself. Sometimes you might try and change the pattern of events, sometimes you might pretend that things were different . . . But somehow, some predestined order always seemed to prevail. Her daughter had brought Ella to Seville, back to a place of mixed memories, and now Holly was forging links of her own here. Which made Ella feel less guilty somehow.

'And why aren't you surprised?' Holly smiled too, picked up her fork again and dipped into the plate of crispy aubergines.

Ella laughed. 'Because he's charming and attractive and funny and you clearly get on so well. And because . . .' But she stopped there. There was so much more she could say. Too much.

'I know.' Holly gave a little roll of the eyes. 'But it's probably hopeless. I mean, what with me living in Dorset and him in Seville. What am I going to do? Come here for a weekend once a month?' Though even as she said this, her dark eyes shone as if she thought it could work, against all odds.

'There are worse things you could do with your weekends,' Ella said lightly. She thought of Caleb. Of course, that had been a very different situation. She'd been married to Felix; she'd had a duty and a responsibility to do the right thing. Nor would it have been so easy, back then, to sustain a long-distance relationship. Now, though, anything seemed possible.

A thought struck her. 'Holly? You're not contemplating moving to Seville?' Her daughter had always had an impulsive streak – and Ella knew where that came from.

'How could I?' Holly took a sip of her beer. 'I'm opening a shop in Bridport, remember?'

'Yes.' Ella was relieved and grateful for her daughter's sensible side.

'One step at a time, Mum. It's very early days for me and Rafa.'

Ella put her hand on her daughter's arm. 'You're absolutely right,' she said. 'There's no need to make any hasty decisions.' One step at a time was plenty fast enough.

In the afternoon, they visited Córdoba's great mosque, the Mezquita, a dazzling maze of arches and pillars made of granite, jasper and marble, which quite took Ella's breath away. Like much of the great architecture in these Andalusian cities, the mosque had evolved over the centuries since it was built in 785 and it now housed an Italianate cathedral within. There was a grand tower, which they climbed for the panoramic view of the city, and a restful patio with a fountain and orange trees where they sat for a while to recover.

Ella had never forgotten the scent of orange blossom – she felt as if it was always branded in her head, in her heart – but here there was a constant reminder. The irony of her daughter opening Bitter Orange in Bridport was not lost on Ella – it looked as if the fragrance of orange blossom would remain in her life forever.

They headed back to Seville on the train. Holly had arranged to have dinner with Rafael and Ella decided to eat something at the hotel and then relax with a book; she was feeling tired, but happy. Her class, the school, even Felix, felt a million miles away right now and she couldn't believe that in a few days she'd be back there, back home. *Where you belong*, she reminded herself. Where she had always belonged.

Almost as soon as they entered the cool white of the hotel foyer, the phone rang and the receptionist beckoned them over. '*Señorita*?' she addressed Holly. 'It is for you.' She indicated the phone in her hand.

Holly frowned. 'I've only given people my mobile number.' But she went over to take the call.

Ella saw her daughter's expression change and her face go pale. She hurried over to Holly's side. 'What is it?'

Holly shook her head. 'Who is this?' she said into the phone.

But whoever it was must have ended the call. Holly was visibly shaking as she too pressed the red button.

'Holly?' Ella took her arm and led her to one of the cane

chairs on the far side of the foyer. 'What's wrong, darling? Who was that?'

'I don't know.' Holly took a deep breath. 'I'm OK. It was just a shock, that's all.'

'What was? What did they say?'

The colour was gradually returning to Holly's cheeks and now she looked angry rather than upset. She glanced around the foyer, at the white pillars and baby grand piano, but the place was deserted apart from the receptionist tapping away on her keyboard and gazing at her computer screen. 'Don't laugh,' she said, 'but it sounded as if whoever was making the call was disguising his voice.'

Ella wasn't laughing. 'What do you mean? What did he sound like?' she asked.

'His voice – it was deep and gravelly and kind of menacing.' Holly shivered. 'It just didn't sound quite real.'

'Was he speaking in English?' Ella asked. Immediately, her thoughts flew to Tomás Pérez and how he had tried to warn Holly off.

'Yes, but with a heavy accent,' Holly confirmed.

'And what did he say?' Ella was conscious of a feeling of dread. It hadn't finished then, this thing with Tomás, Valentina and Rafael.

'He said if I knew what was good for me, I'd leave Seville and go back to England right now.' Holly gave a little laugh but there was no humour in it.

'And?'

'That was it.' Holly stared at her. 'That's all he said. Then he put down the phone.'

'How ridiculous.' But Ella sounded more confident than she actually felt. What the hell was going on here?

'Yes.' Holly nodded. 'It was a bit. It sounded like a cheesy line from some old movie.'

'But still frightening.' Ella put an arm around her. Your children never stopped being your children, even when they were all grown up and independent, even when they had children of their own. That urge to protect was still there, that unrealistic determination that they should pass through life unscathed. For those few moments, as she held her daughter, Ella felt that fierce protective instinct as strongly as she ever had.

When Holly drew away, her expression was resolute. 'How dare he . . . ?' Her dark eyes blazed.

'Do you think it was Tomás?' Ella ventured.

'I don't know.' Holly looked doubtful. 'It didn't sound like Tomás.'

But she'd said herself that whoever it was had disguised his voice. Why would the caller have done that if Holly didn't know him? And even if it wasn't Tomás, he could easily have got someone else to make the call to the hotel for him.

'What are you going to do, darling?' Ella thought of Rafael. Was he as nice and charming as he seemed? Was there some complication surrounding their relationship that Holly was ignorant of? Was that what this was all about?

Holly sat up straighter. 'I'm not going to let this frighten me away, Mum,' she said.

That's my girl, thought Ella. Although . . .

'We're leaving in a few days anyway. But in the meantime, I won't be threatened. Not by anyone.'

Ella admired her spirit. She was so proud of Holly; she was so much braver than Ella had ever been. 'But you must take care, darling,' she said. And a jolt of fear passed through her, like a premonition. 'Please, promise me – you must take care.'

CHAPTER 33

Felix

Dorset, 2018

'Felix,' said his mother. 'What are you going to do?'

They were drinking tea at her house, though Felix would have appreciated something stronger. Only it wasn't yet six o'clock and his mother had always been strict about that sort of thing. About lots of things . . .

He sipped the tea, served, as always, in the thin porcelain cups with the dark red roses, the lip of the cups so delicate and fine that it was a miracle the set had survived since his childhood days and beyond. Felix glanced across at his mother. Her expression, as he'd anticipated, was stern. She expected something of him, he knew. Perhaps, he thought, the cups simply didn't dare break.

'I'm not sure yet,' he said.

'But you must have thought about it,' she shot back.

'Yes,' he conceded. He'd thought of little else. It had been an earth-shattering discovery. Felix didn't think that was an exaggeration. 'But I haven't decided.' It was his life. He still had choices.

He had received the letter in the post, so now he knew, or thought he knew. Of course, there were always exceptions that proved every rule, but Felix was realistic and he doubted that this would be the case.

'Shouldn't you just ask the obvious question, son?' His mother spoke more gently now and her expression was kind. She knew – of course, she knew – how hard it would be.

'I'm not sure,' he said again. He also wasn't sure that he would want to hear Ella's reply.

His mother gave a little shrug and pulled her lilac cardigan closer around her shoulders. 'Well, it depends if you can live with it, I suppose,' she said.

Could he live with it? Felix stretched out his legs and crossed them at the ankles. He thought that he probably could. The most important thing in his life was his family – his wife, his daughter, his mother too. So, he would always do what he could to keep them. He thought of that photograph he'd found. That had told a story, that photo. But it wasn't always a good idea to rock the boat. Someone – or something – was likely to fall out and be lost forever. 'I think I can,' he told his mother.

'And do you blame me?' She looked so sad now that something inside Felix contracted painfully. 'Because I couldn't bear it if—'

'No,' he said. 'I don't blame you for anything. No one could.'

She looked doubtful about this and Felix knew what she was thinking. 'We'll never know, Mum,' he said. 'What was in Colin's head, I mean.' Why he left all those years ago, why he'd barely stayed in touch. Felix supposed that he could ask his brother, but he doubted Colin would tell him. Things like that happened in families, didn't they, and sometimes there were no clear-cut answers, no matter how much you tortured yourself thinking up reasons why.

Their mother had done what their father had wanted – she wasn't to know how it would backfire. But after that, no wonder she had hesitated before telling Felix – she must have been terrified that history would repeat itself, that Felix too would turn away from her.

'But why now?' he asked his mother. 'Why did you decide to tell me now?' It had come as such a shock – finding out about the cystic fibrosis, understanding fully what it might mean.

'It's not easy to find the right time, son,' she said. 'None of it was ever definite, you see. I knew that I should say something. I knew how your father felt. But everything happened so fast. You and Ella . . .'

Yes, he thought. It had been a whirlwind romance – due to Ella's practical circumstances more than anything else. Despite this, of course his mother should have said something. And if she had done, what then? Felix would have had to tell Ella, he would have had to find out more. He might have lost her . . .

'If I thought you'd been trying . . .' His mother's voice trailed.

Yes, then, he supposed, she would have spoken up. He'd done the research. It would be different these days, but back in the 1980s, there was very little chance of doing anything about it.

'At first I thought it was best to let nature take its course. And then . . .'

Yes, he knew what had happened then. And she was right. It would have been devastating.

'Would you rather I'd kept quiet forever?' she asked him.

He glanced across at her; the blue-eyed gaze was unwavering. She was trying to stay strong, bless her. It couldn't have been easy. So often, Felix's mother was misjudged – often by Ella and occasionally even by Felix himself. Even the most demanding orchid had an awful lot to give when it was good and ready. Felix's love for her was undeniable. But it was complicated. Really, it was his mother who loved too much, who clung on so desperately to those she hadn't lost; his mother who never was able to let go.

Felix sighed. And yet, she had kept her suspicions to herself for years, protecting him, unsure what to do for the best. He'd be a fool not to appreciate that. 'No, Mum,' he reassured her. He always reassured her. That was just one of the things he did.

'It's best, isn't it, to be honest?' Her hands were trembling slightly as she spoke.

She was old. She wouldn't be with them forever. Felix felt the lurch of loss as sharply as if she'd gone already. But he wasn't sure about it always being best to be honest. Best for whom exactly?

He'd met people who prided themselves on their honesty even while their harsh words were hurting someone they loved. He'd met people who liked to confess to their wrongdoings because it made them feel better; a burden lifted, a chance to be forgiven. Honesty could be a selfish thing. And his mother? He watched her now as she sipped her tea. She could be selfish too. Did she want to break something apart? Was she thinking of Felix or did she want him all to herself once again?

'I'm sorry, son,' she said. A tear slipped down her lined and powdery cheek and Felix felt bad for thinking that way. Hadn't she always wanted what was best for him?

He got to his feet and knelt in front of her. 'It's OK, Mum,' he said. He put a comforting hand on her arm. It had been a lot for her to hold on to for so many years.

'I've done wrong, Felix,' she said.

'No.' He didn't want her to think that way.

'And that time when you went to Seville with Ella . . .'

'It was a long time ago,' Felix said. 'And I always understood how you felt.'

She ruffled his hair as if he was a boy again. 'More tea, love?' she asked him.

'I'll get it.'

Felix rose and went over to the coffee table and the tray. 'Me and Ella, we've got a lot to talk about,' he said as he poured two more cups.

'You haven't told her about the redundancy yet then?' his mother asked him.

He brought the tea over. She took the cup and saucer and placed it carefully on the little side table, not spilling a drop.

'No.' He could have mentioned it on the phone, but it had felt all wrong. 'Like you just said, Mum, it wasn't the right time.' And as he'd told Ella, face to face was better, at least for that kind of thing.

'She'll understand,' Felix's mother said. 'It wasn't your fault, love, and she'll see that.'

'I know.' He felt such a failure, though. He wanted to be strong for Ella, he wanted to be successful. And it was old-fashioned, he knew, but he didn't want her job to support them. He sat down again, heavily, in the armchair. 'And by the time she comes home . . .' he began.

'You might have heard about that other job,' his mother said.

'Exactly.' She'd been so concerned that he'd told her in the end. He'd needed to talk it through with someone. Felix had been for an interview yesterday and it had seemed to go well enough. The pay wasn't as good as the garden centre, but he'd be working outside and doing something worthwhile. He'd be over the moon if he got it.

'Fingers crossed, love,' his mother said.

'Yes.' Fingers crossed, he thought.

For a few moments, they sipped their tea in companionable silence.

Felix jumped when his mobile rang. He checked who was calling. 'Ella,' he told his mother.

'Talk of the devil,' she said.

Felix picked up the call. He considered going to another room to talk to her, but his mother wouldn't like that. Maybe he could call her back later? 'Ella? Hi, I'm at Mum's—'

'Felix.' She broke in before he could suggest this. 'I just wanted to tell you what's happened.' She sounded strained and on edge.

'What do you mean?' He frowned. 'Is it Holly?' He knew he should have gone with them, damn it.

'What about Holly?' His mother sat up straighter and put her cup of tea down on the side table again.

Felix shook his head at her. He wasn't about to carry on two conversations at once.

'She had a phone call.' Ella was speaking quickly. 'Some man threatening her – we don't know who.'

'Threatening her?' He heard his voice rising. *His little girl . . .*

'Telling her to go back to England.' Ella was really upset by this, Felix could tell. And he didn't like the sound of it either. Men phoning up his daughter and making threats? What was going on, for heaven's sake? He swore under his breath.

From across the room, his mother made a sound of disapproval and Felix glared at her. 'And are you cutting the trip short?' he demanded. 'Have you contacted the police?'

'No,' she said. 'Holly won't. She doesn't want to give anyone the satisfaction of knowing that she's taking it seriously.'

Felix bristled. 'But she should be taking it seriously. You'll have to contact the police yourself, Ella.'

'I wanted to,' Ella said, 'but Holly made me promise. And we don't have any evidence of who it might be . . .'

'Ella.' Felix made his voice sound commanding, something he'd never really had to do before.

'Yes, Felix?'

'Go to the police,' he said. 'Tell them what happened. Stay together. Keep each other safe. Try to persuade Holly to come home. Now.'

'All right.' She paused. 'But she won't come back until she's ready. She won't let anyone scare her away.'

Felix thought he detected a note of pride in her voice. Now, though, wasn't the time for pride. 'This is our daughter we're talking about, Ella,' he said softly.

'Yes.'

He hoped he'd got through to her. But his mind was racing.

'I have to get off the phone now, Felix,' she said. 'I'll call you tomorrow.'

Felix didn't want to let her go. 'Please take care, darling,' he said.

Her voice softened. 'I will. We will.'

'I miss you,' he told her.

'I miss you too.'

When she'd gone, Felix told his mother what had happened.

'What will you do, Felix?' she asked him again for the second time that day. She looked scared. Her fingers were working nervously together around the buttons of her cardigan.

He got to his feet. 'I'm going home,' he said. 'I'm going to go online and book the first flight I can get.'

She blinked at him. 'You're going out there? To Seville?'

All he wanted to do was keep them safe – his wife, his daughter, the life they'd built. This time he wasn't going to hesitate. He wasn't going to let them down. 'Yes,' he said. 'I'm going out there.'

Rather to his surprise, his mother nodded as if she thoroughly approved. 'Well done, Felix, love,' she said. 'You'll be able to sort it out.'

Felix smiled grimly. He didn't know about that, but at least he would be in the right place to help if needed.

A thought seemed to occur to his mother. 'And will you tell Ella?' she asked.

Yes, he would tell Ella. He'd tell her everything and ask her everything too – though perhaps not straightaway. His mother was right. Felix was done with pretending. He would do it and he would deal with the consequences, whatever they might be. Face to face. That was the only way he could make any of it happen.

CHAPTER 34

Holly

Seville, 2018

Holly and Rafael had agreed to meet in a tapas bar just west of the Alameda. The place was always busy, he had told her, and impossible to book, but he was friendly with one of the waiters who had promised to save them a table. 'It is very special tapas,' Rafael had promised. 'It is an experience you will not forget.'

There had been a few too many experiences she wouldn't forget here in Seville, Holly thought, as she walked down Calle Sierpes. As always, she admired the gorgeous tiled doorways, the flamboyant shops selling everything from clocks to hats and fans to pastries, and the little chapel of San José, tucked down a side street but clear to see with its pretty pink, blue and gold facade. The incense being burnt outside drifted down the street to mingle with the more usual fragrances of coffee, tapas and orange blossom. Some good experiences . . . She thought of the touch of Rafael's hands and lips, the closeness, the chemistry. Some, though, not so good.

She thought back to that voice on the phone. The memory gave her the shivers. Whoever it was hadn't said very much, but the tone had certainly been menacing. Her mother hadn't wanted her to even go out tonight, but Holly refused to be intimidated.

'Get a taxi there then, won't you, darling?'

And seeing the concern in her mother's eyes, Holly had agreed, even though she knew already she would do no such thing. She wanted to walk; she needed to think.

Surely Tomás couldn't be responsible for this? Yes, he'd tried to come between her and Rafael, but Holly could hardly blame him for that, given that Valentina harboured such an obvious infatuation. And yes, he'd overstepped the mark when he'd tried to kiss her. But would he have threatened her just to get her to leave Seville? She thought not. And she hoped not. But how well did she know any of them – Rafael included? Who could she really trust?

Once again, her mind drifted into playback, into what had happened between her and Rafael last night. She wanted to trust him so badly.

There had been a strange kind of innocence in his face as he'd touched her, as he'd kissed her. 'Are you sure, Holly?' he had asked and she was oddly moved by this.

It seemed to confirm what she wanted to believe – that he wasn't looking for a one-night stand, that he wasn't just into her because she was a foreigner who would soon be gone, leaving him free again; an experience to add to many others, all of them insignificant and fleeting.

But what was she thinking? Holly stopped in her tracks. She only had Tomás's word about Rafael seducing tourists. It was so ridiculous; such old hat in this day and age. When she talked to Rafael, when she looked at him, the truth seemed very different.

It had to be more than that, she thought, remembering how they had slowly undressed each other, looking into one another's eyes. It had to be much more than that. He had been both passionate and tender. So, why not stop worrying? Why not concentrate on grasping the moment, on loving him?

It had been so good that since then it had been hard to stop thinking about him. She smiled to herself. She couldn't wait to see him to do it all over again.

Rafael was waiting for her at the bar. He greeted her with a lingering kiss on the lips. And a quick glance of concern. 'Are you OK, Holly?' He touched her shoulder.

'Yes. Sorry I'm late.' What with the phone call and the discussion with her mother that had followed, time had run away with her.

'It does not matter,' he assured her. 'I was a little worried. I should have come to the hotel to pick you up, but I was working late, and—'

'I'm fine, Rafa. Honestly.' She brushed the back of her hand gently against his cheek. Though she wasn't and it clearly showed.

His brow cleared. 'A glass of wine then.' He led her to their table inside. The bar was unlike many of those she'd visited up till now with their decorative tiles, old photos on the walls and hams hanging from the ceiling. This was a cool and contemporary space with ice-blue walls, a sleek, polished granite bar and steel chairs.

The red wine from Cadiz was rich and fruity and her first few sips helped Holly unwind.

'How was your day?' Rafael asked, after they'd perused the

menu and ordered a whole string of tapas which Holly was sure would be far too much. Rafael had already told her that the tapas bar prided itself on combining tradition with modernity and that it had won prizes for some of its dishes, especially the egg on boletus and truffle cake and the cheese emulsion with tomato bread, anchovies and green olives. But there were still plenty of the old favourites, such as homemade croquettes and grilled razor clams. Holly and Rafael had ordered a combination of both.

'Eventful.' Holly told him about Córdoba and then, after a brief hesitation, the phone call. She wanted to trust him, but still, she found herself watching for his reaction.

'What?' He stared at her. 'He said what to you?'

Holly repeated the words once more. Rafael was clearly horrified. Of course, he knew nothing about it. She breathed a sigh of relief. How could she have even imagined that he could be involved with anything so horrid? She put a hand to her head. All this was getting to her. What had begun as an innocent business trip to Seville was becoming something darker. Darker and also – she glanced at Rafael – more passionate.

'But I do not understand.' Rafael frowned. 'Why would anyone—?' He broke off as the tapas arrived, two by two.

Holly breathed in deeply. Everything smelt delicious and it was no doubt exactly what she needed. 'I have no idea,' she said, when the waitress had left their table.

'Tomás?' He rolled the name around on his tongue. His dark eyes glittered.

'I really don't think so.' Holly hadn't told him about Tomás's clumsy pass and she didn't intend to. It would only cause more problems between the two men.

'Who then?'

Holly shook her head.

'Have you . . .' – he paused – 'upset somebody?' He began to spoon some of the tapas onto her plate. Artichokes with fried garlic and cod shavings, small deep-fried sardines, a pastry brick shaped like a cigar with cuttlefish and algae. 'Not on purpose,' he added quickly.

Holly raised an eyebrow. 'I don't think so,' she said. 'Not unless you have any other secret admirers.'

He didn't smile. 'You must go to the police, Holly,' he said. 'I will come with you to help translate.'

'Thanks, Rafael, but no.' Holly took her first bite of the cuttlefish. It was delicate and delicious. 'I'm not going to the police,' she said. 'And I'm not cutting short my trip either.' She refused to be scared off. She had a job to do here and no one was going to ruin it for her.

'But—'

She shook her head. 'It was probably nothing,' she said. 'Someone messing about, that's all.' Maybe one of Valentina's friends trying to do the girl a favour by getting rid of her rival. 'I'm not sure we should take it too seriously.'

'At least,' he said, 'I am glad you are not leaving Seville right away, Holly.' He leant forwards. 'Tell me how he sounded again?'

Perhaps he wanted to do some detective work of his own. At any rate, Holly was glad she'd told him and she was also glad of his warm arm around her as they strolled back to the hotel after dinner. It was past midnight, they had lingered over the tapas and the wine, talking into the night and finishing off their meal with a chocolate cake with orange essence and coffee liqueurs.

As they walked, every few minutes he drew her into a dark

doorway or narrow alleyway to kiss her; long sweet kisses that left her weak with wanting him.

Finally, they got back to the orange grove by the hotel. One more kiss and then . . .

'I will wait here until you go inside,' he said.

Holly laughed. 'Don't you want to come in with me?' The intoxicating fragrance of the orange blossom seemed to have taken over all her senses and she was feeling bold.

His dark pupils flared. 'But your mother? What would she think of me?'

'She's very liberal. She wouldn't mind.' Holly had the feeling that her mother was pleased for her. Though admittedly, it might not be ideal if she were to walk in on them in the morning.

'You are very tempting, Holly.' He touched the tip of her nose. 'You are a seductress, I think.'

She grinned. *If only . . .*

'But I must go. I have work early tomorrow morning. Before that, there is a man I must see. And I do not want your mother to think badly of me.' He looked so earnest that she had to laugh.

'OK,' she said. 'Have it your own way.' If only he knew how she was aching for him. But he must know. It was in every touch, every kiss.

'But tomorrow,' he said. 'Can you and your mother come to my workshop in the afternoon?'

Holly was intrigued. 'Yes, we can do that.' She had some calls to make in the morning and she had an appointment with Axel at eleven, but after that, she was free. 'Do you have something special to show us?' she teased.

'Yes,' he said and his expression was serious once again. 'Yes, I do. And then after that . . .'

'After that?' Her heart seemed to skip a beat.

'After that we can be alone,' he promised. And he dropped a last kiss onto her lips. '*Buenos noches*. Goodnight, Holly.'

'Goodnight, Rafa.'

Holly was floating as she walked up the single flight of stairs to her bedroom. The hotel was quiet apart from the soft trickle of water from the marble fountain, the receptionist nowhere in sight – or maybe even in bed by now for it was almost one a.m.

It had been a perfect evening – or at least it would have been if . . . Her mind waltzed off on a tangent and she leant against the wall of the corridor, chuckling softly to herself. There was so little time left. Really, Rafael had shown remarkable restraint. Unfortunately . . .

Her bedroom door was unlocked. Which was odd, because she was sure she'd locked it. Holly frowned. Maybe her mother had needed something and asked the receptionist to open it for her? But she would certainly have made sure to lock it afterwards. Especially after that anonymous phone call.

Holly took a deep breath. She opened the door slowly, cautiously, but of course the room was empty. She exhaled loudly, peered into the en-suite bathroom just in case. Nothing. No one. She sighed. She'd let that damned call get to her. She must have left the door unlocked herself. *Stupid* . . .

She washed her face and cleaned her teeth. She got undressed and slipped her cotton nightdress over her head.

But something wasn't right. She stopped still in the middle of the room. Something felt . . . out of place.

She went over to the desk where she'd left all her paperwork and her laptop. The laptop was open – had she forgotten to close it? – and the paperwork . . . ? Was that how she had left it? Hadn't she squared up the pile, left a Post-it note on top to remind her about the appointment with Axel tomorrow morning? The Post-it note had gone.

She wasn't imagining things. Someone had been in her room, Holly knew it. Someone had been looking through her stuff. She shivered. The same someone who'd made that threatening phone call? Instinctively, she went to the window, looked down into the square. The orange grove was dense and dark, there was not a soul to be seen. Whoever it was, they were long gone and she was sure they wouldn't be coming back.

Holly sat down heavily on the bed. She felt violated. She switched on the bedside lamp. Who had been in here? And what did they want? It was the middle of the night and so things always seemed much worse than they really were. Even so . . . Holly didn't expect to get too much sleep tonight. And tomorrow? Tomorrow, she told herself firmly, was another day.

CHAPTER 35

Ella

Seville, 1988

The countryside beyond the city was made up of olive groves, orchards and agricultural fields and Ella relaxed as Caleb drove, occasionally pointing out landmarks as they passed. They didn't talk much, which suited her; though there were few people with whom she could feel comfortable enough just sitting quietly after such a short acquaintance. She didn't want to think too much about what that meant.

Gradually, the landscape changed again into pale bamboo, dark pine trees and the bright mustard yellow of flowering mimosa growing thick and high up on the banks. Caleb pointed out the fruit farms and the storks nesting at the top of the pines. They bypassed Huelva and drove past windswept Mazagón on the Costa de la Luz.

'And now for a short detour,' said Caleb.

In minutes they had arrived at El Rocío. Ella couldn't believe it. Was this place for real? They got out of the car and wandered along broad streets made up of drifting sand.

'We are on the edge of the Doñana marshes,' Caleb told her. 'But we can get something to eat here before we go down to the beach.'

'OK.' Ella blinked as she looked up. A flock of birds were flying low across the plaza. 'Are those . . . ?'

'Flamingos, *si*.' He shrugged. 'This place is like going back in time.'

It certainly was. Or the filmset of a Western. Ella had already spotted a couple of men on horseback and every house seemed to have a hitching post. She had never seen anywhere quite like it.

They ate a simple tapas lunch of *espinacas con garbanzos*, a hearty, traditional stew of cooked spinach, chickpeas, cumin and garlic, washed down with beer, sitting outside a small bar in the main plaza. It was enough, Ella thought, to watch this particular world go by. Weird, but definitely good weird.

After lunch, they walked back to the car and drove a short distance to their next destination. Caleb parked just off the main road, not in a designated car park, but in a small clearing half hidden by pine trees. Theirs was the only vehicle. 'And here are the Asperillo Cliffs of Doñana,' he said. 'The area is a national park, and one of Europe's greatest wetlands. Again, it is very different from Seville, *non*?'

Ella had to agree that this too seemed a million miles from the city. The scent of the pines and scrubland hung in the air and the place seemed deserted.

'We will walk past the dried-up lake to the high dune at Asperillo,' he said. 'This leads to a very special place.'

Ella was intrigued. 'When did you used to come here?' she asked him as they strolled along the soft sand path scribbled with lizard trails, past low, flat pines and prickly juniper trees that had rooted deep into the shifting dunes.

'When I was a boy.' He led the way down the narrow path. 'At weekends with my family. Mostly I came here with my brother Francisco to swim and make camp.'

Ella was surprised. 'I didn't even know you had a brother.' And why should she? There was so much she didn't know about this man. And yet, here she was walking into the wilderness with him. All around her were sand and juniper, interspersed with gorse bushes and acid-yellow broom. It was an isolated and wild landscape, but there was a sense of tranquillity that drew her.

'I do not have a brother.' His voice almost broke and she heard the starkness behind it. 'Not now.'

'Oh, Caleb.' Ella stopped walking. She didn't know what to say. What did he mean? Had there been a huge family falling-out? Or was it worse than that? 'What happened?'

Caleb stopped walking too. He turned to face her. Into the heavy silence around them the sudden screech of a seabird cut the air. 'He died.' His bleak words dropped into the space between them.

'How?' she whispered.

Caleb turned and walked on. Ella followed and almost immediately the path widened out so that they could walk side by side. Lavender and rock roses grew thick and low in the sand beside the path and their sweet heavy scent filled her nostrils. She waited, aware from his set expression that Caleb was trying to compose himself.

'I have not explained to you everything about Triana,' he said at last.

'What do you mean?'

'It is all the things I told you.' Caleb sighed. He half turned towards her. 'But it has a darker history too. It has sometimes been a bad place. There has been over the years much crime.'

'And your brother was involved in that?' The sand under her feet was becoming more golden, finer and softer and Ella guessed that they were getting closer to the sea. She imagined that if she closed her eyes, she would almost hear the waves rolling onto the shore.

Caleb paused and looked up at the deep blue sky as if it might provide him with some answers. '*Si*. He got involved with some bad people – criminals, I suppose you must call them, a gang.' He walked on, faster now. 'Many men were desperate,' he explained. 'Their families were poor, they would do anything to make money, to survive.'

'I see.' Ella understood how difficult it must have been. But what sort of criminals was he talking about? And had Caleb become involved with them too? Despite the warmth of the day, she felt a small shiver run through her at this thought.

'My father – he died only the year before this happened,' Caleb went on.

'I'm sorry.' Ella knew only too well from her own experience how much such a loss could affect a family.

Caleb nodded in acknowledgement. 'And my brother Francisco, he was angry. Very angry.'

Anger seemed to have no place in this peaceful landscape, but perhaps anger and grief could be a little soothed by it, Ella thought. 'What did he do?' she asked.

Caleb shrugged. 'Whatever they wanted him to do. Whatever they did. Dealing drugs, stealing cars, vandalism, theft . . .

Anything to make money and everything my father would have hated.'

'What about your mother?' Ella wondered aloud. They were still walking side by side on the sandy trail and she couldn't fully read his expression, especially behind his sunglasses. 'What did she say?' She must have been devastated – to lose first her husband and then her son, albeit in different ways.

'She tried to stop him, of course,' Caleb said. 'She cried, she shouted, she threatened, she pleaded. She called in relatives, old family friends, anyone who might be able to calm him down.'

'But no one could?' Ella supposed he was too far gone for that. There must have been so much pressure on him, and perhaps a sense that nothing really mattered anymore.

Caleb pushed aside a bush of wild rosemary that was partially blocking their path and indicated for Ella to go through. As she did so, she smelt the scent of it, almost overpowering as it mingled with the salty sea air.

'No one could,' he confirmed. 'The irony is, I think he was just getting it out of his system.' He walked on beside her. 'I think Francisco was reaching that point at rock bottom when you have to maybe start going up, you know?'

Ella nodded. She knew.

'I tried to stop him too.' Caleb shot his dark and restless glance towards her. 'And on that last night, he promised to stay in with me and practise guitar. He swore he would do that.' His voice broke.

Ella wanted to stop him walking. She wanted to put her arms around him and hold him. The urge to do so was strong. But how could she? It wasn't her place to do any such thing, she reminded herself. 'But he didn't stay in?' she asked softly.

'He could not.' Caleb's voice was strung with frustration as if he was reliving that time. Perhaps he relived it every time he spoke of it. 'One of them came to the house.' He swore under his breath. 'I heard them arguing. Francisco came back up to me. 'One last time,' he said. 'I'm sorry, Caleb, but I have to go.'

'And what happened?' Though Ella could hardly bear to hear.

'There was a car crash.'

'Oh, no.'

'But yes.' Now, at last, Caleb stopped walking. 'Francisco and the man who came to our house, they stole a Mercedes from some rich guy outside a club in town. They went a bit crazy. The other man, he had some coke. Francisco was driving. He had maybe had a few beers, that is all. We do not know exactly what happened. But there was a head-on collision. They both died and the man in the other car, he died also – on impact they said.' He spoke the words matter-of-factly but the intensity of his emotion was there in his set expression, the hard lines of his mouth.

Ella put a hand on his arm. 'I'm so, so sorry, Caleb,' she said again. She wanted to reach out to him, wanted it so badly . . .

'Yes.' He shot her a grateful look. 'I do not talk about it much, you know? As a family we do not talk of it either. But it broke my mama's heart. Broke us all for a while. And Mama . . .' His voice tailed off.

How did you get over such a loss? You could move forward, Ella knew, but you could never move on exactly. She was silent. But Caleb had taken a step away from her and the moment for comforting him had gone. Perhaps, she thought, that was a good thing.

'I never had a brother,' she said at last. 'I suppose you have to remember the happy times you shared?'

'Exactly.' His expression changed as he pointed down the path. Ella could hear birdsong now and a sea breeze was gently lifting the ends of her hair. 'We have almost reached the ocean,' he said. 'Come.'

She followed him, but instead of arriving at the beach, they came to a cliff edge. 'Oh, my God.' Ella realised that they were on the very top, the edge of a very high sand dune. Well, he had warned her. A hundred metres high, hadn't he said? She looked down. The sea glittered far below them. How on earth could they reach the water from here?

'Do not be scared.' Once again, he beckoned her to the edge. 'This is where I come to remember.'

'Here?'

He shook his head and pointed once again. 'Down there,' he said.

'But, how can we . . . ?' Ella felt a bolt of fear. She'd never been brilliant with heights and there was no way she could climb down this massively steep sand dune. She'd fall to her death.

'Trust me,' he said.

Ella wanted to. But now, he was most definitely asking much too much.

CHAPTER 36

Ella

Seville, 1988

She watched as he swiftly climbed a few feet to a fence, where a thick rope had been wound around the wood. She stayed exactly where she was.

'Come here, Ella,' he said. 'Please.'

She took a hesitant step closer. Was she crazy? She thought for a moment of Felix and what he would say if he could see her now and she thought of her life living with his mother that was slowly driving her insane. She smothered a giggle. Maybe it was hysterical but Caleb took it for a 'yes'. Another two steps and she was beside him.

He tied the rope around her waist. 'I go first,' he said. 'You are above me. You will not fall, trust me, but if you do, I am there. All you do is walk normally down the sand and hold on to the rope at the same time.' He paused. 'And do not look down.'

Ella bit her lip. *Walk normally? Do not look down?* It was

practically a precipice. But she allowed him to tie the rope and, as he did so, she looked into his face. He had told her about his brother and she would trust him, she decided. And just hope she lived to tell the tale.

Slowly, gradually, they began walking backwards down the golden and grey sandy cliff-dune, holding the rope. Ella was aware of Caleb just below her, murmuring soft words of encouragement. She stayed calm. One step at a time, she thought. His voice was reassuring, the soft sand felt safe enough. And she would not look down.

'Very good,' he said. 'We are almost there. Just hold on and . . .'

Ouff. They landed on their feet in the sand, not on the beach but on another wooded path with the shore in front of them and the blue sheen of the ocean in the distance beyond.

Caleb took her hand and Ella was relieved because she felt so dizzy. But she felt exhilarated too. She had done it, she was down.

He pointed back at the cliff. 'See the colours,' he said softly. 'They change according to the quality of the light, the time of day.'

'Yes.' She could make out so many different shades of red, yellow, white, ochre and black on cliff walls that were as smooth as caramel in the sunlight. Evidence, she supposed, of how the dunes had been formed.

'Like us, the dunes are continually changing,' he said softly. 'Evolving with the wind and the waves.'

He was still holding her hand and Ella did not pull away. They walked along a path scented with rosemary and pine resin. 'Oh.' Ella stopped walking. Strung between two pine trees in a small clearing was a wide string hammock and from another tree hung a wooden swing made from an old car tyre.

There was a bench and a makeshift table and a small bivouac made of wood.

He let go of her hand. 'Our camp,' he said.

Ella smiled. 'How lovely,' she murmured. It was charming. A secret, hidden retreat. Above the hammock, a windchime made of old fishing net and shells moved and tinkled in the breeze and the carpet on the floor was made up of fallen pine needles. Little wild marigolds and purple thistles grew between the junipers and the pines. In front of them, the broad expanse of sandy beach was deserted. 'What a fabulous location,' she said. Though these words did not in any way do it justice. It was, in fact, a piece of paradise.

'*Si*. You are right.' Caleb took a blanket from his backpack and laid it out on the ground. 'A drink perhaps?' he suggested.

Ella smiled as she watched him produce an insulated cold bag from the backpack which he unzipped to reveal two bottles of beer. 'You've thought of everything,' she remarked.

'Shall we sit?' he said.

They sat on the blanket on the soft pine needles and Ella took the beer he handed to her. The scents of the wild herbs and the pine trees were in her head and, in the distance, she could hear the surf, see the sun glimmering onto the ocean. Ella took a swig of the beer. She didn't think she had ever been anywhere so magical.

'And you, Ella?' he asked her some minutes later. He had stretched out on the blanket now and she was trying not to stare at his flat stomach, at the hard, lean muscles of his upper arms lit up by the filtered rays of the sun as it shone through the branches of the trees above.

'Me?'

'You.' Without warning, he leant up on one elbow, reached

across and tucked a strand of hair away from her face. It was a very intimate gesture.

'You have not always been happy?'

'True.' She kept her voice light. He'd obviously worked that much out. But she wasn't ready to confide – not yet.

'And are you happy now?'

Million-dollar question. Ella sighed. She looked out to sea. Now, at this moment in time, she was content, sitting drinking beer on a blanket amongst the pine needles on the ground, gazing at the ocean, warmed by the sun. But she knew that wasn't what Caleb meant at all.

'My father died when I was seven. That was a big loss for me,' she managed to say.

He nodded encouragingly. 'Yes, of course it was, I know.'

Ella took a deep breath. The sound of the sea was a gentle hiss and a roll in the distance, but it was still calming somehow. 'Me and Mum, we were so sad to lose him, but somehow it never got too bad to bear, because we were a team.' She remembered so well that feeling of solidarity, that knowledge that there was someone who would always be there when needed. She tried to explain. 'We lifted each other up when the other one was feeling down.' Like an emotional see-saw.

'For my family it was like that too,' he said.

Yes, of course, it would have been. How strange it was, she thought, that they had similar experiences of loss and had been drawn together to talk about it. 'But then she met someone,' she went on. Ella couldn't think about her stepfather Kenny without a bad taste sliding into her mouth. 'He wasn't cruel exactly.' Though in certain ways, he was. 'He didn't hit me or anything,' she amended. 'But suddenly, my mum and me, well, we weren't a team anymore.'

'She changed sides?'

'Sort of. She wasn't there for me any longer, at least not in the same way. She stopped thinking about what was best for me. She was too busy thinking about him.' Ella could hear the bitterness in her own voice.

'Perhaps she was scared of him,' Caleb said. 'Perhaps she needed his support and that was the only way to get it.'

'Maybe.' But that didn't stop Ella from feeling betrayed.

'And your husband?' he asked.

She'd known that was coming. 'We met when things at home were getting worse. I wanted to go to teacher training college. Kenny, my stepfather, wanted me to go out to work and bring some money into the house. I just wanted to leave home. But I couldn't get a grant and . . .' Her voice trailed.

'And your mother?'

'She wanted what Kenny wanted.' And Ella didn't think she'd ever forgiven her for that.

'To keep things smooth?' Caleb suggested.

She knew what he meant. The path of least resistance. But Ella had wanted her mother to be a warrior, not a doormat.

'So, finally you met someone who would be on your team for good – was that it?' he asked.

Ella supposed that it was. She put the bottle to her lips and drained the last of her beer. 'Felix offered me an escape route,' she admitted. She put the empty bottle on the ground beside her. 'He proposed. I accepted. Getting married meant that I could move in with him and his mother. We both knew she would never have accepted things otherwise.'

They had discussed it, Ella and Felix. He knew only too well how awful things were at home – she'd only invited him there for supper once and it hadn't gone well; Kenny had ended up picking an argument with Ella's mother, reducing her to tears in front of her daughter's new boyfriend. Felix, Ella knew, had been horrified. 'Which meant I could leave home,' she added.

Caleb's dark eyes widened. 'But you loved him?'

'Oh, yes, I loved him.' Ella wasn't that calculating. She could never have married Felix if not for love. Though now, she wondered how true it all was. What was love really? Viewed in context, part of her feeling for Felix had been connected to the promise of leaving home, though how connected it was, she couldn't say. Perhaps she had loved him partly because he was her escape route. She had been overwhelmingly grateful, she knew that.

'And now?' he whispered.

Ella had been waiting for that question. It had hung unasked since they had arrived in this place. Caleb had shown her somewhere that was special to him; he had shared with her the place that was inextricably linked to the brother he'd adored and the special times they'd spent together. The significance of that wasn't lost on Ella.

'I wanted to come to Seville to save our marriage.' It sounded ridiculously dramatic, even when she just said it to herself in her head. But that's how it was. And she would be honest, she decided.

'Because things were wrong between the two of you?' His voice wasn't giving anything away.

'Yes.' She thought of those things that had gone wrong. 'Since we've lived at Felix's mother's house, gradually everything's become different from the way it was.'

'You have no space to yourselves, no privacy?'

Ella looked around their little hideaway to the vast expanse of beach and ocean. There was certainly privacy here – the best kind of privacy.

'It's not just that,' she said, conscious of a feeling of betrayal. 'Everything's become so predictable, so ordinary.' *Sorry, Felix*, she thought, but that was the truth, and she didn't understand how it had even happened. 'I love my job. But my life with Felix . . . There's no fun in our lives.' She hesitated. 'No passion.'

'That too?' He raised his eyebrows. 'But, lovely Ella, can you not talk about this with your husband? Can you not find a better way to share your lives? One that would make you both happy?'

Miserably, she shook her head. If only it were that simple. 'I thought that coming here would help,' she said. Whereas in fact, it had only made things an awful lot more complicated.

'If your love, your marriage is worth saving . . .' He let the words hang.

Was it? 'I don't know anymore,' she admitted. She told him how Felix had rushed back to the UK when his mother twisted her ankle on the stairs. She probably shouldn't be saying all this, Ella knew that. But after the way in which Caleb had confided in her earlier, after the trust she'd put in him to get down here to the woodland beach hideout, she couldn't help herself. And it was such a relief to finally talk about it. At school, she talked to her colleague Viv sometimes, but she was a relatively new friend and Ella was still cautious about saying too much. After everything Felix and his mother had done for her, it simply didn't seem fair.

But Caleb had touched a raw nerve. Somehow, he had got to her.

'And he just left you here?' He sounded shocked now.

'He didn't want to leave me . . .' She had to defend Felix. Though even as she did so, she looked at Caleb, half mesmerised by the dark intensity of his gaze. Spanish eyes. And she thought of the jewellery box her mother had given her. The song had played while the flamenco dancer twirled around. 'But I wanted to stay.'

He picked up her hand and began to play absent-mindedly with her fingers. *Wasn't that crossing the line?* He seemed, however, totally unaware of the effect his touch was having on her.

'I am very glad that you did not leave Seville,' he said softly.

Just a boy and a girl on a deserted beach. She smiled. 'If not me, there would be some other girl . . .' And it should be some other girl, because she, Ella, was taken.

'No.' His voice was sharp. 'You are not just "some girl" to me, Ella.'

'No?'

'No.'

It was dangerous territory. She looked up and his face was so close, his lips so near. He smelt of rosemary, of pine resin and of the ocean.

'Ella,' he said, and his voice seemed to caress her name. 'You know that you are very much more to me than that.'

CHAPTER 37

Holly

Seville, 2018

Somehow, Holly slept for a few hours. The next morning her mobile rang before she'd even got dressed.

It was Tomás.

She picked up. She waited . . .

'I cannot believe it, Holly,' he said. He sounded very upset. 'I thought we had a business arrangement. What are you doing? How can you think it? Why do you send your *guard dog*' – he almost spat the words – 'to see me in the middle of the night? What the hell is going on, Holly?'

She might ask him the same thing. 'Guard dog?' she repeated weakly.

'You must have told him to come, *sí*? You must have known. It was one o'clock in the morning. And my family . . .'

'Rafael.' It was only just after seven and she'd hardly slept. Holly's mind wasn't yet ready for this conversation. She looked around the hotel room. It didn't seem to belong to her anymore.

'Rafael, *sí*.' Tomás cursed. With some feeling, it had to be said.

Holly groaned. So that was why Rafa hadn't wanted to come back with her last night. He'd already concluded that Tomás was responsible for that phone call. And he'd obviously decided to confront him straightaway. At one o'clock in the morning. *Honestly* . . .

'I had a phone call,' she told Tomás. And that wasn't all. She sat down at her desk and stared at the paperwork which had been rearranged by the intruder.

'So I heard,' he growled back at her.

'A threatening phone call,' she clarified. 'Telling me to leave Seville. I was very upset.' Surely he could understand that? 'But I didn't tell Rafael it had anything to do with you, Tomás.' In fact, if she remembered rightly, she'd said the opposite.

'Hmm.' He sounded slightly mollified. 'But that swine Rafael Delgado – he thought I was the one responsible, for sure.'

Had he really? She supposed he must have. 'Maybe he was just checking.'

'Checking?' he flung back at her. 'At one in the morning?'

OK, it was weak, but the best Holly could manage under the circumstances. 'Oh, I don't know, Tomás.' She flipped through the paperwork. 'I'll speak to him, I promise.' Why would whoever it was have taken the Post-it note? Or had it got dislodged somehow? She peered under the desk. Nothing.

Tomás grunted and swore under his breath.

'I'm so sorry.' Holly didn't know what else to say. 'I hope he didn't wake everybody up.' But of course, he would have. Even the Spanish didn't normally stay up that late.

'Holly, he woke the entire family, and the neighbours too. He hammered on our front door, damn him.'

'I'm really sorry, Tomás,' Holly said again. She pushed the paperwork to one side. She could understand why Tomás was angry, but she too was still upset. And annoyed. And frustrated too. Not only had Rafael wasted a perfectly good opportunity for them to be alone together, for them to make love . . . For a moment, her thoughts wandered.

But he had also jeopardised a perfectly good business arrangement – albeit one that had been fraught with problems from the start. He shouldn't have done that. He had no right to interfere. OK, he must have thought he was helping, he must have assumed that because Holly was female, she needed his protection. But she was an independent woman. And she *didn't* need his protection. At least . . .

She put her head in her hands. Added to all that, she had a headache from too much red wine.

'Maybe he is a fool,' Tomás said. 'And I too am a fool for thinking he was a friend. First, Valentina . . .'

'Please don't start that again, Tomás.' Holly sat back in the chair. She was exhausted and she hadn't even had breakfast yet.

'And now this.' He still sounded very offended.

'You did warn me off, though, Tomás,' Holly felt compelled to say. They couldn't entirely blame Rafael for making assumptions. It had occurred to Holly too, though she had dismissed the idea.

'I warned you about Rafael Delgado,' he agreed. He paused, as if silently adding, *and now you can see why*. 'I did *not* warn you to leave Seville.'

This was undeniably true.

'You're right, Tomás.' Holly kept her voice steady. 'Rafael shouldn't have come charging round to accuse you of anything – and especially not in the middle of the night. But please believe me when I tell you that I didn't ask him to and I had no clue that he was going to.'

'And you do not think I had anything to do with that awful phone call?' he asked. 'Honestly?'

'No, I don't.' Holly was firm. She never had, not really, and she certainly didn't now. Tomás was far too outraged. She thought about telling him the latest development – that someone had broken into her hotel room – but decided against it. Perhaps the fewer people that knew about that, the better.

'Good.' Tomás sounded satisfied at last. 'So, who was it then?'

Holly groaned. 'I don't know, Tomás,' she said wearily. Though she really wished she did.

Once she was dressed and ready to go down to breakfast, Holly called Rafael.

'I am so very sorry, Holly,' he said as soon as he picked up.

'You should be,' she told him. 'Tomás is furious and I don't blame him. I'm surprised he's still willing to do business with me, to be honest.'

'I was worried,' he said. 'I did it for you.'

'I know that.' Holly softened. She was even grateful for that protective instinct; it was nice to feel cared for, after all, especially given what was happening right now. No matter how independent she wanted to be, everyone needed someone to look out for them occasionally. 'But I thought we agreed that Tomás wasn't responsible?' As she was talking, Holly threw a few things in her bag.

'Who knows?' He still sounded unconvinced. 'I wanted to find out for sure.'

'What happened when you went round there?' she asked him.

'I woke him up.'

Yes, she knew that much already. 'And?'

'I demanded an explanation.'

Holly shook her head in despair. 'What did he say?'

She could almost hear him shrug. 'He did not have a clue what I was talking about.'

'Right. And did you believe him?' Holly hoped so. She didn't want any recurrence.

'Maybe,' he conceded.

'You should do,' she told him. They might not be best friends, but it wasn't a great idea for Rafael to antagonise Tomás further. They lived in the same district after all, probably knew a lot of the same people, went to the same parties and bars.

'OK,' he said.

'Promise me you won't go round there again?'

'*Sí*. I promise.'

'Good.' That was all she could do really.

'And now, Holly, you are OK, yes? You had a good night?' Rafael's voice was soft once more; once again he was the attentive lover. There seemed to be so many different roles available to him. It must be the Mediterranean temperament, Holly decided.

But with Rafael too she decided to keep quiet about the break-in. Nothing seemed to have been taken – with the possible exception of a Post-it note – and God knows what else Rafael might be capable of, if he was in full-on protective mode. 'I'm fine,' she said. 'But I have to go now. I'll see you later at the workshop.'

'Holly,' he said.

'Yes, Rafa?'

'Take care.'

*

Over breakfast, Holly told her mother what had happened the night before and as soon as they'd finished their meal, they informed the hotel manager. He was suitably horrified. He would ask all the hotel staff if they knew anything about it, he said. They would change the locks too.

But Holly had already noticed that spare room keys were kept in an unlocked drawer under the reception counter, so presumably when the receptionist was no longer on duty at night, it would be easy enough to sneak into the foyer and pick up a key?

She pointed this out to the manager, who had to agree that this was a possibility.

'Perhaps the keys should be kept in a locked safe,' Holly's mother suggested. 'So that we can all sleep peacefully in our beds at night.'

'*Si, señora*,' the hotel manager agreed. 'I am so sorry. You are quite right. I will arrange it myself.'

Over breakfast, Holly had agreed to her mother's insistence that they tell the police about the break-in. This was more than a threatening phone call; this was an intrusion, a criminal act, and as such it held a menace that was much more insidious.

And so, after they'd spoken to the hotel manager, Holly and her mother headed to the police station. They explained everything with some difficulty to a Spanish policeman who took copious notes, kept them there for two hours and then strongly advised them to keep themselves to themselves and to leave Seville at the earliest opportunity.

'I suppose there's nothing more they can do,' Holly said to her mother as they left the building. After all, the intruder was long gone. But still, she felt better for reporting it.

Their next stop was at Axel Gonzáles the winemaker's,

where talks went much as they had done before. Axel seemed pleased to see them, continued to be enthusiastic about the business opportunity and the idea of the English sampling his orange wine, and insisted on them trying his latest, an orange and sparkling variety which was super fresh and fizzy and went straight to Holly's head in a not unpleasant way. Hair of the dog, she thought. It wasn't even midday.

He showed them inside the bodega where a strong smell of fruity alcohol emanated from rows of wooden barrels, explained his traditional process of fractional blending and how he added the bitter Seville orange peel at a certain stage, in order to give the wine its distinctive bitter-sweet tang. He nodded and smiled a lot and even agreed to Holly's terms.

At which point, as she got down to the question of the costs, the figures and the ordering, he began looking around him from left to right, just as he had done before, as if he expected someone to appear from behind the dark wood panelling or pop up from under the battered counter.

Holly met her mother's curious glance. Something clicked. 'Is there a problem, Axel?' Holly asked. 'You seem a little tense.'

'No, no, no problem.' But he was fiddling with the corkscrew that he'd left on the counter now, twisting it between anxious fingers.

Another glance passed between Holly and her mother. Holly guessed that their thoughts were running along the same lines.

'Are you worried about anything?' Holly persisted.

'Worried?' His brown eyes flickered nervously. 'Not worried, no. Why should I be worried?'

Holly hesitated. She could be wrong, but Axel was the one producer who seemed hesitant about closing their deal. And so . . .

‘Is someone bothering you?’ she asked. ‘Has anyone spoken to you – about me, I mean?’ How could she put this exactly?

‘I say nothing,’ said Axel. ‘Nothing.’

Another glance passed between the two women. Holly was sure now that her instinct was correct.

‘Have you had any trouble?’ her mother put in. ‘About supplying my daughter with your wine, I mean. You can tell us.’

‘Trouble?’ Axel’s eyes widened still further. He looked once again from left to right. ‘No trouble,’ he said.

‘So . . . ?’ Holly pushed the paperwork towards him. ‘Can we agree on a deal? Because I’m going home soon, you know, and we need to finalise this before I leave.’

‘Yes,’ he said. ‘I think, yes. Only . . .’

‘There are other winemakers,’ Holly’s mother said softly. ‘Maybe, we should—’

‘No.’ Axel squared his shoulders. ‘We will do it. And to hell with the consequences.’

The consequences? Holly frowned. That was very dramatic. But . . . She shrugged at her mother. He was a strange man. But his wine was very special. This was a business arrangement. And the quality was key.

After lunch in a café in Triana, and already feeling slightly frazzled after the events of the night and the day – not to mention the effects of Axel’s wine – Holly and her mother made their way to Rafael’s workshop. What did he have to show them? Although she was looking forward to seeing him, Holly wasn’t sure she could cope with any more surprises today.

‘Holly. Ella. Come in.’ Rafael was all smiles and warm welcome. He hugged Holly close, whispered ‘sorry’ again in her ear.

She put her hand on his shoulder and leant in. He smelt of paint and clay. 'Forgiven,' she whispered back.

He beamed. 'I wanted to introduce you both to someone.' He cleared his throat. 'The man who has been my mentor through the past years. The man who helped look after my family after my father died. The man I have to thank for everything – the ceramics, for teaching me to play the flamenco guitar. In fact, he has taught me everything I know.' He seemed very emotional.

'Wow, Rafa, that's some introduction.' A man stepped out of the shadows of the corner of the workshop and came over towards them. Rafael embraced him.

He was older, of course, and his dark hair was salt and pepper grey. But his eyes were dark and intense and Holly could see that he was still a good-looking man.

'This is Holly.' Rafael held out his hand and when Holly took it, he pulled her forwards.

'Holly?' The man smiled and then something in his expression changed. He frowned and then looked from Holly to Rafael and back again. He seemed confused. 'So pleased to meet you at last, Holly,' he said. 'I think of Rafa here as more of a son, you know.'

'And this is Holly's mother, Ella,' said Rafael.

Holly turned as her mother stepped forwards. There was an expression in her mother's eyes that she didn't recognise.

The older man stepped forwards too. He seemed mesmerised. He took Holly's mother's hands in his and just stared at her.

'Hello, Caleb,' Holly's mother said. And a smile stretched across her face like an unexpected beam of sunlight.

'Ella,' he said, and his voice was soft, like a caress. 'Is it really you?'

CHAPTER 38

Ella

Seville, 1988

It was Ella's last night in Seville. And what a night it promised to be.

She dressed with care in a blue skirt that had a bit of a flounce to it, a white silky top and the sandals with the ankle strap. She wrapped herself in a multicoloured fringed shawl she'd bought in Santa Cruz. It made her feel . . .

She hesitated to even think it. But it made her feel as if she belonged.

She added hoop earrings, and applied mascara and a frosted blue eyeshadow which she blended with grey in the inside corners. Her lipstick was earth red. Ella regarded herself in the mirror. With her dark hair and tanned skin, she looked almost like a Spanish *señorita*.

'Oh, Ella,' she whispered. Because she wasn't a Spanish *señorita*. But the excitement dancing in her eyes, the glow on her skin betrayed exactly what she had done. Would everyone be able to tell? And what in heaven's name was she going to do now?

After their shared confidences in the hideout at the Asperillo dune beach, Ella and Caleb had made love.

It had been inevitable, she supposed now. The moment that she felt his lips on hers, the warm touch of his hand on her bare shoulder that sent a slow thrill juddering through her entire body . . . She hadn't been able to break away from him like before. She hadn't wanted to.

Instead he had kissed her, the scent of pine-needle resin on his lips and in the salty air all around and it had seemed like the sweetest thing.

They drew apart and stared at one another. She recognised the flame of passion in his dark eyes and knew that it would be mirrored by her own. 'Caleb.' She whispered his name, tasted it on her tongue.

'Are you certain that this is what you want, Ella?' He was waiting for her. She knew he would pull back if she asked him to. But she didn't. Every inch of her wanted him. Every inch of her seemed to have liquefied into desire.

'Yes. Yes, it's what I want.'

They made love with an urgency almost shocking in its intensity, as if they'd been waiting for each other months or even years, not days. His touch seemed to burn into her, but it wasn't enough; she wanted more, so much more.

When it was over, she was still breathless from it. A feeling of completion stole through her. She trailed her hand over his shoulder, marvelling at the smoothness of his skin, at the feeling in her fingertips. Lovemaking had never been like this with Felix, not even in the early days. And for Ella, there had only ever been Felix. Brief fumbles with other boys in her mid-teens had never amounted to much, until him.

But this. This, then, was what it could be. How would she ever have known?

Afterwards, they ran down to the sea hand in hand, shrieking with exuberance and with that sense of being so wonderfully alive, every last pore of them. They splashed into the shallows, the water cool and inviting on their hot skin. He let go of her hand and dived under, then up to the surface again, droplets of water standing proud on his shoulders, his hair wet and sleek as seal skin, his eyes shining jet black.

They swam and they laughed. They floated on their backs looking up into the blue depths of the cloudless sky and then he lifted her from the water and rained soft, damp kisses all over her body until she begged him to stop. It wasn't enough, and it was far too much. It was Ella's most perfect hour and she had no clue what to do with it or what would come next. All she could think of was now.

They ran back up the beach, their bodies already drying in the sun, and up to the hideout where they made love again.

Ella recalled how their gazes had locked in intensity. 'Already?' she'd mouthed.

'Always,' he'd replied.

Was she quite mad?

Now, Ella touched her red lips. Underneath the make-up, they were bruised by Caleb's lips; she felt that they would be forever. The radiance of their lovemaking was burnt into her skin. Everyone would see it. Everyone would know. And Felix? How could she have betrayed him so easily? How could she have moved so far away from him so quickly? How could she have made love with another man?

She waited for the guilt, and it came, washing over her in great waves that she almost wished she could drown in. But the drowning she had done had been done today, with Caleb. It was no excuse to say that it had seemed like a different time, another world – though it had. Felix had chosen to leave Seville, but that was no excuse either. Even the fact that her marriage had seemed to be falling apart . . . There was no excuse, no reason and Ella would have to live with that.

All she knew was that being with Caleb had seemed right; with him she had felt different, as if he was the missing ingredient she'd always been half looking for. Like Seville, he made her feel alive.

On the way back to the city in the car, Caleb had held her hand; if he had to let go to change gear, he swiftly picked it up again, as if her hand could hold her to him, as if holding her hand would mean that she'd never leave him.

'Tonight, Ella,' he said, when he dropped her at her hotel.

'Tonight,' she'd agreed. Caleb had to help his family with preparations and so Sergio, who was doing any driving that needed to be done, was picking her up as he had done before. It had been less than a week ago and yet now she felt transformed. She had become a different person and so she asked herself yet again – what now?

It was the evening of the family party. Ella would meet Caleb's mother and grandmother. Caleb would be playing flamenco guitar. They would never be able to hide what had happened between them. Everyone would know. And yet that seemed unimportant. What was important, though, was that tonight would be their last time together. It was a painful thought.

She slipped the wedding ring from her finger. *Just for tonight*, she told herself.

Because tomorrow . . . Tomorrow she would be gone.

CHAPTER 39

Ella

Seville, 2018

She should have guessed. Ella felt the warmth of his hands and remembered that warmth from long ago. It had always been so hard to forget. She looked into his dark eyes and remembered how he had looked at her then – as if he wanted to save and recall every last square inch of her forever. That gaze of his had haunted her. Had he remembered her that well? From the way he was looking at her now, from the way he hadn't let go of her hands, she suspected so. *Oh, Caleb*, she thought.

'It's really me,' she said. 'How are you, Caleb?'

He nodded and seemed to recover his composure. He let go of her hands at least. 'I am well,' he said. But he didn't stop looking at her. 'And you, Ella?'

'Yes.' She was still smiling, she realised. *Just the way he said her name . . .* 'Yes, I'm well. It's good to see you.' And it was. She felt transported back thirty years. It all seemed like yesterday.

'You two know each other?' Rafael's surprised voice broke into the tension, the memories of before.

'*Sí*.' At last, Caleb looked away. His gaze fixed on Rafael, then lingered on Holly, then switched back to Ella. 'From a long time ago.'

'Would that be the last time you came to Seville, Mum?' Holly's voice was harsh, almost accusing. 'With Dad, I mean.'

Ella flinched. Suddenly, she couldn't stay here, in this room, with him, with the two young people, with the past. It was overwhelming. 'I'm sorry,' she blurted. 'I have to go. I have a terrible headache.'

'Again?' Holly's voice cut through her. 'You seem to be having a lot of headaches lately, Mum. Funny, that.'

'Yes, it must be the sun.' Ella decided to ignore the sarcasm in her daughter's voice – for now. *Running away* . . . She ignored that voice too. She made her way to the door, not daring to look at Caleb. 'I'll explain later,' she threw over her shoulder to Holly. In seconds, she had escaped once more into the fresh air of the warm Seville afternoon.

Ella hurried away. She hadn't been expecting it. She hadn't been remotely prepared. For heaven's sake. Caleb and Rafael. There'd been so many parallels between the two men, between Ella's experiences back then and Holly's now. She recalled her concern when they'd first met Rafael at the flamenco, when it had first struck her that he and Caleb might even be related. Apart from the possibility that he was Caleb's son . . . this was the biggest parallel of all.

She scurried down the main road, oblivious to the people, the occasional street performer that she would normally linger to listen to; barely noticing fragrances of Spanish tapas and orange trees that usually made her walk more slowly so that she could savour them to the full. She just needed to get away.

And yet it all made perfect sense. The ceramics connection, the flamenco guitar, the closed community of Triana . . .

'Ella!'

She heard his voice. Paused. Turned.

'Ella,' he said again. 'Wait!'

He hurried towards her. He looked very different, she thought, and yet the essence of him was exactly the same. And he had aged well. His dark hair looked good with a smattering of white and grey, he was still in shape – although there was perhaps a little more weight around the belly – and his dark eyes might not be as youthful, but they still burnt with the same intensity as before.

'What is it, Caleb?' she asked when he reached her. Part of her longed to speak with him, to find out all the things she really wanted to know. And part of her wanted to escape. Just like before, she thought.

'I want to talk to you,' he said. 'I need to talk to you.'

She couldn't deny him that. 'All right,' she said. She looked around. What should they do? Go to one of these crowded street cafés or bars? It wasn't ideal.

'We should get away from here,' he said. He seemed about to take her arm, but instead made a gesture that suggested they should walk on.

'OK. But I really do need to get back to the hotel.' Nevertheless, they fell easily into step, just as they had always done.

'Ella . . .' He turned towards her, but seemed lost for words. 'You stayed with your husband then?'

Was he asking if she was still with him? 'Yes,' she said. Felix. For a moment, Ella's pace slowed. What would Felix be doing now? she wondered. He'd be at work in his office in the garden centre, she supposed, wishing he was outside in the open air with his beloved plants. 'And you?' She dared a quick look across at Caleb. 'You're married?'

'I was married, yes.' His eyes clouded. 'My wife died two years ago. Before that, she was ill for a year. She had cancer.' He looked away into the distance towards the Triana Bridge and the river, but she could see his pain. He had loved her then. Ella was glad. She'd only ever wanted good things for Caleb, only ever wanted him to be happy.

'I'm so sorry, Caleb.' Tentatively, she touched his arm. 'Do you have children?'

He shot her a glance. 'A son and a daughter. And you?'

'Just Holly,' she said quickly. Ella had wanted more, but it wasn't to be. And in some ways that was no bad thing. She and Felix had been able to give Holly more than they might otherwise have been able to.

'And Holly . . . ?'

Ella didn't want to go there. She didn't want him to get too close to her other life in England. 'You left Triana then?' she asked him instead. They crossed the road towards the bridge and he didn't take her arm. 'I never thought you would.' He had seemed to belong here so completely. Caleb and his family – they had been an integral part of the community of Triana.

And now Ella and Caleb were standing by the bridge, on the edge of Triana as it were. It was quieter here now that they were off the main street. They paused and he gave the little shrug she remembered.

'Our family, we had our problems,' he said sadly. 'My grandmother died, my mother too . . . I met my wife in Huelva.' He sneaked a glance at Ella and she had to smile. Huelva, of all places. 'So, we lived there, brought up the children there. For a long time, I came back here to Triana every day to work, and then there was Rafa to look out for . . .' His smile was fond as he spoke of Rafael. 'But my family – they were happier in the country.'

'You always said it was your refuge,' Ella murmured. She looked out towards the dense green of the Guadalquivir River, lit up in the afternoon sun. 'The place you were happiest.' She recalled what he had told her that day they went to the dunes in Huelva province. About his brother, the good times in Huelva before his brother died. Though she didn't want to dwell for too long on that afternoon at the Asperillo dune.

'It was, yes.' He looked at her appraisingly, as if surprised she remembered. 'How did you know I'd left Triana?' he asked. 'Did Rafa tell you?'

'No.' Ella shook her head. 'Rafael never mentioned you by name. Maybe he did to Holly, but . . .'

'She would not have known who I was.'

'No, she wouldn't have known. I've never talked of you.' It was pretty obvious why. And now Ella had an awful lot of explaining to do to her daughter.

'Rafa did not mention your name either,' Caleb told her. 'Just Holly this and Holly that and the fact that she had travelled here to Seville with her mother. He is quite smitten, you know.'

'They both are,' she agreed. In the distance, on the other side of the river, she could see the Torre del Oro, the old defence tower, now a maritime museum. In the old days, the young Caleb would have stood here on the banks of the Guadalquivir, pointing out all these landmarks, telling her their history, practising his skills as a tour guide. Now, though . . .

‘So how did you know, Ella?’ he asked her, not letting it drop. ‘How did you know I had left Triana?’

Ella was hesitant. ‘I asked around,’ she admitted. ‘I wanted to . . .’

‘See me again?’ He reached for her hand. He was smiling.

She laughed, but evaded him. ‘You have a high opinion of yourself,’ she teased. But it was a relief that the atmosphere between them had lightened. ‘I just wanted to know what had happened to you, that’s all,’ she said. ‘How you were, how your life had turned out. You know.’

‘I know,’ he said. ‘I wondered about you too – often, I wondered.’

Ella thought about how reluctant she had been to come back here to Seville. She had been scared, of course. But she saw now that she’d had nothing to be scared of, not really. Seeing Caleb was wonderful and the time they’d had together back in the day had been wonderful too. It always would be. Time would never erase that particular memory.

‘Shall we get a drink somewhere?’ he suggested.

But she shook her head. ‘I don’t think so,’ she said. ‘Like I said, I do need to get back to the hotel.’ She might not have a headache, but Ella was still feeling overwhelmed. After trying not to think about the past for so many years, it was pretty shocking when all of a sudden it caught up with you. Literally.

‘Then may I at least walk you back to your hotel and tell you something of how my life has been?’ he asked.

And Ella realised that she didn’t want him to go just yet; there was more she’d like to know. So, ‘Yes,’ she said. ‘That would be lovely.’

As they walked back over the bridge and towards the cobbled streets of Santa Cruz, Ella and Caleb exchanged stories.

Ella told him about her work, about the children she taught, and how things had changed in the classroom since the last time they'd met. She spoke of Dorset and even a bit about Felix.

Caleb told her that after she left, he had indeed worked as a tour guide for a while, but ultimately returned to his first love – ceramics – which he had continued to make for most of his life. He told her how his best friend Antonio – Rafael's father – had died and how he had tried to support the family and help Rafael find his way.

Ella remembered Antonio; a young man as vibrant and alive as Caleb had been.

He spoke of Mariana, the woman he had married, and he told Ella about his two grown-up children; his daughter already had two boys of her own, so they paused while he got out his phone and showed Ella pictures.

'Oh, my,' she said when they came to a picture of Caleb's daughter. And they exchanged a long look before she turned her head away.

They walked on through the maze of narrow streets. They might even, she thought, be just two friends reminiscing about old times. Only they weren't just friends, they had never been just friends and Ella was all too aware of this.

There was still a tension between them, a spark of expectancy that had always been there and never gone away.

'But what am I thinking of?' Caleb suddenly said. 'Rafa, he told me that there has been a problem for you, for Holly. A phone call, he said. A threat of some kind?' There was a deep frown on his face now. 'I will help if I can,' he told her.

'It's got worse since then,' Ella admitted. Now, she was more worried than ever – about Holly, about whoever was trying to frighten her daughter and force them to leave Seville.

'What has happened?'

Ella told him that someone had apparently broken into Holly's hotel room and gone through her things. She told him about Holly's business plans and why they'd come to Seville. Even just telling Caleb was beginning to make her feel better about it all. They passed the flamenco museum and one of the little bars where she and Holly had eaten tapas on more than one occasion. Ella would miss all this, she realised. The warmth, the food, the scent of orange blossom all around . . .

'You did not come back here only to see me then?' he said and put on a sad face.

'The opposite,' she confessed. 'I was terrified of running into you.'

'Am I so scary?'

Ella considered this. 'Actually, yes,' she concluded. Though she wouldn't tell him why.

And finally, she told him about Tomás and their rather odd business meeting with Axel Gonzáles, the winemaker. But he knew, Caleb told her, about Tomás. Rafael had told him already, including the fact that he'd charged round there last night. 'The boy, he is impulsive.' Caleb shook his head sadly.

Ella couldn't help laughing at this. 'Why does he remind me so much of you?'

'Ah.' Caleb pushed down his sunglasses and gave her a sharp look. 'His father Antonio and I were so alike – we could have been brothers.

'You could, yes.' Ella recalled that last night at the flamenco when Caleb had introduced them. Hadn't she thought exactly that at the time?

'But this is worrying,' said Caleb. He glanced down the road and this time he took Ella's arm as they crossed the street.

'Yes, it is.' It felt so strange, his light touch, after all these years. 'What do you think's behind it? Or who?' She'd been right to tell him, Ella was sure. Caleb knew Triana and its ways much better than she or Holly. He had been part of the community for so many years.

'Leave it with me.' They passed an old chapel and a little tiled patio full of terracotta pots and trailing geraniums blossoming in bunches of red and white. Caleb seemed deep in thought. 'I will ask around – discreetly, of course – and see what I can discover.'

'Thanks so much, Caleb.' A sense of relief washed over her. Briefly, once again, she touched his arm.

He glanced across at her, still serious. 'It is nothing, Ella,' he said. 'If anything happened to you – or to Holly . . .' – his expression darkened – 'I would never forgive myself.'

'I should give you my number.' Ella pulled out her phone. 'If you find out anything . . .'

'Yes,' he said. 'Do not worry. I will contact you immediately.'

As they arrived at the orange grove beside their hotel, she and Caleb paused as one. It was such a sweet area – the oranges filling the air with their citrus perfume, the little pathways and archways all leading to the central point of the garden – a deep stone well. On one side of the plaza opposite their hotel, was an old palace with stained glass and wrought-iron balconies next to the French consulate building with the old millstones built into the vintage-pink painted wall; on another side was an ancient monastery with crumbling stone. It was the cutest dead-end road Ella had ever seen – and of course it reminded her of that other hotel, that other time, those other orange trees.

'We have talked of so many things, Ella,' said Caleb. 'And yet we have not yet spoken of the night you left Seville.'

Ella had been expecting this. But it was so long ago, she had been hoping he might leave it be. 'I'm sorry for leaving like that, Caleb,' she said.

'Without saying goodbye,' he reminded her.

'Without saying goodbye.' Though he knew, didn't he, how hard it would have been to say goodbye?

'If you hadn't left the party that night . . .' he said.

There was a pause, a beat of silence. 'I might not have left Seville at all.'

He nodded in acknowledgement of this. 'Or, if you had come back later . . .' He let the words hang.

Ella knew exactly what he was saying. 'Both of our lives would have ended up very differently,' she said. It was obvious enough, but perhaps it had to be acknowledged.

'Yes.' For a few moments, they stared at one another again as they had done earlier in Rafael's workshop, knowing and unknowing. Were they both considering those sliding-door possibilities? Those 'if I had' moments that changed a direction and a life? *Felix*, she thought.

'And now?' he asked.

She had been wondering if he would ask this. She supposed that was why she hadn't wanted to go to a bar with him, why she had run away. Because she was still drawn to Caleb; perhaps she always would be. 'Now?' she whispered.

'Is it too late for us, Ella?'

It couldn't be un-said and she couldn't pretend not to understand. Ella looked out, away from the orange trees, towards the cobbled streets of the Old Town. But she had made the choice. 'I was married, Caleb.' Ella spoke clearly as if she could transmit this truth to them both. 'And I still am.'

'Ella!'

Ella thought she was hearing things. Then she thought she

was seeing things. Because it was Felix's voice and Felix himself was striding over the cobbles towards the orange grove. Ella breathed in the overwhelming citrus perfume. She felt dizzy. It was impossible. Felix couldn't be here – and yet he was.

'So, there you are.' He sounded angry. Well, of course he was angry. Here was his wife loitering in an orange grove with another man.

Ella took a deliberate step away from Caleb, which made her realise just how close together they had been standing. 'Felix. What on earth are you—?'

'Catching up on old times, no doubt.' He glared at Caleb. 'And why should I be surprised about that? He's been in our married life for over thirty years.'

'What?' Ella was at a loss. How did he know about Caleb? Felix didn't seem to be behaving like Felix at all. Ella had never seen him so angry. He was on fire.

He thrust his hand into his pocket and pulled out a battered photo. He practically threw it at Ella.

'You kept it?' It was Caleb's turn to look at her. 'All these years?'

'Yes, all these years,' Felix snapped. 'And now, if you'll excuse me – whoever you are – I wish to talk to my wife alone.'

Ella blinked at him.

'Of course.' Caleb seemed to be waiting for Ella to speak, but words wouldn't come.

'It was good to see you, Ella,' he said at last.

Couldn't he see he was making things worse? Why didn't he just go? 'And you, Caleb,' she said. 'Goodbye.'

And then Ella and Felix were finally alone.

CHAPTER 40

Holly

Seville, 2018

Rafael looked at Holly and Holly looked at Rafael.

'What is going on?' he asked.

'You tell me.' Holly was furious. With Rafael for springing this on them – and maybe she hadn't forgiven him for going to see Tomás after all – with this man Caleb, whoever he might be, and most of all with her mother.

The man, Caleb, had left the workshop a minute ago with a muttered excuse. He'd gone haring off to find Holly's mother, no doubt. And it was obvious why. Her mother had quite clearly had some sort of a relationship with him the last time she had visited Seville. When she had come here with Holly's father! How could she have done such a thing? Especially when Holly's father had been compelled to return to Dorset early when poor Grandma had that fall.

Holly remembered what her mother had told her in Alameda de Hércules. Holly had thought she understood. But she hadn't understood at all. How could her mother be so heartless? So shameless? Holly was shaking. She paced from one side of the cluttered workshop to the other.

'Calm down, *mi cariña*,' said Rafael. '*Tranquila*.'

Holly glared at him. How could she be calm, having made a discovery like this? Her mother – and this man, Caleb? No wonder her mother had been so worried about coming here. Terrified her secret would be revealed, no doubt.

'But how do they know each other?' Poor Rafael was completely at a loss.

Holly promptly forgave him again. She stopped pacing and went over to him. She held on to his arms. She needed to hang on to something solid. 'I think they had an affair,' she said bluntly. 'Years ago, the last time my parents came to Seville.'

'Your parents?' Rafael gawped at her, clearly more confused than ever. 'How could your mother have an affair with Caleb, when she was here with your father? I don't get it, Holly.'

'Dad went home early,' she told him. 'And she . . .' Her voice failed her.

Rafael pulled her closer. 'Your mother? Are you sure about this?'

'Didn't you see the way they looked at one another?' Holly demanded. It was unmistakeable. The way he'd held her mother's hands, so sure of himself. The way Holly's mother had responded, all gooey-eyed. They couldn't take their eyes off each other.

Her poor father. Holly couldn't get over it. No wonder her mother had looked petrified and excited in equal measures the entire time they'd been here. She must have been so worried that she'd run into Caleb – or had she been looking forward to it with anticipation maybe? Oh, the irony. Through Rafael, Holly had led her mother straight to him.

'Well, yes, I did see that,' Rafael admitted. 'But it cannot be, Holly.'

'Why not?'

He let go of her for a moment and spread his hands. 'Because Caleb, he was so happily married. Trust me on this. He and Mariana, his wife, they adored one another. I know it.'

'Maybe he wasn't even married back then,' Holly muttered. 'And he was looking pretty adoringly at my mother too a few minutes ago.'

Rafael nodded. 'They did seem close. But perhaps they were just good friends.'

Holly didn't buy that. 'I don't believe it,' she said. 'But I feel sorry for his wife, whoever she is.'

Rafael frowned. 'She died, Holly. A few years ago. It was cancer. Very tragic. Caleb, he was a broken man.'

'Oh.' That made her feel bad. But then, this whole situation was making her feel bad. 'Sorry.'

'Caleb, he is a good man.' Rafael's voice was stubborn. 'I would trust him with my life.' He took a step away from her. 'Look around you, Holly.'

Holly looked – at the ceramics in various stages of production, at the potter's wheel in the far corner, at the pots of paints and glues, the moulds and transfers that were all part of Rafael's trade. He had learnt all this from his mentor, he'd already told her that. From Caleb.

'I know all that,' she said. 'I know what he means to you.' But this was something else entirely. They had run into one another in an entirely random way in Rafael's workshop. And what now? His wife had died, so Caleb and her mother were going to do it all over again? Holly shuddered.

'Holly, *mi cariña* . . .' Rafael came closer, drew her into his arms once again. 'Please do not be like this. Your mother, she said she would explain to you. Maybe you are mistaken. Maybe . . .'

But then he ran out of words and he kissed her instead. Which was nice. And Holly certainly needed the comfort right now. She clung to him, wanting more of him, wanting the rest of it to go away.

But her mobile rang to interrupt the moment. Her mother? Holly couldn't resist pulling her phone out of her bag and glancing at the screen. Axel Gonzáles. What now? She mouthed 'sorry' to Rafael and picked up.

'I must apologise,' the winemaker began. 'But I cannot do the business with you. It is not possible. I was mistaken. I was wrong. Please find someone else.' The line went dead.

'Axel?' Holly stared at the phone, but he'd gone.

'What is it?' Rafael asked.

'Axel's decided not to supply me with the wine.' Holly tried to call the winemaker back but there was no answer. 'I don't believe it.' *What next?*

'Don't worry, Holly.' Once again, Rafael took her in his arms.

But Holly still felt like crying. What with last night, then her mother, now this . . . Everything seemed to be going wrong. 'Oh, Rafa,' she said. 'Do you think Bitter Orange has been fated from the start?'

'No, no, of course not,' he told her. 'This is something out of your control, Holly.'

'But—'

'There are other winemakers,' he reassured her. 'Let me help you. We can visit them together. There is still time.'

Yes, there was still time. But Holly didn't want any other winemakers. She wanted Axel.

'You know, Holly . . .' Rafael smoothed her hair from her forehead and held her face in his hands.

'Yes?'

'I wish you would stay in Seville for a longer time,' he said wistfully.

'I might have to.' Holly looked into his dark eyes. There was a fleck of green buried deep in the iris that sometimes caught the light. She loved that.

'How much longer?' he asked.

'Long enough to sort out this mess. Long enough to find another wine producer, to make sure I've got all the sources I need.'

'Ah, business,' he said. 'Always the business.'

Holly sighed. Even Rafael didn't seem to get it. 'I've loved being here with you, Rafa,' she told him. 'You know that. But you also know I have to go back to Dorset before too long.'

'Yes?' He adopted a woebegone look.

She laughed. 'Yes. I have to start setting up the shop. There's so much to do.' When she stopped to think about it, she felt overwhelmed by what she'd taken on. Better not stop and think then, she decided. 'And I need to start earning a living.' Though suddenly, with all this, it was hard to find the heart for it.

'Well, I was thinking . . .' Rafael dropped a kiss on her lips, then another, then another. They tasted as sweet as nectar.

Holly responded, wound her arms around his neck and pulled him closer. 'What were you thinking?' she asked.

'That maybe you should stay a lot longer,' he said. 'That maybe, my darling Holly, you should stay forever.'

CHAPTER 41

Ella

Seville, 1988

At the party, Caleb introduced her to his family and friends, keeping a protective arm around her, which didn't escape people's notice; Ella could tell from the curious looks directed their way. And sometimes the looks weren't just curious; from the younger female contingent they were slightly resentful too. But Ella held her head high. Everything that she didn't want to think about still existed – Felix, their marriage, her life in England – but it was outside the bubble. Inside the bubble, she and Caleb were floating and they were alone. It was short-sighted, she knew. At any moment, she'd have to let it back in, face the consequences of what she was doing. But not yet.

The party was taking place in the back room of a bar which looked as if it might often be the venue for gatherings and flamenco shows. The walls were painted deep red and lined with pictures of old Triana, and wooden chairs had been put out around small circular tables placed in a horseshoe shape around the perimeter of the room. At the base of the horseshoe was a small stage area set with chairs and a guitar under an arch of narrow bricks. A table to one side of the stage was laden with bottles of wine and beer and a vast selection of mouth-watering tapas.

'Come and meet Mama,' said Caleb.

Ella felt nervous. What would Caleb's mother think of her, some random British tourist Caleb had become involved with? She was an outsider. Would Caleb's mother resent Ella's intrusion into her son's life?

She needn't have worried, though; Caleb's mother barely reacted to her presence at all. She was small of stature and sweet-faced, but her brown eyes were vague and she seemed disconnected from what was happening around them.

'Mama.' Ella heard the tenderness in Caleb's voice as he spoke first in Spanish, then English for Ella's benefit. 'I want you to meet a very special friend of mine, Ella. Ella, this is my mother.'

Caleb's mother nodded and smiled to her son and to Ella and she proffered her cheek for a kiss, but she didn't speak, and after a moment, Caleb drew Ella away.

'Your mother,' Ella whispered to Caleb, 'is she unwell?'

His expression grew serious. 'She never recovered from the death of my father and my brother.' His words were stark. 'She goes on with her life, she talks only to what is left of her family, or more often she just seems to listen. But most of the time, she is somewhere else.' He pushed his dark hair from his forehead. 'I do not know how much she understands, not even how much she really hears or sees.'

Dementia, thought Ella, or some form of it perhaps. She squeezed Caleb's hand in silent sympathy. His mother had suffered a great loss, but at least she still had the rest of her family close by. Various family members fussed over her, making sure she had a comfortable chair, fetching her a cushion, a drink and some food on a plate. She smiled at one and all, though her eyes remained as glazed as before.

A man who looked very like Caleb himself, greeted Caleb with a slap on the back and a hearty hug. They spoke to one another rapidly in Spanish and Ella could see the newcomer giving her more than one sidelong glance. 'My best friend Antonio.' At last Caleb introduced them. 'This is Ella.'

Antonio grinned. 'You are as beautiful as Caleb told me you were.' He kissed her enthusiastically on both cheeks and Ella laughed.

'I told him about us,' Caleb admitted. He slid an arm around Ella's shoulders. 'Antonio, he is more than a friend. He is like a brother.'

Ella could see that; the affection between the two of them was delightful to witness. And perhaps Caleb's friendship with Antonio might somehow have eased the loss of Francisco, if only a little.

'And now you should meet my grandmother, the true matriarch of our family.' Caleb drew Ella's hand under his arm. 'I must warn you – she does not miss a thing.'

Even more worrying, thought Ella.

The little old lady with snow-white hair was surrounded by a group of people. She was holding court, her veined and jewelled hands gesticulating as she spoke, her back straight and her white head held erect as she surveyed her small audience. Her black eyes lit up when she saw her grandson. And her gaze travelled curiously over Ella, scrutinising every detail of her appearance in seconds; clearly, she was sharp as a pin.

'Buenos tardes, Abuela.' Caleb greeted his grandmother with obvious affection and she smiled and held his face close, looking into his eyes before kissing him firmly on both cheeks.

Caleb brought Ella forward and the old lady spoke to her in rapid Spanish before pulling her in for a kiss on both withered cheeks.

'I'm sorry . . . ?' Ella looked helplessly at Caleb. She had no idea what his grandmother was saying nor how to respond.

Caleb replied to his grandmother and then turned to Ella. 'She says, "so you are the woman who has taken my grandson away."' He grinned broadly.

Ella returned his smile. 'So that's who I am,' she said. She had been wondering. Caleb seemed different here at this family gathering; more relaxed and at ease with himself – and with her. She smiled back at the grandmother uncertainly. Would this strong matriarch with the gimlet gaze approve? Surely not – if she knew the truth?

'Tell your grandmother that you have been showing me your Seville,' she suggested.

Caleb spoke again and the grandmother came back quick as a flash. 'She asks what you think of our city?'

'I love it.'

This was duly translated and the old lady nodded with obvious satisfaction before speaking again. This time, Caleb did not translate; he and his grandmother exchanged more words and from the looks his grandmother sent her way, Ella knew she was under the matriarchal microscope.

Eventually Caleb turned to Ella again. 'She likes you,' he said.

'The feeling's mutual.' Because there was a twinkle of humour in the old woman's black eyes that appealed to Ella and a kindness in her toothy smile that seemed to welcome her too.

‘But she also suspects that you have stolen my heart,’ he added.

Ella shot him a quick glance. They hadn’t talked about hearts or love and she had no intention of starting now. Whatever she felt for this man, this afternoon when they’d made love at Asperillo Beach and now at this family party . . . well, she hadn’t yet acknowledged it as real. As far as Ella was concerned, at this moment there was no past and no future. The present moment was all. And it was very far from real.

‘And it is true.’ Caleb raised one eyebrow and clutched at his chest dramatically. Ella shook her head in mock despair at his play-acting. His grandmother didn’t know then – who she was, where she was from, nor that she was married. Ella felt a fraud.

The old lady spoke some more.

Caleb nodded. ‘She notices that you are scared,’ he told Ella. ‘But she says that you do not have to be.’ He hesitated. ‘She says that you can soon learn Spanish ways.’

Ella looked into the eyes of Caleb’s grandmother, bright as two shiny buttons. Little she knew. If only it were just a question of learning Spanish ways. The old lady was very perceptive. But, even so . . .

‘She says . . .’ Caleb leant closer and whispered into Ella’s hair – ‘that love will always find a way.’

Before Ella could respond to this, the old lady reached out and took her hand. She stared into Ella’s palm, examining the lines; rested the soft-skinned pads of her fingertips on Ella’s wrist and looked up. For a moment Ella thought that she might cry.

But she simply murmured what seemed to be some sort of blessing. Then she took Caleb’s hand and placed Ella’s hand in his.

'Does your grandmother read palms?' Ella asked Caleb. And if so, what might she have seen there?

'Yes.' But he was still smiling. 'Grandmother can see into the future, she says.'

Ella was about to ask more, but the crowd in the room had started clapping and tapping their feet.

'It is time for the music,' said Caleb.

His grandmother patted the wooden seat next to her, to indicate that Ella should sit beside her. Caleb found a cousin who could act as interpreter and then he disappeared to fetch his guitar.

The buzz of conversation continued to hum around Ella but since she couldn't understand a word, she just sat back and let it wash over her. She was still dazed from the events of the daytime. And she couldn't wait to watch and hear Caleb play the flamenco guitar once again.

'Grandmother asks if you love her grandson Caleb?' the young girl cousin asked Ella. She put her head to one side. 'And did you buy your shawl here in Seville? That is my question,' she added.

Ella smiled and nodded. 'I did, yes, from a shop in Santa Cruz.' Because that was by far the easier question.

'And my cousin Caleb?'

'It's not simple,' Ella told her. The last thing she wanted at this point was to be drawn into a conversation about her intentions. For a start, she wasn't sure that she had any. And yet . . .

The girl translated and the old woman spoke. 'Grandmother says that love is simple,' she corrected. 'It is everything, she says.'

'Yes. I know.' This time Ella spoke directly back to Caleb's *abuela* and she was convinced that the old lady understood.

Slowly, she nodded. Caleb's grandmother seemed to know exactly what was in her heart.

Caleb appeared on the small stage with his guitar and the music began. As before, he sat in what Ella now knew to be the flamenco position. He looked good, she thought, in his white shirt and close-fitting black trousers, his dark head bent over the instrument, already totally absorbed. He strummed a few chords and then the notes of the melody began: fluid, plaintive and haunting, as if the music could tunnel into her very soul.

The rhythm of the piece pulsed through the room like a heartbeat, the pace quickened and soon Ella found that her foot was tapping of its own accord and all around her, the group of family and friends were also clapping and tapping their feet along with the rhythm as one.

A man stepped forwards and began to sing. It was a deep, low, resonant sound, that once again seemed to reverberate with emotion and suffering as it rose and fell, as it filled the room. This primitive wail caught at her; the feeling caught at her as if it could pull her in. Ella could sense the spirit of the flamenco sweeping through the space around her and within her as if it were searching for an echo. The atmosphere in the room changed. The tension grew, the mood darkened, the party became more sombre.

As Caleb played, his long brown fingers strumming the chords and rippling over the strings, Ella couldn't take her eyes from him. When she did at last look away, she was conscious that Caleb's grandmother was staring just as much – but at her.

The young cousin had fetched a book, clearly at the grandmother's request, because she handed it to the old lady. And now the grandmother was flicking through it, muttering to herself. She pointed to something written on one of the pages and the cousin took a pen and a fresh piece of paper and began to laboriously copy it out for her while the music played on.

Ella was curious, but she gave them only a cursory glance, because Caleb was still playing. And as he caressed and plucked the notes from his guitar, Ella relived his touch from this afternoon in the hideout at the Asperillo dune. The tension built; she was mesmerised, not just by Caleb and the music he played, not just by the haunting notes of the man who was singing as if his very heart would break, but by the emotion of the piece, the joining of the musicians with these people listening here at the family party, who had become part of the experience, because they all felt it too.

At last, at what seemed to Ella like a moment of no return, the song ended with a spill of those emotions, a whisper, a release. And there it was, Ella recognised it with a shiver: that emotional climax, that moment of *duende* that Caleb had spoken of before.

'*Olé!*' someone shouted. '*Eso es.*'

'*Olé,*' Ella whispered. And once again, when she looked up, the old grandmother was watching her with something that seemed very much like approval.

The lights were dimmed and, in seconds, Caleb was once more by Ella's side, his hand light on her shoulder. Ella reached up and put her hand over his. There were beads of sweat on his brow from the energy he'd put into his playing, and she could see that his neck and collarbone were damp with sweat.

'I have something for you,' he said. He pulled an envelope from the back pocket of his trousers.

Ella opened it. Inside was a photo of herself and Caleb standing by the fountain in the orange grove of the Cathedral gardens. Her breath caught. They looked good together.

She hesitated for a long moment. 'You should have it.' She passed it back to him although she ached to keep it herself.

'I had two copies printed,' he told her.

'Oh.' She couldn't look at him. 'Thanks.' And she tucked the precious photograph carefully into her bag.

Caleb's grandmother was still watching them. She nodded and closed her two hands together in what appeared to be a gesture of acceptance.

'Caleb.' His *abuela* reached forward to speak to him. She spoke for a few moments and then sat back, resting against the red cushion.

'What did she say?' Ella looked up at him.

Caleb leant closer so that his warm lips were almost touching her temple. Ella could feel the heat rising from his body. 'She says that she has seen it,' he said, 'and that therefore it is so.'

Seen it? Seen the future, did she mean? In Ella's palm? But there was no time to question him further. An expectant hush fell around the room. Ella looked at Caleb. What now?

A girl who had been introduced to Ella earlier as Sergio's sister appeared, carrying a cake in front of her like an offering. The rich smell of it seemed to fill the room just like the music had filled it only minutes before. The cake was deep and dusted with icing sugar, and it had a fragrance of oranges, or so it seemed to Ella. She sniffed. A drift of orange blossom, interlaced with the nuttiness of almonds and the sweetness of honey. It seemed an impossibly heady perfume for just a cake.

Once again, Caleb bent so that his head was level with Ella's. 'It is my aunt and uncle's wedding anniversary,' he reminded her. 'And this is a special cake to celebrate the years they have spent together. It is a Seville orange and almond cake. Made to celebrate their love.'

'It smells wonderful.' Ella clapped enthusiastically along with the rest of the family, swept into the atmosphere of festivity as the cake was presented to the aunt and uncle.

The couple smiled and kissed. The aunt blushed and they cut the cake together as if they were a bride and groom once more. What a charming tradition, Ella found herself thinking. She glanced up and once again found the grandmother watching her. The old lady gave a small nod and a smile and Ella smiled back. This family certainly knew how to celebrate. And Ella felt that she'd gained more approval here this evening than she had with Felix's mother in all the years they'd lived together.

Caleb's uncle said a few words, mostly drowned out by cheerful shouting, clapping and laughter from various family members. Then Sergio and his sister cut the rest of the cake and various cousins brought it round on plates for the remainder of the party. There were trays of *fino* too, offered by older male cousins, the sight of which transported Ella back to the evening with Caleb when he had first kissed her. After that, there'd been no going back, she supposed.

Caleb took glasses and plates of cake for them both, passed Ella's over to her and checked that his grandmother had also been served.

The grandmother raised her glass. '*Salud y amor y tiempo para disfrutarlo,*' she said. She nodded to Ella.

'*Salud.*' Ella too raised her glass. 'And . . . ?' She glanced at Caleb. What was the rest of the toast?

'To health and love, and the time to enjoy it,' he said.

But Ella dreaded that there would be no time for her to enjoy it. Time had run away from her and it had almost run out.

Everyone cheered, ate cake and sipped their *fino*. The cake oozed almond oil and tasted bitter-sweet like the oranges of Seville. It was delicious.

'Mmm.' Ella licked her fingers. She took a sip of *fino* and felt for a moment that she was on fire. The sweet richness of the *fino* complemented the almond and orange cake perfectly. It was the best dessert Ella had ever tasted.

A band of musicians appeared, and once again, the music began to play. Not flamenco this time, but some wild gypsy tune that was infectious and got everyone moving. Caleb pulled Ella to her feet. Suddenly, everyone was dancing and the party proper seemed to have begun.

'How did you learn to play the flamenco guitar?' Ella asked Caleb at a pause in the music. She imagined it to be something buried deep in him; he'd had to have learnt it when he was very young.

'From my father. And him from his father. That is how it goes in families. The flamenco takes you or it lets you go.'

'When does it take you?' she wondered.

He laced his fingers in hers. 'Technique, fingerwork, even a sense of rhythm can be taught,' he said. 'But you need something more. And when you have that something more – that is when it takes you.'

'Something more?' Though Ella thought she was beginning to understand.

'Passion,' he said. And his dark eyes seemed to burn into her. 'It is the life force of the flamenco. You need to feel the passion right through to the depths of your soul.'

Was that where he felt it? In the depths of his soul? Ella met his gaze. 'And the *duende*?'

'Yes?'

'What is it exactly?'

He drew her to the side of the room. They stood by a long black curtain. Outside, she could see a few lights illuminating the darkness of this night in Triana.

'Perhaps the *duende* is meant to be mysterious,' he said. 'Perhaps it cannot be defined.' He stroked her hair from her face. Was he teasing her?

'Is that true?' she challenged him.

He moved the curtain aside and they slipped behind it so that they were no longer visible to the rest of the room. She reached up and tangled her fingers into the soft curls of his hair. She hadn't felt free to touch him in front of his family. After all, she didn't belong here and she would be leaving very soon. She had no right at all to imagine herself falling in love with him.

'I believe it is a spirit,' he said. 'A spirit that comes from the earth itself. A feeling even, that you experience deep in your very core.' He took hold of her hands in his and pulled her closer.

Deep in your very core . . . Ella gazed at Caleb as she thought about this. What she had felt when she listened to the music had been powerful and intense. It was a kind of electric energy. And it had seemed to come from something almost primeval; perhaps, as Caleb said, something that couldn't be easily defined.

'Ella.' He was watching her. '*Cariña*.'

'Yes?' She put her hand on the top of his chest, where his white shirt was unbuttoned, where his skin was still hot from the playing and the dancing.

He held her face in his hands. She closed her eyes and thought of the way he played his guitar, the way he had touched her on the Asperillo dune – with tenderness and with passion too. 'There are some things we do not have to define, or even understand.'

Were there? She started thinking about this. But then he kissed her and she stopped thinking. The warm scent of him filled her senses, along with the fragrance of the orange and almond cake that continued to pervade the room. His touch seemed to light her up in a way that she'd never known before. He was right. There were some things she didn't need to define or understand. It was enough sometimes to just feel.

Later, after more dancing and drinking, Caleb's grandmother beckoned her over and pressed a folded piece of paper into her hand. Ella went to look at it but the grandmother stopped her with a gesture from her wrinkled and bejewelled hand. The old lady spoke in Spanish, low and urgent, and Ella strained to understand.

And then Caleb was once again by her side. 'She says that this recipe is known only to the women of this family,' he said. He was speaking softly but he seemed as surprised as Ella. 'It is a great honour,' he breathed. 'She says that this is for you and that she knows you are one of us.'

Ella stared at him. What could she mean? *One of us? Recipe?* She was confused. Of course, she appreciated the sentiment. But . . . Ella leant forward to kiss the grandmother who was leaving the party and clearly exhausted, and all of a sudden, she found herself being kissed by several female cousins all at once.

It was as if they knew something that she did not. It was too much. Ella tucked the recipe into her bag. And it must have been too much for Caleb too, because he was suddenly nowhere to be seen. She felt a rising panic and she knew what she had to do.

Sergio, who had made himself responsible for giving people lifts home, was standing over by the door. The grandmother had disappeared with a different cousin and had already left the room.

Ella waved to Sergio and made her way over. 'Can you drive me back to the hotel?' she asked him.

'Now?' He seemed surprised. She wondered how long parties went on for, here in Triana.

'Please.'

'What about Caleb?' He looked around the room.

Ella couldn't bear this. In that moment when Caleb's grandmother had given her the recipe, it was as if she had woken up, come to her senses with a terrible jolt. What was she thinking of? What was she doing? Whatever it was, she wasn't free to be doing it. 'I don't think I can say goodbye to him,' she said.

'But how can you leave without saying goodbye?' Sergio frowned.

'I don't know,' she whispered. 'But I think that I have to.'

She could see Caleb now. He was standing over in the far corner talking to one of his beautiful Spanish friends. As Ella watched them, the girl tossed her dark head and put her hand possessively on Caleb's arm. He laughed back at her, tilted her chin and dropped a light kiss on her forehead. She pouted. That wasn't enough for her.

This was Caleb's world and Ella wasn't part of it. She couldn't stay here with him – she had a plane to catch tomorrow. Tomorrow, she'd be back in Dorset, back with Felix, back in her life, back to her teaching. It was an ordinary life and nothing like this life, but at least it was hers and she belonged. This beautiful bubble was just a dream. It was thin and unsubstantial. And now that it had burst, she could see it for what it really was. Another world, not Ella's world.

'Please, Sergio,' she said.

He must have caught the desperation in her voice, because

he moved outside and Ella followed him, quickly, pulling the shawl closer around her shoulders.

'That girl, you know, Caleb is not interested in her,' Sergio said, not understanding. 'She is just a kid.'

'But she cares for him.' Ella had seen it written all over her lovely face. 'And he may come to love her in time.' Or if not her, at least there would be someone, someone who, unlike Ella, truly belonged here.

Sergio shrugged. 'Maybe. Who knows?'

Ella flinched. But Sergio wasn't to know how she felt, nor exactly what had happened between Ella and Caleb today. He knew that his cousin wouldn't like her leaving, though. But how could she stay?

Sergio opened the car door and she climbed in. *Be quick*, she thought. If Caleb came after her now . . . She probably wouldn't be able to leave at all.

Sergio started the engine and the car pulled away.

Ella felt the tears rising, but she held them back. She must be sensible. She must be strong. This was a holiday romance, that was all. She had been seduced by this magical springtime, hypnotised by the seductive scent of the thousands of orange trees that lined the streets of Seville. She couldn't let everyone down, everyone who was waiting for her back home – not just Felix but also the children at school; she had worked hard to gain her teaching certificate and after all the problems she'd faced, she couldn't just throw it all away.

'What shall I tell him?' Sergio asked when they got to the hotel. He seemed even more concerned than before. 'What shall I say?'

'Tell him I'm sorry,' Ella said. 'Tell him I just couldn't say goodbye.'

CHAPTER 42

Felix

Seville, 2018

Felix and Ella went to the large airy space that was Plaza Nueva to talk. It had been a long time, he thought, and yet Seville was not really so very different. And the Plaza Nueva with its calm atmosphere, its stately palm trees and formal little gardens laid out around the edges, lined as it was with orange trees and grand buildings like the Hotel Inglaterra and the City Hall, took him right back to that first day with Ella when they had watched the flamenco here in the square.

On the way here, Felix had asked about Holly, and Ella had reassured him that Holly was fine, that their daughter was with Rafael who was trustworthy and would accompany Holly back to the hotel later.

'You're sure?' he asked her. 'She's really fine?'

'She's really fine.'

Felix let out a breath. So, he could relax on that score at least.

'And you haven't discovered anything more?' he asked. 'Nothing else has happened?'

'Not yet, no.' He felt her hesitate. 'Caleb's going to see what he can find out.'

'Right.' Felix tried to quell his irritation at her words. This was Holly they were talking about. What did it matter who helped, so long as their daughter was safe?

When they reached the Plaza Nueva, Ella took his hand – a good or a bad sign? he wondered – and they sat on a bench by the statue. Over the far side of the plaza, instead of flamenco, five young guys were practising a dance routine. Felix guessed there would always be dancing in this square.

'I am so sorry, Felix,' said Ella. 'For . . .' – he felt her hesitate – 'everything.'

He decided not to let go of her hand. 'When I first found that photograph,' he began, 'and by the way, I wasn't poking around in your stuff, I was only trying to fix that stiff drawer.'

'Ah,' said Ella. 'I forgot about that drawer.'

Could she have forgotten about the photograph too? He thought not. 'It made me think – what have I ever really done to deserve you, Ella?'

'Oh, Felix.' She shook her head. He thought there were tears in her eyes. 'You've done so many things. Where would I even be without you?'

'At first, yes, perhaps.' He allowed himself a grim smile as he looked up at the statue. The guy was very imposing. The floor of the plaza had been constructed from granite and marble, Felix could see, a geometric pattern made up of grey, cream and terracotta stone. He didn't remember noticing that, first time around. 'But after that – when I kept you trapped in my mother's house . . .' His voice broke. He didn't want to sound ridiculously melodramatic, but . . . 'You were like a bird with clipped wings.'

'It wasn't your fault, Felix.' Ella slung her other arm around him. 'We were grateful to your mother for helping us out. We didn't have the money to buy our own place, remember.'

'Not at first, we didn't.' He looked down. He couldn't look up, couldn't quite meet her eye. He had to face it – even now, he might lose her and how could he bear that?

'At first?'

Felix took a deep breath. 'After a few years at Mum's, we could have managed it.'

'A few years?' He heard the confusion in her voice. Ella had always left the finances to Felix. 'How many years, Felix?'

'Two or three,' he admitted.

'But we stayed at your mother's for more than five years.' He could feel her processing it, trying to understand. 'Why?'

'I suppose I was too scared to leave her,' he said. Honesty went two ways – if you expected it, you had to give it too.

'Scared, Felix?' Ella's voice was soft. 'But what of?' She hadn't taken her arm away from his shoulders.

'Yes.' And it was a relief to be truthful at last. Felix didn't want a world built on pretence – not anymore. 'I was scared of how Mum would react. Scared of leaving her on her own. Scared that you might realise how weak I really was. And scared of standing on my own two feet, I suppose.' Felix looked up at last. He loved the green trees that surrounded this square; the colour and textures that contrasted with the smooth stone. And he realised that not only had he not observed them, but he hadn't appreciated it all first time around. He hadn't appreciated Seville, and he hadn't appreciated Ella either.

'You were never weak, Felix,' Ella said staunchly. 'You were being kind. You were thinking of others. That's what you always do.'

She hadn't stopped supporting him then. Felix squeezed her hand. 'Thank you, my darling,' he said, 'but I know there've been plenty of times when I should have been stronger.' With his mother in particular.

'It takes a strong man to admit weakness, Felix,' Ella said. 'We've all made mistakes. Me more than anyone.'

There was a silence while they both digested these words. What was Ella's mistake? To get involved with another man while she was still married to Felix? Or to stay married to Felix when they were both aware that they'd grown apart? Because they had grown apart – at least until Holly came along. People often said that a baby wouldn't mend a relationship, but Holly had mended theirs.

'Staying with Mother affected everything,' Felix went on. 'It wasn't good for our marriage. We got to a bad place, you know we did.'

'Yes.' Ella leant her head on his shoulder. 'Yes, we did.'

'And then there was Seville.'

'And then there was Seville,' she echoed.

He sat back and closed his eyes; allowed himself to wallow in the warmth of this place as he had not allowed himself to wallow before. He hadn't even wanted to be here. They had been very young. But Christ, what an idiot he had been. He opened his eyes. 'Will you tell me what happened, Ella?'

Even when Felix found the photograph, he hadn't really wanted to know. Even when his mother tried to tell him all those things, he hadn't wanted to hear. But now . . . He had to know it all if he was to move forward. He'd finally realised that.

He felt her body shift slightly as she fidgeted on the bench. 'I was angry with you,' she said. 'For rushing back. I didn't think your mother really needed you. I thought she was exaggerating what had happened to spoil things for us, to get you back home.'

And Ella had been right to think this. Felix remembered full well how he'd raced back to Dorset, all concern. He remembered how glad his mother had been to see him, how she had apologised profusely for ruining their holiday, how she had expressed disbelief that Ella had stayed behind in Seville . . . And he also remembered that there had been very little wrong with his mother at all. That, he thought now, is when he should have learnt a valuable lesson. Though even then, it might have been too late.

'You were dead right to think that,' he told Ella now. Even at the time, he'd been torn. Even at the time, he'd realised that Ella needed him too; that his very marriage was on the line and he was taking the biggest risk with it.

'And then I met Caleb,' she said.

'So, what was the attraction?' As if he didn't know. But Felix was trying to make light of it. After all, it had been a long time ago, and he'd already admitted that he'd given Ella good reason.

Ella hesitated. She glanced across at Felix, perhaps unsure of his mood. 'He was very kind and attentive.'

'I bet.'

She shot him a glance. 'I wasn't looking for anything to happen. The opposite, in fact. I resisted him at first, Felix, I honestly did.'

'But?' Did he really want to know all the details, even now? Felix heard the birds singing in the trees above them and it felt as though they were mocking him.

'But he swept me off my feet.' She gave a rueful sigh. 'I fell in love with him, Felix,' she said.

Felix tensed. It was worse than he'd allowed himself to think. She loved the man. He eased himself away from her. 'Ella, I want you to know,' he said, 'that I understand how you feel. If it's what you want, I'll release you from our marriage with no bitterness, no recriminations. A clean split.'

There was a pause. It seemed like a long one to Felix.

'But what if I don't want to be released?' She'd lifted her head and was staring at him. His black tulip – elegant and mysterious.

'I don't want you to stay with me out of duty,' he said stubbornly, 'not again.' Because surely that was why she'd stayed with him last time? What other reason could there be? She'd said herself that she'd fallen in love with the guy. What had stood in their way? Only her marriage with a man who had rescued her at a time when she'd desperately needed a friend. 'I don't want you to stay because you feel sorry for me, Ella,' he said. 'It's not enough.'

'I don't feel sorry for you,' she countered. 'I never did. And it wasn't duty either.'

Her hazel eyes were sad and he wanted to stroke her hair, hold her in his arms. But he held back.

'I'm sorry for what happened,' she said. 'I'm sorry I caused you pain. But that's it really.'

'I've been made redundant, Ella,' Felix told her. He may as well get it all out in the open now. He looked away into the square at the statue, at the people going about their business, meeting other people, drinking coffee or beer, at the guys still practising their dance routine accompanied by tinny music blaring from a tiny speaker.

'Really?' Ella blinked at him. 'When did you find out?'

'Six weeks ago,' he admitted.

'Six weeks ago!' She sat up straighter. 'But why didn't you say something?'

He shook his head. He felt bad enough already. All his resolutions to be braver, more honest, to protect his womenfolk . . . They had – with one sighting of this Caleb person – turned to dust. He had known something had to change, but he hadn't wanted it to be like this.

'You've been carrying this alone?' Ella's voice was tender. Could that be right? Tender?

'Mum found out several days ago,' Felix admitted. 'I wanted to tell you first but she guessed and turned up at the house on a weekday in the middle of the morning when I should have been at work.'

To his surprise, Ella chuckled. 'She doesn't miss a thing.'

No, he thought, she doesn't.

'Don't worry, Felix,' Ella said. 'We'll get through this, you'll see.'

'We?' He turned to her. What was she saying? Why was she being so nice? He'd deceived her, hadn't he? He'd put their security at risk. And then there was Caleb, the man she loved, here in Seville.

'I don't want our marriage to end.' She spoke slowly as if she was spelling it out for him. 'I never have.'

'And Caleb?' Though the name grated on his tongue.

'What happened with Caleb is in the past,' she told him. 'There's nothing going on between us now. Holly and I went to Rafael's workshop this afternoon and there he was – it turns out that he's Rafael's mentor. I really had no idea.'

He looked into her face and saw the surprise she'd felt reflected there. 'But you were talking with him,' he said. 'You looked so close. I assumed . . .'

She was shaking her head. 'We were just putting the past to rights,' she said. 'Finding out about the last thirty years. Laying to rest a few ghosts, that's all.'

'So, you don't . . .' – he hesitated – 'still love him?'

'Felix,' she said. 'I love *you*.'

A warm glow that might have come from the late afternoon sun or might have come from Ella's words seemed to wrap itself around him. Could it be true? Felix felt the relief, sweet and warm inside. When he'd seen them standing together like that in the orange grove, he had certainly thought the worst. What had happened in the past was one thing. But what was happening now, that was his chief concern. 'And the photograph?' he managed to say.

Once again, Ella took his hand. 'I won't deny that Caleb meant a lot to me, Felix,' she said. 'I told you, I fell in love with him. I kept the photo as a memory of that time, that's all.' She sighed. 'But I shouldn't have and I'm sorry.'

Felix nodded. She could have left him. But against all the odds, she'd stayed. At last, he took her in his arms and he held her closer than close. He needed Ella now, more than he had ever needed her before. He needed her wit, her wisdom, her love. He even needed her air of mystery. Perhaps he would never know everything about her, but did that really matter? No. Felix had come to terms with a lot of things in the past few days – with the hard fact of his redundancy; with the knowledge that something had to change, that he had to stand alone in a way he'd never really stood alone before, that he had to face up to the reality of his relationship with his mother and deal with it. She was an old lady. He wouldn't be cruel; of course, he wouldn't be cruel – she was his mother and he loved her. But it had to come from him.

'And you know, darling, about the job, something will come up,' Ella said.

He eased them apart. 'It already has, Ella.' And he told her about the National Trust position. He'd been so fortunate, he knew that. It was a bit less than full-time hours but it was a good start.

'That's fantastic news, Felix.' Her eyes were shining. 'You'll love it.'

'Yes,' he said. 'Yes, I think I will.'

'I'm proud of you,' Ella told him.

Felix felt the lump in his throat. There was more. He drew away. 'And Holly?' he asked. He had to address the elephant in the plaza.

'Holly?'

Felix hesitated to say it. 'Does she know about you and Caleb?'

He felt her sigh. 'She may have guessed, earlier on when we came face to face in Rafael's workshop.' Ella hesitated too. 'Some of it, at least,' she said.

Felix nodded.

'I'm so sorry, Felix,' she whispered again.

He knew what she was saying. But this was something he felt strongly about and he had to let her know. 'Ella, it's all in the past. We can put it behind us now.'

Ella held his hand more tightly. 'I'm so glad you came out here, Felix,' she said.

'You are?' He almost felt himself grow an inch or two at her words.

'I am.'

He didn't doubt her. How he loved this woman, Felix thought. He always had.

CHAPTER 43

Ella

Seville, 2018

Later, Ella and Felix went for a drink in the little bar off the plaza near the hotel, sitting at high stools in the window within sight of the orange grove and the hotel entrance. Ella had messaged Holly to tell her where she was, but who knew what sort of mood her daughter would be in? Ella hadn't told her that Felix was here – at least that would be one nice surprise.

It had been a shock to see him, but a good one. Ella was lucky, she knew, that Felix was so understanding. It must have been horrid – finding that photo of Ella and Caleb then seeing her with him here in Seville. And yet Felix had forgiven her – and believed her – without question. Felix was wrong to say he didn't deserve Ella. If anything, it was Ella who didn't deserve him.

How much did Felix know? Ella watched him at the bar ordering glasses of red wine for them both and knew that she must now tell him everything. But it was hard. For so many years, she had hugged the secret to herself, sure that she was doing the best thing for everyone. Now, though . . . It wasn't fair, she realised. She owed Felix a lot more honesty than that. She had taken a lot from her husband, and what she had given him in return had been given in a manner that was less than transparent.

'Felix,' she began when he came over to sit beside her, 'there's something else I need to tell you – about that time, I mean. Something very important.'

He eyed her steadily. Put the glasses down in front of them. 'I think we must tell Holly,' he said. 'Everyone has the right to know – who they are, where they came from . . .'

Ella stared back at him. 'You already know?' She lifted her wine glass to her lips and took a gulp. How could he have guessed? she wondered.

'Mother knew,' he said. 'Or at least, she suspected.'

Ella tried to take this in. 'She knew back then?' she whispered.

'She had a good idea, yes.' Felix's voice remained steady. He took a sip of his own wine and then swirled the deep red liquid around in the glass thoughtfully. 'But she never said a word to me – not until last week, that is.' He smiled ruefully. 'I suppose she kept your secret because she thought it was best for all of us.'

'I see.' Ella stared out of the window at the orange grove. The leaves of the trees were shining glossy green in the late afternoon sun. Felix's words explained a lot. Why Ingrid had never really softened in her attitude towards Ella. Her fierce protectiveness over Felix . . .

'She still surprises me.' Felix shook his head as if in disbelief.

Ella too. 'But what made her suspect in the first place?' she asked him. Was it female intuition? Had Ella returned from Seville that first time looking different somehow? Had there been a glow about her that only another woman would recognise?

Felix sat up straighter. He took a deep breath. 'She told me last week that there was a fifty per cent chance that I was a carrier of cystic fibrosis,' he said.

'What?' Ella stared at him.

'It's a genetic condition. My grandparents were both carriers too. But there's only a one in four chance that a child will go on to have the disease apparently.'

'So . . . ?' Ella struggled to make the connection.

'I've never had any symptoms. But if I turned out to be a carrier . . .' – he paused – 'then it's very likely I'd be infertile. Born without a properly working vas deferens.'

'Vas . . . ?'

'Deferens. The tubes that transport the sperm.' He shrugged. 'Sorry. I've been reading up on it.'

Ella nodded. Of course, he would have.

'It seems that the sperm is there but it never gets very far.'

Ella was still trying to take it all in. 'So, you had the tests for cystic fibrosis?' she asked him.

'Yes, I did. A few days ago.'

She nodded. How could he not? She took a slower sip of her wine this time and thought about what he was telling her. Here they were, sitting in a little Spanish tapas bar in Seville, all old wood and decorative *azulejo* tiles, hams hanging from the ceiling, old photos on the walls, bottles lining the shelves. And this. 'And you are? A carrier, I mean?'

'I am.'

Oh, my goodness, thought Ella. That was a game-changer.

She leant back in her seat. Took another sip of her wine and tried to gather her thoughts. Everything was falling into place. Of course, there would never be a brother or a sister for Holly. Ingrid must have thought this too. The fact that Felix and Holly had been unable to have any more children must have made her theory seem all the more plausible.

'But why didn't your mother ever tell you before?' Ella wondered aloud. 'I mean, if there was a fifty per cent chance you could carry the gene?' Especially when Felix was planning to get married, she meant. Or even before she and Felix had met. It was an important thing to know about yourself. It wasn't the same now; there'd be treatment available. But back then, assisted reproductive technology, or whatever it was called, must still have been in the experimental and no doubt hugely expensive stage and if Felix could never have children . . .

The barman brought over two plates of tapas – spinach and potato croquettes and slices of dark-red paper-thin sweet cured ham.

'My father thought that they should wait until we were both eighteen before they told us,' Felix said. 'Before that, I suppose we would have been too young to understand the implications.'

'Yes.' But that was an awful long time ago.

'Only he died before that time,' Felix reminded her. 'Mum did tell Colin, but it was only six months after Dad's passing, and when Colin just upped and left like he did . . .' His voice tailed off.

Ella realised what he was telling her. 'Your mother thought that was the reason?'

He shrugged. 'She thought it was a possibility. At any rate, it put her off telling me at first.'

Yes. Ella could understand that. Felix and his mother were

so close, but she must have been terrified of losing him after all she had lost already.

Felix put a hand on hers. 'Then you and I met and it seems she sort of stuck her head in the sand and hoped for the best.'

'Oh, my . . .' She must have been so relieved, thought Ella, when she and Felix announced that Ella was pregnant. And then something – Holly's dark Spanish eyes perhaps or the fact that they hadn't gone on to have more children – had made her wonder. It explained a lot. But it was, Ella thought, an irresponsible thing to do. Not to put your child first, not to tell them something so integral to their life, to their identity. And then she thought of Holly. Hadn't she done exactly the same thing?

'She came to a point,' Felix said, 'where she felt that I needed to know the truth.'

The truth . . .

'Were you always sure, Ella?' Felix asked sadly. 'That Holly wasn't mine, I mean?'

'No. Not at first.' Ella remembered exactly how she'd felt. 'When I found out I was pregnant, I simply didn't know what to do.' She felt the tears not far away. Because of course she hadn't known for sure who was her baby's father. 'And I never wanted to deceive you. But . . .'

If she'd had more time, maybe she might even have come to a different decision. Only there had been no time. It had all happened so fast. 'But you were so happy when you found out. I thought it would be the best thing for the baby too. And . . .'

'And?'

'And I thought that it might be' – she put her hand on his – 'a second chance for us.'

He took hold of her hand. 'Oh, it was, Ella,' he said. 'And I'm so glad you made that decision. Holly . . .' His eyes filled.

He didn't have to go on. Holly meant everything to Felix, Ella knew that. 'But it doesn't change the way you feel?' She had to ask.

'No.' He seemed very certain. 'How could it? The love you feel for your child doesn't operate on a light switch.'

Ella nodded. He was right. 'And Holly is very much your child,' she assured him. 'She always has been and she always will be.'

They smiled tentatively at one another. There would be a lot more to say. But this was a start, at least.

'Shall we?' Felix indicated the tapas.

Ella nodded. She took a slice of ham and nibbled it cautiously. It was delicious. But her heart, her body felt so full with all this new knowledge, all these emotions. Felix had been a great father; he still was. As for Caleb . . . Ella wasn't sure what to do about Caleb. She certainly owed him something.

She thought of how she had felt when Holly had first dropped the bombshell of her plans for her shop, Bitter Orange, her daughter's explanation of how the idea had come to her from marmalade and from a heap of bitter Seville oranges. As if the spirit of Seville was already in her blood, even then. And when Ella had walked with her daughter into Triana and witnessed Holly's excitement, when she'd watched Holly's face as she listened, entranced, to the music of the flamenco; when Holly had met Rafael and heard him playing the guitar . . . Ella had worried that she had in some way denied her daughter her cultural birthright.

'We must tell Holly,' Felix said again. A thought seemed to occur to him. He cleared his throat and met her gaze. 'Does Caleb know?'

She shook her head. Though he might have guessed, she supposed. That picture of his daughter . . .

'Then you must tell him.'

'You think so?' Ella hadn't expected him to say that. Her eyes filled. Felix was so generous, he put her to shame.

'He's her biological father.' Felix blinked. Perhaps he was blinking back a tear? Ella couldn't say for sure. 'They may want to meet, Ella. They may want to talk. And they should.'

'I suppose.' Ella wanted that, she really did. But from her daughter's expression when Ella had left Rafael's workshop earlier, she doubted Holly would want to hear what they had to tell her, let alone meet her biological father.

'We should at least give them both the opportunity,' Felix said.

Ella found herself looking at her husband with new respect. 'You've changed, Felix,' she said.

He gave a tight smile. 'Don't worry, Ella,' he said. 'I'm still the same man. It hasn't been easy, finding out all this. But I love you and I love Holly. And I want to be fair to all concerned.'

She leant over and kissed his cheek. That was all he had ever been. 'Thank you,' she said.

When her mobile rang, Ella assumed it was Holly, but she saw immediately that it was Caleb. She hesitated. 'Sorry,' she said to Felix. 'It's Caleb – he might have found out something.'

Felix nodded. 'Take it,' he said, though the expression in his eyes was grim.

'Ella?' Caleb sounded concerned. 'Are you OK?'

'Yes, of course. Do you have some news already?' She waited.

'Yes, I do.' His voice changed. 'I wanted to let you know – I have discovered who was behind the phone call Holly received, and also who broke into her room.'

Ella leant forwards. That was very quick work. 'Who was it?'

'The man, his name is Felipe Romero,' he said.

'Is he from Triana?' she guessed. If Caleb knew him, this seemed likely.

'*Si*. He is not a pleasant man, Ella. Remember I told you about what happened to my brother Francisco?'

'Yes.' She remembered it all.

'Well, he is one of the same gang. A car thief. And he holds a particular grudge against the English.'

'Why?'

'He always got away with it – he had the luck of the devil,' Caleb told her. 'Then one evening, this Romero, he stole an Englishman's car. This time, it was not his lucky day. That Englishman stopped at nothing to find him and eventually got him convicted for the theft.'

Ella could see why the man might hold a grudge and this must be a horrid reminder for Caleb of his brother's death. 'But surely that's no reason to—'

'And he sells Axel Gonzáles's wine in Cadiz and Córdoba.'

'Oh, I see.' Though she didn't, not entirely. 'But why is that a problem?'

'Axel is almost a one-man band,' Caleb said. 'He may not have told you this. He does not produce many bottles of orange wine. If he supplies Holly, then Felipe Romero may not get what he wants. Felipe sees Holly as an outsider – a foreigner out to destroy his business.'

'So, what do you suggest we do?' she asked him. Caleb seemed to know everyone concerned so perhaps he could come up with a solution. She looked out across to the hotel but there was still no sign of Holly. As for Felix – he was being very patient. She watched him as he drained his glass of wine and ordered another for them both.

'I suppose Holly could meet Axel and agree to him supplying fewer bottles,' Caleb said. 'Then everyone, they will be happy.'

Ella wondered why Axel hadn't worked that out for himself. She supposed that he'd been too preoccupied with trying to make Holly and Ella think that his was a bigger concern than it really was.

'I have spoken to Felipe Romero already,' added Caleb. 'He will not bother Holly again.'

Ella registered the tone of his voice and trusted this to be true. 'Thank goodness for that.' She spoke with some feeling. Felix was watching her curiously. 'Thank you, Caleb,' she said. And after all, there was so much to thank him for.

'It was my pleasure,' he said. Almost as if he already knew.

Beside her, Ella was aware of Felix's frown. 'I'll tell Holly as soon as I see her.' She glanced at her watch. She was surprised Holly hadn't come back by now. Ella hoped that was because she wanted to spend as much time as possible with Rafael because they would all be leaving soon, rather than because she was still angry with her mother.

There was a pause. 'And is that all you will tell Holly?' Caleb asked sadly.

Ella glanced at Felix. He nodded. 'Do it,' he mouthed. 'Tell him.'

'How did you know?' she asked Caleb. She seemed to be asking that question a lot lately. Although she thought she already knew the answer to this.

'I told you, I have a daughter,' he said. 'Or should I say, another daughter.'

'Yes.'

'I showed you her picture. You may not have noticed, we were standing in direct sunlight, but Holly . . . she looks so much like my Emilia,' he said. 'I knew it as soon as I set eyes on her.'

Ella didn't doubt it. And although she hadn't said anything, she had noticed the likeness too. Almost from the moment she was born, she'd never doubted Holly's parentage either – Holly had Caleb's high cheekbones and his dark Spanish eyes. Ella looked at Felix once again. He was like an anchor, she thought. She needed him to keep her on the true path, to stop her from drifting too far from safety. 'Felix and I – we plan to tell Holly the truth,' she told Caleb. 'But it will be very hard for her to hear.'

'I am sure,' he said. But she detected a new note of excitement in his voice. 'Do you think she might want to meet me, talk with me, even meet my family?' And his voice was now so full of hope that Ella's heart ached.

'I don't know yet, Caleb,' she said. 'But I'll ask her.'

'Thank you, Ella.' The words seemed to resonate with suppressed emotion and reminded Ella how much she had denied this man too. 'Thank you so much.'

'Perhaps you should thank Felix,' Ella said with an uncertain glance at her husband. 'It was his idea.'

'I would like to.' Caleb was earnest. 'And for looking after Holly all these years.'

'That might be pushing it.' But Ella was almost smiling as she ended the call.

As if the conversation had summoned her here, the door opened and Holly walked into the bar. She scanned the faces and then she spotted Felix. 'Dad!' She rushed towards him.

He held out his arms and she fell into them as if she were a child again.

Ella watched as Felix stroked Holly's hair. 'It's all right, sweetheart,' he soothed.

'It will be now.' Holly drew away to look at him. 'Oh, Dad,' she said. 'I'm so pleased you're here.'

CHAPTER 44

Holly

Seville, 2018

'What did you just say?' If she hadn't been sitting down already, Holly thought she would have fallen. She stared at her mother. 'What did you say?' she repeated.

'Caleb García is your biological father.'

'OK, don't say anything else.' Holly raised her hand as if to stop her. She closed her eyes. Perhaps when she opened them again, the words would have gone away.

They hadn't.

Her mother reached out to her. She took her hands. There was an awful sadness in her hazel eyes that told Holly more than any words that what she'd said was true. 'Holly . . .'

'What are you telling me?' Holly whispered. 'It's not possible.' Though already her mind had gone into overdrive and she knew that somehow, contrary to everything she had ever believed, it was indeed possible. Because otherwise her mother certainly wouldn't say it. But it was too big a thing.

Holly pulled her hands away. She needed much more time to process it.

Earlier, the three of them – Holly's mother, her father and Holly – had stayed in the little bar by the hotel for an hour or so, eating more tapas, drinking wine and catching up.

Holly had been concerned at first. Had Caleb García left Rafael's workshop earlier in order to waylay her mother? And if he had caught up with her, what had occurred between them? And yet now, here was her father, having appeared out of the blue. But thankfully, her parents seemed to be getting on well, so that was a good sign. As for the rest, Holly would get to the bottom of that later when her father wasn't around.

Her mother had begun by telling Holly about some character called Felipe Romero who had a business arrangement with Axel. This Romero man apparently resented Holly, and it was he who had tried to frighten her off so that he could maintain his position as Axel's main wine supplier. The matter had, her mother told her, been resolved.

Holly was both relieved and confused. 'How do you know all this?' she asked her mother. 'And how did it get resolved?'

At which point a sharp glance passed between her parents and her father got to his feet.

'I'm nipping back to the hotel for a while,' he said.

'But you've only just got here.' Holly frowned.

'I want to give you and your mother some space,' he said.

'Space?' Holly looked from her father to her mother and then back again. 'Why do we need space?'

'We have things to talk about, Holly,' her mother said softly.

OK . . .

So, she and her mother had moved to a quieter part of the bar. And now this . . .

Apparently, it was Caleb García who had discovered the perpetrator of the problem Holly was having and Caleb García who had sorted things out with both Axel and Romero. Who did he think he was, some kind of superman? And Caleb García was her biological father. Holly took another gulp of wine and tried to get to grips with it all.

'I can't excuse what I did, Holly,' her mother was saying now. 'You may not be able to forgive me, but—'

'Does Dad know?' Holly blurted.

'Yes, he knows.'

Holly's mind swam with unasked questions. 'Has he . . . always known?' she asked. And if so, how had he felt about it?

'No.' Her mother's voice was steady. 'I never told him. He never knew anything about my relationship with Caleb. But he found out. And so, I was going to tell him the rest of it this evening.' She paused. 'But it turned out that he already knew that too.'

'This evening? So, you kept it a secret all these years?' Holly couldn't believe the deceit of it.

Her mother let out a long sigh. 'It's complicated, Holly,' she said.

How complicated was telling the truth? Holly seethed. 'Has he forgiven you?' she asked. She found herself hoping not. Her mother didn't deserve it.

'He has.' She bent her head. 'He's a good man.'

'Yes,' said Holly pointedly. 'He is.'

Her mother took a deep breath. More revelations? Holly braced herself.

'This isn't an excuse,' she began, 'but you should know that your father and I – we weren't happy when we came to Seville. I didn't even know if we would stay together . . .'

'But you were still married, Mum.'

'Yes, we were.'

'So . . . ?' Holly kept her expression stony. That didn't excuse her behaviour at all. She wasn't even sure what she was supposed to feel. Shocked? Betrayed? Angry? She felt all those things and more.

'When your father cut the holiday short and went home . . .'

Clearly, this was difficult for her mother, but right now Holly had little sympathy. 'The way was clear,' she muttered.

Her mother shook her head. 'It wasn't like that, darling,' she said. 'I know it sounds bad – it was bad, I admit it. But I was angry that he'd gone home and left me here.' Her gesture took in Seville, its narrow streets, its orange groves. 'I thought he didn't care enough about our marriage to try and save it. I was young, I was thoroughly fed up . . .'

She didn't have to elaborate. Holly had already guessed that her grandmother was pulling the strings and that her mother resented it. Holly could see all that. She could understand it. But even if their marriage was about to fall apart . . . Her mother had still been unfaithful, she'd still betrayed him.

'What can I say?' Her mother seemed at a loss. 'I met Caleb and I was . . .' – she hesitated – 'overwhelmed.'

Holly thought of Rafael. She had been overwhelmed by him too, though it was a very different situation. Holly and Rafael were both free to fall in love. Her mother hadn't been free. She thought of what Rafael had said to her about staying in Seville . . . It was still spinning around in her mind. There was certainly a lot to think about.

'I'm not proud of what happened,' her mother said. 'But I fell in love with Caleb – so much so that I almost ended up staying here in Seville.'

'Really?' Holly was shocked. It wasn't simply a holiday romance then? She thought of the recipe for the Seville orange and almond cake that she'd found all those years ago in her mother's old recipe book and her mother's reaction when Holly had eventually baked it. It had meant a lot. He had meant a lot.

She tried to imagine how her life might have been. Holly adored Seville, and if her mother had made a different decision, she would have spent her whole life here. But that would mean that she'd never have lived in Dorset, never known her father even . . . She shook her head. It was too much. She couldn't envisage it, couldn't take it all in.

'I fell in love with the place too,' her mother admitted.

Holly frowned. 'But you couldn't have known – that you were pregnant, I mean?'

'No.' She gave a small smile. 'It was a big surprise.'

A nice surprise? Holly wondered. Presumably not, under the circumstances. What would *she* have done? She had no clue. 'Did you consider . . . ?' Holly didn't quite know how to put this. The whole conversation was surreal. She felt as though suddenly she'd become a completely different person, her whole identity pulled into question, her memories, everything she knew and believed. The man she loved, who had always been her father in every way that mattered, wasn't her father. Or at least . . .

'No.' Her mother seemed to know what she was asking. 'I hadn't wanted to have a child – at least not at that point – and the timing was terrible.'

Holly could imagine.

'But as soon as I knew I was pregnant . . .' – she paused – 'I wanted you.'

Even though she probably didn't even know the identity of her baby's father. Holly sighed.

'I know it's a lot to take in.' Once again, her mother took her hands and this time Holly didn't immediately pull away.

A lot to take in . . . She wasn't joking.

'At the time, I tried to consider what was best for everyone,' her mother went on. 'Which was hopeless, of course.'

'So, you lied to Dad? You pretended I was his baby?'

'You could have been.'

But she wasn't. 'Did you still love Dad?' Holly whispered. 'Or would your marriage really have been over – if not for me, I mean?'

'I did still love your father, yes.' She seemed very sure. 'I loved them both – but in very different ways.'

Holly nodded. That made sense, sort of.

'Your father – Felix, that is – desperately wanted us to have a baby. And here was a baby. You were his miracle.'

Holly shook her head in wonder. But not his miracle, not really. Her mother had deceived them both – and for a very long time. 'Oh, Mum,' she said.

'I know it's hard to understand.'

But in a way it wasn't hard to understand. Who was Holly to take some moral high ground? These things happened. And by not telling the truth, her mother had given her father the very thing that he longed for. Holly took another sip of the rich and fruity red wine. She was half Spanish. When she had arrived in Seville, she had felt as though she was coming home. And she was in love with a Spanish man. In the past few weeks her life had changed beyond recognition. How could that happen?

'I'm so very sorry, darling.' Her mother looked so sad, so repentant.

It was a long time ago. She had been young and her marriage had been in trouble. She had done something she regretted and she'd had to deal with the consequences in the best way she knew how – for all concerned. She shouldn't have to pay for that forever. Holly reached over and gave her a hug. 'If Dad can forgive you,' she said, 'then so can I.'

When Felix returned to the bar a short while later, he looked so unsure of his reception that Holly launched herself into his arms.

'Nothing's changed, Dad,' she said. 'Not for you and me.'

'That's my girl.' And he held her tight, so tight, that Holly gradually started to feel safe again.

CHAPTER 45

Ella

West Dorset, 1988

Ella stared at the thin blue line of the predictor test. It was positive. A feeling of joy swept over her and made her giddy. She put a hand on her stomach in an instinctive gesture of protection. And then she swore softly as reality hit. *Oh my God . . . What now?*

She had one more look, just to make certain, and then she tucked the tester deep amongst the contents of the bathroom bin – she'd be sure to empty it later – and stared at herself in the mirror of the white cabinet. Pregnant. She put her hand over her mouth. That was it then.

It must be Felix's baby. Although they'd been so careful . . . *So careful you hardly make love anymore*, some treacherous voice whispered inside her. But that was because of the way they lived, she reminded herself, unwilling to be party to any more wifely betrayal. So very close to Felix's mother. Felix was desperate to start a family but Ella had been so determined to wait – not just because she wanted to establish herself at the school, but even more importantly, because she'd wanted them to have their own place. She was grateful for everything Ingrid had done, but how could she bring a baby up here? She looked around the confines of the avocado bathroom. It was impossible. Not because it was small, but because every square inch belonged to her mother-in-law.

Felix had agreed to wait and she knew – or at least hoped – that he was as keen to move out as Ella was, when they could afford it. Now, though . . . School and a house of her own didn't seem quite so important. It was, of course it was. But this . . . This was monumental enough to push everything else aside.

And if it wasn't Felix's baby? Ella hadn't intended for that thought to enter her head. She gripped the sides of the sickly green washbasin until her knuckles were white, as if that might make it go away. Then it must be Caleb's. Ella closed her eyes; it was hard to even think his name and yet some days she seemed to repeat it to herself endlessly as if this could somehow transport her back to the warmth of Seville and to what she had found there. *Caleb.*

She and Caleb had taken no precautions whatever on that day on Asperillo Beach. It had been pure madness. Which was why . . .

So many times over the past weeks, Ella had been tempted to chuck it all in; to tell Felix what had happened in Spain, to give in her notice at the school, to leave her husband, to go back to Seville and throw herself into life there; to at least give it a try. Because she missed Caleb so much. It had been such a short, sweet time and yet the intensity of it seemed to have branded itself onto her soul. *Duende*, she thought. It couldn't be explained, but that didn't make it any less real.

She ran the cold tap and splashed some water onto her face. *Wake up, Ella.* It had been over two months – what made her think Caleb would even want her back, especially after the way she'd left him, without even saying goodbye? He wasn't to know that she'd cried herself to sleep that night, that she'd looked out of the hotel bedroom window at four in the morning and ached to see him standing outside under the orange trees. He hadn't come, though, because he knew, just as she knew, that she was going home, that it was hopeless, that she wasn't free.

Ella had tucked the photo of them standing by the fountain in the orange grove beneath the lining of her underwear drawer and she had taped the old García family recipe into the pages of her own recipe book, half hidden in an envelope. She would never make Caleb's grandmother's Seville orange and almond cake. How could she? But equally, she couldn't bear to throw these memories away.

Maybe by now Caleb had fallen in love with some dusky *señorita*, like the girl she'd seen him with at the family party. Maybe he fell in love all the time – with tourists like Ella, with beautiful young Spanish girls. Maybe even now he was showing some other girl the hideout at the Asperillo dune.

But Ella knew this wasn't so. Perhaps she should have trusted it more, whatever it was that had happened between them? She held the towel next to her skin; it was a small comfort. Could she really have fallen in love with Caleb during one crazy week in Seville? Was it even possible?

No, she had told herself every day as she tried to push the image of him from her mind. She had been telling herself this ever since she had arrived back at the airport to be met by a grateful Felix, who had held her in his arms with such a ferocious love that Ella felt bitterly ashamed. She had fallen in love with a romantic dream, that was all. She had been unfaithful to her husband and of course that was unforgiveable, but in her defence, she and Felix had been struggling and it had been almost an other-worldly time. She had, for a while, been living in that world. But now she was back and she must forget her Spanish lover. Felix had done so much for her, and so it was the only way.

Still hugging the towel, Ella examined her reflection. Did she look different already? She thought so. Her eyes seemed too large for her face; they looked apprehensive too. What had she done? Had some outside force stepped in and made the decision for her? Was it too late to go back to Seville – because that was all she wanted to do? Should she write to Caleb? Explain how she felt? How she had been unable to say goodbye? But if Caleb had been wary when his grandmother had told them that Ella belonged to their family, then how would he react if she went back there and told him she was pregnant?

Ella stifled a wild giggle at the thought. Hysteria, probably. He'd be terrified. But in her heart, Ella sensed that this baby was Caleb's; she almost knew it. And she wondered, was this the future that his *abuela* had seen in the palm of Ella's hand?

Was it fair to expect Felix to bring up another man's child? No, it was not. Ella knew from her own experiences what could happen when someone brought up someone else's child, no matter how good their intentions. She hadn't exactly been a child when Kenny came onto the scene and maybe he'd never had good intentions. Felix was worlds away from Kenny. But even so . . .

There were other options. But Ella dismissed this thought the moment it entered her head. She couldn't lose this baby, she couldn't do anything that would make her lose this baby. So, what? Should she leave Felix and bring her child up alone? The irony was that in a way, despite what had happened, going to Seville had helped her marriage, just as she had hoped. On her return, she had felt so guilty and ashamed that she had thrown herself back into it with much more love and affection than she'd been displaying before. Only, it hadn't been enough. Because Felix still wouldn't acknowledge that anything was wrong between them. They had never had the talk that he'd promised they would have, they were still living half a life in his mother's house and, in the end, nothing had changed.

'Ella? Are you OK?' Felix was outside the bathroom.

'Yes, I'm fine.' She put the towel back on the rail, fluffed up her hair, took a deep breath. She hadn't been feeling well lately, now she knew why.

He gave her a sharp look as she came through the door and onto the narrow landing. 'Sure?'

'Sure.'

'You look tired, love,' he said. 'Go downstairs and put your feet up.' He kissed the top of her head. 'Mum's gone out to bridge and I've got something to tell you.'

'All right.' Ella went down the stairs to put the kettle on. She had something to tell Felix too, but she needed more time. Because she had no idea quite how to do it.

Felix was grinning from ear to ear when he came back into the room. 'The bin men are coming tomorrow morning.' He indicated the black plastic bags he was holding. 'So, I'm just going down to –' He broke off. 'Oh, Ella!'

She stared at him. Her brain was processing the information but it was slow.

'When were you going to tell me?' He dumped the bags

unceremoniously on the floor and rushed over, kneeling at her feet. 'You didn't think I'd mind, my darling, did you?'

Oh my God, she thought.

'I saw it,' he said. 'When I was doing the bins. The tester. You're pregnant. That's so . . .' He beamed. 'So wonderful!'

'Felix . . .' His eyes were shining. He was delighted, she could tell. Ella didn't think she'd ever seen him so happy, not even on their wedding day.

'I am so thrilled, I can't tell you.' He was almost weeping now. 'Oh, Ella, oh, my darling . . .'

Ella felt terrible. This was worse than she could have imagined. After everything Felix and his mother had done for her. This was how she had repaid them. She was bad. So bad. It was unforgiveable. The least she could do was be honest with him now.

'Darling, you're crying!' He took a handkerchief from his pocket and tenderly, he wiped away her tears. 'Listen, I know why. I know you didn't want a baby, not yet. I know the timing's not right.'

Ella couldn't look at him. If only that was all it was. If only this really was Felix's baby. Even though that would mean . . . This baby joined her with Caleb forever, she realised. She shook her head. She was so confused. She really had fallen in love, she recognised that now, with a man who was not her husband. And she was still in love with him. It was wrong, all wrong.

'I know that living here has made things a bit tricky,' Felix said. 'I know it hasn't been easy and that I haven't always been—' He broke off. 'But everything's different now.'

'Yes.' It certainly was.

'We'll make it work.' Felix was still speaking. 'Trust me. We'll make it work because we're a family—'

'I can't stay here,' Ella blurted. And then she felt a sense of horror at her own words. Was she talking about Felix mother's house or was she talking about England? Was she talking about Felix even? She wasn't sure.

'You don't have to.' Felix was still beaming.

Ella stared at him. He looked so glad. And that moved her. It seemed to her that nothing could puncture his happiness. Would she be the one to bring him back down to earth? She finally absorbed what he was saying but she didn't understand. Why wouldn't she have to stay here? 'What do you mean, Felix?' she whispered.

'I've been promoted.' He looked proud now. 'With a raise – backdated to last month. And you know what that means, Ella?'

She shook her head. She didn't know what anything meant right now.

'It means that we can finally afford to get our own place.' He was talking fast, breathless in his excitement.

Ella had never seen him like this before. And if he was capable of this, maybe there were other hidden depths she'd never given him credit for?

'I've done the sums. We've saved enough. I was almost sure before, but now . . .' He took her hands. 'Ella, we can move out. We can buy our own home. It'll have to be something small, but we can do it. And we will do it. For our baby.' He buried his head in her lap.

Ella hesitated for only a moment. And then she laid her hand on his head and ran her fingers through his soft fair hair. Oh, Felix, she thought. How could she disappoint him now? How could she take this away from him when he had given her so much? If she told Felix the truth, she would be unburdened; in some ways it would be a selfish act. But if she didn't . . .

No matter how much she loved the idea of Caleb and of Seville, she could feel both of them dancing inexorably away from her. If she had been honest from the moment she returned, it might be different. But now . . . Would this be living a lie? Yes. But what harm would it do? Felix would never know. Felix would be happy. He would give this baby all the love in the world. The child would have a stable upbringing, a home, a future that wouldn't be so uncertain. She had to think of her unborn child.

She continued to thread her fingers through his hair. Felix was a good man, a gentle man. Perhaps there was something missing in Ella's life. Perhaps that something could be found in Seville. But if she left him, Felix would suffer. He would be broken. She couldn't do that to him. It wasn't fair. Felix was right. They could make this work.

A baby – his baby . . . She could give Felix that in atonement for everything she had done. It was what he most wanted, after all. Ella wouldn't write to Caleb. She wouldn't go back to Seville. She would stay here and she would have their baby. She would keep it a secret – Caleb and everything that had happened in Seville in that passionate and crazy week in springtime. That was the best thing that she could do. It didn't matter who was the biological father of this child. This was a child of love. And this child would be the thing that would save them.

CHAPTER 46

Holly

Seville, 2018

Something had changed, though, Holly thought, the following day, as she made her way back over the bridge to Triana to visit Tomás and Sofía. The revelatory news about her true parentage hadn't altered her relationship with the man she thought of as her real father, the man who had brought her up and cared for her. But it had transformed the way she viewed herself. How could it not? Today, she was seeing the world – and especially Seville – through very different eyes: the eyes of a woman who half belonged here – by birth.

Holly knocked on the door of the Pérez family's place. She looked up at the wrought-iron balcony and the decorative tiles, at Sofía's plants and herbs trailing everywhere, their lemony fragrances drifting in the air. It was just as charming as she'd found it on her first visit. Only days ago, but . . . How much had happened since then.

She thought of Rafael. He had asked her to stay, just as

Caleb had probably asked her mother to stay back in 1988. Did this make a difference? How would she answer him now? She'd hardly had time to think about it, but she knew what her answer must be.

'Holly.' Tomás's voice was curt.

'Hello, Tomás. *Buenos días.*' Holly couldn't blame him for being less than friendly. 'I've come to apologise,' she said.

Tomás's manner softened slightly. 'Come in,' he said, and opened the door wider.

'We've found out who was causing all the trouble,' Holly told him as they stood together in the dimly lit hallway. 'I'm so sorry. And I was wondering – can we start again?'

Tomás smiled. 'Come and say hello to my mother.' He led the way up the narrow stairs. 'I must apologise too, Holly,' he said over his shoulder. 'For trying to kiss you, that is. For putting a . . . what do they say?' He frowned.

'I don't know. A spoke in the wheel?' She laughed. Thankfully, he wasn't the type to bear a grudge.

'I was doing it for my sister,' he said. 'She was so angry and upset about you and Rafael. She could not believe that you had just walked into all of our lives and that he had fallen at your feet.' He glanced back at her, an appreciative glance. '*I* could believe it,' he said. 'And after all,' and he winked, 'who could blame me for trying?'

Once again, Holly laughed. 'And Valentina?'

'She will get over it,' he assured her. 'She is too accustomed to getting what she wants, that sister of mine.' He snapped his fingers. 'Just like that, you know?'

Holly could imagine. 'I hope so,' she said. She really didn't want to upset anyone.

Up in the apartment, Sofía waved away Holly's apologies.

Valentina was there too, looking surly, but Sofía pushed her forward.

'Sorry,' the girl muttered.

'Me too.' Holly smiled and was relieved to see the smile returned, even if it didn't quite reach Valentina's dark eyes.

'I speak to her about her behaviour,' Sofía confided to Holly when Valentina had left the room. 'Rafael Delgado, he never encouraged Valentina's affections. It was' – she tapped her head – 'all in her mind.'

Holly was relieved. 'It doesn't matter,' she assured Sofía.

After she'd taken another look at the products she'd ordered and they'd chatted again about the packaging and a few other details, Holly felt much better. Everything seemed to be working out after all and both Tomás and Sofía said goodbye to her with some affection.

Holly felt a surge of renewed energy. And now, she thought, she must go and see Axel. Her parents had both offered to come with her, as had Rafael, but she'd decided to do it alone. Bitter Orange and its suppliers was her business and she still intended for it to be an independent one.

She walked to the bodega, trying not to feel anxious about the forthcoming encounter. '*Buenos días*, Axel,' she said as she peeked around the half-open door.

'Holly. *Buenos días!*' Axel immediately let loose a torrent of Spanish and Holly couldn't help smiling, though she had no idea what he was saying.

'Slow down, Axel,' she begged.

He took a deep breath. 'I am so sorry. I have done everything wrong. I was so worried. I did not know what to do.'

Axel was so repentant that Holly ended up drinking two

glasses of his rich and fruity orange wine before he would be assured that all was well.

She told him that she could take fewer bottles and they came to a new arrangement.

'But in the future,' he said, 'who knows . . . I hope to make more.'

'That sounds good.' Holly climbed down from the bar stool. 'Are you planning on expanding the business, Axel?'

'An assistant,' he enthused. 'Yes. There is perhaps a way. I can see it. The possibility.' He rubbed his hands together. 'Another glass for the road?'

'Definitely not. Thank you.' Otherwise she wouldn't be able to see the road.

'It was the suggestion of Caleb García,' said Axel. 'A good man. A clever man.'

Hmm, thought Holly. She wasn't quite sure how she felt about Caleb being involved in her business dealings – even at a distance and even if he had solved the biggest problem for her already.

Holly said goodbye to Axel and made her way to the café where she was meeting Rafael. But what if she decided to stay in Seville? She was in love with Rafael, she had no doubt about that. But it was very early days. She didn't want to lose him. She knew already that he was special. But she had her new business to think of too. She found herself thinking of her mother. What hope was there of having it all?

Rafael was already sitting outside the café. Holly paused, enjoying the sight of him while he hadn't yet spotted her. He was leaning back in the chair, long legs outstretched, face lifted to the sun, drinking it in, a half-smile on his face.

And then there was Caleb. Her biological father. A man who

was important to Rafael, who was in his life and who would be in hers too if she let him. How could she not? Her mother had said he'd like to meet her properly, but that it was completely up to Holly, of course. Her father had gone even further. 'It might be a good thing to do, Holly,' he'd suggested.

'Good for who?' she'd asked him. 'Or what?' After all, she'd never needed this man before and she didn't need him now. Real fatherhood wasn't just about fertilising an egg and then walking away – though Holly realised that this was unfair; Caleb hadn't even known of her existence until a few days ago and he'd hardly walked away.

Real fatherhood was about the day-to-day stuff. The scuffed knees of childhood, the signature Felix-dish of spaghetti Bolognese on a Saturday night, the protection, the taxi-driving to teenage parties, the unlimited care. So many things that built into a whole castle of memories and love.

'For your peace of mind?' her father had suggested.

And Holly had to admit that she was curious.

Slowly, she walked towards Rafael. There was a moment, when he opened his eyes and saw her. A moment when a slow smile stretched across his face, a moment when he jumped to his feet and came towards her, his eyes telling her that in seconds she would be in his arms.

Holly knew the ways in which she took after her mother. But in what ways did she take after her biological father? Who was he? And did she have the courage to find out?

CHAPTER 47

Ella

Seville, 2018

Ella met up with Caleb again at a coffee bar on the corner of Calle Sierpes near the cathedral. She knew she had to see him one last time – not least because there was so much still left unsaid. She'd chosen somewhere busy, somewhere on the tourist trail, somewhere neutral and away from the memories of Triana. Not because she didn't trust him. Not because she didn't trust herself. But because now, she wanted everything to be straight between them.

They kissed hello, on each cheek, as old friends do, and they sat down at an outside table in the morning sun. It might be a neutral place, but still, orange trees lined the street as they so often did in Seville, and the sweet fragrance of the blossom positively saturated the air.

They talked for a few minutes about the weather, about the number of tourists milling around the plazas and avenues, even about the coffee – which had arrived and was good.

Then they both laughed.

'Thanks for meeting me,' Ella said. 'I know I ran away before. But I wanted you to know – it was good to see you, to hear about what's happened in your life.' She shrugged. 'Everything.' It was all good.

Caleb nodded. 'You too. I thought I would never see you again, Ella.'

She could imagine. 'It must have been a shock.'

'It was.' He laughed. 'And I made a fool of myself all over again, did I not?'

'Never.' She reached across and put a hand on his. This was what she wanted him to know. 'It's still there for me too. The feeling. It always will be. But . . .'

'You made a choice,' he said.

'I did, yes.' Ella leant back in her chair once more and surveyed him. He was still an attractive man. The lines around his mouth and eyes suggested that he'd done a lot of laughing, so perhaps the older Caleb wasn't quite as serious and intense as the younger one had been. 'But that doesn't mean that I didn't . . .' She hesitated.

'Love me?'

He had always been the braver one. 'Yes,' she said. She had loved him all right. When someone made you feel the way Caleb had made her feel, what else could it be but love?

Caleb was silent for a moment. He took a sip of his *cortado*. 'When you left, back then, after Asperillo, after . . .' – he hesitated – 'after everything that had happened between us, I was angry.'

Ella nodded. She didn't doubt it.

'I thought . . .' He put down his glass and she saw his fist clench. 'That I had met the girl of my heart.'

His words moved her more than she could say. Behind her sunglasses, she blinked away a single tear.

'I knew you were married, yes, of course.' He glanced up at her. 'But I thought I could persuade you to give me the chance.'

Only Ella had disappeared before he could even try. 'And then?' she whispered.

'When you left, I saw that it was not the same for you.'

She opened her mouth to protest, but he held up a hand to stop her. 'I saw that I did not mean the same to you,' he said quietly.

Around them people strolled down Calle Sierpes, pointing out the elegant glass shopfronts to one another, exclaiming, taking photographs. Perhaps, Ella thought, she should have been braver. Or perhaps Caleb was right and what she had felt for him had never quite been enough to overcome all the rest of it. Perhaps she would never know the real answer.

'What did you do after that?' she asked him.

His mouth twisted. 'I got drunk. I got angry. I suppose I went a bit crazy for a while.' He shrugged.

'And then?'

He nodded. 'You are right. I know what it is that you are saying. So, yes, I went on with my playing. Life continued. I went on with making my pots, my bowls, my jugs. And then after my mother died, I went to Huelva.'

'And you met Mariana.'

'*Sí*.' Another long look, but his sunglasses prevented her from reading the expression in his eyes; she could only guess. 'And everything, it began to make sense again.'

'I'm glad.' And she really was.

'I am not saying I forgot about you, Ella.' This time, it was Caleb who placed his hand over hers.

Ella understood that. She hadn't forgotten him either. She never would.

'But . . . I let you go.'

And she had done the same, she realised.

'Now, though . . .' He released her hand. 'Now, you come back to Seville. And with my daughter!'

'Yes.' That was something she couldn't deny.

'You are like a hurricane, Ella,' he said. 'You burst into our lives and you turn everything all around and into chaos.'

Ella said nothing. She'd never seen it quite that way.

He slammed a fist on the table and she jumped. 'It was wrong not to tell me about Holly.' He sounded very fierce.

'I know,' she said. What's more, given the choice, she never would have. 'I'm sorry. But Felix—'

'Yes, yes.' He sighed. 'I know about Felix. He is your husband. He loves you. He saved you.' He swore softly under his breath.

'And he desperately wanted a baby,' Ella added. She wouldn't tell him about the cystic fibrosis, though, that was Felix's business.

'*Si*. Of course he did.' Caleb sat back in his chair. He picked up his glass of coffee. The anger seemed to have disappeared as quickly as it had come.

'I did wrong by both of you,' Ella admitted. Did he think she didn't know that?

Caleb shook his head. 'You are a beautiful woman, Ella,' he said. 'A woman who can love. A woman who tries to do the best thing. What can be wrong in that?'

Ella looked down. This was even more difficult than she had expected.

'And perhaps, after all, you have given me something,' Caleb said. 'I hope that you have given me Holly.'

Ella smiled. She hoped so too. Felix had also encouraged

Holly to meet up with him so she hoped that their daughter would at least give Caleb a chance to get to know her a little before they left Seville. Ella had denied them both knowledge of one another – perhaps this would do something to make up for that. 'I think she'll come round,' she told him. 'It's just been rather a shock, that's all.'

'A shock for everyone,' Caleb agreed. He was smiling now. He signalled to the waiter to bring their bill and threw some coins down on the table.

Ella got out her purse but he waved it away with an exasperated shake of his head.

'Thank you for helping Holly,' Ella said. 'I'm so grateful.'

'It was nothing.' Caleb's expression darkened. 'Felipe Romero – he owes me.' He seemed to shake the thought away. 'And if I can, I always will help her, Ella.'

She acknowledged this with a small smile. She knew that this was true and it meant a lot.

'It was worth it, Ella.' He got to his feet and Ella followed suit. 'You and me, I mean.'

Ella thought of that special week she'd spent with him in the springtime of 1988, thirty years ago. And she thought of Holly. 'It definitely was,' she agreed.

'So . . .' Caleb opened his arms and, without hesitation, Ella walked into them. His warmth seemed to close around her. 'Thank you,' he whispered into her hair. 'For everything.'

Ella couldn't speak. She buried her face in his shoulder for one last time.

But the hug ended as it had to end and, once again, she felt him let her go. 'Goodbye, Caleb,' she said.

'Goodbye, Ella.'

And only the scent of orange blossom remained all-pervading in the air as Ella walked away.

CHAPTER 48

Ella

Seville, 2018

It was two days later and they were due to fly back to the UK the following morning.

Ella had gone with Holly to see one of Holly's producers who would be providing a neroli face moisturiser and lip balm for the shop and they were now strolling down the avenue of orange trees outside the Alcázar Palace back towards the hotel where Felix was waiting for them. Beyond the high walls, Ella could hear the parakeets screeching in the palms of the palace gardens.

'I can't believe this is our last afternoon here,' Ella said.

'Mum.' Holly came to a sudden stop. 'I've decided to stay for another few days.'

Ella smiled. She wasn't altogether surprised. 'Because of Rafael?'

'Partly.' A faint blush appeared on her daughter's cheeks. 'Plus, I've still got a few more loose ends to tie up. Rafa's found me another producer of organic orange wine. More like a sherry, really – what they call a *fino* – so with what Axel can let me have, it would work.'

Ella nodded. She knew all about *fino*. She wondered if tying up a few loose ends might include Holly seeing Caleb. She hoped so.

As they walked on through the maze of narrow streets that led to their hotel, Holly looped her hand into Ella's arm – and Ella knew that despite everything and against the odds perhaps, she and her daughter had grown even closer over the past few days. This time in Seville together had certainly strengthened their bond and even after all Ella's revelations . . . Somehow, they had got through it and come out the other side.

Holly had flung plenty of accusations at Ella at first – and who could blame her? But since then . . . She'd asked so many questions over the past few days and Ella had tried to answer as fully and honestly as she could. In a way, that too had brought them closer.

Ella squeezed her daughter's arm. 'I'm sure you're doing the right thing,' she said. 'Follow your instincts and you won't go far wrong.' She hesitated. 'And as for Caleb . . .' The name hung between them but when Ella glanced across at her, she was relieved to see that her daughter wasn't frowning.

'Yes?' And Holly actually smiled.

'I'm not putting you under any pressure,' Ella said. 'And neither is he. Whether you see him or not, it's up to you. But I just wanted to let you know . . .'

'What, Mum?'

'He's a very special man. And' – she paused – 'he always will be.'

*

Later, Felix and Ella sat on the bench in the plaza near the hotel enjoying the late afternoon sunshine.

'How did Holly seem this morning?' Felix asked. 'Do you think she's got over the shock yet?'

'She seems all right,' Ella told him. 'She's still absorbing it. But I think she'll be OK. And she has Rafael here to help her.'

'Do you think she'll move to Seville?' Felix looked glum.

'I don't know.' Ella knew how strong the pull of the city could be . . . She lifted her face to the warmth of the springtime sun. She guessed that Holly would also use this extra time in Seville to decide.

Ella tried not to worry. If anything else went wrong for Holly, then Caleb would help her sort out any problems, she was sure – at least, if Holly gave him the chance. And if their daughter did decide to move to Seville and do something entirely different with her life, it wouldn't be the end of the world. Ella and Felix could come and spend more weekends here. She smiled to herself. Who knew? He might come to love the city as much as Ella did.

'And how about us, Ella?' Felix asked. 'Are we all right now, do you think?'

Ella held his arm more tightly. 'We are,' she said. She watched the sunlight as it dappled the glossy green leaves of the orange trees in the grove at the far end of the plaza; as it highlighted the grain of the bark, and was reflected from the globes of the orange fruit. She had no doubts about that.

'No regrets?'

Ella thought of Caleb; the intensity of his dark eyes, his passion – when he played the flamenco, when he spoke of his family, and most of all when they had made love that day at the Asperillo Dune . . . She hugged that last thought to herself.

It had been a long time ago, and Felix didn't have to know everything.

And then she thought of Felix who had once looked after her at the time when she most needed it, who had loved her every minute of every day since they first met, who had been an amazing father and a wonderful son – giving his mother everything she asked for and more. She thought of the way he cared for and tended his plants, his love of the outdoor life and nature, his calm grey eyes and gentle smile.

She loved him. At first, the love had been built on gratitude and duty. But now . . . Like one of his plants it had grown and blossomed into something quite different, something special that she knew she was lucky to have. Ella breathed in deeply. There was still some orange blossom on the trees in the orange grove and the heady scent seemed to creep deep into her soul.

'No regrets, Felix,' she said. 'It's just another beginning for us, that's all.'

CHAPTER 49

Holly

Seville, 2018

'Thanks for coming.'

Holly regarded him steadily. She could see what was eerily like the reflection of her own eyes, her own bone structure in his face. How bizarre was that? Perhaps it was strange that she'd never questioned how little she looked like the only father she'd ever known, but she really hadn't. Most kids probably went through a stage of feeling distance, of wondering if they were actually the product of their parents at all. But Holly hadn't done that either. She had never questioned anything. More fool her, she thought.

'It's OK,' she said. 'I wanted to . . .' *Find out what you were like.* But she didn't say it. What did you say to a complete stranger who had turned out to be your biological father? 'It's pretty weird, though,' she added. Unreal almost. She felt a sense of loss and a sense of inevitability. It was what it was. End of.

His smile flickered. 'Very weird,' he agreed. It was a crack in the ice, at least, she thought.

Holly could tell he was wondering whether to shake hands or kiss her. She stepped forwards, making the decision for him, lightly kissing the stubble on his cheek, once, twice – the Spanish way.

He looked relieved. 'Shall we sit? What can I get you?'

For their meeting place, Holly had chosen a bar in Triana that she'd often gone to with Rafael. It was simple, clean and decorated with bluc, yellow and white *azulejo* tiles. It was usually busy but rarely full and there was plenty of room to sit outside at tables with red umbrellas where you could linger and watch the world pass by. Or even have a chat with your new father, thought Holly.

'Beer, please,' she said to Caleb and sat down at a wooden table that was half in the sun and half in the shade. That was how she felt. Ambivalent.

She had spent the past few days trying to absorb her mother's story, part of which was Holly's story too. The more details she could discover, the more she could understand – or at least that was the theory. And being here in Seville, while she took on her own Spanishness as it were, had been special. It would take time for her to grow into her new identity – because that was how it felt – but at heart, she was still the same person, with the same hopes, fears and dreams. And Holly held on to that.

'Do you blame my mother?' Holly asked Caleb when he reappeared with two glasses of beer. This was something she'd been wondering about. 'For not telling you about me, I mean?'

He hesitated. Perhaps he hadn't been expecting her to get down to the nitty-gritty so quickly.

'I hardly had time to,' he said after a moment. 'I saw you in Rafa's workshop. I saw your mother. I recognised you . . . I tried to take in what it must mean. And then she was gone and I knew.' He reached into his pocket for his phone, and showed her a picture.

Holly blinked at it. The girl was younger than Holly and wore her hair in a different way. But . . . 'Your daughter?' she murmured.

He nodded. 'Emilia. You're very alike.'

'We are.' So not only a new father but also a half-sister. Holly raised a questioning eyebrow.

'I have a son too.' He found a picture. 'Luis.'

Her half-brother was not so like his father, but he had the same warm smile.

'And grandchildren.' More pictures.

Holly let all this new information slot in. A whole new family, she thought. Around her, the noise and bustle of Triana's main street continued unabated as if nothing momentous had happened at all. Scooters and bicycles wound their way down the road, avoiding all the obstacles. Music blared from restaurants and cafés. In a bar opposite, a young guy was playing a soulful guitar; three teenage boys were laughing and joshing with each other on the pavement nearby; on the table next to them a couple were kissing. Seville. Life. It went on.

'I was a little angry at first,' he admitted. 'But I can only imagine how hard it must have been for your mother – to have found herself in the position that she did. And so . . .' He shrugged.

Very understanding of him. Holly considered his words. It *had* been hard for her mother, she knew. It had taken Holly a while to accept this, a while to fully appreciate what the situation had meant for everybody . . . But now, she had. Everyone was bigger than their socially constructed boundaries, she supposed. 'Yeah.' Holly picked up her beer and took a slug. It was golden, cold and fizzy. *And so . . .*

'Hard for you too,' he said.

He wasn't wrong there and Holly acknowledged this with a small nod. She didn't want to dwell. He was a man who seemed to think a lot about other people's feelings. 'You're a good man,' she said.

He laughed and she liked the way his eyes crinkled at the corners. 'Who told you that?'

'Rafael for one.' She smiled back at him. 'Mum for another. And Axel Gonzáles.' Even her father hadn't had a bad word to say about him.

'Thanks.'

Holly nodded. 'And thank you – for finding out who was behind the Axel business. For sorting it out for me.' That had been a huge relief. It just went to show that even the sunniest places had their shadowy side.

Caleb made a little gesture of dismissal that reminded her of Rafael. 'It was my pleasure. You are doing business in my home town. I am happy to be able to help. Now and at anytime.' He gave her a searching look from those dark eyes and she sensed that he wanted to add *and you are my daughter*, but didn't know if it was just too soon.

'I appreciate that,' she said. She hadn't known quite how to do this, and clearly neither had he. But they were making a good start, she felt. It would take much longer, though, for any of it to feel easy.

Caleb seemed to come to a decision. He held out his glass. 'Here's to getting to know you.'

They clinked glasses. Things definitely weren't as bad as Holly had first thought. She hadn't lost her true father, Felix, and now, she had more understanding of her mother too, because Holly had always known there was something . . . She'd gained an entire Spanish family, including a father who was extraordinarily good at sorting out problems. What's not to like about all that? she thought with a smile.

'Here's to getting to know you too.' Holly could see the warmth in his eyes. And with a slight jolt of surprise, she realised that she meant it.

CHAPTER 50

Holly

Seville, 2018

It was Holly's final night in Seville. All around, the Sevillians were making preparations for the wild and glamorous *Feria de Abril* and Holly would have loved to have experienced it, and with Rafel. But she couldn't justify staying here any longer.

She and Rafael were having dinner in their favourite restaurant and as they lingered over the red wine and tapas, she told him about today's meeting with Caleb.

'Did you like him, Holly?' Rafael put down his fork and picked up her hand.

She knew how important this was to him. Caleb had been quite the father figure to Rafael – which was ironic. But what Caleb had done for this man she loved made it even easier to warm to the father who was still a stranger.

Still, she decided to be honest. 'We didn't throw ourselves into each other's arms, if that's what you're imagining,' she teased. 'It was all very civilised.'

'And very British then.' He pulled a face.

'Although I am half Spanish, remember,' she pointed out.

'Ah, yes, so you are.' He played with her fingers and Holly felt the delicious heat of his touch ripple through her. *Later*, she thought. Their last night, she was sure, would be one to remember.

'I like him,' she admitted. 'I'm looking forward to getting to know him a bit better.'

Rafael beamed. 'That makes me very happy,' he said. 'Because it will make him happy, I know.'

'So, since I am now officially half Spanish . . . ?' Holly slid her hand from his and dug into the tapas. Tonight, they had ordered a delicious mixture of a simple spinach and chickpea stew, ratatouille topped with fried egg, *cazón en adobo* – which turned out to be a kind of white fish marinated in garlic, cumin and paprika – and various melt-in-your-mouth croquettes. Whether they went traditional or contemporary, one of the things Holly loved most about Seville was the tapas.

'You have a way to go before you become ruled by your emotions,' Rafael informed her. 'You will have to live in Spain some time before that happens.' He waggled his eyebrows at her.

Hmm. He might be teasing, but Holly decided to divert the conversation. She hadn't given him her answer yet but clearly, he'd made his own assumptions. And why shouldn't he? He knew as well as she that they were head-spinningly in love with one another. Rafael was the main reason Holly had changed her flight to extend her trip. She couldn't get enough of him. In bed, he was passionate; every touch had the power to thrill. He was good company, he made her laugh, they always had so much to talk about . . . And Holly loved his creativity; his focus and concentration when he was working on the potter's wheel or painting his ceramics with a touch so delicate it made her want to hold her breath for fear of disturbing him. When he held her gaze, she could feel herself melting inside. And when he played the flamenco guitar with that faraway look in his eyes . . . His music seemed to take him to another world, but Holly sensed that it was a world that could include her. And she wanted that, she realised.

Only . . .

It was almost midnight by the time they walked through the narrow streets of Santa Cruz back to the orange grove by the hotel. The pungent scent of the blossom, the rich fruity fragrance of the oranges themselves always seemed stronger when the perfume had settled deep into the blackness of the night.

'I know that you must return to the UK, Holly,' Rafael said softly. 'But when will you come back to me?'

When she didn't reply, he took her in his arms and kissed her; a kiss so full of longing that Holly wanted to drown in it instead of answering his question as she knew she must.

When they drew apart, she saw the question remaining in his eyes, blurred in the shadowy light of the half-moon, but still there. Waiting.

'I don't know, Rafa,' she said. 'There'll be so much to do, with the shop and everything.' She knew how busy she would be. And neither would there be much spare money available for trips to Seville. When would they be able to see each other? She hadn't let herself think of this before; she supposed they would just have to find a way.

'But Holly . . .' He pulled away from her. 'You are still opening the shop?'

She stared back at him. 'Yes, of course I am.' She'd been

planning this venture for more than a year – she'd told him that. Her grandmother had made a serious investment; Holly couldn't let her down. She'd already rented the premises, agreed the contracts; everything was ready. *She* was ready. Rafael knew all that. He'd even helped her source some of her products. How could he imagine that she wouldn't be opening Bitter Orange as planned?

'But I thought . . .' A frown creased his brow. 'You and I . . .'

Holly hated the look of confusion on his face. She desperately wanted to smooth it away.

'You and I have something very special,' she assured him. 'You know how I feel about you, Rafa.'

'But our plans?' He took a step away. He was keeping a distance between them now.

'What plans?' she whispered. They hadn't, in fact, made any concrete plans. He had told her that he loved her, and she had admitted her own reciprocal feelings without hesitation. He had told her that he wanted to live with her one day; even that he wanted to spend his life with her (though privately Holly thought it was far too soon to be making such momentous decisions after knowing one another for such a short time – even for a Spaniard). He'd made all that very clear. But how that was going to happen? Who would give up what in order for that to happen? They hadn't discussed this at all – beyond Rafael asking Holly to stay in Seville.

The anger flared in his eyes now. 'To be together, of course,' he said. 'Have you forgotten, Holly? What we talked of?' He made a fist, stepped away and hit the trunk of the nearest orange tree with a thump.

Holly flinched. That must have hurt. She took a step towards him. Took hold of his bunched fist. 'Yes, I know, Rafa,' she said softly. 'I want all that too.' She brought his hand to her lips and kissed it. 'You know I do. But I can't come here now, not yet.'

'When then?' he asked.

She hesitated. That was a question she was unable to answer. 'I don't know right now. I can't make any promises. I have so many other commitments.'

'Other commitments?' Once again, he pulled away from her. 'And you can make no promises? I do not think you are half Spanish after all, Holly. Other commitments? No promises?' He swore softly. 'What matters most is love.' He crossed his arms over his chest as if his very heart was aching.

In the distance she heard a couple chatting together and laughing. They sounded so carefree that Holly had to bite her lip to stop the tears from coming. 'Yes,' she said. 'I know.' He was right. Only perhaps he was right about the Spanish thing too because the business did matter – it mattered a lot. Her grandmother mattered. Holly's plans – the plans she'd made before meeting Rafael – they mattered.

'So?' He glared at her. He wasn't giving an inch.

'So, there's time,' she said. 'The future . . .' Her voice trailed. 'You and I – after all, we've only just met.'

'But I know what I want.' He was almost shouting now.

Holly winced. She understood his frustration. But it wasn't so easy, was it? Love didn't exist in a vacuum. There were other people – just as there had been for her mother. There were other things, like Holly's business plans. There were even other places. Holly lived in Dorset; Rafael lived in Seville. In 2016 the UK had committed to leaving Europe – much to Holly's distress. They hadn't left – at least not yet. But where did that leave a Spanish man and a British woman who had happened to fall in love?

'And I want you.'

'I want you too.' But it was beginning to sound so hopeless. Holly half turned away towards the little paths that led through the orange grove to the central deep stone well. But there were no answers there. It *was* hopeless – just as it had been for her mother before her, only for different reasons. Rafael was angry and upset and it was Holly's fault; she had got so carried away with enjoying this unexpected and precious time together with him that she hadn't explained anything properly and she hadn't even had the grace to answer his question.

'If you loved me,' Rafael said. And his dark eyes blazed. 'If you loved me . . .'

'I do love you.' But here they were, having their first row. And now Holly was angry too. Was love about trying to take everything away from someone? Everything she had worked for? Everything she had planned? If so, she wanted none of it. Only . . .

'But not enough,' he said.

'If you loved *me*' – she knew tit for tat was childish, but she wanted to make him see – 'then you'd at least try and understand how much I've put into this business.'

'Oh, business,' he scoffed. 'Nothing matters more in life. Is that not right?'

Holly was stung. 'It's important to me,' she said. 'How can you ask me to give up something that's so important to me?'

'And I am not important?'

Oh, honestly. She sighed. 'Yes, yes, of course you are, Rafa. But you don't understand.'

'There you are mistaken,' he flashed back at her. 'I understand only too well.'

Only, he didn't. 'Rafa . . .'

'Goodbye, Holly,' he said.

And before she could say a word to stop him, he was striding down the path and through the orange grove. Walking away from her and out of her life.

Shit. 'Rafael.' Holly whispered his name. But he didn't hear her and he didn't stop walking. 'Rafael.' Louder now. Holly took a step forward. She stopped. She let him go. She watched him disappear from sight. Because . . .

Was it for the best? Holly slowly made her way out of the orange grove, into the hotel and up to her room. She let herself in, walked over to the window and looked down into the circular orange grove with its arches and trellises, its winding paths leading to the secret well within. In the moonlight, the round, bumpy fruit glowed faintly on the trees like far-off planets in some other galaxy.

No, she thought. Because they had lost their last night together and that was a terrible waste. And maybe she'd lost Rafael too, which was even worse.

She had done the same thing that her mother had done thirty years ago. She had left the man she'd fallen in love with in Seville; she'd made a different choice. Her mother had chosen her marriage over Caleb; Holly had chosen her ambitions over Rafael. *Oh, God* . . . She felt the sting of tears in her eyes. She missed him already. She longed for the warmth of his arms, the lilt of his voice, his very slightly crooked smile. Holly flung open the window. But all that was left was the bitter-sweet scent of the orange trees and the darkness of the sultry night sky.

CHAPTER 51

Holly

Dorset, 2019

It was February and Holly was making marmalade. She'd washed and cut the oranges, and squeezed out the juice, and now the fruit and water were simmering gently in the preserving pan. The saucers for testing the setting consistency were in the freezer and now, after two hours, she was ready to check the pith for softness – it couldn't be cooked any further once the sugar was added.

Holly wanted to make enough marmalade to last the whole year – she'd do it in several batches – and so she'd ordered plenty of bitter Seville oranges from the Ave María farm outside Seville. If there were enough left over, she had a plan in mind to make her own aromatic orange gin. In fact, since her visit to Seville last year, she'd discovered all manner of culinary uses for Seville oranges – from bitter-sweet orange vinaigrette, so much more subtle than a lemon dressing, to her latest practice of drying the perfumed peel and adding it to meat casseroles, curries and stews.

It had been a thrill when the oranges arrived. Some were wrapped in the branded Ave María tissue paper that had once protected them from spoilage on long journeys, but was probably used more for sentimental and aesthetic reasons nowadays, and all were packed in the green and orange boxes she'd seen last spring when she and her mother had made that eventful trip to Seville. But a bitter-sweet thrill, she thought. Because the oranges reminded her of Rafael, and of the love that had started with such a sweet promise but ended with bitterness that last night in the orange grove.

The pith was soft to the bite, but not yet disintegrating, so Holly turned off the heat and waited until the muslin package containing the flesh and pips of the oranges was cool enough for her to be able to squeeze it between her finger and thumb to extract all the pectin. As this oozed out through the muslin, she gently scraped it off and returned it to the pan. More pectin would improve the quality of her end product and meant that the marmalade would set more easily.

If she could turn back time, would she have done anything differently? Holly didn't think so. Which didn't mean that she hadn't cared deeply for Rafael – she still missed him, still thought of him often, and she hadn't contemplated embarking on a new relationship; she simply wasn't looking.

Holly added the sugar and salt, and stirred until the sugar dissolved. She upped the heat still further, boiling the mixture hard for fifteen minutes, stirring it occasionally to make sure it didn't catch, skimming off the scum for a clear jelly. She tested it on one of her cold plates – the marmalade wrinkled when she pushed gently with her little finger. A few more minutes should do it, she decided.

'Do you think I made a massive mistake?' Holly had asked

her mother some weeks ago when she'd popped in for a coffee. She seemed the obvious person to ask, and since being back in Bridport, Holly had found that she and her mother spent time together discussing a lot of things, which was definitely one of the pluses to living here. They'd become good friends, almost without Holly noticing.

'No, I don't.' Her mother seemed very sure. 'It just shows, darling, that you value yourself and your business. Which has got to be a good thing.'

'Hmm.' Holly was only half convinced. She had thought that at the time, yes. But since then there had been a lot of long and lonely nights when she'd questioned her decision, nights when Rafael's face seemed near to her in her dreams, when in reality, it was a long, long way away.

'It shows that you value the time you spent on your business course too, your ambition to start your own shop, your dream of a different life. You worked hard for all that and it's no small thing.' Her mother reached over to smooth Holly's hair from her face. 'Giving that all up for Rafael . . . It would never have worked.'

Holly knew she was right. She would never have been happy if she'd had to give up her dream. But the problem was that she now had no one to share it with. That springtime with Rafael in Seville had shown her something else that she could have – something that had nothing to do with business or ambition – and she still wanted it.

Holly sighed. The marmalade mixture had been off the heat for fifteen minutes now and she'd kept stirring to stop it setting. Marmalade had to cool down before it could be decanted into jars.

She had tried to keep in touch with Rafael. After the night

he'd walked away from her in the orange grove, she'd emailed and messaged him regularly, sent him pictures of the shop and cheery little updates on how things were going. In her messages, she stayed upbeat, she didn't get heavy and she didn't apologise for what had happened on that last night. After all, wouldn't she do the same again? She just hoped that with time he might understand her decision.

Holly's jars were prepared and ready on the kitchen counter. She took a deep breath, grasped hold of the handles of her preserving pan and began to pour. It was important to maintain a rhythm and it was hypnotic, watching the vibrant orange jelly slip into the jars, one by one, as she breathed in that scent of Seville and springtime.

Rafael had messaged back from time to time, but it wasn't the same. His messages had got shorter as the year progressed and he'd said little about what he was doing. There was no mention of when they might see one another. No talk of love. Holly paused in her pouring. Had they drifted apart? It had been such a short time together; perhaps it had been unrealistic of her to hope that it would be enough, that they had established enough of a bond, enough strength in their relationship to take them through.

He'd probably met someone else.

Holly felt her stomach flip. She put the empty preserving pan, sticky from the marmalade, down into the sink, squirted in some washing-up liquid and turned on the hot tap. It was ridiculous to feel so bereft at the thought. Only . . . Only, she had hoped. She'd hoped he'd understand that at least for now she had to be here to look after the shop – which was her baby after all.

Holly wiped her hands on her apron and surveyed her

rows of gleaming jars with pleasure. One by one, she popped a waxed paper disc on the top of each, followed by her wet plastic covers, each one bound tightly with a rubber band. But the only thing Rafael had seemed to understand was that she would not be immediately returning to Seville and rushing back into his arms.

At least Bitter Orange was doing pretty well. It was always going to be tough to start up an enterprise like this, especially with so much current uncertainty about the UK's decision to leave Europe. It hadn't been implemented yet and Holly still held out some hope of a turnaround, but she doubted that would happen. She knew she'd taken a risk. But she'd worked hard on getting her website up and running and Bridport was a thriving and popular town – with locals and tourists alike. There were plenty of individual concerns like hers and people also came here for the vibrant street market and to visit the well-established vintage area. Independent shops here had a more than decent chance of surviving and Holly was determined to make hers one of them.

Her kitchen was full of marmalade and that was the way Holly liked it best. She breathed in the rich, glorious smell that she never tired of, took off her apron and ran down to the shop where her father was holding the fort. Holly had moved into the tiny flat upstairs a couple of months ago, and much as she'd basked in the security of living back with her parents for a year, it felt good to have her own space once again.

As for Bridport, she was glad to be back here. The pace of life was slower and she'd never stopped loving the glorious landscape she'd grown up with. She was enjoying spending time with her family, but she'd also reconnected with some of her friends – especially Jess and Will and Susie – and she now felt part of a warm and sociable community where people who came into the shop had more time and often wanted to chat.

In the shop now, a couple were examining the neroli candles, a woman was trying out the tester of orange-scented hand cream, and another younger woman was in the process of paying for a vibrant orange silk scarf and some black socks with an orange tree print – as discovered by Caleb in Seville. Not only was he looking out for new products for Bitter Orange but Holly and Caleb had been emailing regularly, swapping family photographs and news, and Holly was genuinely enjoying finding out more about her new family in Andalusia.

'Maybe,' Holly had said to her mother that same afternoon, 'I might go back to Seville for a few days later this year.'

'To see Rafael?' her mother had asked.

Holly swallowed. 'Perhaps.' That rather depended . . . 'But the stuff we already have here's selling well. I'd like to look around and make some more orders.' Also, in a shop like Bitter Orange, things couldn't stand still. She had to keep sourcing new products, keep the interest going. 'And I'd like to catch up with Caleb,' she added shyly. She wanted to get to know him better and even meet his family – who were her family too; she knew that now for sure.

Her mother got to her feet and pulled her into a hug. 'Oh, Holly,' she said. 'You know we'd always look after the shop for you, and if you can make it in the school holidays . . . ?'

'Thanks, Mum.' Holly wasn't sure she could have done any of this without her family's support. They had all given her something.

'And Rafael?'

Holly nodded, but didn't quite trust herself to speak. It might be too late. Still, she had to find out if there was any chance of a future for them. Although that last night in the orange grove . . . She feared that this was the moment she'd lost him.

Holly looked around the shop with pleasure. Nevertheless, this was her achievement, and she was so proud.

'Hello, love.' Her father had finished the transaction in his usual cheery manner and said goodbye to the customer.

'Hi, Dad.' He was a tremendous asset to the shop, thought Holly. She couldn't afford an assistant, at least not yet, but her father helped out for an hour or two most days. It wasn't working out in the open, as he preferred, but his work with the National Trust gave him enough of that already and he'd assured Holly that he relished the variety. He was growing ornamental orange trees too – cultivating them in his little greenhouse at home and bringing them into the shop when they were ready. They were so pretty and decorative that Holly was almost reluctant to sell them; but she had a business to run, so she had to let them go.

'Mum's cooked supper tonight,' her father told her. 'She guessed you wouldn't have time to do anything yourself – what with the marmalade-making and everything.' He gestured upwards and sniffed appreciatively. The bitter-sweet fragrance of the Seville orange marmalade was drifting down into the shop and Holly could see that at least one customer had registered it.

'Lovely,' said Holly. 'Why don't you get off home, Dad? It's almost closing time already.'

She gave him a quick hug. He was so much happier these days, she thought. He seemed lighter, somehow, as if a burden had been lifted from his shoulders, and Holly was glad. So perhaps the trip to Seville had ended up being eventful for him too.

CHAPTER 52

Ella

Dorset, 2019

Ella gently smoothed out the old and fragile folds of the recipe with her fingertips. She read first the list of ingredients and then the method in Spanish, not fully understanding – just a few words here and there – followed by the version in English, both written by Caleb's young cousin at that flamenco night in Seville.

That night . . . Now the time had come for Ella to make the cake at last. This was the right kind of celebration. By making the Seville orange and almond cake, Ella knew that in some way she was accepting the memories and the magic at last for what they were. And giving thanks for it all.

She glanced across at the bowl of Seville oranges on the kitchen counter, glowing with promise. She'd called in at the shop earlier when she knew that Holly would be upstairs making her marmalade to pick up a bag of the bitter Sevilles from Felix.

It was funny that these oranges had drawn Holly into their mystique all those years ago, when her daughter had first seen them in the farm shop, first decided to make her marmalade. Ella picked up one of the misshapen fruits and held it close to her face, to breathe in the bitter-sweet fragrance she knew so well. An irony of life perhaps? Or maybe the spirit of Seville was already there in Holly, already part of her daughter's inner being. Who knew?

At any rate . . . Ella tipped the oranges into a colander and began to scrub the skins. Holly had made a success of Bitter Orange in the past year. It would always be a niche market, but she'd developed a strong online presence and she was doing, Ella realised, what she wanted to do. And that was the main thing.

Holly wasn't entirely happy, though, and Ella knew the reason why. She placed the scrubbed oranges on the chopping board, took a sharp knife from the drawer and cut into the first one. The sharp-citrus scent was released in a burst, the acid juice flicking like an astringent onto her skin.

Ella and Felix had also come through the past year unscathed. He was enjoying his job with the National Trust, and loving helping Holly out in the shop when he had time to do so. And Ella was still teaching, though she was planning on cutting down her hours soon. The children still needed her, though; her greatest joy was the feeling of satisfaction when an older teenager or twenty-something sought her out to tell her of some special achievement, to thank her for her enthusiasm and patience in their primary school years. Who could want more than that?

Ella gathered the pieces of thick-skinned orange between her palms, dropped them into a pan and carefully picked out the pips, exactly as the recipe advised. She thought of Caleb's grandmother, his *abuela*, the look in the old lady's eyes and her toothy smile as she handed Ella the secret old recipe, thus symbolically welcoming her into the García family. And now Holly was part of that family too.

For a moment, Ella paused, wooden spoon in hand. She hadn't been fully cognisant of the honour, not back then. But later, when she recognised the significance of the gesture, she found herself hoping that Caleb's grandmother had somehow understood. The old lady had given Ella the recipe because she had seen the love – maybe even something of the future – when she looked into Ella's eyes, when she read her palm. But sometimes, even love wasn't quite enough.

Ella added the water, covered the pan and switched on the gas. When they'd arrived back in Dorset from Seville last spring, she'd been worried about facing Ingrid, knowing now that her mother-in-law had guessed her secret. But she needn't have been. Felix's mother must have been doing some thinking too.

'I'm sorry I tried to shut you out, Ella,' she told her. 'Holly wanted to confide in you about her business plans and I persuaded her not to. I shouldn't have done that. I see that now.' Ingrid looked across at Felix and he nodded. 'And I'm sorry I tried to spoil your holiday with Felix in Seville that time before,' she said. Another glance at Felix. Another nod.

Ella stared at her. She could barely believe it. It must have taken some effort on Ingrid's part. She assumed that Felix had put his mother up to it, but even so . . .

'I'm sorry too,' Ella quickly told her. She didn't need to explain what she was apologising for – Ingrid would know. And they'd embraced – slightly awkwardly, it had to be said;

it wasn't something they were accustomed to, after all. But they'd made their peace. Ella and Ingrid would never be best friends, but these days they got along pretty well.

Ella continued to potter around the kitchen, clearing up, checking her watch every so often. After thirty minutes, just as the recipe had promised, she lifted the saucepan lid to see that the oranges were soft and the liquid evaporated. And the smell . . . Ella breathed in deeply. It was divine.

She cracked the eggs, carefully separating them, put the whites into a bowl and whisked them, as the recipe instructed, into stiff peaks. Gradually, she added the castor sugar, beat the rest of the sugar with the yolks and then added the orange mixture and the almonds. She folded in the egg whites, transferred the mix into the prepared baking tin and sprinkled the top with the flaked almonds.

She put the tin in the oven and stood for a moment, hands on hips, feeling a sense of accomplishment – and release. Caleb was right, she thought. It had all been worth it. She had no regrets.

Ella went upstairs to get ready. She and Felix had decided that they would go out for dinner tonight. The cake would be their appetiser.

After she'd changed her clothes, she opened the jewellery box her mother had given her and touched the dancer who stood on the top of the box with her fingertip as she twirled around to the old familiar song, 'Spanish Eyes'. What a bitter irony that song had become for Ella over the years. Only now could she listen to it and smile.

She selected her amber necklace and, as always, when she opened this box, she thought of her own mother, lost when she had passed away, but in reality, lost even more years ago than that. Once, for a long time, Ella had blamed her – for not sticking up for Ella, for being weak, for allowing herself to be bullied by a man like Kenny. But now . . .

The sweet healing scent of almond oil drifted up the stairs. Now, Ella understood. Her mother had been as vulnerable as Ella had been in their home situation under Kenny's brand of coercive control, perhaps even more so. That was why she'd been unable to protect her daughter. Ella's mother hadn't stopped loving her. She hadn't even been weak. She'd tried her best. But the truth was that she'd been a victim too.

'Ella?'

She heard Felix's voice from downstairs.

'Up here,' she called.

'The cake smells amazing.' He came up the stairs grinning.

Ella smiled back at him. Felix had a new lease of life these days. 'Does she have any idea?'

'Absolutely not,' he told her.

Ella held the amber necklace out to Felix. 'Can you do the clasp for me, darling?' She turned around.

He kissed her shoulder and fastened the amber beads around her neck. 'There you go.'

She turned back to face him. 'Thanks, Felix.'

'And thank you too, Ella.'

'What for?'

'For being my wife. For Holly.' He smiled. 'For everything you've given me, my love.'

CHAPTER 53

Holly

Dorset, 2019

Later, after she'd closed the shop, cashed up, stored the marmalade jars in her tiny but cool pantry, showered and changed, Holly walked the ten minutes to her parents' place. She shouldn't mind too much about Rafael, she told herself. She was lucky, she already had so much. And would she really want a man who didn't understand the importance of her career?

Well, perhaps she would, she thought, if it was that particular man.

She knocked lightly on the back door and walked straight into the kitchen. The first thing she noticed was that her grandmother was there – sitting in her usual chair, in deep conversation with Holly's mother. Holly had noticed that the two of them seemed friendlier these days, but tonight they looked . . . conspiratorial.

'Oh, hello, darling!' Her mother jumped to her feet – almost guiltily.

'Hi, Mum. You look nice.'

And then Holly noticed the second thing. A strong scent of baking that took her back to over a year ago. She glanced at her mother in surprise. Almonds? Oranges? 'Mum?' she said. 'What are you making?'

Her mother gave a bright laugh. 'Well, now,' she said. Which told Holly precisely nothing.

'Are we celebrating something?'

Because this was the Seville orange and almond cake, Holly would swear. The celebration cake from her mother's old recipe book. The rich smell of it filled the room; the drift of orange blossom, combined with almonds and honey – as heady a perfume as Holly remembered from the time she had made it before. And yet her mother had never baked this cake. So why now? What was going on? Holly noticed that her father was smiling too.

'Some ceramics have been sent over.' Holly's grandmother eased herself upright. 'For the shop, I gather?'

'Oh?' Holly hadn't noticed them. But here they were, a whole set, laid out on the kitchen table. She moved closer. They were beautiful – plates, dishes, bowls, mugs, all with a subtle blue-wash background and featuring brightly hand-painted orange trees and the kind of decorative buildings that surely could be found in Triana, Seville.

'Wow.' Holly picked up a plate. 'These are amazing.' She held it up to the light; the plate was almost luminescent, the glaze and the colours somehow both delicate and bold.

'Amazing,' echoed her mother.

Holly glanced at her sharply, but her mother gave a little shrug, all innocence.

What was this all about? Had Caleb sent them over?

But why would he send them here and not to the shop? Holly narrowed her eyes as she faced the three of them. They were all grinning. 'Who made these?' she demanded. 'Where did they come from?'

The door to the hallway opened. 'That would be me.' He smiled. 'Do you like them, Holly?'

'Rafa!' For a full moment she stared at him. Then she flew into his arms. 'What are you doing here? How did you . . . ?'

She had so many questions. She seemed to have forgotten that Rafael had expected her to give up her dream and stay in Seville; that he had, almost certainly, moved on. Because at this moment, he was holding her very tightly and that seemed to be all that mattered right now.

'I made them for you,' he whispered into her hair. 'After you left, I missed you so much.' He lowered his voice still further. 'But I talked to Caleb and he made me see. I was selfish. You were right. I should never have expected you to give up your dream. Fight for her, Caleb said. Don't make the same mistake as me.'

Caleb had made him see? Holly gazed at him. She felt ready to give up everything for Rafael at this precise moment. 'I thought you might have met someone,' she murmured.

'I did meet someone,' he said. 'I met you.'

'Oh, Rafa.'

'I designed these ceramics especially for you,' he said proudly. 'When your mother wrote to me.'

At this, Holly glanced around at her mother who definitely had tears in her eyes and was clutching Holly's father's hand as if she intended to hold on to it forever more. Holly's grandmother sniffed – even she looked a bit emotional. Was this a conspiracy after all?

'I told her about the ceramics I was making and she suggested that I might like to bring them over myself. I did not think you were still . . .' – he hesitated – 'interested. Your messages – they were so . . .'

'Light and breezy?' she said. Not interested? How wrong could a man be?

He smiled that lovely, slightly crooked smile that made her heart twist. 'Exactly,' he said. 'But, Ella, she told me that light and breezy was more the English way – the way, that is, of disguising how you really feel.'

Again, Holly turned to look at her mother. *The English way, hmm?*

Holly's mother gave a little shrug. She got up and went over to the kitchen counter. She whipped the cloth away from one of her decorative plates, and turned so that they all could see what was on it.

The cake was deep and dusted with icing sugar. 'Traditionally, the cake is made to celebrate love.' Her mother picked up the plate and held it out as if it were an offering.

'Oh, Mum. It looks fantastic.'

Holly turned back to Rafael. Light and breezy was clearly never going to work with this man. 'How long will you stay?' she asked him, just as he had once asked her.

Perhaps this was a private conversation and they shouldn't really be having it in front of her entire family. But on the other hand, her family seemed to have engineered the whole thing. Even now, her mother was cutting the cake and her father was handing out plates to everyone.

'As long as it takes,' said Rafael.

Holly took the plate from her father. She took a bite of the cake, her eyes not leaving Rafael's. As long as it takes to do what? she wondered.

The cake oozed almond oil and tasted bitter-sweet like the oranges of Seville. It was delicious. Holly didn't know the answer. But she couldn't wait to find out.

Acknowledgements

It has been a fabulous experience writing this novel – not least because during the writing and the researching, I fell in love with the city of Seville. People told me I would, and they were so right.

I know Andalusia quite well – I've been travelling there every year for thirteen years now. I take lovely writing groups to the Finca el Cerrillo, a restored two-hundred-year-old farmhouse, high in the foothills of the Sierra de Almijara (see my website rosannaley.com for details!). But until last year, I hadn't visited Seville.

I've visited other cities in Spain, but I found Seville to be very special. The people are welcoming and friendly, the food and wine are delicious, the architecture is stunning, the surrounding landscape is glorious; there is sunshine, fabulous flamenco and, of course, all those vibrant bitter orange trees . . . I would go back there in a heartbeat.

I'm also a big fan of Seville orange marmalade (you probably guessed that already!) and my favourite marmalade ever was made by Mary Eggleston of Cattistock, Dorset. Sadly, Mary is no longer able to make her marmalade, but I would like to thank her for all the jars I have enjoyed over the years and also for being my inspiration. (And if anyone knows of someone who makes delicious homemade Seville marmalade, please get in touch.)

On the subject of Seville oranges, I'd like to give big thanks to the charming José Manuel Bautista of the Ave María orange farm in Mairena del Alcor. José showed us round the farm on my research visit and was so knowledgeable and interesting that I felt I needed to put him in the book as a real person, just as the Ave María is a real farm growing real organic oranges. Fortunately for me, he agreed to this! Thanks, José, for your time, your enthusiasm and your passion. I hope that I have done the Ave María justice. (And thanks for the bag of oranges you gave us at the end of our visit too.)

As always, I have tried to immerse myself in the spirit of the place I am writing about and here are some of the books that have helped me do this. Giles Tremlett's *Ghosts of Spain* (Faber & Faber) gives an insight on Spanish history, and Laurie Lee's *A Rose for Winter* (Vintage) is the most charming account of the author's travels in Andalusia. I found *City of Sorrows* by Susan Nadathur (Azahur Books) insightful and fascinating. Jason Webster's fabulous *Duende* provides evocative descriptions of flamenco – both the music and the dancing. Jason happens to live in the same town as me, so I'd also like to thank his wife Salud for her beautiful flamenco dancing which I was fortunate enough to witness at a party some years ago.

Thank you so much to the wonderful team at Quercus who continue to be supportive and lovely. My editor, the brilliant Stefanie Bierwerth, Jon Butler, Milly Reid my excellent publicist, Katie Sadler, Kat Burdon, Laura McKerrell and everyone else who has worked on this novel. Thanks once again to Lorraine Green for her perceptive and sensitive copy-editing.

Big thanks and love to my agent, Laura Longrigg of MBA, for her support, encouragement and friendship and grateful thanks also to Louisa Pritchard of LPA who works with MBA and overseas publishers.

Thanks to my family and friends, without whom I would crumble slowly into a corner. Special hugs to Grey for being my research companion, photographer and sounding board, to Alexa for her creative photographic work and for all her help with Instagram, and to Luke and Agata and Ana (with extra thanks for 'socially constructed boundaries') and James for everything they do.

I was very sad to lose my dear friend the author June Tate in 2019. June and I first met as novice writers in a writing group in West Sussex almost thirty years ago and we were firm friends since that day. I always thought of June as my biggest supporter – though thankfully she could also be a fierce critic. June was funny, honest and brave – three qualities I very much admire. I miss her.

Thank you to all my writing friends, especially Maria Donovan, who is so generous with her time and expertise. Thanks also to Claire Dyer, Gail Aldwin, Jane Cable, Laura James, Tracy Rees, Tracy Corbett, Peter Guttridge, Isabelle Broom and all those lovely supportive people who do all the retweeting and sharing that we writers need to help us along the social media way. You know who you are and sorry that there are too many names to mention. Thanks to Tim Deal for everything. Thank you, Wendy Tomlins, for all the support you continue to give me – you are a star. Thanks to all my lovely friends in Bridport and the surrounding area for your support, companionship and cake! Thank you to writers in the groups I meet with – in the RNA, in Andalusia, in Dorset. Thanks to all the writers whose books I love reading (again, too many to mention!). And to all the libraries and library staff who do so much to promote reading and who also provide a fantastic service to their communities. Thanks to the book bloggers! You are great! Your reviews, your posts and your passion for books mean so much.

And finally, thanks to all you wonderful readers – please, never stop . . .

www.rosannaley.com

Twitter: @RosannaLey

Facebook: @RosannaLeyNovels

Instagram: @rosannaleyauthor